PENNIES ON A DEAD
WOMAN'S EYES

PENNIES ON A DEAD WOMAN'S EYES

MARCIA MULLER

THE MYSTERIOUS PRESS
New York · Tokyo · Sweden
Published by Warner Books

 A Time Warner Company

With thanks to Robert P. Samoian,
deputy district attorney, County of Los Angeles,
for providing those finishing touches.

Copyright © 1992 by Marcia Muller
All rights reserved.

 Mysterious Press books are published by
Warner Books, Inc., 1271 Avenue of the Americas, New York, NY 10020.

 A Time Warner Company

The Mysterious Press name and logo are trademarks of Warner Books, Inc.
Printed in the United States of America
First printing: July 1992

10 9 8 7 6 5 4 3 2 1

Library of Congress Cataloging in Publication Data
Muller, Marcia.
    Pennies on a dead woman's eyes / Marcia Muller.
        p.   cm.
    ISBN 0-89296-454-5
    I. Title.
PS3563.U397P4   1992
813'.54—dc20   91-58025
                                                    CIP

For Helene Piazza

Part One

The Victims

One

■ ■ ■

At first they were going to kill me. Then they changed their minds and only took away thirty-six years of my life."

The older woman was perched beside me on the guardrail of the road leading to the telecommunications tower at the top of Bernal Heights. Wind gusted across the barren hillside and loosened tendrils of her white hair; the pale afternoon sunlight transformed them to a shimmering spiderweb. She stared toward the spires of downtown San Francisco, eyes narrowed against the glare. Smog blanketed the Bay Area today from the eastern hills to the city itself, making the panorama look like an old-time sepia-toned photograph.

After a moment she added, "*Only* took away thirty-six years. And my husband. My child. The entire middle of my life."

I waited, not wanting to interrupt the flow of her thoughts.

"And all the time I was innocent," she said. "They kept me as long as they did because I wouldn't admit to it. Wouldn't express remorse or tell them what they wanted to hear. If I hadn't almost died of a heart attack, I'd still be in prison."

I'd expected the claim of innocence, but now that she'd made it, I had no immediate response. I've never been one for snap judgments, and I certainly wasn't going to make one in this case. When I didn't reply, she faced me, fixed me with an insistent stare. Her eyes were a curious translucent aquamarine, sunk deep in their sockets and edged with pale lashes. I shifted on the guardrail, pulled back slightly.

The woman, Lis Benedict, and I had climbed the hill from her daughter's house on one of the steep little streets below. Doctor's orders to walk vigorously once a day, she'd said, plus the house was small and she couldn't stand the confinement. In truth, I preferred to talk with her in the open. The murder for which she'd been convicted had been an unusually vicious one involving multiple stabbing and mutilation, and, though old and frail, she had an aggressive, temperamental manner that made me uneasy.

"Miss McCone," she said, "you have no idea what it's like to lose that much of your life."

"No, I don't."

"The worst thing is that you become permanently stuck in the past. This old woman who exists here in the nineteen nineties—this embarrassment and guilty burden for her daughter—she isn't the real me. The real Lis Benedict is still back in nineteen fifty-six."

"And the years you spent in prison?"

"A bad dream that I'm still waiting to wake from." She gestured at the cityscape below. Almost all of San Francisco was visible, from Hunters Point to the Golden Gate Bridge. Ironically, one of the few places we couldn't see was the exclusive Seacliff district south of the bridge, where the murder had been committed.

"Look out there," she commanded. "In nineteen fifty-six most of those downtown skyscrapers, including that hideous pyramid, weren't built yet. So I simply don't see them. That ugly red tower on Sutro Heights—I ignore it. But once there was a huge oil storage tank on the far side of Potrero Hill; for me it's still there. Playland-at-the-Beach, Fleishhacker Pool, the City of Paris: the landmarks of my youth are gone. *And yet I still see them.*"

An unusual mind-set, I thought, but probably not uncommon for newly released prisoners. I considered it for a moment, tried to imagine how it would feel to return to a world that had been altered by a span of nearly four decades.

She seemed to take my silence for lack of understanding. Thrusting her face close to mine, she asked, "Am I making myself clear?"

Again I shifted away. "Yes, you are. What would it take to bring you into the present?"

"I'm not sure anything could."

"Then why pursue this?"

"I told you before, for my daughter's sake. Judy has begged me and begged me to agree to have my case reinvestigated. I've got no resistance left, and I suppose I owe it to her. You see, she was the one who discovered the evidence they used to convict me. She was only ten years old at the time. The prosecutor, Joseph Stameroff, manipulated her into testifying against me. Later, when her father didn't want her, Stameroff and his wife adopted her and did their best to turn her totally against me. But Judy always loved me, and reestablished contact when she became an adult. She even dropped the Stameroff name and started using Benedict again. Six weeks ago when the governor commuted my sentence because of my health, she invited me to live with her. This is the only thing she's ever asked of me. How can I refuse?"

"Maybe the best way for both of you to get on with your lives is to let the past go."

Emotion mottled her parchment-pale skin. "I wish that were possible. But Judy feels so terribly guilty about her part in what happened to me. She's repressed most of her memories of the murder and the trial, and she's spent her whole life running— San Francisco to Los Angeles, Los Angeles to New York, back to San Francisco again. When she finally settled down here, she buried herself in her work. This relationship with your Jack Stuart is the first normal one she's had that I know of, but even that is connected to my case."

Jack Stuart was our criminal-law specialist at All Souls Legal Cooperative. I didn't know all that much about his relationship with Lis Benedict's daughter, but what she'd said about Judy's earlier life didn't ring true. She'd been an actress, and her career path had taken her from amateur productions in San Francisco to commercials and occasional TV roles in Hollywood to soap operas in New York. She'd once told me she finally got tired of the daily grind of daytime TV and opted to return home, where she'd borrowed money from her wealthy adoptive father and set herself up as a producer, bringing off-Broadway shows to a small downtown theater. Jack had met her at a fund-raiser for an actors' workshop that she sponsored, and although I'd socialized with them a number of times, I'd seen no indication that their relationship was strongly involved with her mother's murder conviction. Lis Benedict, I suspected, was overplaying that aspect of Judy's life, and it made me wonder if she might not be guilty of something less than maternal altruism.

I said, "So Judy is the only one who wants your case reinvestigated?"

"Yes."

"Don't you also stand to gain from it?"

She bristled at that. "For your information, Miss McCone, I stand to gain very little. Jack plans to take my case before the Historical Tribunal rather than actually request a new trial."

That fact hadn't come up in my brief conversation with him earlier, and the omission annoyed me. Obviously it was deliberate.

San Francisco is a city that takes great pride in its history, and at that time it boasted two quasi-judicial bodies that conducted mock trials before actual presiding judges—the Court of Historical Review and the Historical Tribunal. The former scheduled its hearings during the noon hour, when attorneys, often in period costume, argued issues of some importance— was Fatty Arbuckle guilty of the murder for which he was convicted in 1921?—and questions of pure whimsy—was Groucho Marx a genius or just funny? The Historical Tribunal's proceedings were lengthier, extending an entire weekend, and more serious. Neither, however, had true legal jurisdiction, and I was fairly sure that Jack had neglected to tell me of his intention so as to avoid an argument about whether All Souls' chief investigator should devote her time to researching an old case for a mock trial.

I asked, "Why *not* go for a new trial?"

Lis Benedict looked away, seemed to be studying a ship in the channel beyond Hunters Point with great interest. Her pallor was pronounced in the direct sunlight; beneath the flaccid flesh, her bone structure seemed to have crumbled, leaving only a hint of the once-elegant contours of her cheeks and brow. With surprise, I realized she had been striking when young, perhaps even beautiful.

After a moment she turned to me, pain naked in her aquamarine eyes. "Because I *am* history, Miss McCone. The Historical Tribunal may rule in my favor, but there will never be any true exoneration for me."

I bit my lip, feeling the full force of her hopelessness.

"*Will* you help Jack prepare my case, Miss McCone?"

Not answering, I stared at the smog-shrouded hills across the bay, their contours as blurred as the true facts of a thirty-six-year-old homicide case. This woman, I thought, had been through absolute hell—infinite varieties and refinements of hell that I couldn't even begin to imagine. What was I to tell her? *I'm sorry, but I've had a rough time of it this past year, and I can't risk becoming involved in yet another case where I might get torn up emotionally. I used up all my reserves on other clients, other victims. I've got nothing left for you.*

In my peripheral vision I saw Lis Benedict's hands clench together, gnarled knuckles going white, but she didn't repeat her request. I wished I could simply agree, relieve her anxiety, but something in me held back. The crime—the vicious slashing and mutilation of her husband's twenty-one-year-old lover—was absolutely repugnant to me. And much as I pitied Mrs. Benedict, I had to admit that I didn't really like her. Not well enough, at least, to do battle with Hank Zahn, my nominal boss at All Souls, who would say I had no business wasting my time and the co-op's money on such an investigation.

Finally I said, "Let me think about it over the weekend. We'll talk again on Monday."

The sudden sag of her shoulders told of her disappointment, but she didn't voice it. She must have become skilled at stifling vain protests during all those years when parole had repeatedly been denied her. "I'll expect to hear from you then." She stood, waited for me.

"You go ahead," I told her. "I want to sit awhile."

She shook my hand and moved toward the narrow strip of blacktop that curled between the white telecommunications tower and the access road below. I watched her go: a thin, erect figure clad in a long navy sweater and slacks, walking carefully but proudly, and never looking back.

When she rounded the curve and disappeared from sight, I got up and crossed the pebbled ground to where the cliff dropped off to the roofs of distant houses. I selected a smooth slab of rock and sat down cross-legged, feeling out of sorts and emotionally stingy.

Two painful cases in the course of one year had left me professionally burned out, all my zest and caring and passion reduced to ashes. I could feel it even now, sitting here in the sun on a fine spring afternoon: a torpor, a flatness. For six months I'd toed a careful line, creating a work life that was productive, comfortable, and safe. But all the while I'd been tensed against an event that would shatter that balance. Whether Lis Benedict was guilty or innocent didn't matter; the reopening of this long-ago murder case, rife with details that would turn the stomach of the most seasoned homicide investigator, had the dangerous power to do that.

The Two Penny Murder, as it had come to be called, was a San Francisco legend, on a par with Phoenix's Trunk Murders and Los Angeles's Black Dahlia Case. In the early hours of Saturday, June 23, 1956, the badly mutilated body of post-debutante Cordelia McKittridge was discovered by a gardener in a dovecote on a three-acre estate belonging to the Institute for North American Studies, a think tank dedicated to pondering issues of public policy and national defense. Cordy, as she was called, had literally been hacked to death the night before with a pair of gardening shears. Her body had then been laid out ritualistically, as if it were in a coffin; a final bizarre touch was a penny covering either eye.

Suspicion naturally centered on the think tank staff, an elite corps of intellectuals recruited from the most prestigious universities in the country. While lofty-minded, they apparently also had their earthy side; at least two were rumored to be having affairs with Cordy, a member of a wealthy family whose fortune went back to the days of the Nevada silver boom. Since her debut at the Winter Cotillion two years before, Cordy had delighted in shocking proper San Francisco society, and the dovecote—a small circular structure with high-beamed rafters, nestled on a wooded bluff above the Pacific—had been the scene of many a tryst. On the night of her death she reportedly had an appointment for a rendezvous with biochemist Vincent Benedict, but Benedict and his colleagues were gathered at a banquet at a financial district restaurant that evening. Prosecuting attorney Joseph Stameroff would later argue that the assignation was a setup engineered by Benedict's wife, Lisbeth, and that the resulting confrontation had been bloody and final.

That, anyway, was what the jury at Lis Benedict's trial had believed. At the time there were rumors of the involvement of people in high places, collusion between the police and the prosecutor's office, influence brought to bear by the rich and powerful family of the victim—the usual talk that surfaced in high-visibility murder cases that combined society, wealth, power, and sex—but in the end no one gave them much credence. Lis Benedict was sentenced to die in the gas chamber, was reprieved at the last hour, and then had her sentence commuted to life in prison. Every time she came up for parole, the former prosecutor and a representative of the McKittridge family's law firm appeared at the hearing and argued successfully against her release.

That was virtually all I knew about the Two Penny Murder—facts I'd gleaned from a newspaper update that had run when Mrs. Benedict got out of prison. And the only reason I'd read it in the first place was my connection with Judy. Gruesome murders hold no fascination for me; I've seen too much ugliness in my work as a private investigator to relish gory accounts of true crime, current or historical. I supposed I could take a look at the trial transcript over the weekend. . . .

For a moment I stopped thinking about it, emptied my mind, and tipped my head back, feeling the sun on my face. I'd often climbed up here to the little-used public land at the tip of Bernal Heights during my years at All Souls, some dozen steep blocks away on the northwestern incline. A barren russet outcropping, it towers above the ill-assorted small dwellings that crowd the lower slopes, standing fast in the face of nature's worst assaults. While much of the city is built on sandy fill that shifts or even liquefies during an earth tremor, this hill is bedrock; while other areas are easily altered by wind, rain, or tide, the elements have little impact here. I suppose a good part of the place's appeal for me is its homely permanence, which seems to embody a refreshing honesty and truth.

Honesty and truth: commodities that are generally in short supply for an investigator. How much of either was Lis Benedict offering me? The woman seemed sincere, but so do many murderers who claim innocence of the crimes for which they've been imprisoned. My conversation with her had been too brief to allow me to take an accurate reading.

Finally I got up, brushed off the seat of my jeans, and started downhill. At the far side of the access road I angled along several blocks to where I'd left my car on Wool Street near Judy's house. The homes I passed were an odd mixture: frame cottages, stucco row houses, small apartment buildings, classic Victorians. Many had vegetable gardens; a few had illegal chicken coops. There is a hint of the rural about Bernal Heights, which may be why it attracts couples with young children, newly arrived émigrés from Mexico, aging and nostalgic hippies, and oddball institutions such as All Souls.

As I rounded the corner of Wool Street, I saw a crowd in front of Judy's white Victorian. Concerned, I quickened my pace. The crowd—not large, since it was midafternoon on a Friday— milled about, murmuring in subdued voices. Lis Benedict stood just inside the low picket fence staring at the house's facade. As I went closer, I saw words spray-painted in red on the clapboard: Murderer . . . Killer . . . Bucher. They hadn't gotten all the spellings right, but the meaning was clear.

I pushed through the gawkers and touched Mrs. Benedict's arm. "Who did this? Did you see?"

She shook her head, unable to look away from the words. The paint was so fresh that it still dribbled. It speckled the white clapboard like a huge blood-spatter pattern. Judy was going to be horrified when she returned from the theater and saw this.

I turned and shouted to the people behind us, "Did anyone see who did this?"

More murmurs. Then a man in coveralls said, "A kid, looked Mexican. Ran off that way." He pointed downhill toward Mission Street. "Shouldn't be hard to find him. He's got that red enamel all over his hands."

I turned back to Lis Benedict. She hadn't moved. Her shoulders slumped, and the proud tilt of her head had vanished. I touched her arm again; slowly she looked at me. Her eyes were dull, their translucence muddied.

She said, "They warned me."

"Who did?"

"Voices on the phone."

"You've received threatening phone calls? Why didn't you tell me?"

She swallowed, took a deep breath, grasped my hand to steady herself. "I wanted you to decide whether or not to help me on the merits of my case alone. If I'd mentioned the calls, it would have sounded as if I were begging. I never beg. My life has been demeaning enough without stooping to that."

Pride, stubborn pride. It could get you hurt, even killed. "When did you receive the calls?"

"They started on Tuesday, have been coming regularly ever since."

"How often?"

"Two or three times a day."

"What do they say?"

"The same as it does up there." She motioned at the house. "Even worse."

"Threats?"

"Not exactly. Just that I should leave the city, that I'm not wanted here."

Anonymous phone calls: the refuge of cowards. I shook my head angrily. "You said 'voices.' Is it a different one each time?"

"I can't tell."

"Male or female?"

"Male, with a Spanish accent."

The people behind us were starting to leave. I watched them, wondering if a neighbor might be responsible for the calls. Any number of them might not want Lis Benedict living so close by.

She said something I didn't catch.

"What?"

"I'll have to go somewhere else."

"They're just crank calls. Ignore them."

"But this . . ." She gestured weakly at the house.

"A kid's malicious mischief."

"Kids can be dangerous. I can't risk my daughter's safety." She leaned heavily on my arm—no longer the haughty, unpleasant woman, but merely a vulnerable old lady.

My anger was high. I cautioned myself against allowing my emotions to influence my decision about whether to investigate her case. "Don't do anything hasty," I told her. "At least talk it over with Judy first."

She didn't reply. Her eyes were once again focused on the red spatter pattern. She shuddered, pushed me away, and stumbled toward the house's door—as if she'd suddenly remembered a blood-splashed scene thirty-six years in the past.

Two

■ ■ ■

I made sure Lis Benedict was securely inside the cottage. Then I went looking for a kid with red hands.

The business establishments that I passed as I hurried along the crowded sidewalks of Mission Street reflected the influence not only of the area's working-class Irish and Italian settlers and today's predominantly Hispanic population, but also recent encroachments of other cultures. Scattered among the small bodegas were Asian produce shops. Tacquerias abounded, but so did Vietnamese restaurants and sushi bars. The Remedy Lounge, All Souls' favorite watering hole, had been owned for more than forty years by the O'Flanagan family, and Spanish-language videos were still the staple at the rental shop, but a karate studio, a Filipino travel agency, and a Zen meditation center all foretold a new order.

While the various cultures remained relatively segregated on the street, inside City Amusement Arcade the melting-pot process prevailed. The appeal of video games knows no ethnic boundaries; kids of diverse backgrounds and appearances, speaking at least a half dozen languages, hunched over the glowing machines. The air was stale and far too warm, thick with smoke and redolent of cheap after-shave and sweat. I stopped inside the door and waited.

After a moment a slender young man wearing an expensive leather jacket emerged from one of the aisles. He glared at me as he took a comb from his pocket and ran it through his luxuriant black hair. I smiled. His scowl intensified, and he jerked his head toward the door. I went back outside and halfway down the block to a decrepit sandwich shop called the Serving Spoon. There I bought two cups of black coffee and sat in one of the booths. A few minutes later Tony Nueva came in and took the seat across from me.

"Jesus, McCone," he said, "why do you have to stand around the arcade looking like you're my dope connection?"

"It's more likely people will think I'm your parole officer."

"Shit, why would I have a P.O.? I'm a businessman is all."

"Right." At only nineteen, Tony Nueva had built a minor financial empire on a base of various semilegal activities, not the least of which was selling information to the highest bidder. The fact that he was still alive, much less thriving, testified to a certain warped genius.

He sipped his coffee and made a face. "What do you need?"

"Sometime during the past hour, a Hispanic kid painted graffiti on a house up on Wool Street. The spray can leaked, and the kid came away with red hands. I want to know who he is."

Tony rolled the Styrofoam cup between his palms. "Graffiti artists are a dime a dozen. Some nights there're more of them than riders waiting for buses at the Muni stops."

"Still, you can find out."

"Why you so interested?"

"This is no ordinary incident. There's a possibility somebody hired him to do it."

"I don't know, McCone."

"Come on, Tony, I've got faith in you. White Victorian. Red spray enamel." I gave him the address. "It's twenty bucks to you when you deliver."

"Now wait a minute! I got overhead—"

"Ten now, ten when you deliver." I had the bill ready and pushed it across the table.

Tony made a disgusted sound and pocketed it. Ritual dance

of informant and buyer ended, he said, "I'll have it for you by five. You gonna be in your office?"

"Yes."

"Talk to you later."

. . .

The big Victorian that houses All Souls was wrapped in scaffolding and its scabrous brown facade had been prepped for painting, but as I cut through the grassy triangle across the street, I didn't see any workmen. That in itself was a bad sign and should have prepared me for the chaos that reigned just inside the front door.

The first person I saw was an overall-clad man who apparently had tracked light-colored paint onto the newly refinished hardwood floor of the foyer. Another worker stood beside him, shouting and flailing a crowbar dangerously close to the antique chandelier. My assistant, Rae Kelleher, faced him, arms akimbo, her flushed face complementing her auburn hair. And Ted Smalley, our usually unflappable office manager, looked on with alarm.

"Ain't my fuckin' fault!" The man with the crowbar ended his tirade.

"It is, too, you idiot!" Rae exclaimed. "Don't you *dare* try to duck responsibility. You're dealing with a law firm, you know."

"Goddamn roof's rotten."

"Don't you try to blame your ineptitude on the roof!"

The worker gaped at her as if she'd said a filthy word—and one he wasn't familiar with, to boot.

"Color's not coming out," the painter whined plaintively.

The others ignored him.

"Rae, please," Ted said, "let's talk reasonably—"

"You keep out of this!" She grabbed at the crowbar as it grazed one of the chandelier's fluted-glass shades. "That was an expensive brass bed you crushed," she told the workman.

"*I* didn't crush it. Fuckin' piece of roof fell on it."

"Still, you're liable." Rae looked at Ted. "He *is* liable, isn't he? Oh, shit, why am I asking you? You're not a lawyer. Where's Hank when I need him?"

Ted spotted me in the doorway and rolled his eyes. "Now I know why Hank and Anne-Marie picked this week to leave for Hawaii," he said.

"What am I supposed to do with thirty gallons of paint that looks like what I find in my kid's diaper?"

"If you don't pay for that bed, I'll sue!"

"The hell you say!"

I slammed the front door and shouted, "Everybody shut up!" Quite incredibly, they did.

Ted quickly seized control. "You," he said to the painter, "go outside and get something to clean this floor. We'll talk about the color problem on Monday."

Exit the painter, muttering.

Ted turned to Rae. "That roof *is* in bad shape, and I happen to know that your brass bed is a cheap imitation. I'm sure our insurance will cover its replacement."

She hesitated. I could tell she was torn between the pleasure of laying into the workman again and the wisdom of staying in Ted's good graces so he'd file a claim.

Ted asked the workman, "Are those skylights going to need special bracing so the roof'll support them?"

He nodded.

"How much?"

The workman opened his mouth, then glanced at Rae. Suddenly downcast, her lower lip aquiver, she'd undergone a transformation from litigious bitch from hell to Little Match Girl. "Aw, I'll do it for a hundred," he said.

Rae looked up and bestowed a glowing smile on him.

Ted sighed, waving his hands in dismissal. "Go ahead, then." As Rae and her newfound admirer started upstairs, he ground his teeth and muttered, "Now the roof's rotten. What next?"

I merely patted his shoulder and went to check my message box. Three slips, nothing of importance.

Ted sighed again and flopped into his desk chair. His computer equipment, steel file cabinets, fax machine, copier, and shelves of reference books looked out of place in the elegantly wainscoted foyer. Ted himself complemented the decor—a slender fine-featured man with a handsome goatee who had recently taken to wearing brocade vests over ruffled shirts. Appearances seldom deceive more than Ted's, however; under his foppish exterior there beats the heart of an efficiency expert.

He said, "It was a bad decision to buy this dump."

From a purely practical standpoint I agreed, but sentiment made me say, "Well, the landlord was going to sell whether we bought or not. Can you picture us anyplace else?"

"No, but the corporation's going to have to pour one hell of a lot of money into this building just to keep it standing." He paused, listening to the echo of what he'd said. "The corporation. My God, I never thought we'd be All Souls Legal Cooperative, Inc. What's happened to us?"

"We got successful."

At a time when law firms all over the nation were cutting staff and raising fees, All Souls was expanding and holding down membership fees in its legal plan. While partners in stuffy downtown firms groused about the loss of gentility that came from treating a law practice as a business, All Souls had aggressively added services to attract clients. Members, who paid fees on a sliding scale based on their incomes, could now call an 800 number for consultation with paralegal workers about minor problems. And we'd marketed the plan to major local employers; several now included it as part of their benefits packages.

Success necessitated changes, hence our somewhat dubious entry into the real-estate market. But the Victorian, which comprised both offices and living quarters for some of the staff, couldn't begin to house all our operations. We now rented a second building directly across the triangular park out front, and negotiations were under way for a third. And to reinforce our successful image, our newly purchased headquarters was being spruced up, supposedly painted pale gray with black and white trim—or if the painter could be believed, the color of what he found in his baby's diaper.

I winked at Ted and went upstairs to my office, thinking about changes. When I'd first come to work here, nearly all the partners lived in the house rent free because they made such dismal salaries. Now only Rae, Ted, Jack Stuart, business specialist Larry Koslowski, and tax attorney Pam Ogata chose to remain; their salaries were competitive with those of other firms, and they paid going-market rent. Once I'd known everyone who worked here on a fairly intimate basis; now if I ventured over to our other building, I was apt not to recognize some of the support staff. Ted, in fact, used to be our only secretary; now he wore the title of office manager. And Hank Zahn complained that he spent more time in administrative meetings than in client consultations or in court.

But the important things hadn't changed, I reminded myself. We were still a young, energetic firm that cared more for its clients than for its profit and was committed to the principle of affordable high-quality legal representation for low- and middle-income people. Most of us still gathered in the big kitchen at the rear of the house on Friday afternoons for a happy hour. Meals for anywhere from two to twenty were frequently whipped up on the spur of the moment; a good poker or gin rummy game could be gotten up day or night; commiseration or congratulations or just plain good company was always available. And while many of us admitted to feeling jaded on a bad day, we also confessed to harboring fugitive ideals on a good one. All Souls was, in truth, the closest thing that many of us had to a home and an extended family, and I couldn't begin to imagine life without it.

In my office at the front of the second floor, I dumped my bag and jacket on the chaise longue and stuck the message slips under a paperweight. Then I sat down at the parsons-table desk in the window bay and scrawled my signature on some letters that were waiting atop my in-box. There was a thick, unfamiliar file folder lying next to the blotter; I pulled it toward me: *State of California v. Lisbeth Ingrid Benedict.*

"Jack," I whispered, "leave me alone."

As I shoved the file away and leaned back in my chair, my eyes rested on the deep tangerine rose in the bud vase on the corner of my desk. It had arrived, as they always did, on Tuesday morning—a gift from my lover, Hy Ripinsky, who lived on a small sheep ranch in the high desert country east of Yosemite, near the Nevada border. Last fall when he sent me the first of the weekly roses, its color was yellow—my favorite. But when we became lovers two months ago, he said yellow wasn't passionate enough, and the tangerine ones began arriving. This one was wilted now from the unseasonable heat we'd been experiencing, but I would leave it in the vase until the new one came—my way of keeping Hy close even when we were apart.

Uneasily, as if someone might be spying on me, I reached for my bottom stack tray where, under a pile of blank expense forms, I kept a file labeled "Ripinsky, Heino." I'd started it the previous November, when reports on him that I'd requested from the National Crime Information Center and the California Criminal Justice Information System had been forwarded to me by an acquaintance on the SFPD. There had been nothing damning or even very interesting in them, except for an early arrest for lassoing a streetlight in the Mono County seat of Bridgeport and a series of later ones related to environmental movement protests. I hadn't needed the reports any longer; the investigation I'd been conducting up at Tufa Lake was ended, and by all rights I should have thrown them away. But instead I had set up the file, and by now I knew its dry, factual contents by heart.

I removed my hand from the stack tray. No amount of further examination of the documents and my notes would tell me what I wanted to know. There wasn't the remotest possibility that the reports contained an as-yet-unnoticed clue to the blank nine-year period in his life.

Hy's whereabouts and activities during that period were unknown to anyone, and he refused to talk about them, even to me. Rumors abounded in Vernon, the small town on the shore of Tufa Lake where he'd been raised. Some people claimed he'd been CIA; others claimed he must have been a drug smuggler, since he never seemed to lack for money after his return. Theories ran the gamut from the possible (he'd been in prison) to the improbable (he'd fought as a mercenary) to the absurd (he'd been kept by a wealthy old woman who had died and left him her entire estate). I discounted even the most realistic of them, because none fit the man I had come to care for.

As we grew closer, I'd thought that he'd tell me about those years, or at least explain why discussion of them was off limits. But every time the subject came up, he closed off in such a forbidding way that I knew pressing him would end the relationship. And so I merely wondered and brooded and repeatedly pored over his file.

It would be easy, I'd often thought, for an investigator of my experience and contacts to uncover Hy's secret. Even the most closemouthed people let hints slip; even the most careful leave traces of their past. But aside from checking with the CIA and the FBI, which would "neither confirm nor deny" Hy's past employment, I'd managed to control myself. So far . . .

Even the simple act of setting up a file was a violation. I felt ashamed every time I saw the neatly typed label, wrestled with guilt every time I opened the folder. And I also had to question my motives: Did I want to know about those years because the understanding would bring me closer to Hy, or was I merely curious? Did his silence disturb me because it erected a barrier between us or because it hurt my pride?

I moved my hand toward the stack tray again. I should destroy the file and forget it. If I ripped it up and tossed it in the waste-basket right now, by Monday the trash would have been col-lected and I wouldn't even be tempted to retrieve the pieces.

But I wasn't ready to do that—not yet.

Three

■ ■ ■

By the time I went down to the kitchen, the Friday happy hour was under way. Ted was there, setting out chips and salsa. Rae was there, too, and surprisingly, so were the painter and the man who was installing the skylights—minus his crowbar. Larry Koslowski, our resident health nut, was blending some god-awful cocktail of natural fruit juices and mysterious powders, and arguing with Pam Ogata about the merits of tofu hot dogs. A couple of the secretaries from the other building wandered in, followed by the neighbors' German shepherd. The shepherd lay down quietly on the rag rug in front of the sink and watched us with its soft, intelligent eyes; I was certain he found the goings-on bizarre and pointless. As I fetched a glass of white wine, I stopped to pat him and said, "Sometimes I agree with you, guy." He looked up to see if I had any food and then ignored me.

Jack Stuart sat at the round oak table near the windows. Jack, so the women claim, is the co-op's hunk, and I have to admit that a body honed lean by frequent rock climbing, a craggy face that only improves with age, and a thick shock of silvering hair add up to a pretty attractive package. A while back I had my chances with him when he became ridiculously

21

smitten with me on the rebound from his divorce, and there are still times when I regret how prudently I ignored his overtures.

I went up to the table and took the chair next to him, figuring I'd clear the air about the Benedict matter. Jack's face lit up when he saw me. "Well?"

"I found the file you put on my desk."

"You read it yet?"

"My God, I've only been back here half an hour. Why didn't you tell me this was a case for the Historical Tribunal?"

"You wouldn't have gone to see her if I had."

"And you also conveniently timed this for when Hank's on vacation and can't throw a fit about me wasting my time."

"Guilty again. You going to shoot me for my subterfuge?" He said it lightly, but his brows immediately drew together in consternation. I knew he was thinking of a night the previous summer when he'd seen a coldly murderous side of me that few people had known existed. It was a night that had almost severed my close ties to my friends at the co-op, continued to strain them whenever the memory surfaced.

"Hey," I said, "it's okay."

"Thoughtless of me."

"Look, Jack, you can't tippy-toe around the subject forever. I've put it behind me, and you should, too."

He nodded. "So tell me—what'd you think of Lis?"

"At first I didn't like her. She's got a mighty thick protective shell, and it makes her come off as pushy and abrasive. Of course, I realize a woman like her would have to develop that in order to survive in prison. She's not your average ex-con."

"No. She's well educated—Bryn Mawr—and was raised in Scarsdale. That, plus the victim's own background, was one of the things that made the Two Penny Murder so intriguing."

"And notorious. Those pennies—am I right in thinking there was something unusual about them, besides their being placed on Cordy McKittridge's eyes?"

"Uh-huh. They were war-issue lead pennies."

"That's a misnomer; they weren't made of lead. They were zinc-coated steel, minted only in nineteen forty-three, due to the wartime copper shortage."

Jack raised his eyebrows. "Where'd you lay your hands on that piece of trivia?"

"When we were kids, my brother Joey was willed a coin collection by one of our uncles. I was horribly jealous and would sneak into his room to study it, before he went and sold it so he could buy a surfboard."

"Joey sounds like a sentimental fool."

"Oh, he's been in the running for village idiot all his life, but I love him anyway. To get back to Lis Benedict—her tough shell took quite a beating this afternoon." I told him about the graffiti. "Did you know she's also received phone threats telling her to get out of town?"

"I had no idea, and I'm sure Judy doesn't either."

"She wouldn't have told me about them except for the graffiti. I've got Tony Nueva working on that, trying to get a line on the kid who did it. There's a possibility somebody hired him."

"Why do you think that?"

"Because the phone caller used the same words that were painted on Judy's house. This sounds like a campaign of harassment rather than a kid acting on a whim."

Jack rubbed his chin. "Poor Lis. Why would anyone want to harass her now?"

"Well, people don't forgive, I guess. Or forget, given the recent publicity. What about the McKittridge family? They kept blocking her parole."

"Harassment's not their style. And most of them are dead now, except for Cordy's brother, who lives in England."

"Tell me about them. All I know is that their money went back to the Nevada silver boom."

"The McKittridges were once the cream of San Francisco society: mansion in Pacific Heights, country estate in Hillsborough, ranch in the Napa Valley. The old man was a member of the Pacific Union Club. Cordy was your classic tall, aristocratic blonde, went to the right school—Katherine Delmar Burke—and came out at the Winter Cotillion at the Sheraton Palace. But then everything went haywire."

"She rebelled."

"Uh-huh. Refused to go to college, started running with a wild crowd. Affairs with married men, dabbling in the bohemian culture, lots of booze and marijuana. Sign of the times, I guess: in fifty-four, the insulated little world of our social circle was falling apart. The war had changed everything."

I was silent for a moment, toying with the stem of my wineglass. The German shepherd wandered over and rested his head on Jack's knee. Jack fed him a taco chip.

"Jack," I said after a moment, "do you really believe Lis Benedict is innocent?"

"I do."

Why was he so definite? I wondered. Certainly not because he was in love with Judy. Jack was a good criminal lawyer, and in the course of his career he'd heard even more lies and bullshit than I had. He wouldn't allow his emotions, however strong, to blind him to the facts.

"You sound as if you think otherwise," he added.

"I'm not sure."

"Read the transcript."

"Jack, I have to warn you, I feel a tremendous resistance to this case."

"I told Judy you would. And frankly I don't blame you. But how much trouble would it be to go over the transcript?"

"Not much. I suppose I could look at it this weekend. And I do want to find out who's responsible for those phone calls and the graffiti." I glanced at my watch. "What's keeping Nueva, anyway? He said he'd report by five, and it's almost six now. I've never known him to come up empty-handed on something this simple—much less pass up an extra ten bucks."

Rae came up next to me. "Shar, I'm going to run some errands before I go over to your house," she said. "Can I have a spare key in case you're not home when I get there?"

"Sure. Ask Ted for his."

She nodded and headed for the door.

Jack raised his eyebrows.

"I've acquired a temporary roommate. Her garret's open to the air until the skylights are installed, so I offered her the use of my guest room."

"Skylights—Jesus. I don't know why Hank's such a soft touch where Rae's concerned. He spoils her rotten. She's already preempted a third of the attic for her living space; why does she need skylights too?"

I shrugged. "There's something about Rae that makes people want to spoil her rotten."

"Guess so. How come she's staying with you instead of Willie?"

"He's up in Reno this weekend opening a new store, and I don't think she likes to stay in that big house of his when he's not there." Willie Whelan, Rae's current love, had expanded his chain of cut-rate jewelry stores to Nevada. Soon most of the newlyweds who had tied the knot in the West's marriage Mecca would be up to their eyeballs in debt to him. "Rae's promised to help me get my garden in shape for spring planting," I added.

"A little late, aren't you? It's already the end of May."

"Not as late as last year; I didn't get so much as a petunia into the ground. Rae and I have a hot weekend planned: hard work in the garden followed by a culinary experiment with Larry's mushroom enchilada recipe, and then early to bed—alone."

"Hy's not flying down?"

Hy is a pilot and owns a Citabria Decathlon, a small aerobatic plane that is a sheer, sometimes scary, thrill to fly in. "I haven't heard from him, so I assume not. But you never know; he's one of the world's truly unpredictable souls." And puzzling ones, I added to myself. "Anyway, the most I'm hoping for from the weekend is that this weather will hold so I can laze on my deck on Sunday and contemplate the fruits of our labors." I paused. "Do you and Judy have plans for tomorrow night?"

"No. It's one of those hot weekends for us, too. Why?"

"I was thinking you might come for mushroom enchiladas. Bring Lis, too. It would be a good chance for all of us to talk, since I intend to go over that transcript tonight." Even as I spoke, a plan took form: I'd read up on the case, feed everybody, make some provocative comments that would pique Rae's interest, and turn the case over to her. The easy way out, maybe, but Rae was a good investigator, and I could always help—more effectively because I could maintain a certain objective distance.

Jack looked skeptical. "Dinner sounds fine, but I don't know about the enchiladas. Koslowski's recipes . . ."

"Rae's had them, and she says they're good. Trying them is part of my campaign to begin eating more healthfully."

"You're just a bundle of good intentions these days, aren't you?"

"So far I'm only working on my minor flaws. The major ones would take more effort than I can put forth right now."

"Well, we'll be happy to come to dinner. It'll do Lis good to get out of the house. We'll bring some wine—something robust to drown out the peculiar undertaste that all Larry's recipes have."

I smiled. "Tomorrow night at seven, then."

After I'd set my empty wineglass in the sink, I went down the hall to Ted's desk, to see if someone might have taken a call from Tony Nueva and neglected to locate me. Surprisingly, Ted had returned to the foyer, was sitting in his chair staring into space. I hesitated, not wishing to intrude, but he glanced my way and motioned for me to come in.

"Don't mind me," he said. "I'm just brooding."

"About something specific or everything in general?"

"Oh . . ." He shrugged.

I waited, but he didn't go on. During the past six months I'd noticed a worrisome change in Ted. He was as efficient and devoted to his work as ever, but at times I could tell he felt overburdened. He laughed and joked as much as ever, but often his humor had a bitter edge. And more and more I found him staring blankly like this or aimlessly wandering through the house.

Of course, I reasoned, these were hard times for a gay person. Ted had lost his oldest friend to AIDS, more recent friends and former lovers, too. So far—thank God—he'd tested negative for HIV, but the prospect of a positive result always cast enough of a shadow so that Ted had engaged in no relationships for quite some time.

Loneliness, I thought now, was the crux of his problem. Throwing himself into his work couldn't fill the void; neither could any amount of laughter and joking and socializing. And much as we at All Souls loved him, that still couldn't take the place of the love of one special person. Still, you have to try to help. . . .

I perched on the edge of his desk. "Want to talk?"

He shrugged again. "Nothing to talk about. It's just more of the same."

"I'm always here for you."

"I know that. Friends like you are what keep me from hanging myself from the roof beam."

"That's just as well—the skylight guy says it's rotten, remember?"

He smiled faintly.

"By the way," I added, "did Tony Nueva call me while you were sitting here?"

"Nobody's called, and I don't see any message in your box."

"Odd. Well, I'm out of here. See you Monday."

As I went upstairs to fetch my jacket and bag, I wondered about Tony. This was the first time since I'd been using him that he'd failed to deliver when promised.

Four

■ ■ ■

The evidence at this trial will show that the defendant, Lisbeth Ingrid Benedict, had the motive, the opportunity, and the means to murder Cordelia McKittridge. It will further show that Mrs. Benedict made complicated and well-thought-out preparations for her crime, and that she went to the dovecote on the Seacliff property belonging to the Institute for North American Studies on the evening of Friday, June twenty-second, with full intent to kill the young woman she had lured there.

The portion of the transcript containing Deputy District Attorney Joseph Stameroff's opening statement lay on my kitchen counter. I wanted to go over both it and the closing statement before my dinner guests arrived in two hours. Now I left off reading and went to stir the lumpy grayish white mixture in the cast-iron skillet on the stove.

Stameroff had argued persuasively for the People, and the state's case, while circumstantial, had been strong. But there were a few holes, made obvious by the passage of time and my own detachment. Holes that might lead to various avenues of inquiry.

I gave the mushroom mixture a final stir and went back to my reading.

> The evidence at this trial will show Lisbeth Benedict's motive to be age-old and unoriginal: a betrayed wife's jealousy of her husband's younger paramour. The defendant's solution to the problem of a faithless husband was also age-old and unoriginal, but she took advantage of her opportunities in a creative manner.
>
> The opportunity: The evidence will show that Mrs. Benedict was aware of her husband Vincent's habit of meeting with Miss McKittridge at the dovecote on the think tank's property. That she knew he set up these assignations by note rather than by telephone. That she was aware that on the night of June twenty-second her husband, his colleagues, and their spouses would be at a banquet in honor of visiting Secretary of State John Foster Dulles at the Blue Fox restaurant downtown—an event no one would miss.

A bubbling noise came from the stove; the heat under the skillet was too high. I adjusted it, then picked up the wooden spoon and tasted a mushroom. It had no more flavor than cardboard, was overpowered by the green chilies. And the sauce . . . it must have been the low-fat cottage cheese that had given it that lumpy consistency. The yogurt didn't help the flavor, and the lack of salt . . . Quickly I grabbed the shaker and dumped in a couple of teaspoonfuls, then pulled the transcript closer, stirring as I read.

> The means: The evidence will show that Lisbeth Benedict had studied calligraphy, was in fact an excellent calligrapher, and was in the habit of signing her husband's name to checks when it was not possible to obtain his signature. That she was fully capable of creating a note that Cordelia McKittridge would believe came from her lover, requesting that she meet him at the dovecote on the evening of June twenty-second. That Mrs. Benedict came down with a convenient and

unconfirmed case of food poisoning on the afternoon
of June twenty-second and was allegedly forced to can-
cel out of the dinner for the secretary of state. That the
household staff had been given the evening off, and
that Mrs. Benedict and her ten-year-old daughter Judy
were the only persons at the estate from six o'clock
until midnight. The only persons save for one other:
Cordelia McKittridge.

I tasted the mushroom mixture again. The salt had done
absolutely nothing for the dreadful concoction. Tossing the
looming specter of high blood pressure to the winds, I grabbed
the shaker and dumped in a whole handful. On the back burner
sat a second skillet containing a tomato-based sauce to be
poured over the filled enchiladas. I hesitated before tasting it.
That oily sheen on its surface—what could have caused it?
Health food wasn't supposed to be greasy. I dipped the spoon
into the skillet and sampled a small amount. Oh, that was nasty
stuff! Shuddering, I went back to the transcript.

The People, ladies and gentlemen of the jury, cannot
presume to know exactly what went on in that isolated
dovecote between Lisbeth Benedict and Cordelia
McKittridge. We can assume that angry words were
spoken on both sides; we can assume that emotions
ran high. The evidence will show that Cordelia McKittridge was attacked with a pair of gardening shears,
that she was badly mutilated, that she died of exsan-
guination—that is to say, she bled to death on the
floor of the dovecote. Testimony from Mrs. Benedict's
own daughter will show that the defendant returned
to the mansion shortly after ten that evening with red
stains on her dress, stains that she later—much later,
after she was arrested for the crime—attempted to explain as ink stains. But, ladies and gentlemen, it
would have taken a great deal of ink to make those
stains; Cordelia McKittridge lost practically all her
blood.

I looked up from the page, glanced at the skillet containing the red sauce, then tried to wipe the obvious from my mind with a flurry of activity. I dumped in some garlic powder, followed by more cumin and chili powder. Stirred furiously and tasted.

"Oh, my God!"

Whatever restraints I'd imposed upon myself in the interests of sound nutrition fell by the wayside. I snatched up a bottle of red cooking wine and poured with abandon. As the vile concoction simmered, I read on.

A crime of passion, you say? Violent and reprehensible, but understandable as a product of momentary insanity? No, ladies and gentlemen of the jury, it was not.

The evidence we are about to present will show that the murder weapon—those sharp and deadly shears— was not seized either in an unanticipated fit of rage or in self-defense. The shears were kept, not in the dovecote, but in the gardener's shed, had in fact been in the shed when the gardener locked it before going home at five that afternoon. And a duplicate key to that shed was kept on a Peg-Board in the pantry of the mansion, easily accessible to any of the residents. Lisbeth Benedict went to the dovecote with those shears in hand, prepared to do murder.

You may recall that we have stated that Lisbeth Benedict took advantage of her opportunities in a creative manner. Creativity was one of the hallmarks of this crime. Lisbeth Benedict took with her to the dovecote not only the shears with which she killed Cordelia McKittridge but also two symbolic objects. And she came away from there with an even more symbolic object.

The objects that the defendant took with her were two pennies. It could be claimed that everyone has at least one pair of pennies with him at any given time, but these were not ordinary coins. They were war-issue pennies, no longer in wide circulation. And although we cannot presume to know what significance they held for Lisbeth Benedict, we do know what she did with them. After Cordelia McKittridge had bled to death there on the floor of the dovecote, the defendant laid her body out as if for burial and placed one of those pennies over either eye.

And the symbolic object she took away with her? A ring. An amethyst ring that the evidence will show had been given to Miss McKittridge by the defendant's husband. A ring that was later found among the defendant's things by her daughter, Judy, after the family had moved from the estate to their own home, where outsiders would have no access to their possessions. A ring, ladies and gentlemen of the jury, that was not merely removed from Cordelia McKittridge's hand but *hacked* from it—along with the finger on which she wore it.

I pushed the transcript away. Right there was the reason I didn't want to reinvestigate this case. Perhaps what had been done to Cordy McKittridge was mild in comparison to what went on today, but it still repulsed me. And just as I refused to watch splatter movies or read lovingly crafted fiction or true-crime accounts dwelling on mutilation and sadism, I didn't have to deal with this.

I was beginning to very much regret having included Lis Benedict in my dinner invitation. How could I sit at the same table with her when I still harbored doubts that she was innocent of this atrocity?

The heat had edged up under the mushroom mixture again. It bubbled, and a grayish white blob flew through the air and onto the counter. I glared at it, consulted the recipe. What was I supposed to do next with this horrible concoction? Wrap it in corn tortillas. Pour the oily sauce over them. Top with Monterey Jack cheese and bake.

Oh, no, I wouldn't! I wasn't wasting perfectly good tortillas and cheese on *this*. I hefted the pan containing the mushroom mixture, carried it to the sink, and dumped it into the Disposall. Then I went back for the tomato sauce.

Just as I tipped the skillet over the sink, Rae came in from the backyard, face rosy from a day in the sun, fresh crop of freckles blossoming on the bridge of her nose. In her hand she carried a pair of gardening shears.

My eyes rested on them, and I recoiled. Looked at the thick red mixture washing down the drain. And thought, *The finger. Good God, what happened to Cordy's finger?*

Rae stared at me. "Shar, are you okay? What's going on here?"

"This stuff is inedible, that's what! I thought you said Larry made these for you and they were good."

"Well, that's how I remember them. But I'd fortified myself with wine. You always have to do that when Larry cooks."

"Now you tell me! Listen, I need you to go to the store right away."

"What for?"

"For something to eat!"

She laughed and set the shears on the counter. "All right. I suppose this is my fault . . . sort of. What do you need?"

"Sourdough—a couple of loaves. Shredded Parmesan—lots. Spaghetti. And you'd better get something for us to snack on; it's going to take a while for my spaghetti sauce to defrost."

Rae grabbed her car keys from the table and went down the hall. I tidied the kitchen, put the spaghetti sauce into the microwave, and took a glass of wine and the trial transcript outside to the deck.

The early evening was unusually warm and clear. Mellow rays of sun showed a transformed backyard. Rae and I had tamed wild vegetation and weeded overrun flower beds; all that remained was planting. Tomorrow, I thought as I sat on one of the lounges, I might make a run to the big nursery out on Bayshore Boulevard. I'd buy colorful flowers, whatever the nursery people could recommend that needed little watering, since drought-induced rationing was still on.

I heard a scrabbling sound and looked up in time to see an orange cat face peer over the back fence. Ralph, home for his supper. Moments later he was joined by his calico sister, Alice. For a few seconds both looked stunned at the loss of their jungle. Then, adaptable creatures that they were, they bounded down and raced for the house, Allie hissing as Ralph leapt over her on the steps. He gave her a condescending look and stalked inside to the food bowl. Allie flopped at my feet, and I scratched her with my toes as I went back to the transcript.

The prosecutor's closing argument repeated the points he'd made in his opening statement, tying them more firmly to the evidence and dwelling on the heinousness of the crime. I skimmed it, then rechecked several portions of the actual testimony. There were a number of areas in the state's case that seemed weak to me, but most of these had gone unchallenged by Lis Benedict's attorney, a public defender and not a particularly good one.

I wondered about her legal representation. Her husband, by all accounts, had been well paid, and Lis's own family was affluent. Surely they could have afforded a better attorney. And what about the well-funded Institute for North American Studies? Why hadn't they come to the aid of their staff member's wife? I couldn't pinpoint specific instances, but my impression was that no one had given Lis much support. Perhaps the rumors of a cover-up had some basis; perhaps Lis *had* been sacrificed to protect someone or something more important than she.

I reviewed my mental list of weaknesses in the evidence. First, the note that Lis had allegedly forged to lure Cordy McKittridge to the dovecote. A friend of Cordy, Louise Wingfield, had testified as to its existence, but she had never actually read it. Wingfield had merely recognized what she thought was Vincent Benedict's handwriting on the envelope. Any competent attorney could have demolished the testimony, but Lis's public defender had passed the witness.

A second and, to me, vitally important area that had gone unexplored was the issue of the men in Cordy's life. Her promiscuity had been whitewashed at the trial, the affair with Vincent Benedict made to seem a great, albeit illicit, love. But the recent recap of the case that had appeared in the *Examiner* pointed out that Cordy had been wild, was said to have engaged in affairs with *two or more* men at the Institute. Who was that other man—or men? Why hadn't Lis's attorney used Cordy's reputation to cast suspicion on someone other than his client?

The pennies that had been used to close Cordy's eyes bothered me, too. Joseph Stameroff had mentioned them in his opening statement, but then made no attempt either to tie them to the defendant or to explain their symbolism. As he'd said, they were unusual coins, no longer in wide circulation; surely proving they belonged to Lis Benedict would have cemented his case. And yet, after the initial mention, he'd let the subject drop.

Finally, the testimony of the state's star witness, ten-year-old Judy Benedict, was extremely tenuous. All she had been able to say about the stains on her mother's clothing was that they were large and red. No clothing of Lis's with either ink stains or bloodstains had ever been recovered. The evidence of the ring that Judy had found among her mother's possessions after the family moved from Seacliff to a house in the nearby Outer Richmond district was straightforward enough; but Deputy District Attorney Stameroff's contention that outsiders would have had no access to the residence seemed farfetched, and there was no proof that the ring hadn't been placed beforehand in one of the boxes the Benedicts moved from Seacliff. Again, the public defender had not raised this important issue.

I paged back through the transcript and reread Judy's testimony. Even in this dry form, the words showed a strong rapport between the prosecutor and his witness. Ten was a highly suggestible age, and a young girl whose mother was in jail and whose father seemed to have little or no interest in her would have been eager to please an adult who cared. I didn't doubt that Stameroff and his wife had been genuinely fond of Judy; after all, they'd taken her as their own daughter after the trial. But it was possible that the prosecutor had exerted undue influence over her; the case had high visibility, and a conviction would have been sure to further his political career. And it had: today Joseph Stameroff was a justice on the state supreme court.

Yes, I thought, there were plenty of avenues that warranted investigation. Talk with Lis Benedict, with Judy, with Joseph Stameroff. Find out about the public defender . . . what was his name? Harry Moylan. Find out if Moylan was still alive and, if so, talk with him. The same for other witnesses, other members of the Institute staff. And what about Vincent Benedict?

Why had he given his daughter up for adoption, and what had happened to him?

Then there were present events that needed looking into—the phone calls to Lis and the graffiti. At first I'd tended to doubt they were connected to the old case, except in a very peripheral way, but now I wasn't so sure. Tony Nueva had yet to contact me, which meant he'd come up empty-handed and was too proud to admit it. That bothered me most of all; a secret that Tony couldn't ferret out was a closely guarded one. I'd have to check with him—

Abruptly I applied the mental brakes, reminding myself that this was going to be Rae's case. And was surprised to feel a twinge of regret. . . .

Five

■ ■ ■

For a while I thought the mushroom-enchilada disaster might have set the tone for the evening. First Jack called, sounding uncharacteristically curt, to say they would be half an hour late. Not five minutes later Hy phoned from Tufa Lake. He'd started to fly to the city, he said, but the Citabria had developed minor engine trouble and it had taken him all day to repair it. Maybe he'd try again around midweek if I'd be available. I said I would and hung up feeling disgruntled. I hadn't expected to see Hy this weekend, but now that I knew of his aborted trip, I missed him keenly.

By seven the spaghetti sauce was simmering, the garlic bread was ready for the broiler, and the salad was crisping. An evening chill had set in, so I laid logs in the freestanding fireplace I'd recently installed in my informal sitting room. Rae set out the sinful hors d'oeuvre tray she'd bought at our favorite Italian deli, and we sat down to wait for my overdue guests.

At seven-fifty Jack and Judy arrived, without Lis and acting as if they'd just had a fight. As I hung up their coats, Jack drew me aside. There had been another graffiti incident, he said, this one in the middle of last night, and Lis was seriously depressed. "She keeps insisting that she should go away. When we tried

37

to persuade her to come along tonight, she told us she wasn't fit to eat at the same table with normal people."

I thought of my earlier reservations about having invited her and immediately felt ashamed. It occurred to me that while I knew a great deal about crime and its immediate effects, I'd given very little thought to its long-range impact, particularly upon parolees.

Jack took the wine he'd brought to the kitchen, where Rae was getting out glasses. Judy had gone into the sitting room, so I followed and found her warming her hands in front of the fire. She was tall and so thin that her pleated gabardine trousers hung in exaggerated folds. Her hair was the color Lis's must once have been, creamy blond, and pulled atop her head in an artful knot; short wisps trailed against her high forehead and at the nape of her long neck. Her eyes, behind large round glasses, were quietly expressive.

For as long as I'd known Judy, I'd sensed an intriguing quality in her that I couldn't put a name to. Now one came to me: fey. It was a word that my Aunt Clarisse, whom the family considered just plain spooky, had used frequently in the lurid bedtime stories that kept us cowering under the covers long after we should have been asleep—and that, to my adult thinking, hinted at mild sadomasochistic tendencies. I'd once looked up the word "fey"; it was of Scots origin, as was Clarisse, and meant "under a spell, marked by apprehension of calamity, death, or evil; otherworldly." Being something of a born labeler, I felt better now that I'd finally named the elusive quality in Judy, but doing so served only to emphasize the contradiction in her makeup. One seldom thought of a tough-minded and successful theatrical producer as fey.

She came toward me and took my hands in hers. "Thank you for inviting us. I'm sorry my mother couldn't make it." She seemed to stumble over the appellation, as if speaking or thinking of Lis as her parent didn't come easily.

"Jack told me about the new graffiti. What did it say this time?"

"More of the same. The fellow down the block whitewashed over it for me, but you can still see it, and I suppose they'll be back."

"I've got somebody working on finding the kid who did it."

She shrugged, unencouraged. "I'm afraid the damage to Lis has already been done."

"Is she really determined to go away?"

"That's what she says. She claims bad things happen in threes—Lis is, and always has been, extremely superstitious. Strange, in someone of her intelligence. She thinks that if she leaves, it'll break the spell. But I doubt she'll make any immediate move; she's much too depressed."

Jack and Rae entered, carrying wine. As we sat down I steered the conversation to more pleasant subjects—an automatic response due to my mother's habit of forbidding the discussion of disturbing things before eating because it was bad for the digestion. Rae told a few of her Willie Whelan stories, which inspired laughter, and the tension I'd felt between Jack and Judy eased. It wasn't until we were relaxing around the table over coffee and chocolate truffles—Rae had outdone herself at the deli—that our talk returned to Lis Benedict.

"So," Jack said to me, "are you going to help me prepare my case for the Historical Tribunal?"

"I haven't decided yet." I'd outlined the case to Rae the night before and attempted to further pique her interest by reading her sections of the transcript. Now I glanced at her, but she was unheedfully picking chocolate crumbs from her plate with her forefinger.

Jack's lips twitched in annoyance. "You've read the transcript?"

"Yes."

"Well, what more do you need to help you decide?"

"A better idea of whether it's feasible to investigate. There are a number of things about the case that bear looking into, but I'm not sure it's possible."

"Why not?"

"The availability of witnesses, for one thing. A lot of them are bound to be dead." I looked at Judy. "I can talk to you, but your memories of the murder and trial won't be as accurate as those of someone who was an adult at the time."

She nodded. "Most are pretty hazy. Others are nonexistent."

"What about the night of the murder and the bloodstains on your mother's clothing?"

"That I don't remember at all. My testimony at the trial seems like something someone else said. My father claims I've repressed it for good."

"You mean Joseph Stameroff?"

"Yes."

"What about your biological father? What happened to him?"

"He died back in the sixties."

"Fairly young, wasn't he?"

"Forty-six, my age. He was an alcoholic; the booze killed him. Vincent Benedict," she added as if speaking of a person she'd merely read about, "was never very stable. He blamed himself for what happened to Lis, because of his affair with Cordy McKittridge. He blamed himself for Cordy's death; I think he really loved her. And, of course, he blamed himself for abandoning me."

"Exactly why did he give you up for adoption?"

"He knew he couldn't take care of a child. By the time Lis was sentenced to die, Vincent Benedict could barely take care of himself."

I glanced at Rae again. Her eyes met mine and she quickly looked away. Then she got up and began clearing the table.

This was not going as I'd hoped. I turned back to Judy. "What about finding Cordy's ring?"

"Now, *that* I remember." She drew in her breath and looked at Jack, who put a reassuring hand on her shoulder. "You know how there are certain milestones in your life?" she asked. " 'This happened before, this happened after?' Well, that night is mine. After the trial I used to daydream a new ending, where I didn't go up to the attic and come down with the ring. Even when I was old enough to know daydreaming doesn't change anything, I held on to that fantasy." She paused, added in a softer voice, "I still do."

The thought of living with so much guilt was something I could scarcely comprehend. "Tell me about that night."

She shifted uneasily, candlelight from the tapers on the table reflecting unsteadily in her round lenses. "We'd moved away

from Seacliff," she began. "Nobody wanted to live there after
. . . what happened, especially Vincent . . . my father. He found
us a house on Lake Street, not far away. I remember not liking
it much. At the mansion, I'd had the run of the grounds, and I
loved my attic room; it was like an eagle's aerie from where I
could spy on the world unobserved. Anyway, they'd sent me to
theater day camp down the Peninsula that summer—this was
early in July—and I needed a costume for the next week's production. Nobody would help me get one together. Dr. Eyestone
and his wife were there, and the Sheridans, and they were all
having cocktails."

I recalled one of the names from the transcript. "Russell Eyestone was director of the think tank, right?"

"Yes."

"Is he still living?"

"He died about two years ago. His son, Leonard, runs the
Institute now."

"And the Sheridans—who were they?"

"He was on staff, a physicist, I believe. I don't know what
happened to them; they moved back east after the trial."

"What about the Institute? Is it still located in Seacliff?"

"No. As soon as Russell Eyestone died, Leonard began building a new physical plant on the Embarcadero. The old one, he
said in a newspaper interview, was outmoded. The new building's very modern, very plush. I hear the Seacliff property, what
hasn't already been sold off, is on the market."

"Okay, you were saying that your parents were having cocktails with the Eyestones and Sheridans at your house on Lake
Street. . . ."

"It was more of a conference than a party. There had been a
lot of those: very tense, very worried conversation about what
effect the murder would have on the future of the Institute. And
they were always accompanied by plenty of booze. No one was
paying any attention to me." She paused, seemed to be replaying the memory.

When she didn't go on, Jack prompted her. "You needed a
costume."

"Yes, a costume. Earlier that week I'd seen my mother take a box of clothes to the attic—things that were out of style but too good to throw away. I went up there and rooted through it and came up with the ring."

"Where?" I asked.

"In what part of the box, you mean? I don't recall."

Judy's transcribed testimony had said the ring was in the pocket of a blue brocade dress. "You're sure you don't?"

"As I said, there are a lot of gaps in my memory."

"Did you recognize the ring as Cordy's?" I asked. "For that matter, did you know Cordy?"

"Everybody at the Institute knew her. Her parents were good friends of the Eyestones, and she came by to see them frequently. Too frequently, if you ask me."

"Why?"

"Well, it's not natural for a twenty-one-year-old to be that interested in her parents' friends. Even I suspected what she was really after." Judy's lips tightened. Her dislike of the young woman lived, even though Cordy was decades dead. "I suppose I also suspected who had given her the ring. When it appeared on her finger a few weeks before the murder, it fascinated me. Fascinated my mother, too, judging from the way she looked at it."

Another reason to disbelieve Lis Benedict's claim of innocence. "Okay, you found the ring in the box. . . ."

She nodded, staring at the flickering candle flames. "I took it downstairs to show my parents. I knew Cordy had been killed, although I wasn't too clear on the details, and I realized the ring shouldn't be in our attic. When Mama saw it . . . I'll never forget her face."

"Describe her reaction."

"Shocked at first. Then she got really quiet, scared. Daddy made me take him upstairs and show him where I'd found the ring. When we came back down, Mama had shut herself in the kitchen, and . . . everybody else was whispering, looking funny."

Judy's voice had risen to a childish pitch. The second time she called Lis "Mama," I glanced at Jack. He'd noticed the change, too; frown lines were etched between his brows. His eyes met mine, clearly uneasy.

Judy, he'd once told me, had a tendency toward the melodramatic—not surprising, given that she'd been an actress. But this abrupt shift felt a bit eerie. . . .

"What happened then?" I asked, aware my own voice was unusually hushed.

"Daddy was . . . He went into the kitchen and started shouting at Mama. I don't remember what he said. Mama shouted back. And then he hit her. She screamed. He kept hitting her and she kept screaming until Dr. Eyestone and Dr. Sheridan went out there and made him stop. And then the police came."

"Who called them?"

Her face grew very still; she seemed to be momentarily mesmerized by the candle flames. She drew a shuddering breath.

Jack put his hand on her shoulder. "Judy?"

She shrugged his hand off. "My God," she said, "*I* did. I called the police!"

"Why?" I asked. "To protect your mother?"

She shook her head, clearly confused. "I guess so, but I'd never done that before when my father beat her."

"Did that happen often?"

"When he drank. And he drank often."

Jack said, "You never told me any of that."

She pursed her lips in irritation. He noticed, drew back. I'd seen them behave this same way a couple of times: she'd project emotional neediness; he'd become solicitous; then she'd seem to reach a saturation point and turn on him in annoyance, and he'd withdraw.

Into the awkward silence, I said, "Had the drinking and physical abuse been going on long?"

Judy didn't reply immediately; she seemed to be trying to get her temper under control. "For as long as I can remember. My parents were married in 'forty-three, when he was still in graduate school. He'd never done anything but go to school, and I think he felt trapped in the marriage. And in his job; he was the junior staff member at the Institute, and people stuck him with routine work. Plus he was good-looking and could be charming when he had to, so they were always using him for P.R. purposes." She paused. "I guess he felt trapped by me, too. He sure got rid of me in a hurry when Mama was arrested."

She turned to Jack, lips curling down in a way that begged forgiveness for her earlier annoyance. "The reason I never mentioned the abuse to you is that I only remembered it recently. And I only remembered about calling the police right now." She glanced at me. "Lately that's been happening a lot. Lis will say something, or I'll see something that reminds me of my childhood, and—bingo!—I'm right back in the past, and it's all so clear."

I asked, "What else have you remembered?"

"Nothing like this. Just the way a place looked or something a person said. I don't know why it happens—or why it happened just now."

I looked at the candle flames, where she'd been staring as she spoke of that long-ago night. They flickered in a draft, colors shading from gold at their tips, through red and purple, to cobalt at their bases. "You were talking about Cordy's ring. Maybe the amethyst in the flames triggered the memory."

"Maybe. But why now, so many years later?"

"Lis is back in your life."

"She's been in my life since I turned twenty-one and got in touch with her in prison."

"But not on a day-to-day basis. Not living under the same roof."

"I guess that's why." Her face fell into weary lines. She reached for Jack's hand, entwined her fingers with his. He squeezed them comfortingly; the pattern was entering another cycle.

After a bit she said, "My God, what else do you suppose I'm going to remember? What *else* did I do to my mother?"

"You didn't *do* anything," he told her. "You were a child, not responsible."

I glanced at Rae, who was standing behind Judy's chair, arms folded across her breasts. She wore the expression she gets when she wants to clear the air about something, but all she said was "I think we could use an after-dinner drink."

Jack demurred, but the rest of us opted for sherry. When Rae had served it and sat back down, I asked Judy, "Do you recall how you felt about having to testify against your mother?"

"Oddly enough, I wanted to—one more thing to feel guilty

about. I was angry with her. Because she'd killed Cordy—or so I thought at the time—I'd lost everything."

"What happened to you after she was arrested?"

"For about two weeks my father tried to hold things together. He hired a woman to come in and cook and be there when I got back from theater camp; he came home on time and didn't drink so much. But then on July twenty-sixth—I remember the exact date because it was the day after the *Andrea Doria* and the *Stockholm* collided and everybody was talking about it—he came home . . . well, really plastered. He drank at the kitchen table most of the night until he passed out. And the next afternoon he sent me to stay with the Eyestones. They kept me for a couple of weeks, and then I went to a foster home. And except for a few short visits, I never saw my father again. I lost everything."

"What about your mother?" Rae asked. "Did you see her in jail?" Her voice held an edge of emotion; she herself had lost both parents at an early age and been raised by a grandmother who had made it plain she didn't really want her.

"A few times."

I asked, "What was her reaction to you testifying?"

"She told me to do what I had to. To tell the truth and never regret it. Even at the time I thought that was strange. I knew if they convicted her, they would kill her."

"Have you talked about that since?"

"All she'll say is that she didn't want to make it any harder on me than it already was. But doesn't that sound kind of flimsy?"

"Maybe not," I said, thinking of my own mother. "Some parents can be very selfless where their children are concerned. Who did you first tell about the blood on your mother's clothing? And when?"

"Red stains, not blood. I don't remember."

"And when did you first meet Joseph Stameroff?"

"In the foster home, about a week after I went there, months before the trial. He came to talk with me and brought me a teddy bear. I told him I was too old for stuffed animals, and he said nobody was too old for them, that sometimes you needed something to hug and tell your secrets to. He understood . . . a lot of things."

"Lis claims he and his wife tried to turn you against her."

Judy's lips compressed. After a moment she said, "There's a good deal Lis can't comprehend about my relationship with my parents . . . adoptive parents."

Jack said gently, "But she has good reason to think he might have influenced you. He's pressured you to have nothing to do with her all along, ever since you first contacted her in prison. He made it clear he didn't want her living in your house. And since he heard about the mock trial, he's virtually badgered you, trying to talk you out of it."

She looked at him, face tense with anger. "How do you know about that?"

"About his feelings about the trial? I can infer it, from things you've let slip. And he called me at the office last week, attempting to apply pressure. He also phoned Lis today while you were out running errands—and it's not the first time."

"He did? She told you that?"

Jack nodded.

Judy was silent for a moment. Finally she said, "Speaking of Lis, we ought to be getting back to her."

Jack didn't seem surprised at the abrupt switch of subject. He merely checked his watch, said, "Jesus, it's after midnight," and stood up. As Judy rose, he asked me, "Will I be hearing from you before Monday?"

"Possibly. Will you be available tomorrow?"

"All day. I'm prepping for a trial on Tuesday."

"Then maybe I'll stop by." I followed them to the door and watched them walk down my narrow, congested street to where Jack had wedged his van. Then I went back inside and joined Rae by the fire.

Immediately she said, "Don't ask me to take it on."

"I . . . How'd you know?"

"You've been trying to hook me since last night. 'Rae, listen to this! Rae, this case would be such a challenge!' " Her imitation of my rather transparent efforts was unflatteringly accurate.

"Pretty obvious, wasn't I?"

"You should never try to manipulate people. You're just not very good at it."

"And you really don't want to take this on."

"Not unless you order me to. My caseload, as you well know, is heavy. I don't want to give our clients short shrift because of this . . . research project of Jack's."

"You don't approve of it."

"No, and probably not for the same reasons you don't, but that's my affair." She poured us more sherry and sat cross-legged on the floor in front of the fireplace. "What I don't understand is why you're considering it at all."

"Well, Jack's really committed to it. And it *could* be a challenge. But there's something that bothers me besides the obvious distasteful aspect. There's too much emotion swirling around."

"You mean between Jack and Judy. And the mother and the adoptive father."

"And around the events of the case itself. Even in the trial transcript, I could feel it."

"You've never been one to back away from emotion."

"Maybe I'm learning." Yesterday afternoon I'd told Jack that I'd gotten over the previous summer's violent events and put them behind me, but that wasn't completely true. And there had been other violent events up at Tufa Lake last fall that had left me newly scarred and tender.

The truth was, I didn't want to become involved in yet another case that would make me care; all too often when that happened, people around me got hurt. I'd already felt the pull of this case, in spite of the elapsed decades and the dryness of the court documents, and that made me distinctly uneasy. If I could be sucked in by events so many years in the past, how would I ever be safe from those of the present?

But I couldn't explain that to Rae, so I simply added, "Right now I'm not up to anything more than routine investigating."

"Isn't that what historical research is?"

I shrugged, stared at the dwindling flames in the fireplace. As they licked at the logs, the darker shades of the spectrum flickered: cobalt, emerald, amethyst, blood red. . . .

Blood red and amethyst. The color of murder, the color of

memory. Perhaps the depths that harbored such memories as Judy's were best left unplumbed. Or were they? Which was better—to probe them and risk the pain of unpleasant revelations? Or to keep the lid on and risk the spiritual infection that stems from repressed secrets?

Similar questions, I realized, applied to my own life. Which was better—to tread a narrow middle ground of noninvolvement and remain safe? Or to let go, give myself to the investigation wholeheartedly, and risk the pain of unpleasant consequences?

I kept on staring at the fire, feeling my emotional tie lines slacken. Their ends, already raveled, were disentwining, casting me adrift. Anxiety nibbled at me. I resisted, then let it in. In time it would grow to a low-level fear that would constantly be with me and carry me through whatever lay ahead. Fear was my old companion—the only one, I'd recently had to acknowledge, that made me come fully alive.

Six

■ ■ ■

On Sunday mornings the Mission district undergoes a brief transformation. Church bells toll. Cars double-park along Dolores Street near the Mission. Neatly dressed families, old women in hats, and workingmen in their only suits crowd the sidewalks after Mass. Children run to corner groceries for loaves of sourdough and thick newspapers; young couples push baby strollers and window-shop at the cheap-furniture stores along Valencia. And for a few hours the Mission is once again an old-fashioned place where God's laws are supreme and no sin is so bad that it can't be forgiven in the confessional.

In contrast, the interior of City Amusement Arcade seemed seedier than usual when I entered it at a little after eleven. Stale smoke clogged my nostrils, and the reek of Lysol wasn't strong enough to mask a stench of vomit. The young men who hunched over the machines might have been the same who were there on Friday. Oblivious to their dismal surroundings, they focused on the flickering screens; when stimulated by the images, they responded—rats in an unsanitary laboratory maze. It occurred to me that, for most of them, manipulation of such electronic devices might be the only skill they'd ever acquire, conquering such nonhuman adversaries the only triumph they'd ever claim.

Unfortunately Tony Nueva wasn't among them. I hunted up the arcade's manager, a one-armed Vietnam vet called Buck, and asked if he'd been in yet. He hadn't, Buck told me. Tony had a "real foxy lady" and liked to take it easy on Sunday mornings, if I knew what he meant.

I knew what he meant, and the thought of Tony lazing between the sheets while he still hadn't delivered my information did nothing to improve my mood. But when I went back outside, I saw my informant getting out of a garishly painted low-rider at the curb. The young Latina at its wheel bore about as much resemblance to Buck's figurative fox as a bedraggled fur boa does to the real animal.

When he saw me, Tony frowned, then put on a nonchalant grin. "So, McCone," he said, "what's happening?"

The greeting was too hearty. I eyed him thoughtfully. Today he wore a new-looking buttery suede shirt, and on his slender wrist was a silver watch with a turquoise-encrusted band. I'd never seen that watch before; he hadn't worn it on Friday. And it was a sure thing he hadn't bought it with my ten dollars.

He saw me looking at the watch, and his grin faded. Quickly he adjusted his shirt cuff to cover it.

"How come I haven't heard from you?" I demanded.

"Jesus, McCone! A beautiful morning like this, I just got laid, and now you want to start on me?"

"I want either my information or my ten bucks."

"Look, just give me time."

"You've had time."

"I told you it might be tough to get a line on—"

"Who'd you sell out to, Tony?"

It was a guess, but an accurate one. His mouth twitched and his eyes darted from side to side, as if looking for a way out. "I don't know what the hell you're talking about."

His cuff had ridden up, exposing the watch again. "Somebody must have paid you good money," I said, motioning at it.

He yanked at the cuff. "So I make good money."

"By selling out to the highest bidder."

"Jesus, McCone!" He took out his wallet, extracted a ten, and thrust it toward me. "Here—you want your money, you take it."

That confirmed my suspicion; Tony had never parted willingly with even as small an amount as ten dollars before. I took the bill, said, "You know, you've got a pretty decent reputation among the people who use you. Something like this could blow it."

"That a threat?"

"Call it a friendly warning."

"Well, you know what you can do with your warning, McCone." He pushed past me and slammed through the door to the arcade.

•   •   •

I had a couple of errands to run in the neighborhood, so by the time I arrived at All Souls it was already ten to one. The Victorian held a sleepy Sunday-afternoon hush; flies buzzed in the front window bay, and the living room was warm and stuffy. I went directly to Jack's combined office and living space at the rear of the second floor. The door was open, and papers were strewn on his worktable, but he wasn't there.

So much for prepping for the upcoming trial, I thought. A few months ago I would have assumed the good weather had lured him out to go rock climbing, but since he met Judy, he'd pretty much abandoned the dangerous sport. He'd only taken it up in order to keep his mind off his divorce, and I supposed that the injuries he'd sustained had taught him that there is worse pain than that of a broken heart.

Back downstairs, I went to the law library and dragged out the various phone directories that Ted stores there. Some preliminary checking revealed no listings in the area for any of the witnesses at Lis Benedict's trial. I noted the number and address of the Institute for North American Studies. Then I went back to Jack's office; apparently he'd gone for the afternoon.

Well, I didn't need him to deliver to Lis Benedict the news of my decision to go ahead with the case. I could do that in person. I decided to walk up the hill to Wool Street.

The residents of Bernal Heights were out in full force: cultivating their gardens, walking their dogs, playing ball with their children, chatting with their neighbors. I spotted one of our clients and stopped to admire his rosebushes; a woman Larry Koslowski occasionally dated was building a picket fence, and I paused to ask how it was going. Wool Street was relatively deserted, although a friendly black cat bounded up and chattered at me. I talked back at it as I climbed to the middle of the block.

My mellow mood soured when I saw the facade of Judy's house. The whitewash the neighbor had applied only minimally covered the ugly words; they were faded to pink, but still easy to read. When I rang the bell, no one came to the door. I rang again and stood well back so anyone looking out the window could see who was there, but got no answer.

Perhaps Jack and Judy had decided to get Lis out of the house, I thought. They might have taken her to the park or to lunch over in Marin. Then I remembered the vigorous walks her doctor had prescribed. I'd climb up to the tower; even if she wasn't there, the exercise would do me good.

More people were using the public land this afternoon than on Friday, but it was not nearly as crowded as the city's more scenic areas would be. I didn't pass anyone as I followed the curve of the blacktop, saw only distant figures on the lower inclines. But when I topped the final rise, I spied Lis Benedict at the cliff's edge where the drop-off was most precipitous.

She stood very still, wrapped in a black wool cape that fell in folds to her calves. The bright sunlight made a shining halo of her white hair. As I reached the guardrail, a sudden gust of wind caught the cape and blew it into great flapping wings. Lis leaned forward, balancing on the tips of her toes.

I had a vision of a bird of prey taking off from the cliff, soaring high, then plummeting to seize a small animal from the jagged rocks below. Unease stirred in me as I slipped over the rail.

Lis leaned out farther. I started to call to her, then quickened my pace instead. For a moment she stood poised on the very edge of the cliff, looking down at the city that, for her, was caught in a time warp. Then she rocked back on her heels and drew the cape around her, her body seeming to shrink within its engulfing folds.

I sighed and slowed down, relaxing. Told myself my anxiety had been foolish, unwarranted. But I knew otherwise.

After a moment Lis turned away from the cliff and began walking my way. Her face was drawn with resignation; it didn't change when she saw me. As I approached her, she stumbled. I took her arm.

"Are you all right?" I asked.

She nodded.

"We missed you last night."

"Did you?" The words were shaded by disbelief.

"Yes. I understand there was another graffiti incident. More phone calls, too?"

She hesitated a beat before replying, "Yes, three last night and again around noon today."

"Plus a call from Joseph Stameroff."

". . . Yes."

"What did he say?"

"He tried, as he called it, to reason with me about what the mock trial might do to Judy."

"Did he threaten you in any way?"

"No."

"What did you tell him?"

"I didn't tell him anything. He didn't give me a chance. That's the kind of man he is."

"Are the phone calls the reason you came up here? To get away so you wouldn't have to answer them?"

She merely made a weary gesture, allowed me to help her settle on the guardrail.

I said, "You should stay away from the edge of the cliff, Lis."

Her eyes met mine; the knowledge that I'd seen her near-leap made their translucence more pronounced. Saying nothing, she looked away. After a moment she asked, "Why did you come up here?"

"To talk with you. I've decided to investigate your case."

"Why?"

Surprised at her reaction, I took a moment to formulate a reply. "Because I read the transcript and found some loose ends

that bear looking into. Because it's important to Jack and Judy
. . . and to you."

She laughed dryly. "What's important to me doesn't matter
to you, Miss McCone. It's plain you don't like or believe me.
That's all right; I can live with it so long as you don't let it get
in the way of your job."

Instead of taking offense at what she'd said, I felt relieved to
have everything out in the open. "You're right, but I don't have
to like my clients in order to investigate professionally. And as
for believing or not believing you, there are enough of those
loose ends to make me wonder. I wouldn't take this on unless
I had some doubts about the prosecution's case."

"Lawyers take on clients they know are guilty."

"It's a lawyer's job to provide the best possible defense for the
client, guilty or not. My job, on the other hand, is to get at the
truth. I don't have any patience with being tricked or lied to. If I
find out you're hoping I'll prove you didn't kill Cordy McKittridge
when in fact you did, I'll not only drop the case but make the
truth public."

"So you're an idealist, Miss McCone."

"I'm not sure what I am anymore." Not after the past few
years, I wasn't. Not after the things I'd seen, been forced to do.
And certainly not after the things I'd sometimes had to *stop*
myself from doing.

Fortunately, Lis Benedict's focus was inward; she didn't ask
what had caused the uncertainty. "I used to be an idealist," she
said, "but prison cures you of that—rapidly. Our system of
justice does, too. I stopped believing in justice the day they
arrested me. I stopped believing in compassion the day they took
me to Corona—that's where they kept condemned women in
the fifties, until it was time to drive them to the gas chamber
at San Quentin."

"What about when the governor granted a stay of execution
and then clemency?"

She laughed derisively. "I knew what was operating there."

"What?"

She tensed and didn't reply, as if she'd been voicing random
thoughts and now realized she'd said too much. But too much
about what?

I studied her, wondering if I could press for an answer. No, I decided, better to get her talking about something else. "What about prison?" I asked. "Do you ever get used to it?"

"In a way. At first it's like being dropped into a whole different universe, particularly for someone who was raised the way I was. The physical surroundings are bad, of course, but the inability to make your own decisions is even worse. And the feeling of being set apart from the other inmates is worse yet. After a while that changes. You learn to make small decisions: What brand of toothpaste will I buy this month? What book will I check out of the library this week? What daydream will I use to put myself to sleep tonight?"

I thought of Judy's comment about her daydreams; apparently her mother had similarly eased her pain.

"After a while," Lis went on, "you begin to accept the other inmates and they begin to accept you. It doesn't matter that for the most part they're badly educated and poor, or that some are just plain insane. They become your family, because they're all you have. And to them it doesn't matter that you've had advantages they haven't. They become proud of you, in fact. 'That's my college-lady friend,' one woman would tell her visitors. As I grew older, the younger ones saw me as a surrogate parent and would tell me their troubles or their mad fantasies. Some of them called me Mom, and in a strange way, I liked that."

She paused, then added in a softer tone, "You can become adapted to anything, I guess, but there was one time of day when I always hurt. Early evening was my favorite time of day . . . before. A time of peace and hope. After I went to prison it became the loneliest, saddest time, because I knew there would never be any hope again. I cried in the early evening, before the wells dried up and I stopped crying for good."

The simple words touched me deeply, all the more so because she'd spoken in a manner that did not ask for sympathy: *This is how it was; this is why I am as I am.* No more.

"There's hope now," I said.

"No, it's too late for me. But not for Judy."

"Then for Judy's sake let's get started on this." I took my notebook from my bag. "I've done some preliminary checking, but I haven't been able to locate most of the people who were connected with your case. How about Joseph Stameroff? What are my chances of talking with him?"

"Not very good, I'm afraid."

"Is there any possibility he could be behind the graffiti and phone calls?"

She considered, then shook her head. "He wouldn't do that to Judy. To me, perhaps, but not to her."

"I'll ask her to work on him, then. Maybe she can persuade him to discuss the case with me. Now, Leonard Eyestone—I'll call his office first thing tomorrow and try to set up an appointment. And this Louise Wingfield, the friend of Cordy who testified about the note—I've heard of her. Society matron, got a big divorce settlement about fifteen years ago, took back her maiden name. Since then she's used the money to establish a foundation that aids minority kids. I've got a connection who may be able to persuade her to see me. What about your attorney?"

"Harry Moylan? He's been dead for years."

"Why a public defender, anyway?"

"He was all I could afford."

"Surely on your husband's salary—"

"My husband was an alcoholic, Miss McCone. The first item in an alcoholic's budget is liquor. Most months we could barely meet our expenses."

"And the Institute didn't offer to help?"

"They were only too glad to wash their hands of me. My alleged crime placed their government contracts in jeopardy. Russell Eyestone was a cold man. If you speak with Leonard, you'll find he's much like his father."

"And your family—did you appeal to them?"

"There would have been no point in that. Years before, I'd quarreled with them over Vincent's drinking and bad treatment of me. Once I was arrested, they broke off whatever tenuous contact we had."

There was no bitterness in her tone, no regret; the years in prison had dried those emotions up, too. "Okay," I said, "what about the Sheridans, the couple who were at your house the night Judy found Cordy's ring?"

"I have no idea what happened to Bob and Jane. For all I know, they might be dead."

"Are there any other Institute staff members I should speak with?"

"Most were older than Vincent and I, and have died."

"Domestic help at the estate?"

"Dead or scattered. I can't imagine how you could locate any of them."

I closed my unused notebook and turned to a more sensitive topic. "Mrs. Benedict—"

"Please—Lis. I'm not used to formality."

"Lis," I agreed, "if you'll return the favor. Now I need to ask you a few questions that may make you think I doubt your account of the night of the murder. I don't want you to take offense; I'm doing it only for purposes of clarification."

"All right."

"Was food poisoning the real reason you didn't attend the banquet for Dulles?"

"I was ill, yes."

"And the stains Judy saw on your clothing—were they actually ink?"

"I was a calligrapher, and working on a project involving red ink."

"You were doing calligraphy even though you were too ill to attend a banquet for the secretary of state?"

"I felt better by then."

"Where were you working on this project?"

"Where . . . ?"

"Judy testified that you *returned* to the house from somewhere with stains in your dress."

"Judy was mistaken. A child awakened by a noise is easily confused."

"What sort of noise?"

"Why, almost any kind."

"No—I mean, Judy, specifically, that night."

"I . . . don't know."

"But she'd been awakened—"

"And saw me downstairs with stains on my dress and assumed I'd been outside. I usually did my calligraphy work on the big table in the library."

"I see. And so far as you know, there was no one on the estate that night but you and Judy?"

". . . That's right."

I didn't like what her reaction to the series of questions had told me. Most people can't entirely mask a lie. They betray themselves with physical gestures, changes in posture and voice level, innumerable small signs. In Lis's case it was a faint tic at the right corner of her mouth. No matter how candidly she met my eyes, she couldn't control that, and the questions about Judy seeing the stains on her dress had especially aggravated it.

Lis was hiding something, but what? What could have been— still *was*—so important that she would have died in the gas chamber in order to keep it secret?

As I studied her, she lowered her eyes, pleating the fabric of her cape between her fingers.

After a moment I asked, "Can you think of anyone else I should talk with?"

"No."

"Was there a friend you confided in?"

"About what?"

"Your husband's affair with Cordy McKittridge. Your feelings toward her."

She rose suddenly and moved toward the cliff's edge. Uneasy again, I followed. She stopped at a safe distance, however, facing southwest toward the Golden Gate. Beyond the rust-red towers of the bridge a bank of fog hovered, ready to reclaim the city once darkness fell.

Lis said, "From here I can see almost every place except where it happened."

"Maybe that's just as well."

"I don't think so. I have to face the nightmare if I'm going to go through with the mock trial."

"But not by looking at Seacliff and brooding. You wouldn't recognize much, anyway; it's all changed."

"You're probably right."

"Lis, I asked you a question. Did you tell anyone about your feelings toward Cordy?"

She continued to stare at the cityscape. After a moment she said, "I spoke of Cordy McKittridge to two people, and two people only—my husband and my daughter."

"And what did you say?"

She turned candid aquamarine eyes on me. This time there was no evidence of the facial tic. "I told them that I wished Cordy were dead. I said I would gladly cut her heart out."

Seven

■ ■ ■

What kind of woman would say a thing like that to her ten-year-old daughter?" I asked Jack.

He shrugged, clearly troubled.

We were seated on the sofa in his office at a little after nine on Monday morning. The worktable was still strewn with papers, but they looked as if they hadn't been touched since yesterday. I was on my third cup of coffee; he'd downed at least that many and still seemed half asleep.

"Dammit!" I pounded the arm of the sofa with my fist and only succeeded in hurting myself. "She didn't even act as if she thought she'd done anything wrong."

"Don't get all riled up," he told me absently.

"How do you expect me not to? I should have trusted my initial instincts and stayed the hell out of this. How on earth can you justify this . . . farce?"

Jack stood and poured himself yet another mug of coffee from the percolator on a side table. "I happen to believe in her innocence. I don't feel called upon to make a character judgment, as you seem to."

"And you also happen to be in love with her daughter."

"True."

"When's the mock trial?"

"It's not calendared yet. The Historical Tribunal considers this an important issue, since the defendant is still living. They're trying to assemble an impressive jury." Jack's expression turned sour; I knew he didn't care for the Tribunal's publicity-hungry organizer, a retired attorney named James Wald.

"Going to turn it into a media circus, are they?"

"Not if Rudy Valle has anything to say about it." John "Rudy" Valle was the superior court judge who presided over the Tribunal's sessions. "Valle's a brilliant jurist and an amateur historian. He takes the proceedings very seriously."

"And the jury—where do they get them?"

"They're volunteers selected from a permanent roster. Most're legal experts, historians, journalists, crime writers. The trial's conducted pretty much like an actual one, except the witnesses are also volunteers—many with acting experience—who've been briefed on the facts their testimony is to cover."

"So whatever I find out in my research will be told to them, and they'll act the parts of the various people who participated in the real trial?"

"Essentially."

"What if a real witness wanted to play himself or herself? Would they allow it?"

"You're thinking of Judy and Lis. We've talked about it, but I'm not sure it's a good idea. The Tribunal, particularly James Wald, would love it, of course."

I tried to imagine the proceedings. I'd often had to testify in both civil and criminal cases; even during occasional moments of courtroom levity, I was aware of an underlying seriousness. But in a mock trial—didn't the word "mock" imply a certain level of frivolity?

I said, "It sounds like half theatrical production and half trial. Only in this case, they'll be fiddling around with Judy's and Lis's lives—"

There was a resounding thump against the rear wall of the building. Jack and I exchanged alarmed glances. When I looked at the window, a blue-and-white striped cap appeared; the cheery face of one of the painters followed. He grinned idiotically at us and waggled his eyebrows.

I got up, stalked over there, and yanked the blinds shut.

"God! Ever since they started, it's been like a bad Marx Brothers comedy around here." Returning to the sofa, I added, "What I was trying to say before we were interrupted is that I'm not terribly comfortable with the idea of a mock trial. I can't shake the idea that it's a silly exercise that could have serious repercussions."

There was a horrendous crash overhead. Jack tipped his head back and glared at the ceiling. "Now we've got to listen to that! Goddamn manipulative little bitch and her skylights!"

The outburst was totally uncharacteristic of him. I stared, speechless.

"Sorry," he said. "I know you're fond of Rae. I like her, too. It's just that I think she takes unfair advantage."

"Rae's like a lot of people who've had unhappy childhoods: she's making up for it by stepping on toes."

"Well, I wish she'd hurry up and even the score and cut it out. To get back to what we were talking about, let me ask you this: did you ever suspect that I might be aiming at something more than a mock trial?"

I frowned. "Lis said—"

"I know—she's history. And I also know she's deathly afraid of going back into a real court of law. I don't blame her. But maybe if you come up with new evidence . . . That's why I wanted so badly for you to investigate. If anyone can find out what actually happened back then, it's you."

Big compliment; heavy burden to carry. "You flatter me."

Jack's phone buzzed. He crossed to the worktable, spoke, then held the receiver out. "For you. Ted."

Ted said, "I've got a message for you from somebody named Alison. You're to meet with Louise Wingfield at Project Helping Hands on Sixteenth Street at ten-thirty."

"Thanks." I replaced the receiver and turned to Jack. "Someone I know who works in the nonprofit sector talked to the friend of McKittridge who testified about finding the note; she's arranged an appointment for me. I was afraid Wingfield would refuse to discuss the case, but apparently she's open to it."

"I doubt you'll find that people are hostile after all these years."

"Somebody's hostile, Jack. If you want proof, just take a look at the front of Judy's house."

.   .   .

Project Helping Hands occupied a storefront in the grubby heart of the Mission. It had once been a bookstore-and-café; the bar still held steaming urns and towers of Styrofoam cups. Young men and women, most of them Hispanic, sat at the tables toward the front, drinking coffee, talking, reading. The nearby shelves housed a jumbled assortment of pamphlets, used textbooks, college and trade school catalogs, and nearly every self-help manual ever written.

The rear of the space was broken up into cubicles for counselors and administrators, and in one of them I found Louise Wingfield. She was a tall, vigorous woman dressed in black jeans and a soft, much-washed chambray shirt; her gray hair was stylishly short, and her fingers were stained with ink and nicotine. As she waved me into a wooden chair wedged between her desk and the cubicle's flimsy wall, she spoke into the phone, jabbing at the air for emphasis.

"Gordon, this young man is our most promising college candidate, and he deserves your support. You *must* meet with him this week so you can write the recommendation in time for your alma mater's early decision deadline. . . . No, I will not write it for your signature; that sets a bad example for our clients. . . . *Why?* Because, dear, we're trying to turn these disadvantaged young people into outstanding citizens and leaders, and one thing outstanding citizens and leaders do *not* do is give recommendations to people they've never met. . . . Friday at four? Fine, dear, he'll be there."

Louise Wingfield replaced the receiver and gave me a bright smile as she scrawled a note on a scratch pad. "The only reason Gordon Kane takes that kind of crap from me," she said, "is because I caught my son and him pig-drunk in my greenhouse when they were only fourteen and gave them both a hiding they've never forgotten. Gordon's still scared shitless of me."

I smiled as I took out my notepad. Gordon Kane was a formidable power in San Francisco business and society, and so proper it was rumored that royalty worried about using the correct fork at his table. The images of him "pig-drunk" and "scared shitless" were highly amusing. "You certainly have impressive resources to call upon for your clients."

Wingfield ripped the top sheet off the pad and tossed it into her out-box. "Nobody's impressive once you've seen him vomiting on your clean floor. But yes, I'm fortunate to have been born into our little golden circle, as one society editor dubbed it. We know everything about one another, both the good and the bad; consequently, we all owe one another favors." She leaned back in her creaky swivel chair, looked levelly at me, and added, "I hear you want to talk about Cordy."

"That's right. Did Alison tell you why?"

"She did. It came as no surprise. Joseph Stameroff has been obsessing for weeks about the prospect of a mock trial and what it could do to his precious adopted daughter. Leonard Eyestone—the present director of the Institute for North American Studies—isn't too thrilled, either."

"You know both of them?"

"They're part of our golden circle—Leonard born into it, and Joe a naturalized citizen because of his acquired prestige and wealth. And they're also two of those impressive resources you mentioned, as is Judy Benedict." She paused. "Frankly, I can't say I sympathize with Judy's biological mother's cause. Thirty-six years ago—even twenty—I wouldn't have spoken with you. But a lot's happened to me since I stopped being a society wife, and that kind of experience gives one a different perspective on the past. What one realizes often isn't pretty."

"Such as what you've realized about Cordy McKittridge?"

"Cordy, among others. Including myself." Wingfield shook a cigarette from a pack on the desk. "Do you mind if I smoke?"

I shook my head.

"Good. The few close friends I have from the old days are all into fitness—for themselves and everybody else. I read an article a couple of years ago that coined a wonderful term for that type—'health Nazis.' But down here"—she motioned around us—"and in the other neighborhood centers my foundation runs, the clients smoke, so it's difficult for me to quit. Minority group members don't think much about purifying the temples of their souls; they're too busy trying to keep body and soul together. Besides, smoking's a small wickedness compared to the others available to them, and it gives a great deal of pleasure." She lit the cigarette, inhaled, and made a face. "Not that I recommend it."

"About Cordy . . ." I began.

"Sorry, I tend to ramble about pet peeves. Anyway, Cordy." For a moment her eyes narrowed and she appeared to sort through her memories. "You know, even though I now see her and those days for what they were, a part of me feels such a . . . an affection for them. The early fifties . . ."

"Tell me about them."

She tipped farther back in the chair, smoked contemplatively. "Cordy and I had known each other forever. I was a couple of years ahead of her at Burke, though, and for school kids two years is a big gap, so we didn't really become friends until the summer after my sophomore year at Stanford, when my parents bought a small ranch near the McKittridges' summer place in the Napa Valley. Cordy had just graduated from Burke and was resisting her parents' plans for her debut, as well as their pleas that she attend college, or at least finishing school. The debut thing—I'd managed to avoid that myself, so I supported her, but I did try to talk her into giving college a whirl. We spent a lot of time that summer riding and swimming and talking."

A slender young Hispanic man with an acne-scarred face and stringy hair that fell to his shoulders came to the door of the cubicle. Wingfield looked at him, then gestured impatiently with her cigarette hand, laying a trail of smoke in the air. "Later, Rick." He nodded and went away.

She continued, "I really thought Cordy should go on with her education. She was very bright, in spite of the fact that she tried to give the opposite impression, as was fashionable in those days. But in the end she agreed to make her debut and stayed at home doing . . . whatever it was she did. It was while we were nipping gin in the powder room at the Sheraton Palace during the Winter Cotillion that she talked me into going in on renting the apartment."

"What apartment was that? According to the trial transcript, Cordy lived at her parents' home."

"It never came out at the trial; a great deal was hushed up, for reasons that will become obvious. The flat was in North Beach, on an alley off upper Grant Avenue. Very bohemian, above an Italian bakery. Only one girl actually lived there, but six of us used it for our . . . we called them adventures."

"Who were the others?"

"My roommate from Stanford. Two former Burke girls who attended Mills College in Oakland. A girl named Melissa—the one who lived there full time. I never got to know Melissa well; she was really Cordy's friend and not around a whole lot."

"And these adventures—I take it you mean sexual."

"Occasionally they were, but compared to what goes on today, they were pretty tame. Mainly we dressed more wildly than we were allowed to at home or at school, ran around to places our parents wouldn't approve of with people they wouldn't want us to know, stayed out late. We gave parties that artists and intellectuals came to, experimented with marijuana. On weekends when our parents thought us safely tucked away in the college libraries or visiting school friends, we'd be right under their noses in San Francisco."

It was just the sort of dual life a frivolous society girl would embark on: daring on the surface, but safe enough; if she got in over her head, she could always flee home to the monied nest. But even that degree of duality interested me, given what had happened to Cordy McKittridge. I asked, "What places did you run around to? And who were these people your parents wouldn't have wanted you to know?"

"Well, there were the clubs: Sinaloa, Ann's Four-forty, the Hungry I, the Forbidden City with its Chinese showgirls. Coffeehouses. This wasn't really the Beat era yet, but the city was full of bohemians. We met artists, poets, actors, all kinds of writers and intellectuals. Wild-eyed socialists, even Communists, I suppose. And there were less savory places: gambling rooms in Chinatown where they would let Caucasians in; back rooms behind Fillmore district bars; after-hours jazz clubs, blind pigs."

Wingfield paused, chuckling. "We had some narrow escapes.

At the Forbidden City we ran into one of my parents' neighbors; the only thing that saved us was that he was with a woman other than his wife. Another time my roommate's father turned up at Bimbo's—and he was from Santa Barbara. Fortunately we got out of there before he saw us." Suddenly her expression sobered. "And there was Cordy's abortion."

"When was that?"

"August of the summer before she died, right before she . . . started with Vincent. I went with her to the clinic in Ensenada. It was . . . awful. On the way home she passed out at L.A. Airport and I was afraid she'd hemorrhaged, but it was only the heat."

I jotted notes on my pad. "Who was the man?"

"Cordy wouldn't say. I always suspected it was Leonard Eyestone; she'd been seeing him off and on. But if it was, neither ever admitted to it. Have you spoken with Leonard?"

"I'm hoping to meet with him later today."

"Well, Leonard's an odd duck—not at all the type of man Cordy usually went with. A Ph.D. in economics. Anyway, I'd seen her with only a few other men the year before our trip to Mexico, and no one as frequently as Leonard. Whoever it was had to have had money; the abortion was expensive, and we went first class."

"The man couldn't have been one of your wild-eyed socialists, then. This brings us to Vincent Benedict. Was Cordy in love with him?"

Wingfield's lips tightened. "In her limited way. One of the things I've been forced to face about Cordy is that she didn't love anyone. Especially herself."

"And those notes she received from Benedict setting up their assignations—I gather they went to the North Beach flat rather than to her parents' home?"

Wingfield nodded.

"Did you ever read any of them?"

"No."

"But you were certain they came from Benedict. Why?"

"His handwriting was distinctive. Bold black writing on gray vellum notepaper. No return address, city postmark."

"But how did you *know* they were from him?"

"Because Cordy confided to Melissa, who told me. Cordy would always act different when they came—smug, smiling, and secretive."

"When did she start with Benedict?"

"Right after we came back from Mexico."

"Did you know Benedict?"

"Yes. Cordy took me to the Institute a few times, even fixed me up with a date for one of their cocktail parties. I knew most of the people there. It was one of those times that she pointed out the dovecote to me—the house's architect was an Anglophile, so there had to be a dovecote—and said it was a very romantic place."

"And you took her statement to mean that was where she met Benedict."

"I *knew* that was what she meant; Cordy had her ways of making things perfectly clear without actually saying them. I got mad at her when she started hinting around about the cote, and told her to grow up."

"When was that?"

"A couple of months before she died."

"But given the way you were sneaking around behind your parents' backs—that wasn't very grown up, either."

Wingfield shrugged. "Maybe I'd become tired of all that by then. I was about to graduate from Stanford and had to make some hard decisions about my future. Somehow helling around in the clubs and having affairs with married men didn't seem very intriguing anymore."

"How many other people knew about Cordy's and Vincent's meetings in the cote?"

"I'm not sure. It's possible quite a few did, the way gossip circulates in this town."

"Lis Benedict?"

"Well, given that she killed Cordy—"

"Assume for the moment that she didn't."

"Well . . . it's still probable that she would have known."

"I take it you were also acquainted with Lis."

"Yes."

"How did she behave toward Cordy?"

"She was equally pleasant to Cordy and to me, in a kind of

remote way. Mrs. Benedict was well bred and always acted the lady. That's why I was so shocked when they arrested her for the murder."

"But you believed that she'd done it."

"Yes."

"And do you now?"

". . . I don't know. At the time I wanted to believe she had because I wanted the whole thing over and done with so I could get on with my life. Now . . . well, I still can't imagine who else could have."

"That's what I'm trying to figure out." I looked down at my pad; my notes were sparse. "Ms. Wingfield, do you think this dual life you and Cordy and your friends indulged in could have led to her murder?"

She considered, shook her head. "As I said before, we were really pretty innocent. It was a very minor rebellion against the sterility and conservatism we saw at home and at school."

"I didn't think San Francisco or San Franciscans were ever sterile or conservative, even in the fifties."

"Then you don't know how things really were. After the war San Francisco had to grapple with a tremendous inferiority complex and paranoia. The way it coped was to conform."

"I'm not sure I understand."

Wingfield's face became animated; I suspected that in spite of the painful memories, she was enjoying this discussion of the past. "In the spring of forty-five," she began, "the city was host to the charter conference of the United Nations. Three thousand visitors representing some twenty-seven countries and the world press crowded into town. The parties and entertainments . . . well, they were spectacular. I know, because my parents gave one at our house on Lafayette Square. Several hundred people—including some men in turbans—attended. For years afterward my mother would relate that they drank over a hundred bottles of Korbel champagne, nearly that many cocktails, and smoked a hundred dollars' worth of cigarettes and cigars. I don't know what the canapés cost because at that point in her story my father would turn cross as a bear and tell her to shut up. . . .

"I'm rambling again. The point is that for two months San

Francisco was party-giver to the world. When the U.N. charter was signed and the delegates left, the leaders of society and industry were certain the city would be selected as home to the organization. You can imagine their shock when New York was chosen instead. And at that point the city changed; everyone decided they had to out–New York New York. Skyscrapers went up. Corporations were lured here. With them came the executive families, the executive tracts in the suburbs where we'd once had our country estates. Strangers invaded our clubs and our neighborhoods, our restaurants, shops, and schools. And instead of welcoming the newcomers, our socialites withdrew into the narrow confines of their supremely boring lives. And the children of society, like Cordy and me, rebelled."

"And what became of those children of society?"

"They're dead, like Cordy. Or as boring as their parents, like the two girls from Mills College who shared the flat. Or they've changed with the times, as I have."

"Speaking of the others who shared the flat—can you put me in touch with them?"

"No. My roommate from Stanford died ten years ago. I'm no longer close to the women from Mills, but from what I know of their lives, I can assure you that they'd want nothing to do with your investigation."

"What about Melissa?"

"Melissa I know nothing about. I haven't seen her since before Cordy died. Cordy's murder destroyed what little enthusiasm I had for the wild life; I collected the things I kept at the flat, spent the summer dating eligible men, and accepted the first halfway decent proposal of marriage. In a sense, Cordy's death doomed me to a living death in a bad marriage—until fifteen years ago, when I broke free of it."

"Do you recall Melissa's last name?"

Wingfield frowned, lit another cigarette. "I can't . . . That's odd. I knew it at one time, and I'm usually very good with names. Bird? No, *a* bird. Wren? Finch? No . . . Cardinal!"

"Melissa Cardinal. And you say you don't know how Cordy met her?"

"No. Cordy was always picking up strays."

"What did Melissa do? Was she a student?"

"No. She worked, and her job involved traveling, because she was in and out of the flat. She was . . . yes, a flight attendant."

"For what airline?"

"One of the big ones with international routes. I remember her showing us things she'd bought in Paris and London."

It was possible I might be able to locate Melissa Cardinal— just barely possible. I made a note, then asked Wingfield if she could think of anything else that might have had bearing on Cordy's death.

She thought for close to a minute, eyes narrowed against the smoke from her forgotten cigarette. Finally she noticed it and stubbed it out, shaking her head. "I can't recall a thing. Is this really so important at such a late date?"

"It's important to Lis Benedict. She was convicted—unjustly, I think. And even though they didn't execute her, she spent most of her adult life in prison."

Wingfield nodded. "It's odd," she said, "but if Lis *was* unjustly convicted, she and I have a good deal in common. Cordy's murder marked the beginning of a living death for both of us."

Eight

■ ■ ■

Before I went back to the office, I stopped at a corner grocery and bought a Coke and some microwaveable popcorn—not much of a lunch, but all I saw that appealed to me. Besides, popcorn contained fiber, and wasn't fiber one of the big nutritional buzzwords these days? I nuked it, as my nephew Andrew says, in the co-op's microwave, then carried it upstairs, losing a couple of handfuls to passersby, including one of the painters.

There had been no messages in my box in the foyer, but I found a pink slip on my desk on top of a stack of letters to be signed. The message was from Leonard Eyestone's office at the Institute for North American Studies, where I'd called early that morning to request an appointment. Since it was the noon hour, I put the slip aside for later, then called Rae on the intercom.

"Have you developed any good informants in the Mission's Hispanic community?" I asked her.

"A couple, but neither is as reliable as your Tony Nueva."

"Well, Nueva's no longer mine." I ran through the particulars on the graffiti incidents for her, then asked, "Will you contact your informants and see what they can come up with?"

She agreed, verified a couple of details, and hung up.

72

I signed the waiting letters, then turned my attention to setting in motion the machinery for a trace on Melissa Cardinal. Finding her—if she was still alive—would be tricky, perhaps impossible. First I checked the area phone books in the law library, unsuccessfully. The next logical step should have been an inquiry to the Department of Motor Vehicles, but I used my contact there sparingly in light of the DMV's strict confidentiality rules. I could check Vital Statistics for a record of a marriage or death, but that would entail a personal visit to City Hall and perhaps to offices in the adjacent counties—a time-consuming procedure that wouldn't necessarily produce results. I sat down on a stool beside the cluttered library table and pondered how to short-circuit the process.

Wingfield had told me that Cardinal was a flight attendant for an airline with overseas routes. She would have retired long ago—after all, those were the days when they made women quit upon marriage or when they reached a certain age—but flight attendants were unionized, and unions kept records. In the Yellow Pages I found a listing for the International Union of Flight Attendants in Burlingame, near SFO. I hurried back upstairs and made an exploratory call, but learned that their confidentiality was as stringent as that of the DMV. Sign of the times, I thought. We're all mildly paranoid—and for good reason.

All right, which airlines with San Francisco—based crews had held routes to Europe in the mid-fifties? Who would know? I consulted my Rolodex and called my travel agent, Toni Alexander. I was in luck, Toni told me; one of her employees had been in the business then. She spoke with her, came back on the line, and told me my best bet would be to try TWA. Before I hung up, Toni mentioned a fare to Hawaii that was so low I actually did a quick review of my finances. But funds were shorter than usual after installing the new fireplace, accommodations in the islands were expensive, and I didn't want to go alone, anyway. I doubted I could entice Hy into taking a trip; those exasperatingly blank years away from Tufa Lake seemed to have cured him of wanderlust.

TWA's central records, Toni had said, were maintained at Kansas City. I got the number from Information, dialed, and spoke with a Ms. Cook. She insisted on calling back to verify that I was actually with All Souls. When Ted put her through to me, her tone was less guarded.

Now for the story I'd manufactured, designed to elicit Ms. Cook's sympathy in case my request required extra effort on her part. "My problem is a little unusual," I said. "Our deceased client was a very eccentric woman, worth millions. I've often wondered if having money makes people strange or if it just gives them the idea they're entitled to let it all hang out, if you know what I mean."

Ms. Cook laughed; the ice was broken.

"Anyway," I went on, "our client traveled extensively and chose to draw up a will leaving her estate to people who had been of service on her journeys. A fairly substantial bequest goes to a TWA flight attendant named Melissa Cardinal. That's the good part. The bad part is that our client's last contact with Ms. Cardinal dates from nineteen fifty-six."

"That *is* unusual."

"Would it be possible for you to look up Ms. Cardinal's employment records? I'd like to get a Social Security number, last known address, or name of next of kin."

"Given enough time, I'm sure I can, but I can't give it priority. It may be several days before I give you a response."

"Since our client waited thirty-some years to express her appreciation to Ms. Cardinal, I don't suppose a few more days will hurt."

Ms. Cook said she'd get back to me as soon as possible. When I finally thanked her and hung up, it was nearly two, time to return the call from Leonard Eyestone's office. I dialed the Institute; a secretary told me Eyestone had an opening at three. Setting aside the mound of paperwork I'd reluctantly been contemplating, I headed for the Embarcadero.

·   ·   ·

The Institute's new headquarters, a gleaming white building at the south end of the shoreline boulevard near China Basin, reminded me of an avant-garde church. Its many windows arched gracefully; its cruciform wings radiated from a glass dome like that of a basilica. As I opened the wide front door, I wondered if Eyestone had chosen the orthodox design to signify that this was a shrine to the intellect.

The majority of the ground level was reception area, marble-floored and stark white. Three tiers of gallery rose above it, drawing my gaze upward to the glass dome. Its halves were drawn back like an open clam shell, exposing the sky; a salt-scented breeze spiraled down, rustling the fronds of the palms behind the semicircular desk. The strikingly attractive blond woman seated there smiled at my surprised expression. "It works on a sensor," she said. "When the temperature's right, it opens automatically."

"What if the temperature's right but it's raining?"

For a moment she looked nonplussed, then shrugged. "I'm sure the sensor takes moisture into account."

It probably did, I thought. Nowadays they had sensors for everything—everything except the tragedies resulting from rage and frustration and craziness that threatened to rip our world apart.

The woman took my name and spoke into her telephone. Soon a young man came down the stairway from the second-story gallery and introduced himself as Alex, Dr. Eyestone's appointments secretary. Alex was as attractive as the reception-ist and so fashionably dressed that he might have stepped off the cover of *GQ*, but a dullness of expression hinted that not much was going on behind his long-lashed eyes. The shrine to the intellect seemed to favor the physical over the mental in its acolytes.

Eyestone's office had a large anteroom on the bay side of the gallery. Alex led me across it to a pair of carved double doors and ushered me through them with ceremony. The inner sanc-tum was as glaringly white as the building's lobby, with a vista that swept from Treasure Island to Alcatraz.

My first impression was that the room was full of . . . stuff. Furniture: blue sofas and sand-colored chairs and bleached teak bookcases and an enormous old mahogany desk. Photo-graphs: all of men, shaking hands and smiling and posturing for the camera. Sculptures and the kind of mechanical toys that are presented to the man who has everything. Framed certificates and Oriental vases and little boxes in ivory and silver and gold. Golfing trophies and a wall rack containing dozens of exotic pipes. A huge stuffed koala bear in a tuxedo jacket sat on a stool at the wet bar. The bear's glassy eyes were dust-filmed, and he looked depressed, one arm outstretched on the bar as if he could use a drink. I glanced from him to the man who came around the desk, arm also outstretched.

"What's his name?" I asked.

"Hasn't any. He's only there to suggest that we academics have a sense of humor."

"Do you?"

"Only in rare instances." Leonard Eyestone clasped my hand, appraising me intently. He was of medium height and stocky, with silver-gray hair. His head looked too large for his body, and his blue eyes bulged slightly. When he smiled, there was an exaggerated tilt to the right side of his lips. Not an attractive man by any means, but one with character and sensitivity in his face. Something about him brought to mind the word "bruised"; I wondered briefly if any of the invisible contusions had to do with what had happened to Cordy McKittridge.

Eyestone led me to a grouping of chairs by the window wall. After offering me a drink, which I refused, he sat opposite me. "Now, Ms. McCone," he said, "I understand you wish to talk about the McKittridge case. Frankly, I find your attempt at resurrecting it counterproductive."

Odd phrasing. "What do you mean?"

"What can you hope to accomplish?"

"Possibly I can salvage what's left of two badly damaged lives."

He frowned, fingers toying with an ivory-handled letter opener on the table beside him. After a moment he said, "I take it you mean Judy and Lis Benedict. Ms. Benedict has had every opportunity to make a good life for herself, and from all indications she's succeeded. As for Lisbeth, I have no sympathy there. She chose ruin the night she hacked Cordy McKittridge to death."

"You speak as if you've kept track of both the Benedicts."

"I've monitored their situations from time to time."

"Why?"

He shrugged. "Wouldn't you, had you been close to the central characters in such a grisly drama?"

"You were close to the family?"

"To Vincent, anyway."

"And what do you remember of the night of the murder?"

"Nothing that contradicts the reported facts, if that's what you're hoping for."

"Tell me about it anyway."

"I have nothing exceptional to tell. I didn't live on the premises at the time, hadn't been there all day, hadn't seen Lisbeth, Judy, or Cordy in a couple of days. I was at the banquet for Dulles at the Blue Fox. Vincent was there, too, as were all the other staff members and their wives—save Lisbeth. Why go over this? Obviously you've studied the trial transcript."

"Even a cursory study of that transcript indicates that certain facts didn't come out at the trial."

"Ah, the old cover-up theory. Why is it that the notion of conspiracies is so attractive to people?"

"Because very often conspiracies exist." I hesitated, then added, "Let me ask you this: if you don't approve of my investigation of the case, why did you agree to see me?"

Eyestone smiled, features skewing. "Why, Ms. McCone, I neither approve nor disapprove. Frankly, I agreed to this meeting because I was curious about you."

"About me?"

"Yes. You may not be aware of it, but you enjoy a certain reputation in San Francisco. In exchange for the opportunity to meet you face to face, I'll be glad to tell you whatever you wish to know—within reason."

"What's 'within reason'?"

His smile broadened. "Test your limits and find out."

I felt as if I were involved in some sort of competition with Leonard Eyestone—one in which I knew neither the rules nor the prize for winning. "All right. Tell me what kind of woman Lis Benedict was back then."

He looked surprised; obviously he'd expected a different question. "She was . . . well bred, intelligent, articulate. She dabbled in hobbies—the calligraphy, for instance. I sensed frustration and anger in her, primarily because of Vincent's drinking and womanizing, but it may also have had to do with the fact that she had nothing to put her considerable talents to. I also sensed fear in her."

"Of what?"

"Of a good many things. Lisbeth Benedict was—still is, as far as I know—an extremely superstitious woman. By nature, superstitious people are fearful; they guard carefully against mishap with rituals."

"I take it you're not superstitious?"

He shook his head. "I'm a social scientist, with the emphasis on scientist. A pragmatist. And I'm seldom afraid—probably because I have very little imagination. One has to be able to visualize dire consequences in order to fear them."

I hadn't ever thought of it that way, but what he said made sense. I had a good deal of imagination, and whenever I found myself in a dangerous situation, I had to turn it off by force of will.

"What about Vincent Benedict?" I asked. "He was an alcoholic, a wife-beater. What did Cordy and his other women see in him?"

"Pain."

"I don't understand."

"The man had an aura of deep psychic pain—carefully cultivated, of course. He consciously projected the image of an unrecognized genius, misunderstood and undervalued by everyone, and stoically suffering in silence. Women lapped it up; they wanted to kiss him and make it all better. It didn't hurt that he was extremely handsome in a dissipated way." Eyestone spoke without rancor, as if on some level he admired Benedict's pose.

"I have the impression, though, that Cordy wasn't just another of Vincent's women."

"You're correct. He was planning to divorce Lisbeth and marry her."

"Had he told Lis of his intention?"

"Yes."

"Why wasn't that used against her at the trial?"

"I presume because Vincent didn't want his wife to go to the gas chamber."

"But you knew about it. Others must have, too."

"I doubt that. Vincent didn't tell me until the week before the trial began, and in the strictest confidence."

"And you told no one?"

"No. In fact, I've never spoken of it until today."

I hesitated, taking time to formulate my next question. "It was rumored that there were other men in Cordy's life besides Vincent. Someone else at the Institute."

"Yes."

"Who?"

He shrugged, smiling slyly.

"You?"

"So people said."

"*You*, Dr. Eyestone?"

"Such an irritated look, Ms. McCone! Yes, I admit I was involved with Cordy."

"Yet you and Vincent were friends."

"Some male friendships transcend territorial squabbling over women. Besides, my affair with Cordy was over long before she died, before she took up with Vincent."

"How long?"

"Since the previous summer, when she aborted our child."

Louise Wingfield's suspicion had been correct, then. "Whose idea was the abortion, yours or Cordy's?"

"Hers. I would gladly have married her, but she'd tired of me by then. She said she would have the abortion no matter what, so I gave her the money to buy a safe one. I cared enough that I didn't want her to risk her life at the hands of some butcher." Eyestone looked away from me. It was a moment before he looked back.

It surprised me that the memory of Cordy's rejection could still cause him pain. I thought of Judy Benedict's dislike of the woman, as strong now as thirty-six years before. Cordy's persona had been powerful, if it could tug so hard from the grave.

Eyestone glanced at his watch. "Is there anything else, Ms. McCone? I have another appointment in two minutes."

"Nothing that we can cover in two minutes. I'd like to talk with you again. I'm interested in the Institute—about what a think tank actually does."

He winced exaggeratedly. "Bad phrase. Don't use it again. It emerged long ago in the popular press; we didn't care for it then, and we still don't. But why are you interested in us? Surely the operations of the Institute have no bearing on Cordy's death."

"Probably not, but I like to develop the context in which a crime took place."

He squinted, studying me intently in the glare from the window. After a moment he said, "Every man enjoys talking about his work. I'll be glad to meet with you again. Call Alex and arrange an appointment—next week would be best."

"I'll do that."

We rose simultaneously, and Eyestone escorted me out and through the anteroom. It was completely deserted, and I saw no one in the lobby below who seemed to be waiting for an appointment. On the gallery, Eyestone clasped my hand, lips quirking lopsidedly. "I've enjoyed our talk, Ms. McCone," he said. "You've lived up to your reputation."

Now, what did that mean? Before I could ask, Eyestone went back into his office.

.   .   .

At All Souls I put thoughts of the case aside and slogged through my neglected paperwork. It was after seven when I finished. I'd planned to go home and read over the Benedict trial transcript once more, but my verbal sparring with Leonard Eyestone had stimulated me. What I wanted was active investigation, but I seemed to have temporarily run out of leads. Perhaps I needed some inspiration.

I picked up the phone receiver and dialed Project Helping Hands. Louise Wingfield was still there, as much of a workaholic as I. She responded with enthusiasm when I suggested she come along with me on a journey into the past.

Nine

■ ■ ■

I know a fellow investigator, an Italian-American and native San Franciscan in his late fifties who frequently bemoans the death of the old North Beach. Although I haven't lived here long enough to remember those days, I fully understand what my friend, a self-admitted nostalgiac, means. Chinatown has spilled over into what used to be Little Italy; topless clubs and bars and T-shirt shops form a sleazy neon-lighted hub at Broadway and Columbus. Trendy restaurants have supplanted many of the generations-old Italian establishments, and high rents are driving families out. But there are still pockets of the once-dominant culture, where the odors of crusty sourdough and oregano and espresso drift on the air and the official language is that of the native land. To me, North Beach is an exciting place where cultures clash and mix, bohemian life-styles abound, and a good meal of pasta and strong red wine can be had for under twenty dollars. If you can find a parking space, that is.

I got lucky that evening: a space opened up on Washington Square in the shadow of the twin-towered Saints Peter and Paul Church. Superstitiously I crossed my fingers to ensure further good fortune and hurried uphill toward the corner of Greenwich and upper Grant, where Louise Wingfield had said she'd meet me. The warmth of the afternoon had dissipated, and fog was drifting in—thin fingers that reached into the narrow alleyways and curled around the neon signs and streetlights, lending them an old-timey softness.

Wingfield, bundled in a down jacket, scarf, and knitted cap, leaned against one of the street poles at the corner. She was smoking and staring up the hill. When she heard my footsteps she glanced around, then straightened and dropped her cigarette on the pavement, crushing it out and nudging it into the gutter with her foot. She faced me, expression wistful, smile edged with pain.

"It's still there," she said.

"The flat?"

"Probably, but I'm talking about the bakery." She gestured at the next block, where a fog-muted sign said, Fabrizio Pastries.

"The same name?" I asked.

"The same sign, even."

"Why don't we go in there, see if it's still run by your former landlord?" As we began walking uphill, I added, "I take it you haven't been back here since you gave up the flat?"

"No. After I married, we never came to North Beach. It wasn't a place where—as my former husband would say—our kind of people went. Since my divorce I haven't had any reason to come here. And I suppose I haven't wanted to be reminded of those old days. Of Cordy . . ."

The bakery had plate-glass windows fronting on the sidewalk. Displayed in them were round loaves of sourdough, slabs of focaccia, handmade breadsticks, and an ornate custard-filled cake. Inside, behind a counter at the rear of the shop, stood a good-looking curly-headed man of about forty. As we entered, he flashed us a broad welcoming smile. I trailed behind Wingfield, examining the trays of cookies with various intriguing shapes and toppings. When I spied some cannoli stuffed with candied fruit and chocolate, I felt a sharp pang of hunger. So much for nutritionally sound fiber-heavy lunches.

The man noticed the yearning expression on my face and came over, smiling again. "Here, have a taste." He placed one of the little fried horns on a square of waxed paper and handed it across the counter. My mouth watered painfully as I bit into it. Ricotta, citron, and that bitter, bitter chocolate—just a step short of heaven.

I asked, "How on earth do you make this?"

"It's an old family secret."

"This is a family business?"

"Has been for over fifty years. The old man started it back before I was born."

"And how long have you been running it?"

"Only five years, since the old man retired. I served a long, tough apprenticeship, but it was worth it."

"I don't suppose you'd remember my friend." I motioned at Wingfield. "She rented the upstairs flat back in the mid-fifties."

He glanced at Louise, shook his head apologetically. "I remember that Pop let out the flat, yes. That was when he decided that my sister and I ought to grow up in the suburbs. We moved to Daly City, lived in a tract house. That was what people thought they wanted in the fifties: everything modern, nice and hygienic, nice and boring. My sister and I, we moved back here, and now I live in the flat with my family. Whatever my kids' lives are going to be, I guarantee they won't be boring."

I asked, "Does your father still live in Daly City?"

"Are you kidding? After my mother died, he wanted to come back here as much as my sister and me. He's got an apartment a couple of blocks away, and most nights this time you can find him enjoying his retirement with his cronies over at Reno's."

"That's a bar?"

Wingfield answered for him. "A bar in the finest North Beach tradition."

The baker nodded. "You've been there?"

"Many a time, back in the old days."

"And my old man, Frank Fabrizio, was your landlord. What do you know. Listen, why don't you go over to Reno's, say hello to him? The old man would get a kick out of it."

I said, "I think we'll do that." Then I glanced at the tray of cannoli. "But before we do, could I get a half dozen of those?"

.   .   .

To get to Reno's we cut through the mist-clogged alley. Wing-field stopped midway and pointed out the stairway to the flat. A black iron grille barred the tiny entry; the windows above were softly lit behind sheer white draperies.

"It's all the same," Wingfield said. "It's as if I'd moved out of there yesterday. I half expect to see Cordy come down those stairs in her favorite ice-blue taffeta shirtwaist." Then she hugged herself, shivering. "How did I get to be so old while this stayed the same?"

"You're not that old."

"I didn't think so till now. But my body feels so . . . perishable, while this"—she kicked viciously at the concrete stoop—"just goes on and on."

There was real anger in her voice, and it surprised me. Wing-field wasn't yet sixty and very hardy, but I supposed our concep-tions of age were all relative. I myself was already braced against the day when my own body would begin to fail me and one by one I'd be forced to abandon the things I loved to do, the dreams I hadn't yet fulfilled. And I knew there was no soothing word I could offer Louise, nothing that would temper her rage at the steady onslaught of time.

I said gently, "Let's go on to Reno's. We could both use a drink."

The bar was old North Beach: dimly lighted, with dark panel-ing, checkerboard tile floor, and deep red hangings. The ex-posed brick wall was honeycombed with niches containing pseudoclassical statues, and over the bar hung a badly executed gilt-framed oil painting of a Tuscan landscape. At one table a pair of old men hunched intently over an inlaid chessboard; at another a lone party who might have been a poet scribbled desultorily on a tattered legal pad. A middle-aged couple locked hands in a booth, faces strained in mute desperation.

There was only one other customer: a balding, wrinkled man who could have been the baker aged more than a quarter of a century. He perched on a stool at the far end of the bar, glass of red wine in front of him, conversing with the grizzled bar-tender. I tapped Wingfield's arm and pointed him out. She nod-ded and moved his way.

As we approached, the men broke off their conversation—a

spirited discussion of our mayor's failings—and turned interested eyes toward us. Frank Fabrizio's twinkled in mild lechery—obviously a man who appreciated women both young and old. Wingfield allowed herself a small smile of pleasure at the compliment, then slid onto the stool next to him. I sat on the other side of her as the bartender slapped two cocktail napkins onto the polished surface. After we'd ordered glasses of the house red, Louise lit a cigarette, turned to Frank Fabrizio, and introduced herself. "I was one of the girls who rented your upstairs flat back in the mid-fifties," she said. "Your son told us you'd be here, so I stopped in to say hello."

He studied her, furrows deepening around his eyes. "You look familiar, some. Of course we're all older now—hah, Reno?"

The bartender set down our glasses with a philosophical shrug.

Fabrizio shook his head in amusement. "Funny how people turn up after all these years. You girls sure were hell-raisers back then."

"Well . . ."

"The wife, rest her soul, always complained. Said we might as well've turned our flat into a bordello. You ever notice how the women who pride themselves on their virtue have very dirty minds? Anyway, I stuck up for you girls. Said you were just sowing some wild oats. I figure everybody, male or female, is entitled to, if they've got the nerve."

The old man seemed to like to hear himself talk and would probably ramble unchecked if allowed to. I leaned around Wingfield, told him my name and occupation, and added, "I'm trying to locate one of the other tenants of the flat—Melissa Cardinal. Do you remember her?"

"Sure, there's nothing wrong with my memory. What's she done?"

"Nothing. Louise just wants to see her again, and asked me to help find her."

"Well, I remember her like she was back then. Little blond girl. Nice shape." Fabrizio's hands described Melissa's curves. "When that one came around to pay the rent, the wife didn't let me out of her sight."

"When was the last time you saw Melissa?"

Fabrizio's prompt response took me by surprise. "Two weeks ago."

I glanced at Wingfield. She frowned.

"Where?"

"Over on Broadway, near Chinatown. She hasn't aged well, not like you." He winked at Wingfield. "Damned blowsy looking, doesn't keep herself up. I wouldn't've recognized her except the guy she was with used her name. Funny about that, too: he wasn't her type. A gentleman. Good haircut, good suit, real quality."

"What were they doing?"

"Coming out of a bar. It wasn't his type of place, any more than she was his type of woman. And they were arguing."

"About what?"

"I couldn't make out the words. But I caught the tone: whine, whine, carp. I got enough of that from the wife to recognize it."

"Melissa was doing the whining?"

"Uh-huh."

"And the man?"

"He wasn't too happy with her, but he was trying to be nice. Like I said, a gentleman, didn't want a public scene."

"Can you describe him?"

"Well, I didn't see him face on. And I was looking more at Melissa than him. Younger than me, from the way he held himself. Gray hair? White? Well, plenty of hair at any rate." Ruefully he patted his own balding pate.

"Height? Weight?"

"Medium, I guess."

"Anything else?"

"Like I said, he had his back to me, and I was paying more attention to Melissa. I really saw him as a type, you know?"

I knew. Unfortunately, it was a type that populated San Francisco in large numbers. "What's the name of the bar?"

"The Haven."

I'd noticed it—a typical Broadway dive. "What time of day was this?"

"I was coming back from my morning walk to the produce stand on Jackson, so maybe eleven-thirty, quarter to twelve."

It would do no good to go over to the Haven tonight, then; I'd have to check tomorrow when the daytime shift was on. But it was my best lead to Melissa so far, and if she was a regular, someone might know where she lived.

I asked, "Is that the first time since she rented your flat that you've seen Melissa?"

"She's been around the neighborhood for years, but so far as I know, she only goes out at night. And to tell you the truth, I never connected that blowsy dame with the little stewardess until I heard the guy say her name." Fabrizio's features grew glum, and he pulled heavily at his wine. After a moment he looked at Wingfield and added, "It's a bitch, isn't it—what time does to us all?"

She nodded in silent reply.

.　　.　　.

The conversation with Frank Fabrizio had depressed Louise. As we walked downhill toward Washington Square she was silent, hands thrust deep in her jacket pockets. Finally I said, "I saw Leonard Eyestone this afternoon. An odd man, but interesting. He admitted he was responsible for Cordy's pregnancy."

"Just like that?"

"With no hesitation, once he acknowledged that he was the other man at the Institute whom she'd been involved with."

"Well, he must have figured it didn't matter at this point. Water under the bridge, over the dam, whatever. On the surface, the affair might seem peculiar, but Leonard has a brilliant mind, and Cordy, whatever her other failings, was not stupid."

"He said he would have married her, but she'd tired of him."

Wingfield's lips tightened. "Inability to sustain interest in things and people was one of the failings I just mentioned."

"She sustained an interest in Vincent Benedict long enough to make him want to leave his wife and marry her. Eyestone also told me that."

"I doubt the wedding would ever have taken place."

"You think she would have tired of him, too?"

"Maybe not tired, but . . . consider the situation. Vincent was going to divorce Lis. A divorce would have been costly, especially with a child involved. Also, this was in the days before no-fault; Lis would have named Cordy as corespondent. And when that happened, Cordy's family would have cut her off instantly. Vincent would have had to pay alimony, provide child support, plus support Cordy on his salary from the Institute—which was good, but not all that generous. It never would have worked out; Miss McKittridge was used to, and liked, her luxuries."

I thought about that. "And if Cordy had broken it off after Vincent asked Lis for the divorce?"

"Potentially explosive."

"But Vincent, according to all the witnesses, was at the Dulles banquet and reception the night Cordy was killed."

"And Lis was not."

We had reached my MG. Wingfield said, "I'm going to have to trouble you for a lift. My car's in the shop, and one of my volunteers dropped me off here."

"Are you hungry?"

"Not particularly. You?"

"No." But I hesitated, unwilling to put an end to the evening. "How do you feel about indulging in more nostalgia?"

"Not terribly enthusiastic. But what do you have in mind?"

"I want to take a look at the estate in Seacliff."

"Why?"

"The same reason I wanted to see the location of the flat. Going to crime scenes or places that figure in a case is a habit of mine. It helps me get a feel for what happened."

"Even so many years after the fact?"

"Yes."

She compressed her lips, shifted her weight indecisively.

I said, "I'll drop you off and go alone."

". . . No, I'll go with you. It'll be easier for you to find the place if I direct you. And it's time I confronted the past."

"Lis Benedict said something like that just yesterday."

"Did she? Well then, as I speculated this morning, Lis and I have more in common than I realized. We're both victims of what happened to Cordy."

.   .   .

The area of exclusive homes called Seacliff is spread over a bluff south of the Golden Gate, high above the open sea. Sandwiched between Bakers Beach and Lincoln Park, it is not set off from the adjacent Richmond district by walls or security gates, but imposing stone pillars mark its boundaries. Once one passes through them, it quickly becomes apparent that this is an enclave of wealth and privilege. The lots are large by city standards, and the houses are custom-built. The landscaping is elaborate, the views breathtaking. A mere estimate of the maintenance cost for one of those establishments is enough to make a modest property owner like me cringe.

That night a strange, motionless fog gripped the terrain outside the Gate. It made the pavement slick, the curves of the winding streets dangerous; blurred the contours of the great homes that sprawled on the promontory; muted light and sound. Beneath it I sensed hidden life and activity—deceptively quiet and faintly menacing.

Wingfield directed me, with a few errors and some back-tracking, through the maze to El Camino del Mar. The houses on the bluff crowded together to take advantage of the view, but as we neared Lincoln Park, a long stone wall overhung with vegetation appeared, then a driveway flanked by pillars. A For Sale sign was prominently displayed on one of them.

"Stop here," Louise whispered. Her fingers grasped my right hand where it rested on the wheel—tense and icy.

I guided the MG to the curb and leaned forward, trying to glimpse the house. All I saw above the cypress trees on the other side of the wall was a dark monolith with a steeply peaked roofline. I took my foot off the brake and let the car inch forward.

Wingfield said, "You'd better not drive in there. The police patrol frequently, you know."

"Then we'll walk in. If anyone comes along, we'll tell them we're prospective buyers." I motioned at the sign on the pillar.

"Prospective buyers wandering around at night?"

"Why not? If I were about to pay what they must be asking for this, I'd want to see the property at night as well as during the day, wouldn't you?"

She shrugged but got out of the car.

Except for the cry of foghorns and the muted restive motion

of the sea, it was very quiet there. Cold moisture touched my cheeks; I could taste and smell its brininess. I crossed to the driveway and started up, Wingfield a bit behind me. The drive cut through the cypress grove that I'd glimpsed across the wall; when I reached the other side of it, I stopped, staring up at the mansion.

It was a tall house with dormer windows on the third story. English in style, half-timbered above the brick, flanked by thorny pyracantha hedges. An enormous leaded-glass window rose beside the door, its small diamond-shaped panes dark and lusterless. Much of the brick was covered with climbing ivy, and below the slate tiles of the roof the rain gutters were choked with the vines. Several small security spots cast deceptive patterns of light and shadow.

The driveway bled out into an oval parking area with room for at least a dozen cars. I started across it, then realized Wingfield wasn't following. She stood at the edge of the cypress grove staring at the house as I had. Her arms hung limp at her sides, but as I watched she hugged herself; even at a distance I could see her shiver. I motioned for her to join me, and she did, reluctantly.

"Where was the dovecote?" I asked.

"Over there." She motioned to our right, where the grounds sloped toward the edge of the bluff. "They tore it down as soon as the trial was over. For years they tried to sell the lot, but there were no takers."

I peered over at the lot. It was heavily wooded, misshapen Monterey pines dark against the motionless fog. If I had crossed to the bluff's edge, I would have had a view of tumbled rock and waves breaking on the crescent of China Beach. Beautiful as this place probably was in daylight, at night it seemed desolate. Even the empty mansion looked more inviting.

I asked Wingfield, "Why no takers, given the value of oceanfront land?"

"The slope of the lot makes it extremely difficult to build on, plus there was the stigma of the murder. That's faded by now, but the lot is still priced too high, as is the mansion."

"But some of the property was sold off?"

"Yes, in the late fifties. The house that we passed just before the wall began used to belong to the Institute; it was used for conference rooms and staff quarters. But after the murder fewer and fewer people wanted to live on the premises, so it was sold."

"What was the reason for the staff living here in the first place?"

"Russell Eyestone wanted to keep his handpicked intellectuals cloistered in a little community where they could feed on one another's genius."

"You sound cynical."

"Well, I didn't come here all that often, but when I did I never heard anything remotely resembling lofty discourse."

"What *did* you hear?"

"The same kind of cocktail-time chatter and gossip I heard at home. Money talk, plenty of it. Politics—they were as conservative as they come. And pretty vicious gossip. Academics can be some of the worst backbiters in existence."

"Leonard Eyestone claims they don't have much of a sense of humor, either."

"Leonard should know. He laughs only at other people's expense."

"Tell me, who and what did they gossip about?"

"People I didn't know. Things that didn't interest me."

"And you say cocktail-time chatter. Did a lot of drinking go on?"

"Hard drinking. It was no secret that Vincent Benedict was a serious alcoholic, and the others usually managed to keep up with him. It's frightening to think that such people had so much influence on this country's public and defense policies."

"The Institute's influence was that powerful?"

"Yes. I don't know exactly which contracts they've held or what studies they've conducted, but they're a premier think tank, on a par with RAND or Brookings. When the Institute speaks, the decision-makers listen."

I made a mental note to remember to call Eyestone's secretary for the appointment to discuss the think tank.

A foghorn bellowed again up by the Gate—a plaintive cry, like that of a wandering soul searching for comfort.

Wingfield shivered, violently this time. "Let's go," she said.

There was nothing to see here, but something held me. "Go back to the car," I told her. "I'll be there in a couple of minutes."

"Don't take too long." She hurried down the walk into the mist, hunching to light a cigarette.

I faced the house again, acutely aware of its silence, my eyes probing the darkness. I tried to picture what it would have been like with light in its many-paned windows and music and laughter drifting through them into the night. The image would not materialize.

I pivoted and looked to the north, where the waters of the bay became those of the sea. A wall of white blocked my view. Had it been foggy on that June night so many years before? Had Cordy McKittridge's killer used that fog as cover, moving stealthily through it to the dovecote? Had the fog also masked the murderer's bloody departure?

The questions smashed my mental dam, and images washed over me. A shadowy form of indeterminate sex gliding across the lawn and slipping through the foliage. Fingers of light spilling from inside the cote, briefly pulling the mist aside. And inside the cote: rough brick walls across which more shadows fell. Shadows in attitudes of anger, rage, violence. And the long blades of the garden shears shining . . . slashing. Blood flowing . . . spattering. . . .

I blinked. Whipped around. Stared hard at the vacant lot, then at the dark mansion.

No evil here now, I told myself, only an empty house waiting for real estate agents to troop through with clients. The other homes in the vicinity were solid, lighted, tenanted. The dovecote no longer existed. This was simply a pleasant neighborhood where people conducted their lives in style and luxury.

But memories of evil still lived in the minds of some people. Memories of evil still lived in this fog-clotted darkness.

Ten

■ ■ ■

When I woke the next morning, gray light filtered through the mini-blinds and I could feel fog-damp in the air. I lay bundled up in my quilts for a while, listening to Rae, whose room at All Souls was still open to the sky, getting ready to go to work. Even after she left, I remained in bed, fighting a peculiar leaden feeling and trying to identify what was troubling me.

Well, if pressed, I could have thought of plenty of troubling things, from the purely personal to the global, from the important to the mundane, but none of them was what weighed down on me. Actually, "troubling" wasn't the right word. Call it . . . haunting.

I recalled the specters that had passed before me the previous night in Seacliff, others that had clouded my dreams. Started to push them away, then told myself, No, take a good look at them in the daylight.

What I saw wasn't a pretty picture, but then, murder, even one so far in the past, never was. And the murder *had* happened long ago, to someone I'd never known. So why the vivid images and nightmares? Why the feeling of not being safe from violent, time-trapped emotions?

93

I shivered, pulled the quilts closer. Call it a morbid preoccupation with the crime; call it a weird psychic link, even. But whatever the label, last night as I'd stood in front of that house in Seacliff, I'd *felt* how it had been on June 22, 1956. Altered as the landscape was, I'd *seen* the gardens, the dovecote. And later, in my dreams, I'd sensed what might have gone on there. I knew, and yet I didn't know. . . .

All of which added up to the fact that I'd become too involved in this case and was in serious danger of becoming unhealthily obsessed. When your objectivity goes like that, it's time to back off—call it quits, say you gave it your best shot, and go on to something else before you do your client and yourself irreparable harm.

But it was too late for that now. Once I'd committed myself to an investigation, I couldn't just abandon it. An obligation to the client, yes, but even more to myself. I wouldn't be able to live with the knowledge that I'd allowed bad dreams to frighten me away from the truth.

If I'd truly wanted to escape involvement in this case, I would never have gone to Seacliff the night before. Would never have opened those moldering trial transcripts. Would never have climbed to the tip of Bernal Heights and talked with Lis in the first place.

Too late now. Maybe it had always been too late.

.   .   .

As soon as I had dressed and poured my coffee, I called All Souls and spoke with Rae. Had either of her informants come up with anything on the graffiti incidents? I asked. She said no, but she'd keep after them. Next I had her transfer me to Jack and asked if Judy had made any headway in persuading her adoptive father to talk with me. He didn't know; Judy was out of town on business, but he'd ask her when she returned that night. Finally I called the Haven, the bar on the edge of Chinatown where Frank Fabrizio had seen Melissa Cardinal; a recording told me it opened at eleven.

That would leave me plenty of time to speak with Lis Benedict. I collected my bag and briefcase and headed for Bernal Heights.

The fog made the steeply canted little street dismal; the streaky pink letters on the facade of the white Victorian gave it a trashed, abandoned aura. I pushed the bell, received no reply. Used the knocker and waited. After a moment the curtain on the window of the front room moved. Then the chain rattled and Lis opened the door.

She looked haggard. Her white hair straggled and her black robe gaped at the breasts. She drew it together and fastened it before she motioned me inside. The house felt cold and smelled of stale cooking odors. A small formal parlor to the right was as dusty and unused as the one in my own house.

Wordlessly Lis beckoned me to follow her down the narrow hallway to a kitchen and dining area. In spite of the warm earth tones and comfortable furnishings, the room was cheerless; outside a sliding glass door, mist lurked in the foliage beyond the deck.

A half-full mug of coffee sat on the table next to a newspaper open to the want ads. On the breakfast bar a TV with its volume turned off showed an exercise class, the participants' pasted-on smiles more like grimaces of pain. Lis smiled at me in much the same way and offered coffee.

I accepted and sat at the table. The newspaper was Sunday's; the ads were the rentals. Lis returned with a mug, moving haltingly, as if today she felt the full burden of her years. As she sat, she pushed the paper aside. "I'd offer you breakfast, but I'm afraid the cupboard is bare."

How automatically she minded her p's and q's, even after all the time in prison. I assured her that I rarely ate in the morning, then asked, "Does the name Melissa Cardinal mean anything to you?"

She thought, then shook her head. "It's a curious name. I'm sure I'd remember it if I'd ever heard it."

"Even if you'd heard it before you went to prison?"

"Prison didn't dull my brain," she retorted with some sharpness. "Who is she?"

"A former roommate of Cordy McKittridge." I explained what Wingfield had told me about the apartment.

"I've never heard any of that. It never came out at my trial. Is Melissa Cardinal important to my case?"

"I'm not sure, but I want to talk with her, if she's still alive."
I sipped coffee, set the mug down, and leaned my forearms on
the table. "Lis, I spoke with Leonard Eyestone yesterday. He
claims your husband confided that he'd asked you for a divorce
so he could marry Cordy."

Her face underwent a sudden change—sagging, crumpling.
She reached blindly for her coffee mug and upset a saltshaker
that sat on a trivet between us. Automatically she brushed up
the salt and tossed it over her shoulder. "I guess I should have
told you about that."

"Why didn't you?"

"I've lived so long with . . . Do you remember what I said
about my daydreams?"

I nodded.

"One of them was that Vincent had never decided to leave me.
If I pretended that he still loved me, that Cordy was simply one
of his unimportant affairs, the days in prison were easier to get
through. When you pretend so hard and for so long, after a
while you come to believe it."

"I see. Is there anything else that you've been pretending
about?"

She got up and moved to the sliding glass door. Stared silently
at the fog.

"Lis, is there anything else I should know?"

The phone trilled. Lis jerked violently, clawing at the drapery
beside the door. From her panicked expression, I knew it wasn't
the first time this morning that the phone had rung.

I said, "I'll get it," and crossed to the breakfast bar. Pitching
my voice lower and trying to make it sound older, I said, "Hello?"
into the mouthpiece.

There was a click as the connection broke.

I replaced the receiver. Lis watched me, still clutching the
drapery, her face like bleached parchment. With an effort she
let go and crept to her chair.

"How often are you getting the anonymous calls?" I asked.

"Oh . . . several times a day. At least a dozen over the past
twenty-four hours. And then there's . . . Judy's adoptive father."

"He's tried to pressure you again?"

"Twice. Joseph Stameroff is as persistent now as when he was with the district attorney's office. Somehow he's gotten it into his head that he can simply bludgeon Judy and me into giving up. It's gotten so that between him and the other phone calls, I can't sleep. I can't even bring myself to go out to the store or to take my walk."

"For God's sake, why don't you unplug the phone? Why doesn't Judy get the number changed?"

"Judy's away, since Sunday night. I can't leave the phone off the hook; she might call."

When Jack had mentioned Judy being out of town, it occurred to me that she'd chosen a very bad time to leave Lis alone. "Where is she?"

"New York. Something to do with a stage play she's bringing here." Lis must have seen my disapproval, because she quickly added, "She didn't want to go. I insisted. I've ruined too much for her as is, without damaging her career."

I felt a flash of irritation. "Stop being a martyr. *You* didn't do anything to Judy. What happened was done to both of you, and frankly, you got by far the worse deal. Judy's done well for herself, so let go of the idea that the past has somehow crippled her."

Lis was silent, looking down at the table.

Briskly I added, "What you need is some food in the house. Do you want me to go to the grocery store?"

". . . No. The woman next door has offered. Mrs. Skillman. It's time I accepted her kindness."

"Good. You should get to know your neighbors; you won't feel so alone then. I'm going to All Souls now, and I'll talk with Jack. He'll probably come over later, check on you. In the meantime . . ." I glanced around the room—at the silent, flickering TV screen, the rumpled newspaper, the menacing presence of the phone on the breakfast bar. "In the meantime, try to keep your mind off your problems," I ended lamely.

She nodded and got up to see me out.

I waited until I heard the dead bolt turn and the chain fasten before I went down the porch steps.

.   .   .

Jack looked every bit as haggard as Lis. He sat behind his worktable, papers strewn over its entire surface. I could have sworn he'd done nothing with them since Sunday.

I leaned in the doorframe until he noticed me. "Thought you had a case going to trial today," I commented.

He shrugged wearily. "The judge is out sick."

"Lucky for you."

"Why?"

"You're too preoccupied to do well by your client. And I hate to burden you any more than you already are, but . . ." I told him about my visit to Lis.

"Jesus," he said. A pounding noise came from above, where Rae's attic room was. He glared at the ceiling.

"That been going on all morning?"

"Yes. It's driving me insane. The guy promises he'll be done by noon. Did you say you told Lis I'd check in on her?"

"I said probably."

"Good. I'll just call her."

"What's the matter? You don't want to see her?"

"Not really." He hesitated. "Shar, I don't admit it to Judy, but Lis makes me uncomfortable."

"You *do* think she killed McKittridge."

"No, I don't. But like any criminal lawyer, I've got a good shit detector, and I know there's something not right about the woman. There's a lot she's not telling us. I don't know . . . Maybe old Joe Stameroff is right. Maybe she *shouldn't* be living there."

He looked so uncharacteristically confused and forlorn that I transferred my sympathy from Lis to him. "Listen, give it a rest. Lis'll be all right. A neighbor is going to fetch groceries for her, and maybe they'll visit for a while. I find it hard to believe that someone who survived all those years in prison can't survive until Judy comes home tonight."

Jack looked torn. "Well, maybe I'll give her a call. It's the least I can do. Are you making any progress?"

"Some." I stepped back into the hallway. "And if I'm to make anymore, I'd better get cracking."

As it turned out, progress had been made for me. On my desk was a message from Ms. Cook at TWA in Kansas City. Melissa Cardinal's records had been easy to access, it said, because she was receiving disability payments from the airline for injuries suffered in a crash in 1961. Her current address was on James Alley off Jackson Street in Chinatown.

.   .   .

James Alley had none of the picturesque trappings usually associated with Chinatown. It was just a grimy half block with vehicles pulled up on either narrow strip of sidewalk and trash cans standing by the back doors of shops and restaurants. The smell of cooking oil, Oriental spices, and garbage hung on the air; the pavement was littered and dog-fouled; dirty curtains masked the windows above the commercial establishments. Melissa Cardinal's address was an entryway between two reeking Dumpsters; the glass in its door wore a covering of steel mesh.

I pushed her bell and after a while received an answering buzz. The door opened onto a steep, dark stairway that smelled of cats. I looked up, saw no one, and began climbing. At the first landing I looked up again and spied a bulky figure in the shadows. "Ms. Cardinal?"

"Formal, aren't you?" an old-woman voice said.

"I'm sorry?"

"Oh." Confused. "I was expecting . . . Who are you?"

"Sharon McCone, from All Souls Legal Cooperative." I started up the last flight of stairs.

"What do you want?"

"To ask you a few questions about a case I'm working on." It was so dark in the hallway that I still couldn't see her clearly. Didn't the landlord believe in light bulbs?

"I'm busy. I'm expecting—"

"This will only take a few minutes."

The woman sighed. "All right. I've got that long." She turned her back and led me into her apartment. From behind, her faded white-blond hair looked as if it had been lopped off without the aid of a mirror; ragged hanks hung down, forming an uneven line above the collar of her shapeless flowered dress. The apartment was nearly as dark as the hall, but smelled better.

"Have a seat." Melissa Cardinal motioned toward a lumpy sofa.

I sat, expecting her to turn on a light. Instead she lowered herself into a recliner, sighing heavily. A white cat jumped onto her lap, and she cuddled it possessively. Now I was able to see her better, and what I saw was a shock.

Melissa Cardinal's facial features were cruelly scarred. The flesh on her left cheek was pitted and puckered, the corner of her mouth warped in a perpetual one-sided grin. Seen from the right, she would have appeared perfectly normal, but from the left the disfigurement was jarring. The plane crash, I thought, back in sixty-one.

My expression must have betrayed my surprise, because she touched a pudgy hand to her cheek—briefly, before beginning to stroke the cat. In order not to compound her discomfort, I got out my notepad while glancing around the room. It was shabbily furnished, except for a tall glass-fronted cabinet full of animal figurines, carefully arranged and probably lovingly dusted.

I felt a swift stab of sympathy for Melissa Cardinal, living alone in semidarkness with her disfigurement. It was no wonder Frank Fabrizio hadn't recognized her until the man she was with spoke her name; at that, he must have seen only her good side.

"So what do you want to know?" Cardinal asked defensively, as if she sensed my sympathy and wanted none of it.

"I understand you were a friend of Cordy McKittridge."

She started so violently that the cat flew off her lap. "Cordy! Cordy's been dead years and years now."

"One of our attorneys has asked me to reinvestigate the case. I understand that you—"

"I can't talk about Cordy."

"Why not?"

"I just can't, is all." She tried to get up, pushing hard on the arms of the recliner, but sank back helplessly. "You better go. I'm expecting company."

"Ms. Cardinal, there's no reason to get upset. As you said, Cordy's been dead a very long time. It can't hurt to talk about—"

"It can't?" Her eyes glittered. "Shows how much *you* know."

"How can it hurt?"

Silence.

"Has someone told you not to talk about Cordy? Threatened you?"

Melissa Cardinal looked around for her cat, located it under the glass-fronted cabinet. She made a clicking noise with her tongue, and the animal leapt onto her lap. Melissa cradled its furry body against her breasts like a shield.

I tried a less intimidating tack. "Do you remember Frank Fabrizio? The baker who rented the flat to you and Cordy and your other friends?"

"Sure I remember Frank. I see him around the neighborhood, but he doesn't see me."

"Why not?"

"Because I only go out at night, that's why." She touched her cheek gingerly, as if it still hurt. "Over thirty years it's been now, but I can't face the daylight, much less a mirror. I used to be pretty, you know—an airline hostess, flew all over the world. Then there was the crash, fall of sixty-one, at Orly. One of the passengers, a little boy traveling alone, didn't get evacuated with the others. I went back for him. Wasn't heroism—just what I'd been trained to do. He got out without a scratch, but I was so badly burned that two operations wouldn't fix it any more than this. And you know what? His parents never even thanked me."

"I'm sorry."

"No sorrier than I am." Her voice grew bitter and weary. "Look, I don't want to remember Cordy or the days when I was still pretty. Please go away."

Pressuring vulnerable people like Melissa Cardinal is something I thoroughly dislike, but a necessary part of my job. I said, "Did you know that Frank Fabrizio saw you one morning a couple of weeks ago?"

"I never go out—" She broke off, remembering.

"He saw you and a companion outside the Haven."

For a moment I thought she'd deny being there, but then she asked almost shyly, "What did he say about me?"

"That you'd aged well," I lied.

She nodded. "Frank always had his eye out for me, and I guess I led him on a little. Gave me a kick—his wife was such a prune-face. But he must've seen me from my good side. Otherwise . . ."

"Why did you go out that morning, Ms. Cardinal?"

"What?"

"If you never go out in the daytime, you must have had a good reason. Was it because of the man Frank saw you with?"

"What man?"

"Frank described him as medium height, well dressed, a gentleman."

". . . Oh, him. That was just somebody who bought me a drink at the bar."

"So you went out by yourself at eleven o'clock in the morning to have a drink—that's all?"

"Why else?"

I just looked at her. Before she looked away, I caught a glint of fear in her eyes.

"Ms. Cardinal," I said, "if you're in trouble, I can help you."

"Why would I be in trouble?" But she clutched so hard at the cat that it yowled in protest. She released it, and it again bounced to the floor.

I took one of my cards from my bag and wrote my home number on the back. "You can reach me at one of these numbers day or night, if you need help or want to talk." I stood and extended it to her. When she didn't take it, I set it on the table.

"Miss McCone," she called after me as I went toward the door, "I'm sorry, but I just can't risk it."

"Risk what?"

She shook her head. "Please go. I don't have much of a life, but I'm not suicidal."

Eleven

■ ■ ■

After I left Melissa Cardinal, I went over to the Haven and tried to get a better description of the man Frank Fabrizio had seen her with. The bartender said he'd worked the early shift every day for six weeks running, but at first he claimed not to remember Cardinal. Ten of my dollars later, his memory improved to the point that he remembered her but not the man. Five additional dollars bought me a description of the man that conflicted with Fabrizio's in several respects. The barkeep, who was very short, said the man was tall; he thought his hair might have been blond, rather than gray or white. Distinguishing features? Well, he'd paid more attention to the woman, gross-looking as she was. Would he call the customer with her a gentleman? Well, he wasn't the sort of guy you usually served in the Haven, but you get all kinds.

What now? I thought as I stepped out of the murky bar and into the sun glare that was breaking through the fog. I really wanted to talk with Justice Joseph Stameroff, but that would have to wait at least until Judy returned from New York. I'd also have liked to question Leonard Eyestone about the workings of the Institute for North American Studies, but the director had said he couldn't talk again until next week. Why such a delay?

103

A busy schedule—or a desire to avoid further conversation? I supposed in the meantime I could do library research on the subject, but that seemed unnecessarily time-consuming.

Still undecided, I headed crosstown in the general direction of All Souls, but at Market and Church I pulled into the parking lot of Safeway and used the pay phone. Jack, conveniently, was manning Ted's desk over the noon hour. I had no urgent messages, he said, and nothing at all from Rae, who had gone to lunch with Willie Whelan.

"So he's back from Reno," I commented. "Even if her skylights aren't done on schedule today, my house'll be my own again. Undoubtedly she'll prefer his bed to my guest room."

"Undoubtedly. But, Shar, you're not going to like this: Willie hinted to me that he brought her back a diamond ring."

"The new store opening must have been a wild success. God, what if she actually marries him?" It was a prospect I couldn't bear to contemplate. After all, hadn't I already suffered with Rae through the demise of her first ill-starred union?

Jack said, "If she does, she ought to be committed. There used to be a law in this state that you could get fifty dollars for turning in a lunatic. Wonder if it's still on the books?" He paused, then asked, "You coming back to the office?"

I'd intended to, but quickly I said, no. I couldn't stomach yet another microwaved meal at my desk; I couldn't deal with painters grinning idiotically at me through every window; and I certainly couldn't stand to witness Rae's raptures should she indeed return from lunch with a diamond. "I'll be at home until further notice," I told Jack.

At the Safeway fish counter I bought a container of marinated mussels, then added a freshly baked sourdough roll and a pint of pear ice to my shopping basket. When playing hooky, I told myself, do so in style.

There was an accident at Thirtieth and Church involving the streetcar and a delivery truck, and access to my own little tail end of Church, beyond where the car tracks turn and stop, was blocked. I had to detour to the south, and by the time I entered my street from the far end, grumpy and hungry, it had been nearly an hour since I'd talked with Jack.

And there, right smack in front of my house, stood a big gray Lincoln Towncar whose dark-suited driver seemed oblivious to the fact that he was causing any number of my neighbors excessive inconvenience. On top of that, he was blocking my driveway. I came to a stop and leaned on my horn, gesturing.

The driver looked up, then spoke to someone in the backseat.

I stuck my head out my window and shouted, "You're blocking my driveway!"

He ignored me, kept right on talking to his passenger.

Who was this person keeping me from my own driveway— and my long overdue lunch? I leaned farther out the window and hollered, "Get that goddamn thing out of my way!"

My neighbor across the street, who was trying to get *out* of her driveway, gave me the thumbs-up sign. The driver of the Lincoln looked around and frowned. Then he started it and backed up a few feet.

I pulled the MG into the drive, grabbed my grocery sack, and got out. The Lincoln's driver was at its rear door now, opening it. I strode over there and said, "Look, you're making trouble for a lot of people by blocking a narrow street like this."

The driver shrugged and turned toward the man who was emerging from the car.

He was perhaps seventy—tallish and slender, with a lined face that suggested intelligence and reflectiveness. He had a full head of white hair and hard gray eyes that didn't even try to mask their arrogance. From newspaper photos I recognized Justice Joseph Stameroff of the State of California Supreme Court.

Stameroff looked down his long nose at me, then glanced along the street, his eyes resting on my neighbor's car, whose rear bumper was nearly touching the Lincoln. His expression made it clear that he found visiting such a place distasteful.

The look brought my anger to a full boil. I said, "Tell your driver to move the car. Where the hell did you learn your manners—in a barn?"

Spots of color appeared on the justice's cheekbones. "And where, young woman, did you learn to speak to your elders that way?"

"Just because you've lived a long time doesn't give you the automatic right to be inconsiderate." *Shut up, McCone. This man's Judy's father; you're trying to get him to talk with you about the case—remember?* "And just because you're a justice on the state supreme court doesn't make you above the law." *My God, you'll never learn, will you?*

Surprisingly, Stameroff's lips rippled in what I supposed was as close to a smile as he ever got. "Miss McCone," he said, "I'll forgive your rudeness if you'll forgive me mine."

". . . Fair enough."

"Now, if you'll invite me into your home, we'll talk. My driver will take the car around the block." He turned to the man and added, "Twenty minutes should be sufficient."

As I led him up the steps of my brown-shingled cottage, Stameroff commented, "I see this is one of the earthquake houses."

"You're familiar with them?" I shook my front-door key loose from the others on the ring.

"Reasonably. Some forty-six hundred were built as temporary housing after the quake and fire of oh-six. Two or three rooms; yours must have been one of the three-roomers. Stoves, but no plumbing. Tenants became owners if they moved the houses to new sites at their own expense by August of oh-seven."

And that recital told me that Stameroff enjoyed showing off his knowledge. I flattered him. "You're well versed."

"History was my first love, before the law."

Inside the cottage I considered where to take him for our talk and opted for the informal sitting room. As I led him down the hallway, I noticed he was studying the interior with keen interest.

"You've done a great deal with the cottage," he said. "How many rooms is it now?"

"Six. Two of them, as well as the garage and basement area, were added by previous owners. I added the sixth and a deck, and I modernized the kitchen and bathroom."

"By yourself?"

"Some by myself, some by hiring contractors."

"You young women are so enterprising these days." The words sounded fatherly and indulgent—and condescending as hell.

"It's been an interesting project" was all I replied. I motioned for him to be seated and took my groceries to the kitchen.

When I returned, Stameroff was perched on the edge of a chair, his arrogant eyes skipping from the ash-clogged fireplace to a tumbled stack of paperbacks on the rug, to a finger-smudged wineglass on the coffee table, to my scuffed athletic shoes lying loose-laced and pigeon-toed underneath it. Suddenly I saw the room as he did: not as a warm, cheerful haven but as the shabby lair of an uppity woman who was also a poor housekeeper. Being unfairly made to feel defensive only increased my annoyance with him, and I sat down on the sofa, offering neither refreshment nor apology.

"I assume," I said, "that you spoke with Jack Stuart, who told you I would be at home this afternoon?"

"Yes. My daughter has been urging me to meet with you, and I had some free time, so I decided to come here. What we have to say is best said in privacy."

"I appreciate your talking with me. While I can't expect you to sympathize with my investigation—"

"That's fortunate, Miss McCone, because I have no sympathy whatsoever. I am here, in fact, to ask that you cease your efforts on Mrs. Benedict's behalf."

Not surprising. "Why?"

"Because I love my daughter, and your dredging up the painful past can only hurt her."

"She doesn't feel that way. Shouldn't the decision be hers to make?"

He sighed. "Judy has always been a . . . problematical child. It's small wonder, of course, considering what happened to her at the vulnerable age of ten. She overdramatizes, and tends to bring difficulties upon herself. First there was the business of reestablishing contact with her biological mother. For close to twenty-five years she visited her at Frontera—where Mrs. Benedict was moved in the sixties—whenever she could, and Mrs. Benedict filled her head with lies. Next came the nonsense of bringing the woman into her home. With that, it has gone far enough. I cannot . . . I *will* not allow this exhumation of a past that is better left buried."

"Justice Stameroff," I said, "Judy is forty-six years old."

He frowned. "I know my daughter's age."

"Then you must also know that she's an adult woman, capable of making her own decisions."

"I'm afraid you don't understand the situation. Judy is a grown woman, yes, but in many respects she's like a child. A willful child who wants her way regardless of the consequences."

"The consequences to whom?"

"To her, of course."

"I'm not sure your main concern is for your daughter."

"For whom else would it be?"

"Yourself."

His eyes narrowed. "Explain that."

"Justice Stameroff, I'm not at all convinced that Lis Benedict killed Cordy McKittridge. If I were to prove she didn't, it would reverse your victory in the case—a victory that put you on the road to the state supreme court."

"I hardly think it would affect my tenure there."

"Unless there was some sort of cover-up or collusion at the time of the trial."

He heaved an exaggerated sigh. "Not the old conspiracy theory again! Miss McCone, I thought better of you."

"Leonard Eyestone laughed at the conspiracy theory, too. But something has made me wonder if it isn't true: in fifty-six you were only a deputy D.A., fairly junior on the staff. Why were you chosen to prosecute Lis Benedict? It was a high-profile case; why not the D.A. himself?"

Stameroff spent a moment framing his answer. "The district attorney himself was in poor health; he'd already announced he wouldn't run for another term. The prosecutor's office was looking for someone who had potential as well as trial experience on crimes such as Lis Benedict's. I was the obvious choice."

"Or perhaps you were the obvious choice because you were young and willing to compromise in order to further your ambitions."

Stameroff's reaction was mild, considering what I'd accused him of. "If you believe that nonsense, then you're a fool."

I didn't respond, merely looked into his eyes and waited.

"A fool," he repeated. "Do you realize what you're risking by undertaking this ridiculous cause?"

"You tell me."

"I *have* told you. My daughter's happiness, perhaps her emotional stability, is at stake."

"And what else?"

"I'm sure this case will not enhance your career. Or your employers'."

"Ah, there it is. I knew it had to come down to this."

"To what, Miss McCone?"

I got up, began to pace. "What would the first step be, Justice Stameroff? Costly but essentially harmless destruction, like the graffiti sprayed over the facade of Judy's house? Or an attempt to wear me down psychologically, like the anonymous phone calls that have been troubling Lis? And when those things didn't work, what next? Bodily harm?"

For a moment Stameroff seemed incapable of speech. "Would I do that to my own daughter? Only a monster would resort to such tactics, no matter how much he wanted to get that woman out of her house!"

"Then for your sake, I hope you haven't. But I suppose when it came to me, you wouldn't feel called upon to resort to such clandestine tactics. You're very highly placed, and you have friends in even higher places. A call to the right person. . . . Of course, you couldn't exert pressure on All Souls; you tried with Jack Stuart, and it got you nowhere. You might attempt to influence the state board that licenses me, but you know what? To civil servants like them, there's something that smells very bad about illegal coercion from a man who's sworn to uphold the law."

Slowly Stameroff rose from the chair—an old man with a failing body, but still a formidable adversary. "I will not tolerate any more of this kind of talk! I will not tolerate your meddling. You cannot fly in the faces of the people who count."

The people who count.

No phrase could have triggered more rage in me. I turned, faced him down. "Who are these people, Stameroff? Your friends? The ones at the top of the political power structure? The ones with enough money to buy whatever and whomever they please? Just who the hell are they, Stameroff?"

He compressed his lips, glanced around. It was obvious he wanted out of my house, but he also wanted to have the last word.

"Who are they?" I insisted. "Are the people who count the ones who know the truth about Cordy McKittridge's murder? Who know the truth and have good reason to fear it?"

Stameroff's tongue flicked over his lips. He busied his hands with adjusting the hang of his suit coat. Finally he said, "I will not dignify your questions with a response. Suffice it to say, this is your last warning. You will not be allowed to perpetrate this offense against justice. Justice was served thirty-six years ago when Lisbeth Benedict was sentenced to die in the gas chamber. My only regret is that I wasn't able to watch her strangle on the cyanide. I will not allow justice to be further subverted—not at this late date! And certainly not by you."

I looked directly into his eyes—eyes that now made me understand what the old westerners had meant when they spoke of the eyes of a hanging judge—and said, "That's the first time I've heard someone refer to righting a wrong as 'subversion.' "

His mouth worked, and he clamped his lips together again. Then he turned on his heel and left the room. Moments later the front door slammed violently behind him.

.   .   .

I spent the rest of the afternoon on routine work in my home office, and the early evening digging out the remaining blackberry-vine roots from my backyard, while contemplating exactly how much trouble I'd gotten myself into. A good deal, I decided, but I wasn't at all sorry. I was thoroughly sick of the Joseph Stameroffs of the world, who thought they could trample all over the rest of us. In attempting to intimidate me, Stameroff would find out some of us weren't so easily frightened.

Tough talk, McCone, I told myself. Not at all bad for one of those uppity enterprising young women. We'll see how brave you are when the pressure starts coming down.

With renewed frenzy, I resumed my attack on the blackberry roots.

By nine, when I was lying on the sofa listening to some CDs of big band music—a recent enthusiasm, brought on by a re-reading of *The Last Convertible*—I had to conclude that any desire to drop the Benedict case was gone. Anger made me want to press on with it—and that in itself gave me caution. Very few things I'd ever undertaken in anger had turned out well. What I needed was advice—both legal and personal—as well as official sanction from All Souls. Hank could provide both; I'd call him tomorrow at the condo he and Anne-Marie had rented on Kauai.

And if he did give me the green light? I wondered, jiggling my foot to Glenn Miller's "American Patrol" and sending Allie flying from the sofa's arm. Investigate very discreetly and hope that Stameroff wouldn't catch wind of it? Or go full tilt and place myself and All Souls in even greater jeopardy? Bad choice to be forced to make.

I didn't like either option any better by the time the CDs had cycled twice, so I gave up and went to bed.

.　　.　　.

At first I didn't know what the ringing was. I'd been dreaming at such a deep level that I couldn't hold the images long enough to identify them. I pushed myself up on one elbow, tossing my hair out of my face. The digital clock showed two-seventeen. The phone kept ringing. I grabbed the receiver, prepared to snarl at a drunk calling the wrong number.

Jack's voice—agitated, forming words I couldn't grasp.

"What? Say that again?"

"Come over here right away."

"Why? Where?"

"Sharon, wake up! I already told you—Judy's house. Lis has been killed."

Twelve

∎ ∎ ∎

There always are crowds when police cars and an ambulance arrive in a residential area, even at two-forty in the morning. The small one in front of Judy's house parted, at first I thought for me; then I realized they were bringing the body out, and I stepped back, looking away as the bag on the stretcher went past.

A uniformed patrolwoman guarded the door. I told her who I was; she spoke with someone else, then motioned me inside. Jack and Judy sat on the sofa in the little formal parlor I'd glimpsed that morning. She was rumpled and red-eyed; he wore running shoes that didn't match. She must have come home late, found Lis, and called and woken him.

With them was Bart Wallace, an inspector on the Homicide detail. A wiry black man with gray hair and silver-framed glasses, Wallace was one of the department's best detectives. I'd known and liked him for years, respected his abilities, and trusted his judgment. It was a relief to see he'd caught the call.

Wallace came forward and shook my hand. "Mr. Stuart says you may have some information that could be helpful to us."

"I hope so." I glanced at Jack, but his attention was focused on Judy. She sat still as stone, eyes on the floor in front of her.

Jack had his arm around her shoulders, but she seemed barely aware of his presence, not at all aware of Wallace's or mine.

Bart noticed, too. He said softly, "We'll go back to the kitchen, where Ms. Benedict found her mother."

I nodded and followed him into the hall. "When did she find her?" I whispered.

"Twelve-fifty, the call came in. She'd just returned on the red-eye from New York."

"And how did it happen?"

"Benedict was shot in the head. Looks like a contact shot: star-shaped wound, flaps outward, no blackening."

"Someone she knew, then?"

"Maybe not. It was a forced entry. You been here before, know the layout?"

"Yes."

"Sliding glass door to the backyard was broken. Signs of a struggle in the eating area—chair tipped over, coffee cup knocked off the table. Gun was beside her—thirty-two, belongs to the daughter. Says she bought it for protection."

"So Lis Benedict was trying to scare off an intruder. He took the gun away from her and killed her." It was a prime argument against untrained individuals having access to firearms.

"Looks like," Wallace said.

Poor Lis, I thought. Alone here, frightened, helpless against someone younger and stronger. I remembered my leave-taking of her: I'd become irritated, told her to stop being a martyr. And I'd told her Jack would probably stop by later, but he hadn't wanted to.

I put my regret away for now and motioned at the kitchen. "Is it okay to go in?"

"Lab crew's finished."

We entered the room where I'd talked with Lis that morning. The signs of a struggle, while not numerous, were readily apparent. The chair where she'd sat had been knocked on its side. Her coffee cup lay shattered next to the chalk outline of her body. A fern had fallen from a stand near the glass door, was trampled and wilted. I looked at the door: jagged shards protruded from its frame, and smaller ones were scattered on the terra-cotta tile. On the table the coffee cup I'd drunk from was filmed with fingerprint powder.

"The prints on that are probably mine," I said, pointing it out. "I came by around nine-thirty yesterday morning, stayed maybe half an hour. Do you have a fix on the time of death?"

"Yeah. Neighbor to the right, Adele Skillman, heard the shot. About six-fifteen, she says. A little while later she heard somebody run down the path between the houses."

Six-fifteen. I thought again of Lis, alone and helpless. Judy had been out of reach, unaware of the crippling depression into which the increasingly frequent anonymous phone calls had plunged her mother. And Jack? He might not even have bothered to call Lis, taking to heart what I'd said: *I find it hard to believe that someone who survived all those years in prison can't survive until Judy comes home tonight.*

Well, she hadn't survived, had she? And perhaps my words to Jack made me, in some indirect way, partly responsible. Where had *I* been while Lis was dying? At home, obsessing about Joseph Stameroff and how I might have put myself and All Souls in jeopardy.

Stameroff, I thought now. Could Stameroff be involved in this? He hadn't made an outright denial when I suggested he might have arranged for the graffiti and phone calls. Could this have been a professional hit?

Wallace was watching me closely. "Something wrong?"

I wasn't ready to bring Justice Stameroff into the conversation yet, so I said, "Feeling guilty, I guess. She was my client, and I didn't like her much. When something like this happens to a person you don't care for, you feel guilty for a lot of irrational reasons." I looked at the smashed glass door again. "Bart, this Adele Skillman—she heard the shot, but not the glass breaking?"

"Right."

That bothered me. It had to do with something I'd learned during the seemingly endless years of renovating my house, but I couldn't quite grasp it. "So what did she do after she heard the shot and the person running?"

"Nothing. Didn't want to—"

"Get involved."

"Yeah."

We were silent for a moment. Then Wallace said, "Tell me about your investigation. Stuart gave me rough outlines, and of course I know the victim's history. Now let's hear what you've got."

I perched on the edge of the table, and he leaned against the breakfast bar as I went over the details. When I finished, he closed his notepad and slipped it into the inside pocket of his suit jacket. "That's good stuff. You think of anything else, be sure to let me know."

I hesitated. The concept of a state supreme court justice ordering a professional hit might be farfetched, but my talk with Stameroff had bearing on Lis Benedict's final attempt to clear her name—and that attempt could possibly have led to her death. Withholding the details of my conversation with Stameroff would have been withholding evidence. "Bart," I said, "there *is* something else," and told him about the justice's visit to my house.

Wallace's expression grew very grave. When I finished he was silent for some time. "You've really handed me a can of worms, you know that?"

"Yes."

He took off his glasses and rubbed the bridge of his nose where they'd made deep indentations. "Christ, I hate these cases that turn politically sensitive! I'm going to have to talk with my lieutenant about this, and he'll have to go to the captain. . . . Listen, Sharon, I want you to promise not to discuss this with anyone else."

"Of course."

"And lay off the investigating for now. You don't want to go stirring things up, even by looking into this old murder. Those . . . what was it Stameroff called them? Those 'people who count' can play rough."

I nodded and slipped off the table. My gaze rested on the outline of where Lis had fallen, and my eyes stung with tears. It didn't matter that I hadn't liked the woman; this was a terrible end to a terrible life.

Not much escaped Wallace; he put his arm around my shoulders and guided me toward the door. "If it's any consolation," he said, "it doesn't get any easier for me, either."

He and I spoke briefly with Jack, Wallace stressing that I was to put my investigation of the McKittridge case on hold. Jack was distracted, his mind on Judy. "It was a bad idea in the first place," he said, and went to comfort her.

·　·　·

At home I brooded in what remained of the darkness. Brooded not only about Lis Benedict but about the other, living victims of the McKittridge murder. Brooded about all the victims I'd seen during my time in the business. About all the predators I'd seen do the victimizing. And about all the reasons why. . . .

As the sitting room windows were taking on gray definition, the doorbell shrilled. I started, flooded with that uneasiness such untimely summonses cause. Went down the hall and peered through the peephole. My neighbor, Will Curley, a short-haul trucker whose route throughout the Bay Area took him away at all sorts of ungodly hours, stood on the steps. Under the bill of his Giants cap, his face was angry.

"Have you seen this?" he demanded as soon as I opened the door.

I stepped outside and looked where he pointed. The shingles on the front of my house were streaked with red; it had soaked in and bled, but I could still make out the words: DEAD WOMAN. Sprayed two, three . . . no, four times.

Numbly I touched the nearest patch of paint. Still tacky. Had it been done as I sat wrapped in an afghan on the sofa, or earlier, while I was at the murder scene? Or even earlier than that, while I slept? I could have missed it while leaving and coming home in the dark. I'd been upset and in a hurry, and the porch light had burned out the night before last.

Dead woman. Me, if I didn't leave the Benedict case alone. I thought of Wallace's words: "Those 'people who count' can play rough."

Will was waiting for me to do something—scream, curse, cry,

anything but just stand there. Finally I asked, "Do you know how I can get that off?"

He frowned, clearly puzzled by my mild reaction. "Probably you'll have to reshingle. Is this a mob thing or what? The wife said a limo was hanging around yesterday and that you were talking to a couple of guys in dark suits."

I smiled weakly. "You've seen too many *Godfather* movies. The guy with the big car—it wasn't a limo—is on our side of the law." Or at least he was supposed to be, I reminded myself.

"Then who did this?"

"I wish I knew."

"You find out, come to me. I'll take care of him."

"I'd rather you asked around for a cheap shingler."

"I got a cousin in the building trades—he'll get you a good price." Then Will peered at my face, checking to see if I was really all right. "Anything else you need, just give a holler."

"Thanks, Will." As he jogged down the block toward his truck, I felt a wave of gratitude for having found this oasis of neighborliness. Then I went inside and called Bart Wallace at his office.

"You remember something else?" he asked.

"No, but there's been a new development." I explained about the graffiti.

" 'Dead woman,' " he said. "I don't like that one bit. I've been in conference with my lieutenant for the last hour, and now he's with the captain, but my gut feeling is that I'm going to have to move slow on the Stameroff angle." He paused. "Tell you what—I'll send a lab crew out there to take pictures and paint samples. Maybe we can get a match with the stuff at Benedict's. You okay?"

"I'm not frightened, if that's what you mean. In fact, I'm starting to get really pissed off."

Wallace was silent for a moment. "Sharon, why don't you go away for a few days? Memorial Day weekend's coming up. Have yourself a little vacation."

"Why? I doubt I'm in any real danger."

"You don't know that. Besides, you keep on getting pissed, it'll be the ruin of my case." He tried to make a joke of it, but there was real concern for me behind the words. "Think about it, will you? There's nothing you can do here."

"Bart, I do have other work besides the Benedict case."

"Well, think about it anyway. If you decide to go, just let me know where I can reach you." Abruptly he hung up.

As I ground coffee beans, I considered Wallace's suggestion. Leaving town seemed like running away, but on the other hand, I really couldn't do anything about the Benedict case or the graffiti. My remaining caseload was light, and I'd already requested this coming Friday off, so why not take a couple more days on either end of the long weekend? I could sort through the facts and my impressions of the case in a different environment; something might occur to me that would aid Wallace's investigation.

But *could* I leave, given what had just been done to my house? What if the perpetrator returned, wreaked even more costly havoc?

Of course I could leave. Through Wallace I could arrange for extra police patrols on my street; it stood to further his case if they apprehended the vandal. And Ted could be persuaded to periodically check on the house; he had a proprietary interest in Ralph and Alice—they'd originally belonged to his childhood friend Harry, who had died of AIDS—and always fed them when I went out of town. Plus there were vigilant neighbors like Will Curley. Sure I could leave.

And there was an added factor that made the prospect of getting away attractive: I'd feared I was becoming obsessive about the McKittridge murder, and now I could feel the pull of that long-ago crime even more strongly. I needed to sort through not only the facts and my impressions but also my feelings. With distance, perhaps I could regain control.

After I'd finished my first cup of coffee, I made my arrangements. Then I called Hy. Said I needed to get away for a while. He heard the seriousness in my voice and without question told me he'd meet me at Oakland Airport in four hours. We'd fly over the Sierra Nevada. He'd take me to the Great White Mountains, where bristlecone pines, the oldest living things on earth, grow. We'd watch the tule elk, the wild mustangs, the golden eagles. We'd make love under the black star-shot sky. We'd listen to the silence.

Uneasiness nudged me. I reminded him that I hated the oppressive silence of the mountains.

That was because I'd never really listened to it, he said. Once I learned to do that, the silence of the Great Whites would soothe me. Strengthen me, so I'd return home prepared to face whatever was driving me from the city.

I wasn't totally convinced, but I agreed and started packing. And realized I'd made all my arrangements without once doubting that Hy would fly here for me—just as he hadn't doubted I would fly off to the Great Whites with him.

In that moment I understood that we knew each other as fully as was necessary. There might be blanks and empty spaces in both our lives that we chose not to fill in, but what counted was the essence of a person, and almost from the first we'd instinctively grasped that.

On the way to Oakland I stopped in at my office and destroyed the file labeled "Ripinsky, Heino."

Part Two

The Predators

Thirteen

■ ■ ■

Flames flickering against rough stone, Hy warming his back as he sat on the raised hearth. Shifting light leaving his hawk-nosed face in shadow, playing on the dark blond hair that curled over the collar of his wool shirt.

I crossed the room, stepping over our joined sleeping bags, and handed him the beer I'd fetched from the ice chest. Then I placed my own on the rough pine floor and sat beside him, my thigh pressing against his.

"You've been awful quiet the last few days, McCone," he said. "Come to any conclusions yet?"

"Some, but nothing major."

He nodded, didn't press me.

We'd flown in the Citabria to a landing strip at the northern Inyo County town of Big Pine. There we had picked up supplies and a rental Jeep and driven along Death Valley Road into the Great Whites, to this two-room cabin belonging to one of the many nameless, faceless friends who owed Hy favors. We'd done all the things he'd said we would, and more. I'd learned to listen to the silence. This was our last night here; tomorrow— Wednesday—we'd fly to Oakland, and Hy would continue on an unexplained mission to San Diego.

123

"What about you?" I asked. "Are you ready to tell me why you're making this trip to my hometown?"

"I've got to talk to an old buddy about a business proposition he's made me."

"What kind of proposition?"

"I'll tell you about it if it works out."

"Something to do with the foundation?" Watch it, I warned myself; you're getting too inquisitive.

Surprisingly, he grinned, teeth flashing white under his droopy mustache. "No, you nosy person. To tell the truth, environmental work's kind of paled for me. Not the cause—the work itself. That foundation directorship my late wife so generously set up for me doesn't take half my time. As for the rest of it . . . maybe I'm just tired of getting busted to save the trees. The trees'll get saved sooner or later, but by some kid with a good fund-raising apparatus and a PR firm, not by an old jailbird like me."

The word "old" didn't fit him, but "jailbird" certainly did. I'd never known anyone who had done more jail time for more noble causes than Hy. "Sounds to me like you're getting restless."

"That I am." He glanced at me, frowned, then put his hand under my chin and tipped my face up toward his. "Look, McCone, I feel a change coming on. It's a good change, and a lot of it's due to you. But I've never been much of a talker, at least about myself, so don't rush me, okay?"

I let the subject drop. He'd tell me what he wanted me to know in his own good time, and in his own way.

The silence that fell was comfortable. Wind baffled around the stone chimney behind us. I shrank deeper into the luxurious warmth of my down jacket, conscious of the heat of Hy's thigh through my jeans. Minutes ticked by before he said, "You never called that cop back."

I'd phoned Bart Wallace from Big Pine, to let him know I'd be incommunicado for a few days. Friday afternoon Hy and I had driven back into town for more supplies and spent the evening eating, drinking, and dancing at a country-and-western bar, but I'd made no effort to check in with the inspector. "No point in it. He wouldn't have gotten anything conclusive from the coroner's office or the lab yet, and the higher-ups had advised him to tread very lightly as far as the Stameroff angle is concerned. Treading lightly gets you nowhere with a bastard like that."

"So what're you going to do? Let them cover it up, like they did thirty-six years ago?"

The question annoyed me. He should have known by then that I'd never been a quitter. This trip—my flight from the city and the case—was merely a respite. And part of the reason I hadn't called Wallace again was that I'd been playing for time, hoping that one nagging piece of information would shake itself free from the mass of useless data that we all carry in some remote corner of our minds. Something *had* been wrong about Lis's murder scene. Something . . . but I just couldn't grasp it.

Because of my irritation, my voice sounded sharp when I replied, "You're jumping to a conclusion, Hy. Stameroff may be just a concerned and overprotective father."

He didn't react to my tone, merely said, "You know you don't believe that. Sure as hell he's covering something up, and take it from me, McCone, cover-ups are bad shit."

I looked at him with interest, hoping he'd go on. We all knew cover-ups were bad, but Hy had spoken with a vehemence that was obviously born of bitter personal experience. He saw my expression, however, and his own became closed, guarded.

"Well," I said after a moment, "cover-up or not, it isn't my case anymore."

Hy pulled at his beer, looking thoughtful. "What is it with you, McCone? You're not afraid—not of the good Justice Stameroff or the scumbag with the spray paint. You're pissed off, but you're not afraid you'll lose control; you've faced that fear twice now, and you know you won't step over the line. So why this resistance? You could still research the old case for the Historical Tribunal. Nobody can stop you from doing that."

I moved away from his side, swiveled on the hearth and looked into the flames. Cobalt, emerald, amethyst, blood red—pulling hypnotically at me in the same way my dream visions of the events of June 22, 1956, had . . . .

"McCone?"

"I hear what you're telling me."

"And?"

"I'll think on it."

He nodded, satisfied. After a bit he said, "Those pennies on the dead woman's eyes—the symbolism's pretty obvious." I'd filled him in on the cases, past and present, in bits and pieces over the last five days.

"Closing one's eyes to something," I said. "A statement about the victim: she should have closed her eyes to whatever it was that got her killed. Or maybe a warning to somebody else."

"But why *lead* pennies? Not easy to come by, even then. Lead: a very reactive metal, highly toxic. And then there's the symbolism again: heavy, gray, inert."

"Those war-issue pennies weren't actually lead. They were zinc-coated steel. Only minted one year, nineteen forty-three."

Unlike Jack, Hy seemed to find nothing odd about my having such a fact at my command. "Wonder how many people know that, though? Zinc—not much symbolism there, other than the association with the color white. Steel—an alloy, man-made—symbolizes strength. The eleventh wedding anniversary is the steel anniversary." He laughed reminiscently. "I know, because my parents divorced in their eleventh year of marriage, and my mother used to carry on about how there had been no steel, no strength, in the relationship. There was plenty of steel in her second marriage, though; it lasted till death did them part."

Again I glanced at him with interest. Hy had a way of imparting bits and pieces of his life—fragments that didn't quite add up—and intriguing me all the more.

"Lead's chemical designation is Pb," he went on, "atomic number eighty-two. Zinc's is Zn, thirty. Nothing in that, I guess."

Now I just plain stared. "Since when do you know so much about chemistry?"

"Oh, I looked into it some, once. You can't help but have a nodding acquaintance with mineralogy, what with all the mining that goes on in my part of the state."

I shook my head. The wide range of Hy's interests never failed to amaze me. So far I'd learned that he was a western history and fiction buff; could fly and repair an airplane; had mastered the diplomatic process of fund-raising for environmental causes but also possessed a confrontational style that I'd once heard described as a cross between that of Genghis Khan and the kamikaze pilots. In addition, he could speak with authority on folk medicine, animal husbandry, native American art, meteorology, and antique firearms—and do so in four languages. Now it appeared that he'd not only read the table of chemical elements but memorized it.

"What?" he asked.

"I'm impressed."

"Hell, McCone, why do you think I learned that stuff? Struck me as a good way to get women." In more serious tones he added, "You know, to a collector those coins might be considered fake, since they weren't made of copper."

"But they were minted by the government."

"I mean, to a purist. Collectors can be weird, you know."

"Do I ever." Hy was a purist where his western fiction collection was concerned. He'd once told me that he didn't consider a book to be a complete first edition unless the dust jacket was the exact same one it had worn when it left the warehouse.

"So," he went on, "the coins could be taken to represent a falseness. And here's one more bit of symbolism for you: in the Old West, they put coins over a dead person's eyes because of a superstition that a corpse with open eyes was looking for the next one to die."

"Interesting, but like all the other symbols, what does it *mean* in terms of this particular case?"

"Damned if I know. You ever think of this: maybe the coins weren't all that central. In focusing on them, the cops might've overlooked something else."

I had thought of that. "You mean the ring. And the missing finger."

"Right."

"Okay, explain the meaning of *that*."

"Well, if the Benedict woman actually killed McKittridge, it would be obvious: remove the ring, the husband's gift to her, by hacking off the ring finger, where the wedding ring would go." Hy drained his beer and smiled at me. "But why spoil our last night here by getting into that kind of gore? Frankly, I feel more interested in physical acts than in symbolic ones."

"Do you, now?"

"Uh-huh."

As I moved closer to him, he pitched his empty bottle toward the trash bag. It missed and shattered with a loud pop. We both started, then laughed.

"Gun-shy," Hy whispered as he pulled me down onto our sleeping bags.

Sometime toward morning I woke, twisted in the padded flannel, Hy's arm heavy across my breasts. Woke from a dream of gunfire in which I was both the pursuer and the pursued. And knew instantly what had bothered me about Lis Benedict's murder scene.

Fourteen

■ ■ ■

The next morning I said goodbye to Hy on the tarmac at Oakland Airport's North Field. He planned, he said, to refuel and fly on to San Diego. Inside the terminal I found a pay phone and called Bart Wallace.

"Where've you been?" he demanded. "I thought you were going to check in with me again."

"I said I'd try. Where I was they don't have phone booths on every corner—in fact, they don't have corners."

"Then you had no business being there." Bart was a confirmed urban dweller; he'd once confided to me that even houseplants made him twitchy. "There're a couple of details I want to check with you," he added. "I've got a statement ready for you to sign, plus the results of the lab work on the graffiti on your house. Besides, I was worried about you."

"Why?"

Wallace didn't reply. In the background I could hear a woman's voice. Bart said, "I'll be ready in three minutes," then came back on the line. "Sharon? You got any time to talk this morning?"

"Yes. I can get there—"

"Better make it someplace else. How about Judy Benedict's

house around eleven? There're a couple of things I want to look at before we take the seal off."

"Good, I'll see you then." There were a couple of things I wanted to look at, too.

.   .   .

Before I went to Bernal Heights, I swung by my own neighborhood to check on my house. The ugly red words on the shingles looked garish in the morning sun, but otherwise everything seemed in good order. Ralph and Allie greeted me at the front door, yowling indignantly for their breakfast. "Nice to be considered nothing more than an adjunct to a can opener," I told them sourly.

I went back to the kitchen, opened some of the gummy stuff they favored, and soothed the savage beasts. There was a note on the counter from Ted, saying he'd stayed over on the weekend and received only one late-night call full of heavy breathing—which, I thought, could have been made by any of the twisted, lonely souls in our city's population. The note also said that somebody had phoned about reshingling the facade and would send a written estimate.

I played the tape on my answering machine, found nothing of consequence, then called All Souls. Jack was in court, but I spoke with Rae. One of her Mission district informants had told her that Tony Nueva had left town abruptly on Friday. That was interesting, since I'd seldom known Tony to leave the Mission, much less the city. Perhaps Buck, the manager of the video arcade, would know something about this sudden trip; I'd pay him a visit later.

.   .   .

Wallace's unmarked car was pulling into the driveway when I parked opposite Judy's house. As I crossed the street, he and a woman got out. The woman was about my height—five six— with a honey tan complexion and dark brown ringlets cropped close to her head. Her features were strong and handsome, her movements brisk, her elegantly tailored jacket and slim-legged pants deceptively functional.

"Sharon, meet my partner," Wallace said. "Adah Joslyn, Sharon McCone."

I'd read about Adah Joslyn in the paper, but hadn't realized she was teamed with Wallace. She'd been an inspector only a few years before transferring to the elite homicide detail—a promotion that greatly furthered our chief's aim to move women and minorities throughout the department until its composition reflected that of the community as a whole. In Joslyn, the public affairs office had found—and exploited for all they could—a virtual gold mine: not only was she a woman, half black, and relatively young, but she was also half Jewish.

We shook hands, appraising each other, said simultaneously, "I've heard of you," and burst out laughing.

"Thought you two might get on," Wallace commented. He mounted the steps of the house, where a yellow plastic police-line strip stretched across the door, removed it, and fiddled with a bunch of keys.

"Where's Judy Benedict staying?" I asked as Joslyn and I followed.

"Her office at the theater downtown. Bart says she's still really torn up over her mother's death. Makes it difficult to get information out of her. And of course the father's still hovering around, being overprotective."

"Overprotective or—"

Wallace said, "Save it for later, after I've shown Adah the scene. She just came back from vacation this morning, hasn't even gone over the reports yet."

It was cold inside the little house; the parlor curtains were drawn, shrouding the room and the hallway in darkness. Wallace led us to the dining area where Lis had died. The only alteration since the night of the murder was a sheet of plywood nailed over the broken glass door.

Wallace began pointing out details of the scene to Joslyn. I watched for a bit, then said, "I'll be right back," and went down the hall and out the front door. The boundary fence was flush against the house on its right, but a path ran along at the left. I followed it, found it ended at an unlocked gate that opened onto the deck outside the glass door. As I retraced my steps, I checked out the side of the house; there were no windows overlooking the path, and a storage shed protruded next to the dining area. I thumped the wall; the house seemed solidly built and well insulated.

When I went back into the dining area, Wallace was pointing out a spot on the wall where a section of paneling had been removed. "Stray bullet went in here."

"Two shots were fired?" I asked.

They both looked surprised, as if they'd forgotten I was there. "Right," Wallace said. "Benedict was only shot once, but her hands tested positive for nitrate. We figure she fired a wild shot before the killer took the gun away and used it on her."

"Interesting." I looked around, spotted the TV on the breakfast bar. "Can I try an experiment?"

"What?"

"I want to turn the TV up as loud as it'll go for a few minutes."

Wallace gave me a puzzled look but said, "Go ahead."

I did, then hurried back outside. At no point along the path could I clearly hear the sound. Wallace and Joslyn had their hands over their ears when I returned. As soon as she saw me, Adah hit the off button.

"Jesus," she said, "did you have to tune in on that Pillsbury Doughboy commercial?"

I grinned. "He's on my list, too—along with the Snuggle Bear, Mrs. Butterworth, and both Orville and his grandson."

Wallace frowned, obviously not a man who took serious offense at TV commercials. "What the hell was all that about?"

"You mean turning on the TV? I wanted to find out if I could hear it outside. I could, but just barely."

"So?"

"This house is well insulated for sound. A gunshot would be louder than the TV, of course, but someone next door would probably have dismissed it as a car backfiring."

"But the neighbor was definite about hearing a shot. Remember, the glass door was broken; that made it audible."

I asked, "Have you ever broken a door like that?"

Both Wallace and Joslyn shook their heads.

"Has either of you ever worked Burglary?"

"No," they replied.

"Well, when I was remodeling my house, I had an officer from Burglary come out and advise me on how to protect myself against break-ins. And you know what he told me? When one of those glass doors shatters, it sounds exactly like a gunshot."

They looked at each other, then back at me. "And?" Joslyn prompted.

"I think that the shot the neighbor heard—when was that?"

"Six-fifteen."

"The shot she heard at six fifteen was actually the door breaking."

"Then why didn't she hear two shots shortly afterward? With the door broken—"

"Maybe whoever broke the glass didn't shoot Benedict."

Wallace looked skeptical, but said, "Go on."

"Assume someone came to the front door and got no answer. Someone, perhaps, who had an appointment with Benedict and expected her to be here. He or she then went down the path and looked through the back door. Benedict was lying on the floor. The person broke the glass, found she was dead, panicked, and ran."

Wallace pulled out a chair and sat, looking thoughtful. "If she was shot before six-fifteen, that would explain a discrepancy in the M.E.'s report."

"What?" I asked.

"Degree of rigor—it was more than you'd expect."

Joslyn said, "I haven't seen the report yet, but rigor varies with temperature. Couldn't it have been accelerated by heat?"

Wallace shook his head. "The cold coming through the door during the five or so hours before the daughter found her would have inhibited it."

I added, "And even before the door was broken, it was cold in here. I noticed when I stopped by that morning."

"Stomach content analysis tell you anything?" Joslyn asked Wallace.

"Only that she hadn't been eating."

I said, "When I was here she told me there wasn't any food in the house. She'd been too depressed to go shopping."

"One of the things I wanted to double-check with you," Wallace said to me. "You left the victim at ten that morning?"

"Latest."

"You talk with her on the phone at any time afterward?"

"No. Jack Stuart might have."

"He says no; so does the daughter."

Joslyn said, "You checked the daughter's alibi, of course."

"Her ticket on the red-eye was used. Flight attendants didn't remember her, but that doesn't mean anything. Given what I know of the situation, I didn't see any need to check further."

Joslyn nodded, but I could see she didn't like the presumption. And, I supposed, the possibility of Judy being involved in Lis's death was something they should consider. She could have come home earlier than she'd said, and either sold or given away her other return ticket at the airport in New York.

Wallace's thoughts were elsewhere, however. He said to me, "Benedict could have died at any time from ten that morning to six fifteen that night, assuming your theory about the glass door is correct. The other thing I wanted to ask you: did she ever seem suicidal?"

Over the weekend I'd considered that. "She had tendencies." I explained about seeing her at the cliff's edge.

"You know," Joslyn said when I finished, "if she was a suicide, the advanced state of rigor could have been brought on by cadaveric spasm. The extreme tension suicides undergo at the time of death *can* bring on immediate stiffening."

Wallace shook his head. "No way. If she'd shot herself and gone into spasm, she'd still have been clutching the gun. But it was loose on the floor beside her."

"But that doesn't rule out suicide," I said. "Not all suicides go into spasm."

"Two shots were fired," Bart reminded me.

"So she was inexperienced with guns. She missed the first time."

He nodded. "Okay. If we accept your theory about the glass door—and I think it's a good one—what we've got is either a suicide or a murder by someone Benedict knew and let in the front door. In the latter scenario, she had the gun handy because she didn't trust the person. They got into an argument, she started waving the gun around, fired a shot, he took it away and killed her." Wallace's eyes met mine; I knew he was thinking how well Joseph Stameroff fit the scenario.

"Adah," he added, "will you run next door, see if that Mrs. Skillman's there? Ask her if she heard anything earlier that might have been shots or if she noticed whether Benedict had any visitors. And try the folks across the street and on the other side of the house while you're at it."

Joslyn nodded and hurried out.

"Okay," I said to Wallace, "this brings us to Joe Stameroff. What's your superiors' stance on him?"

"Pretty damned frustrating. Officially we're supposed to give Joe the old kid-gloves treatment, but they also want him closely looked at. You tell me how the hell we can investigate him without him noticing." He paused, then added, "God, I'd love to see that arrogant bastard get what's coming to him!"

I'd seldom heard Bart speak so passionately. "You sound as if there's history between the two of you."

Wallace seemed to be debating how much to tell me. In a moment he replied, "Let's just say that I didn't like him as a prosecutor or a superior court judge, and I like him even less now that he's sitting on the state supreme court."

I wanted to probe for specifics, but decided to let it drop for the moment. "You mentioned the lab report about the graffiti on my house."

"Yeah. We took paint samples and pictures from both there and here. Paint was a match. I don't know if you're aware of it, but graffiti's like handwriting in that certain characteristics recur. Not as reliable, of course, but our expert thinks the same person might have done both."

I was mulling that over when Joslyn rejoined us. "Skillman says she was gone all day, only got back a little before six. Nobody's home at the other houses. You want me to canvass the rest of the block?"

Wallace shook his head and stood up. "I'll do it. Why don't you go grab some lunch with Sharon and let her fill you in on what's in her statement? Afterward she can run you back to the Hall and sign it."

I had more questions for him, but he started for the front

door, adding to Joslyn, "And talk with her about what we dis-
cussed earlier, will you?"

"Hey," I called after him.

He kept on going.

"Come on," Joslyn said. "Let's get out of here before he
changes his mind and I miss lunch."

Fifteen

■ ■ ■

Adah said she knew a good place to eat down the hill in the little shopping area on Cortland Avenue, so we left my car and walked there. Nestled among the groceries, liquor stores, taverns, and small shops was a ramshackle red bungalow overgrown by bougainvillea, with a hand-painted sign that said Twylla's Creole.

"I never noticed this before," I said.

She smiled. "A lot of people miss it. It's been here forever. Twylla Hopper, lady who runs it, is an old friend of my folks." She led me up rickety front steps and into a dim hallway scented with rich, spicy aromas. "Twylla moved here from New Orleans about the same time my dad came to work in the shipyards during World War Two. She started cooking for homesick friends; now she's a little local institution."

Two rooms opened on either side of the hall: pink-walled, with cracked plaster; crammed with rickety chairs and tables covered by worn flower-sprigged oilcloth. Nearly all the tables were taken. Joslyn moved toward one by a window, where a single daisy reposed in a jelly jar. The flatware didn't match, and neither did the dishes; the napkins were faded cloth, carefully darned.

"Twylla doesn't mess around with frills," Joslyn said as we sat, "but I can guarantee you a damn good jambalaya."

"I'll take your recommendation."

"We'll make it two." She held up her fingers to a young man waiting on the next table, and he nodded. "Twylla's grandson," she explained. "He knows it's my usual."

"You live in Bernal Heights, then?"

She shook her head. "Grew up here, a few blocks away on Powhattan. Now I've got a studio in the Marina. I needed to put some distance between myself and the folks. You know how that is."

"Yes, I do." I'd chosen to attend college at Berkeley rather than one of the southern California campuses and then remained on in the Bay Area in order to put that same kind of distance between myself and my emotionally engulfing family.

"One of the problems with my folks," Joslyn added, "is that they weren't wild about me becoming a cop. Police work hasn't ever been held in real high regard by the people on Red Hill."

"Red Hill?"

"You've never heard Bernal Heights called that?"

"No."

"Funny, I thought that was why those bleeding-heart liberals you work for located here. As legend goes, you're smack in the middle of a former Communist hotbed."

"No kidding. When was this?"

"From the twenties on. Communism may be dead damn near everyplace else, but there're still a few cells of very old Commies here today."

"Do you know that for a fact?"

"Well, I don't *know* any card carriers, but . . . take my folks, for instance. Dad's an old Socialist labor organizer, and Mom has a Marxist study group that's been meeting every Wednesday for decades. It was one of those opposites-attract marriages made in postwar bohemian heaven: he's black, working-class, and a tough pragmatist; she's a college-educated Jewish intellectual with a rebellious streak. The way they go at it over their ideological differences, it's a wonder they've survived."

"They sound interesting."

"Oh, they're interesting, all right. Particularly if you don't have to live with them." She smiled fondly. "So tell me about this research you've been doing on the McKittridge case and how it feeds into this homicide. Like Bart said, I only got back from vacation this morning, and I haven't had time to read the reports."

Steaming bowls of jambalaya arrived. I used the interruption to ignore her request and pose a question of my own. "What is it that Bart wants you to talk to me about?"

She frowned, clearly displeased at having lost control of the conversation. In a moment she said, "He's hoping you'll keep on researching that old case."

"Why? Does he think it's linked to the present one?"

"I can't tell. He claims not, but at the same time he's very interested in the McKittridge homicide. What I suspect is that he's hoping you'll turn up something incriminating on Justice Stameroff."

"Something incriminating him in the McKittridge murder?"

"I don't think even Bart knows exactly what he's looking for. But I do know he wants to see Stameroff brought down."

"What's the history between them, anyway?"

Adah shrugged, toyed with her spoon.

Even though Wallace and Joslyn were offering me quasi-official sanction to proceed with a course of action I'd already more or less determined to pursue, I felt somewhat leery. "How come Bart didn't talk with me about this back at the house?"

"Oh, you know how he is—he hates to ask a favor."

"Mmm." But that didn't sound like Bart; we'd traded favors on numerous occasions. And Joslyn was avoiding my eyes now, which didn't strike me as in character, either.

"Okay," I said after a moment, "if Jack Stuart and Judy think we should go ahead with preparing the case to clear her mother's name before the Historical Tribunal, I'll do it. But that's the only way I can justify spending the time. And there's something I need from you—the department's original files on the McKittridge case."

"Sure. They may not be all that easy to access, but I'll have Records expedite it. Now brief me on what's in the statement Bart wants you to sign; it'll save me time."

Between spoonfuls of the excellent jambalaya, I outlined what

I'd told Wallace on the night of the murder. When I finished, Adah considered for a moment. "All that makes me suspect that somebody got stirred up by Benedict getting released and you digging into that old killing," she said.

"That's the conclusion I've come to. It would be obvious to anyone that if I turned up new evidence, Jack Stuart would petition to have the case reopened rather than merely present it at a mock trial."

"So who looks good to you?"

I shrugged, shook my head. What could I tell her? That I'd forged an odd psychic link to the events of June 22, 1956? That I knew what had happened, yet didn't know? Could sense but not conceptualize it? Sure.

To circumvent her question, I said, "Why am I still uncomfortable about Bart not approaching me directly about this?"

She looked down at her empty bowl. "I told you, he doesn't like to ask a favor. Besides, he wants you to deal exclusively with me on this."

"How come?"

"It's safer. If someone's watching you—and they probably are, given that your house was vandalized—they'll assume we're just personal friends."

"That doesn't wash, Adah. If they're keeping tabs on me, they're keeping tabs on the police investigation, too. They'll know it's your case."

"Okay." She glanced around, lowered her voice. "What I just told you was Bart's rationalization. But we're neither of us dumb broads, right? I know what Bart means is that it's safer for *him* if I'm your liaison. If the departmental brass is watching us and the shit flies because we've co-opted a P.I. to look into areas that we can't because of their kid-gloves policy vis-à-vis Stameroff, I don't have as much to lose. Bart's got a mortgage and a couple of kids in college; I've got a month-to-month on my studio and a tankful of tropical fish."

"How do you feel about taking all the heat?"

"Not great, but it goes with the lack of seniority. And I'm a natural-born risk taker. Bart isn't."

If I'd been in Adah Joslyn's place, however, I wouldn't have accepted that kind of risk—at least not without some major concession. And since Adah, as she put it, was not a dumb broad, I was certain she'd extracted said concession from her partner. I'd have loved to know what.

Also, I knew Bart Wallace wasn't the sort of man to ask a partner to assume a risk alone—not without a strong belief that it was worthwhile and necessary. Again I wondered what the history between Bart and the justice was, and if the inspector didn't have too personal a stake in this case.

.   .   .

After I signed the statement waiting for me at the Hall of Justice, I told Joslyn that I'd probably spend most of the afternoon at the public library, then detoured to City Amusement Arcade. Buck confirmed that Tony Nueva hadn't been in since Friday afternoon. Tony seldom went anywhere without telling Buck where he could be reached and when he'd be back, but when I pressed him, the manager claimed he didn't know. If I wanted, he said, I could ask Tony's fox, Linda Bautista; she worked in the next block at Wig Wonderland.

The windows of the shop displayed an astonishing assortment of hair mounted on disembodied, featureless heads. Some of the wigs were so blatantly synthetic that they glistened; a more select and natural-looking group clustered around a sign that said, Genuine Asian Hair Grown in Taiwan. I entertained a fleeting vision of a plain at the edge of the South China Sea, where hair plants grew like the artichoke plants on the Monterey Peninsula.

The only person in the shop was the woman I'd seen with Tony on Sunday morning. She wore a cap of synthetic blond ringlets and stood in front of the sales counter, swiping with a feather duster at the heads displayed there. When the bell on the door tinkled, she looked my way, frowning as she tried to remember where she'd seen me.

I explained who I was and said I had business with Tony. The lines of her face went rigid. "Don't you dare say that name to me!"

"I thought you and Tony were friends."

"Hah!" She folded her arms, cloaking herself in tattered dignity. "Not anymore, we're not. Bastard ran out on me Friday night, took our emergency money and stuck me with the rent."

"Do you know where he went?"

"To his relatives."

"Where?"

"National City? Chula Vista? One of them damn places between San Diego and the border." She made a gesture of dismissal. "You know what I say to him? I say good riddance. Tony promises and promises, but he sure don't deliver."

"What did he promise?"

"The ring, the wedding chapel in Reno, two nights at Circus Circus. We were gonna play the slots, blackjack, win big. What a bunch of shit! All I got was an empty stash box and the rent coming due."

"You don't think he's coming back?"

"He better not. But he won't anyway, not after the beating he took. He'll hole up down there forever."

"What beating? When?"

Linda Bautista regarded me silently, then stretched out her hand for money, fingers flicking in a grotesque imitation of her runaway lover. I sighed, reached into my bag, and handed her a ten.

"What happened," she began, stuffing the bill into the V of her pink blouse, "was Tony had this scheme. Week before last he got some bucks off of this guy who'd been hired to do somebody."

"You mean commit a murder?"

"Jesus, no!" Linda's hand flew to her breast. "Nothing like that! Just cause some trouble, you know?"

"Go on."

"Well, anyway, then around the middle of last week Tony found out something else had gone down—something bigger. So he decided to hit the guy again. And the guy beat the crap out of him."

"This guy—who hired him?"

"I don't know. Tony said it was somebody big, but Tony's just a lot of talk and no action. He was supposed to get all this money the second time so we could go off to Reno, and now look at me. I got nineteen bucks in the bank and the rent coming due, and

I wouldn't marry him if he came crawling back and kissed my ass."

Behind the defiance in her eyes I could see real disappointment. The dreams that Tony Nueva had shattered weren't big dreams, but they were likely to be the best Linda Bautista would ever have. Fool that I am, I took another ten from my bag and handed it to her along with one of my cards. "Linda, this is an advance. If you hear from Tony, find out where he is and let me know. Or if you remember anything else he said about the guy he was trying to get the money from, give me a call."

She looked down at the card and bill in her hand, then closed her fingers tightly over them. "You're not gonna hurt him or anything?"

"No, I just need to ask him some questions."

"That's good. Tony's an asshole, but I kind of . . ." For a moment her lower lip trembled. She got it under control, added, "It's just that I thought he was different—you know? But he turned out like all the rest. I don't get it. I mean, look at me. What's *wrong* with me?"

Her hands swept out and down, from the glistening fake curls to the too-bright skirt and blouse hugging her too-plump frame to her cheap pink plastic heels. She was all tricked up—a victim of the myth that illusion is necessary to entice and entrap the male. Women all start out believing the myth to one degree or another, and too many of us never figure out that real women don't trade in illusion—any more than real men buy into it.

Sixteen

■ ■ ■

After I left Linda Bautista, I checked in at All Souls and told Jack about my conversation with Bart Wallace and Adah Joslyn. He felt confident that Judy would want to go ahead with preparations for the mock trial, and promised to set up a meeting with her for me. Next I went to my office and buzzed Rae on the intercom. She came upstairs, and we spent half an hour reviewing her caseload. As she got up to leave, I remembered what Jack had said last week about her prospects of a diamond ring from Willie Whelan. No such trinket shone on her left hand.

"Uh, how's Willie?" I asked.

Rae's round face became pinched. "I'd rather not talk about him."

"What happened?"

"I just can't talk about it now, okay?" Her mouth twitched in anger, and she whirled and rushed out the door.

Another he-done-me-wrong story, I thought. And more hard times ahead for Rae.

I repacked my briefcase and went down to the foyer. Ted wasn't at his desk, but one of the painters sat on its edge, gabbing on the phone. I gave him a reproving look as I moved the tag on my message box so Ted would know I was out; the painter merely grinned vacuously.

Earlier I'd noticed that the facade of the building finally looked more or less as intended, but along the sides the color still resembled the stuff of baby diapers. If only, I thought, Hank hadn't been persuaded to buy the paint at discount from the failing store of one of Larry Koslowski's clients. If only the client hadn't recommended his second cousin, the painting contractor. If only All Souls wasn't blundering, rather than forthrightly striding, into the twenty-first century. . . .

.　　　.　　　.

One of the advantages I enjoyed in college was being a demonic researcher. While others were only deciding on the subjects of their term papers, I could be found in a carrel in the library, heavy tomes stacked around me as I relentlessly filled index cards with obscure facts and figures. I'd spend whole weekends in the shadow world of the microfilm room digesting useless details that would have entirely escaped a less obsessive individual, and I would emerge curiously refreshed and satisfied. But now that research was more than a pleasant intellectual exercise, I chafed at the enforced inactivity. And when I surfaced red-eyed and irritable from the main branch of the public library into the five o'clock bustle of Civic Center Plaza, I felt like one of the Mole People.

What I'd gleaned during the past few hours, however, was highly informative. Think tanks, for instance: they came in widely divergent varieties, from small private research-and-development firms, to nonprofit institutions generally affiliated with universities, to elite entities like RAND and the Institute for North American Studies, which were closely tied to the federal government. The main factor they held in common, as far as I could tell, was the generation of what insiders referred to as "paper alchemy"—written studies and reports that made evaluations, suggested policies or long-range plans, promulgated theories, or described techniques. It wasn't uncommon for the entire yearly output of a think tank holding a hundred million dollars' worth of contracts to fit into a single briefcase.

The R&D industry is a vague one—difficult to quantify or describe. It employs some of the most intelligent and powerful people in this country, and the breadth and depth of its influence on our government can only be guessed at. And because of this influence, particularly upon the upper echelons of the Departments of Defense and State, it is an industry with very scary potential.

Top secret security clearances, unmarked buildings with uniformed guards on every door, hush-hush conferences with high government officials, for-your-eyes-only reports, quick-response work for the Joint Chiefs of Staff—there is enough cloak-and-dagger stuff going on in the think tank industry to satisfy even the most devoted fan of spy fiction. And when you throw in dangerous variables—alcoholism, megalomania, kinky sex, psychological quirks, dubious loyalties—you come up with a horrifying scenario worthy of an apocalyptic film.

In light of what I knew of the Institute for North American Studies, thinking about that scenario virtually made me shudder.

But the stuff of bad dreams wasn't all my research had revealed. I'd also checked into the types of contracts the Institute had held at the time of Cordy McKittridge's murder: cold war containment; public support for the use of atomic weapons in limited warfare; "biological alteration" for military purposes; procedures for reestablishing the federal government after a global nuclear war. John Foster Dulles's visit to San Francisco was occasioned by the State Department's announcement of the award of a multimillion dollar contract to the Institute for a major study on the domestic security threat within the United States.

Which told me that the Institute had been enlisted in the later stages of the Communist witch-hunt of the fifties. Had to some degree abetted the work begun by the likes of Senator Joseph McCarthy and FBI Director J. Edgar Hoover—a ruthless probe into the private affairs of citizens that, in my opinion, had destroyed as many innocent lives as the Spanish Inquisition.

I wondered how Adah Joslyn, formerly of Red Hill, offspring

of an alliance between a Socialist and a Marxist, would react to that information.

I'd also checked the local newspaper coverage of both the Dulles banquet and the McKittridge murder. The photographs of Cordy—lovely, blond, patrician—left me uneasy; again I felt the odd pull of the case; it was as if I'd come across the picture of a long-dead friend. The coverage of her murder had been as all-out and lurid as I'd expected. In contrast, the Dulles banquet and an exclusive reception afterward for state and local dignitaries had been closed to the press. Aside from photographs showing the Dulles entourage arriving at the St. Francis Hotel where the reception had been held, the only pictures from inside the event were "official" shots by the Institute's photographer, Roy Loomis. In one of those, Dulles posed with both Eyestones, Russell and Leonard. The three men were dressed nearly alike, in conservatively styled formal wear, but there the resemblance stopped. Dulles was the pugnacious, bespectacled man I'd often seen in photographs. Russell Eyestone looked handsome, imposing, seemed to tower head and shoulders above his son, in spite of them being of a size. Leonard looked shrunken, anemic; the expression he put on for the camera seemed vaguely hunted, as if he dearly wanted to escape the impressive shadow of his father.

Before I left the library, I'd called Jack and learned that Judy wanted to meet with me at six at Artists' Showcase, the theater where she staged her productions. I retrieved my car from the plaza garage and inched along busy Golden Gate Avenue toward Market.

The area where Golden Gate and Taylor intersect with Market is undergoing a transition, but of what sort it's hard to say. There are theaters and restaurants catering to playgoers, hotels both upscale and down. Children of the Southeast Asian refugees who have settled in the Tenderloin skateboard on the sidewalks; hookers jealously guard their turf; and of course there are the crazies.

One of them, a black woman with a wild mane of purple hair and needle tracks on her thin arms, stood on the corner not far from where I'd parked, haranguing the passing cars. Something to do with them giving their money to her, since Jesus didn't need it anyway. As I walked up the block toward the theater, I passed a pair of hookers leaning against the facade of a defunct sandwich shop. One said, "Lunatic Lady's really on a roll tonight," and the other replied, "Yeah, she don't watch it, *I* gonna get on a roll, and then she wish she talked nicer 'bout Jesus."

I reached the theater and moved toward its front entrance, but stopped abruptly, my attention arrested by a woman walking up the block from Market. A tall woman with light fine-spun hair, wrapped in a long cape whose folds billowed in the wind. For a moment I caught my breath, seized by the irrational notion that it was Lis Benedict. Then Judy saw me and waved. I relaxed, but a vague uneasiness stayed with me.

As she came up to me, Judy saw how I was looking at the cape and smiled. "Yes, it's Lis's. I wanted something to remember her by, and I've always liked this." She led me to the entrance of the theater and tapped on one of the glass doors for a security guard to admit us.

The lobby was dim and cold; stale cigarette smoke lay over a base of mustiness. The guard flicked switches on a light panel before he went away, and a huge chandelier blazed crystal and gilt. Its rays revealed tired red carpet and hangings, more gilt and crystal, walls of marbleized mirrors. The theater, I thought, had not been upgraded since Judy took over the lease.

She was looking around, mouth pulled down critically, as if seeing it through my eyes. Motioning at an old-fashioned round sofa with tufted red upholstery, she said, "Let's talk here. My office is a mess since I've been living in it."

We sat, her black cape ruffling around her like a nesting bird's feathers.

"Are you planning to move back to your house eventually?" I asked.

"I don't know. Right now I think it might be better to sell it."

"I'm sorry I couldn't attend the funeral." It had been held on Tuesday, when I was still high in the Great Whites.

"That's okay. It was small, the way Lis would have wanted it—except for the press, of course."

The security guard emerged from the main part of the theater, and for a moment the open door emitted a babble of voices and the sound of hammering.

"Pandemonium as usual back there," Judy said.

I hadn't noticed what was on the marquee, so I asked, "Is *Deadfall* still running?" It was a mystery play that I wanted to see; Jack had offered comps for its opening night, but I'd had another engagement.

"Only for another week. Then I've booked a psychological drama that's been something of a runaway success off-Broadway."

"Obviously you're doing well here."

"Yes, I am. Sometimes it almost makes up for not succeeding as an actress, but . . . I go backstage, they're all rushing around, the tension crackles. I can feel it, but I'm no longer a part of it." She sighed.

"You *did* have a long acting career, though."

"If you can call what I did acting. I just never got any breaks. I keep thinking that if I'd had the right material, been able to give one really great performance, it would have made all the difference. But maybe not." She looked pensive for a moment, then abruptly switched the subject. "Sharon, I want to apologize for my father's behavior last week. Jack told me he went to your house and bullied you. He . . . he means well, but he can be so high-handed."

"No apology necessary." From *you*, I added silently. "How do you feel about going ahead with the mock trial?"

"I want to more than ever now."

"Is your father still opposed?"

"Yes."

"Will that pose a problem for you?"

"No more than it did before. I can handle him." She leaned toward me, eyes filled with an intensity that was augmented by the glare of the chandelier on her round lenses. Her fingers grasped my arm, almost painfully. Again I was reminded of her mother.

"I want the trial," she said. "I want it for Lis's sake, to clear her name. But I want it for me, too. I have to settle this. You understand, don't you?"

I nodded, removing my arm from her grasp. "We'll go ahead, then. But I'm going to have to ask you a question. Please don't take offense."

"I'll try not to."

"Could your father—Joseph Stameroff, I mean—have planted in your mind some of the testimony you gave at Lis's trial?"

"He . . . wouldn't have done that."

"But *could* he have? Say, during his pretrial visits to you in the foster home."

She frowned; I could tell she was working hard at controlling her temper.

"Think about it, Judy: you've said you don't remember the things you testified to, that it was as if they'd happened to somebody else."

"I also told you there's a lot I don't remember. I never realized how much until it started coming back." She shivered, pulled the black folds of the cape around her.

"Have you remembered other things since we last talked?"

"Yes."

"Tell me about them."

"Well . . . the day after Lis . . . died, I had . . . it wasn't a dream so much as an image, when I was just on the edge of sleeping. In the image I was on the third floor of the house— the one in Seacliff—looking out the window of my old room at night. There was a heavy fog. The towers of the bridge were lit up, but the mist made them look . . . unreal. And there was something in the dark under the window. I was afraid, really afraid." She shook her head. "This is stupid, but just talking about it frightens me."

"Sometimes mental images can be more frightening than reality, especially when they're not all that clear. This thing under the window—was it a person? An animal?"

"I don't know."

"Did it move? Stay in one place?"

"It moved. I was afraid it would come into the house, up to my room."

"Did it?"

"I don't know. That's all there was."

I considered. During my library research, I'd learned that

there had been an unusually heavy fog the night of the McKittridge murder—the kind of fog I'd imagined as I stood in front of the Seacliff house last week, the kind of fog Judy described. It seemed to me that the image she'd seen while half asleep could actually be a true memory of that night. And the thing that moved in the dark? Cordy's killer?

Judy said, suddenly and vehemently, "I wish it would *all* come back! I need to know!"

Much as I understood that, and much as I wanted the old case resolved, I felt I should caution her. "Maybe it's better if you don't remember. You must have had a powerful reason for repressing as much as you have."

"No, it's *not* better. I can't live with this . . . void any longer. I can't get on with my life until I know that Lis was telling the truth about not committing that murder."

"Have you seen anyone about these memories? A therapist?"

Her expression became closed; she shook her head.

"Maybe you should."

"Let me handle this in my own way, will you?" The words were clipped, almost angry. Before I could frame a reply, she demanded, "Now, how are you going to proceed with this case?"

Swallowing my annoyance, I said, "I did want to talk with your father again, but from what you tell me, that's impossible. I need to speak a second time with Leonard Eyestone. And I want to tour the Seacliff property."

"How do you plan to manage that?"

"The house is for sale. I'll call my real-estate broker and arrange to see it."

"For an expensive property like that, you may have to prequalify before they'll show it."

"The broker is a friend; she'll find a way."

"Why do you want to go there?"

"Just to see where it all happened."

"I haven't set foot on that property since my parents and I moved to Lake Street right after the murder." Conflicting emotions washed over her face—discomfort, hesitancy, and finally eagerness. "Sharon," she said, "take me with you."

The request took me completely by surprise. Quickly I searched for a way to dissuade her.

"Please," she added. "It might help me remember."

"I'm not sure that's wise." What if a calling-up of her memories precipitated a major emotional crisis?

"You're treating me like a child, the way my father does. With him it's always 'Judy, you don't want to know. You don't want to remember.' Well, I *do*, dammit!"

"All I'm saying is that maybe that's not the right way to remember."

"Let me be the judge of that." She thrust her jaw forward and added, "If you don't take me, I'll go on my own. Any broker would be glad to show me the property; I can trade on the Stameroff name."

Our eyes locked; hers were intractable. After a moment I said, "Let me see what I can arrange."

.   .   .

As soon as I got home, I unearthed an old address book and called a friend from college, Mary Norton, who was now a therapist at a Sacramento Street clinic. Mary was just coming out of a group session and had my call transferred to her office. It had been more than two years since we'd gotten together, so we swapped news and gossip for close to ten minutes before I could get to my reason for calling. After briefly outlining Judy Benedict's experience with resurfacing memories, I asked, "Does this sort of thing happen often? And how accurate are the memories?"

"To answer your first question, repressed memory is a fairly common phenomenon. We see it a lot in abused children. Was this woman abused sexually or physically?"

"I doubt it, but the father was an alcoholic and frequently beat the mother, so the environment was abusive."

"And you say she's forgotten most of the events surrounding the murder and the trial?"

"Yes. She says her testimony sounds as if it happened to someone else."

"That's consistent. If a child suffers one single traumatic event, she usually won't be capable of repressing it. But in this case, where it was a continuing trauma . . . Is the woman a self-blamer?"

"She feels guilty because she testified against her mother."

"And probably about a lot of other things, too. Children, especially those who have been abused in any way, tend to believe they're responsible for the bad things that happen in their lives."

"Okay," I said, "the repression is brought on by a series of events that the child's mind can't handle. As protection, the memory shuts down. What makes it come back?"

"Sometimes when the grown individual's ego structure is strong enough to handle them, the memories just filter to the surface in response to mild stimuli. As in your client's case, where her mother had come back into her everyday life. Or it can be more dramatic. You remember that murder trial down the Peninsula a few years ago? The Susan Nason case?"

"Yes." Eight-year-old Susan Nason's 1969 murder had gone unsolved until 1989, when her best friend came forward, saying that she had seen her own father kill her playmate. The long-repressed memory was triggered by the friend seeing the same expression in her young daughter's eyes as she'd seen in Susan's immediately before she died; psychologists for the prosecution had so well documented the phenomenon that the jury returned a first-degree verdict.

"That was a textbook example of spontaneous unblocking," Mary said. "As for the accuracy of the memories, they're often clearer and far more detailed than ordinary memory, as if they've been frozen or preserved. Sometimes they may have been distorted by shock or fear—in which case it takes some interpretation to get at the facts—but most of the time a true memory is easily distinguished because of the richness of detail."

I consulted the scribbled notes I'd been making. "You say the memory becomes unblocked when the individual's ego structure can withstand it. What if a person receives a strong stimulus before she's ready to deal with the memory? Will it come anyway?"

"It might, and that can cause further trauma. What are you trying to get at, Sharon?"

I explained about Judy's insistence on visiting the Seacliff property. "I'm afraid it might push her over the edge."

Mary hesitated. "Well, I don't know her, and there's no way to predict reactions except on a case-by-case basis. But I'd say that if she wants to recall that badly, she's probably ready. Is she seeing anyone about this?"

"No. I tried to broach the subject, but she closed off entirely."

"Why, do you think?"

"She strikes me as someone who wants to handle her problems on her own."

"Maybe she can."

"Maybe, but I can't form any opinion of how stable she is, particularly now that her mother's been murdered. And I'm in a bind, because if I don't take her along, she'll probably go on her own."

"And that could do her more harm than if she went with someone."

"So what should I do?"

Again Mary hesitated. "You know I can't advise you without evaluating her, but . . . in a case such as the one you describe, it would be better if she saw the property in the company of someone she cares for and trusts."

Jack. Of course—I'd take both of them. "Thanks for the non-advice, Mary."

"Any time. And my advice to you is to do better about keeping in touch."

I promised I would. Then I dialed my real estate broker, Cathy Potter, and left a message on her answering machine. By this time I was starving, so I went to the kitchen and put a frozen lasagna in the microwave. While the oven whirred and the food whirled, I considered calling Hy later on, then remembered he'd gone to San Diego. Maybe it was just as well I didn't have a number for him; I wasn't really in a talkative mood.

The microwave beeped. I dumped the lasagna onto a plate and wolfed it down while paging through an L.L. Bean catalog. The Benedict trial transcript lay on the table beneath that morning's unread newspaper; my fingers inched toward it, and I pulled them back as if it were hot to the touch.

Not tonight, I cautioned myself. No bad dreams for one night, at least.

I got up, tidied the kitchen. My gaze kept creeping toward the transcript. I went into the sitting room, considered a couple of novels waiting to be read, consulted the *TV Guide*. I could still feel the pull from the kitchen. Finally I surrendered, got the transcript, and paged through it—looking once again for the reasons why.

·   ·   ·

The anonymous phone call came at five minutes after three that morning. The voice was male, heavily accented.

It said, "You don't want to die, you lay off the Benedict thing."

Seventeen

■ ■ ■

At eight-ten the next morning I opened my front door and found garbage strewn all over my walk. Slick, slimy garbage—and not mine, either—that looked and smelled as if it had been rotting for weeks.

A choking mixture of nausea and rage rose in my throat; I went back inside, slamming the door and leaning against it. Maybe it won't be there when I go out again, I told myself. Maybe some Good Samaritan who likes handling garbage and hosing down walks will happen along.

Yeah—and maybe pigs would fly and I'd win the lottery.

I returned to the kitchen and poured my second cup of coffee. The cordless phone receiver sat amid a welter of grocery coupons and junk mail on the table; I picked it up and punched out the number for SFPD Homicide. Joslyn was already in, and unconscionably cheerful. "Hey, Sharon, what've you got for me?" she asked.

"What I've got is about a ton of garbage all over my front walk."

"Kids or dogs get into it?"

"No, it appears to have been trucked here especially for me."

"Jesus, I know they've got mail-order catalogs for everything, but couldn't you have stuck with the Sharper Image?" Then she added more seriously, "You figure this to be a variation on the graffiti?"

"Uh-huh. Along with the death threat that came by phone in the middle of the night."

"Getting creative, isn't he? What've you been doing to bring this down?"

Briefly I reported my activities since I'd last seen her.

When I finished, she said, "Look, I thought you realized you were to keep out of our case. You should have left Nueva to us."

"You've admitted the two cases could be connected. If you aren't sure by now, you're suffering from linkage blindness. What you're asking—for me to investigate the past but drop everything pertaining to the present—isn't feasible *or* productive."

She was silent.

"I've reported everything to you. I'm saving you legwork. What more do you want?"

"I want you to be careful you don't jeopardize our investigation—or our jobs. From now on don't call me here; you've got my home number."

"You and Bart really *are* paranoid."

"We've got every right to be, given who we're going up against." She hung up, leaving me open-mouthed and more than a bit irritated.

For a moment I considered calling her back. After all, I was doing her a favor, and what I'd gotten so far for my pains was a sleepless night and some garbage. But then I reconsidered. Police powers over private investigators are wide and discretionary when there's a homicide involved; I didn't want Joslyn ordering me not to investigate at all. So instead of venting my annoyance on her, I put on old jeans and a T-shirt and went outside to tend to the mess. As I shoveled and hosed down the walk, I was interrupted several times by neighbors, either wanting to know what had happened or expressing disapproval because I was wasting water. Afterward I took a long hot shower—wasting water again, but behind closed doors.

. . .

The stench of the garbage cans along James Alley didn't faze me after my earlier task, and as I rang Melissa Cardinal's bell, I felt in no mood to put up with nonsense from anyone. Cardinal peered around the door to her building, then tried to close it when she saw me. I put my shoulder to it and pushed my way inside. Her mouth dropped open and she backed away, eyes clouded by fear.

I took her arm, gently but firmly, and guided her toward the stairway. "We have to talk, Melissa."

"I told you before—"

"I know what you told me, but look at yourself: you're so frightened you came all the way down here rather than buzz me in. And it's not me you're afraid of, is it?"

She'd offered resistance to starting up the stairs, but now she sagged, putting weight on my hand.

"Come on," I said. "Maybe I can help you."

"Nobody can help me." But she grasped the railing and climbed laboriously.

Inside the apartment, Cardinal retreated to her recliner, looking around anxiously for her cat. I spotted it cowering under the glass-fronted cabinet, picked it up, and set it in her lap. The gesture reassured her. She cradled the animal, fingers drawing comfort from its fur.

"Now," I said as I sat on the sofa, "we are going to discuss why you're afraid to talk about Cordy McKittridge. First, who was the man you met at the Haven?"

"I told you, just a man."

"Does this man have a name?"

"I don't know his name. He just bought me a drink at the bar, that's all."

"Come on, Melissa—you've already told me you never go out in the daytime. You weren't at the Haven because you had a sudden urge for a drink, and that particular man wasn't just a casual pickup."

"Is that what you think—that I'm so ugly nobody would offer to buy me a drink?"

"Melissa, the man knew you; he called you by name. That's

what attracted Frank Fabrizio's attention. And you were arguing with him; Frank noticed that, too."

"Frank's an old man. His hearing's probably going. For all I know, he could be senile."

"He's not senile, and his hearing's perfectly good. Melissa, why didn't you let the man come here to your apartment?"

Her eyes darted around, glittering in a stray shaft of sunlight.

I said, "Because you were afraid of him, right?"

Silence.

I tried another tack. "Melissa, what you know about Cordy's murder has become dangerous to you."

"I don't know *anything* about that murder! I wasn't even in the city that day. I was working a Rome flight that left that morning."

"But you knew Cordy—knew her well."

"Those girls were just people I got together with to share the rent."

"You mean Cordy got them together. You and she were friends from before, and then she enlisted some of her other friends. Louise Wingfield told me so."

A knowing light came into her eyes, and malice twisted her lips into a hideous smile. "Louise Wingfield?" she asked. "Is that who this is about? You think I'm in danger because I know about her and Vincent Benedict?"

"Louise and . . . Benedict?"

"Sure. I don't suppose she bothered to tell you about that. Louise was in love with him before he started seeing Cordy. Cordy was going with Leonard Eyestone and introduced the two of them. They carried on a hot affair for almost a year. I know, because where they carried it on was one of the bedrooms of that flat in North Beach."

"And then?"

"Then Cordy had her abortion and broke it off with Eyestone. And she went after Benedict, never mind that Louise was in love with him. Took him right away from her, never mind that Louise was her best friend. After that, Vincent wouldn't come to the flat—he couldn't face Louise—but we all knew what was going on. And we all knew how much Louise hated Cordy. She tried to cover it up, but her eyes . . . they *watched* Cordy, full of hate, like she was waiting for something bad to happen to her."

I considered Louise Wingfield. She'd been forthcoming with me, I thought, but only up to a point. Perhaps she'd hoped her candor would disarm me, discourage me from digging further and unearthing this particularly damning fact. And when I'd kept on investigating—well, Wingfield *did* have a close connection with the Mission district Hispanic community.

I asked, "Exactly when did Cordy start seeing Benedict?"

"Right after she and Louise got back from Mexico."

They'd gone to the abortion clinic in August of the year before the murder. That would have given Wingfield's resentment of her friend nine months to smolder.

"Melissa," I asked, "have you told anyone else about Louise and Benedict?"

She shook her head.

"Then don't. From now on I want you to be very careful. Do you still have that card with my home number on it?"

She motioned toward the table beside her, where the card was anchored under the base of a lamp.

"Good. If anyone attempts to harm or threaten you, call me immediately. Day or night, at home or at my office."

For a moment she looked hesitant, as if she wanted to tell me something. Her eyes flicked to the glass-fronted cabinet, and she shook her head. "Louise isn't going to hurt me, if that's what you're thinking."

"You never know."

"*I* know."

"Then who *are* you afraid of?"

She closed her eyes, shook her head again.

"All right," I said. "You have my card. Call me when you're ready to talk."

"Are you going to tell Louise what I told you?"

"Yes. The best way to deal with this is to ask her about it."

•   •   •

"I didn't *hide* my relationship with Vincent Benedict from you," Louise Wingfield said.

"You were candid about everything else. Why conceal that?"

Wingfield ground out her cigarette in the ashtray on the desk between us. "Hide! Conceal! Don't you have any concept of a person's right to privacy?"

"I do. But the concept that seems more pertinent here is a person's desire not to incriminate herself."

"*Incriminate* myself? Have you lost your mind?" Wingfield's expression was both outraged and horrified. "You can't suspect that I killed Cordy!"

"I can quote Melissa Cardinal almost verbatim: 'Her eyes watched Cordy, full of hate, like she was waiting for something bad to happen to her.'"

"What would Melissa know? She was never there."

"Apparently she was there enough to observe what was really going on."

"*Really* going on?" Wingfield laughed bitterly. "At this point, who knows the reality of the situation? Anyway, how can you take the word of an angry old recluse over mine?"

The way she described Melissa gave me pause. Before, when the subject of her former roommate came up, Wingfield had at first claimed not to know her last name—a bird, she'd said, a wren or a finch—and not to know her whereabouts. I hadn't mentioned anything about Melissa's present circumstances when I'd come here and confronted her.

"Why do you think she's angry?" I asked.

"Who wouldn't be? She's disfigured and living in two shabby little rooms on Social Security and disability."

I didn't reply. Let the silence lengthen until Wingfield looked down, groping for her cigarette pack. She found it, shook one out, and lit it before I asked, "How long have you known where Melissa is?"

"Since last Tuesday. Didn't I tell you? No, it was Monday night when we went to North Beach and Seacliff. Melissa called me the next morning. It was a surprise, seeing as we'd just been talking about her with Frank Fabrizio the night before."

"What did she want?"

"To see me. I went over to her apartment, heard her out."

So that was who Melissa had been waiting for when I'd arrived last Tuesday. She'd said, "Formal, aren't you?"—expecting

Louise—then had been confused at seeing a stranger on the stairs.

"What did she want?" I asked.

"Money."

"Money not to tell about you and Vincent Benedict?"

She hesitated, then nodded. "I may as well admit to the affair; I'm not a good liar."

"Did you give her any?"

"I did not. I offered to help her, because she's so obviously in need, but I told her she would also have to help herself. There's an excellent seniors center in her area, one with a counseling program, but Melissa wasn't interested. So I told her to do what she wished with her information about Vincent and me, and left."

"You weren't afraid of what use she'd put it to?"

"Naturally I didn't want her to tell anyone. I hoped she'd just forget it, as she probably would have if you hadn't gone to talk with her today. I can see it's lowered your opinion of me considerably, but that's about the maximum damage I expect to bear. I didn't kill Cordy; my alibi for that night, as they say on the TV cop shows, is ironclad, still alive, and probably still willing to back me up. My old friends might be titillated if the story came out, but I stopped caring what society thought of me when I left my husband and created a scandal by battling in court for my fair share of our community property. My life is different now, and nothing that happened in the bad old days can hurt me."

I had to admire her forthrightness—unless it was calculated to misdirect me. "For your sake, I hope you're right about that," I said. "May I ask you a few more questions?"

"If they won't take too much time."

"You met Vincent Benedict through Cordy?"

"Yes, at a party at the Institute in August of fifty-four."

"And this was when she was seeing Leonard?"

"Yes again."

"Have you remembered anything about where or when Cordy met Melissa?"

"No. I assume it must have been in the fall of fifty-three, when she got the idea about going in on the apartment. But I was at

Stanford and pretty much out of touch. I honestly don't know what she was doing then, or who her friends were."

"Would she have been seeing Leonard as early as then?"

"Perhaps. She wasn't seeing anyone else, at least not anyone in our circle; her escort for the cotillion was the son of her father's business partner."

"Why wasn't she escorted by Leonard?"

Wingfield smiled. "I can see you're not a disciple of Emily Post—thank God. Cotillion escorts are usually college boys, not men over thirty."

"So Cordy ran with an older crowd?"

"Even in high school. If you want to know how long she was seeing Leonard, why don't you ask him?"

"I will. You can count on that."

Eighteen

■ ■ ■

No workmen's trucks clogged the street in front of All Souls, and as far as I could tell, the paint on either side of the Victorian now matched that on the facade. Ted was leafing through an office-supply catalog at his desk, a red-and-white flower lei draped around his shoulders.

"Hank's back!" I exclaimed.

Ted smiled benignly as he handed me a stack of messages.

Quickly I checked the tag on Jack's box; it indicated he was out. Then I hurried down the hall to Hank's office. My boss—and dear friend—was hunched over his paper-strewn rolltop, running a hand through his steel-wool hair as he tried to decipher chicken scratchings on a legal pad. When I knocked, he looked up and broke into a wide grin.

I said, "How come all hell breaks loose when you leave here, and harmony is restored the instant you return?"

"Because I got the magic touch, baby." He sang the words, getting up to hug me.

"Vacation seems to have agreed with you. How's Anne-Marie?"

"Off to save the rain forests."

"Really?" Anne-Marie Altman, Hank's wife, was chief counsel

for a coalition of environmentalist groups, including the foundation that Hy directed.

"Well, she's off to Sacramento, anyway. Just for a few days." Hank opened his briefcase, extracted a small tissue-wrapped package, and handed it to me.

"Oh, boy—my present!" I sat down in the client's chair and fumbled with the bow. We've always been big on gifts at All Souls, and Hank's are the best because he picks each with the individual firmly in mind. This time mine was a small piece of coral, sun-bleached and deceptively delicate-looking.

"You remembered," I said. For years I'd carried a piece of coral from a Hawaiian vacation in the zipper compartment of my purse; then one day it just hadn't been there, and I'd found myself more upset than the situation warranted. Subconsciously I'd then realized, I must have thought it a talisman against disaster, and though I prided myself on not being superstitious, for a long time after its loss I'd missed it. Now I took the new coral and tucked it deep inside my bag.

Hank said, "Keep safe."

"But never secure."

"Huh?"

"Old proverb. In a way, it's what I've lived by." Then I began to fill him in on Rae's and my activities during his absence, ending with the Benedict case. "What do you know about Joseph Stameroff?" I asked when I finished.

Hank took off his thick horn-rimmed glasses and nibbled on one well-gnawed earpiece. "Stameroff's bad news. Conservative as they come. He's swung the vote on some Neanderthal decisions in the area of civil rights."

"Can he—or could he ever—be bought?"

"Sure he can be bought; we all can, for the right price. But if you want to know if he *has* been . . . I'd say yes. Stameroff's not that good a jurist; he's gotten as far as he has because he's done favors."

"For whom?"

Hank shrugged.

"Do you think he might have engineered a cover-up in the Benedict case? He was a deputy D.A. at the time; suddenly he got handed this high-visibility prosecution. Why, unless some-body thought he'd be easily manipulated?"

"Have you asked Stameroff about that?"

"He says he was the 'obvious choice' for the case. Something to do with him having trial experience in similar types of crimes."

"Hmm. Well, I don't know all that much about the Benedict case—seeing as I was a mere child in fifty-six."

"Okay, hazard a guess."

"What you tell me makes me think it's possible there was a cover-up." Hank continued to gnaw at his glasses frame. "You sound pretty wrapped up in this."

". . . I guess I am."

"What about Jack? Do you think he's putting in too much time on what's basically a personal cause?"

"Maybe."

"And you, too?"

"Well, it's not my personal cause."

"But you've personalized it."

"Yes."

"Is it important?"

"Yes."

"Then keep on it. In the meantime I'll make some discreet inquiries about Stameroff."

Hank didn't have to put himself out, and the offer told me that the facts of the case had touched him where he lived. More than any of the attorneys at All Souls, Hank feels the burden of his oath to uphold justice; more than any of us, he is the champion of the underdog.

I thanked him for the coral and went up to my office. I easily dealt with my messages, a small amount of paperwork, and some phone calls. Then I swiveled in my desk chair and stared out the bay window, watching the play of light and shadow on the houses across the triangular park and thinking about Louise Wingfield. It bothered me a great deal that she'd initially concealed her affair with Vincent Benedict, but perhaps she *had* merely been preserving her right to privacy. And I had only Melissa Cardinal's word about how much Louise had hated Cordy.

How much credence could I place in anything Cardinal might tell me? The woman was an extortionist. She hadn't succeeded with Wingfield, but perhaps she'd attempted the same with someone else—the man at the Haven, for instance. Maybe he'd found some way to turn the tables that made Melissa afraid.

Who was Melissa, anyway? There had to be more to her past than her job as a flight attendant. How had she come to know Cordy? If I found the answer to that question, I suspected, any number of other things would become clear.

I needed to backtrack on Melissa, I decided, from her present address on James Alley all the way to the early fifties—

Someone rapped on the doorframe. I swiveled, saw Jack. He asked, "Got a minute?"

"Sure."

He came in, shoved aside my tape recorder and camera bag, and perched at the foot of the chaise longue. "We have a problem."

"More trouble with Stameroff?"

"Of a sort. I've just come from a meeting with James Wald, organizer of the Historical Tribunal. They've got a jury and have calendared the mock trial for this weekend."

"*What?* Why so soon?"

"Because Joe Stameroff approached both Wald and Judge Valle about reprising his role as prosecutor. Wald, the old publicity hound, couldn't resist the opportunity to capitalize both on Lis's murder and on having a state supreme court justice as a participant. Rudy's interested in it from a jurist's standpoint; he wants to see the Benedict prosecution reenacted."

"But why this weekend?"

"Stameroff insisted, said it was the only free time he'd have for months. In my opinion, he's trying to get it over with before your investigation uncovers anything else."

"The bastard." I drummed my fingers on the desk. "Stameroff must really have something to hide. He's setting up a situation that's potentially dangerous to him in the hope he can somehow control it."

"And the way it looks now, he probably can."

"So what's your defense?"

"Reasonable doubt—something the original defense attorney never thought about."

"And when do you meet with the people who are playing the roles of the witnesses?"

"Tomorrow morning."

"Can you alter the content of what you tell them to testify to after that?"

"At any point up until they go on the stand. And remember, the defense doesn't present until Sunday."

"Then we've got time."

"You still think you can find new evidence?"

I shrugged. "To start with, let's sit down and see what we've got." I grabbed my files and we went downstairs to the law library, where we spread everything out on the trestle table. Rae heard us and came out of her cubbyhole under the stairs, still grumpy and uncommunicative. She brightened as Jack and I began drawing up a list of things to do, and soon was immersed in the files. It was quite a reversal of her earlier refusal to become involved in the case, but I wasn't about to mention that. Instead I began making a list of what needed to be done.

I took care of two items on the list immediately: making an appointment to talk with Leonard Eyestone in the morning and contacting Cathy Potter about getting access to the Seacliff house. Then I returned my attention to Melissa Cardinal.

"Anything we can find out about her past may help," I told Rae. "Will you check public records?"

"Sure. I have lots of time on my hands." She scowled but didn't elaborate.

Jack and I exchanged looks that said neither of us was willing to plumb the depths of Rae's displeasure. I said, "There's a Ms. Cook at TWA personnel in Kansas City who thinks we're trying to trace Melissa because of a bequest from one of our clients. Call her and see if she'll give you Melissa's Social Security number, or anything else from her personnel jacket."

"Right. If I'm lucky at Vital Stats and get the names of her parents, I'll run by Voter Registration. They might have addresses and occupations for them."

"Melissa herself might have been old enough to vote in the early fifties; check for her, too." I looked up as Ted came to the door with a large Jiffy bag.

"For you, Shar," he said. "Was messengered over from the Hall of Justice."

I took the package, saw it came from Adah Joslyn. "Original SFPD files on the Benedict case, I bet. Jack, do you want to go over them first? Right now I want to make a run to North Beach and talk again with that bartender at the Haven and with Frank Fabrizio, the man who rented the flat to the bunch of them. Why don't we gather back here around dinnertime?"

They both nodded. Rae said, "I'll pick up a pizza."

"What about Judy?" I asked Jack. "Shouldn't she be in on this?"

For an instant he hesitated, a shadow moving across his craggy features. "I'll see if she can make it" was all he said.

.   .   .

The memory of the bartender at the Haven hadn't improved since the week before; if anything, it was worse. He didn't even attempt to hold me up for money this time, and that made me wonder if his mental lapse had been induced by an infusion of cash—and if so, from whom. I left my car nearby and walked the several uphill blocks to Fabrizio Pastries. Frank Fabrizio's son told me his father was a man of regular habits; this time of day he could be found taking the sun in Washington Square.

It was another beautiful spring afternoon, and to the casual observer the square must have looked postcard-perfect. Old men and women sunned themselves on the benches; children, many of them in Catholic school uniforms, were playing; lovers and singles sprawled on the grass; youths congregated, talking among themselves as they watched the pretty girls. But to a practiced observer like me, the scene was far from idyllic. Too many of the old people showed signs of being in extremely reduced circumstances; among the children ran youthful purveyors of crack; eight out of ten people sleeping on the grass called no other place home; a good many of the young men's conversations centered on drugs and illicit deals; too many of the pretty girls were prostitutes.

It saddened me that time and experience had conditioned me

to see more of the bad than of the good. But in a way I was better off than the younger, more idealistic McCone, whose faith had repeatedly been shattered as ugly truths were revealed. Besides, I wasn't so cynical that I couldn't recognize the good when I did see it, so jaded that I couldn't seize and hold the rare perfect moment—was I?

I was saved from further soul-searching when I spotted Frank Fabrizio on a bench under a shade tree. He leaned back, arms folded across his chest, eyes closed—a contented old man taking his pleasure in a fine afternoon. As I approached, one of his eyes opened. He straightened, smiling.

"You're the detective friend of my former tenant," he said as I sat beside him. "Did you ever find the little stewardess?"

"I did. You were right—it's terrible what time does to us." Briefly I described Melissa Cardinal's current circumstances.

Fabrizio's face grew doleful. "Such a waste," he said. "You know, I got aches and pains, some mornings it's damned hard to get out of bed, but it's nothing, compared. And the killer is that she did it to herself. Shut herself in and let her life seep away."

"She's badly scarred—"

"Scars." He made an impatient sound. "Scars on the face are nothing. It's when you let them spread to the soul . . . Ah, well, who am I to talk? And it's done, it's done."

"Mr. Fabrizio, when you originally rented that flat, was it only to Melissa?"

"She's the one answered my ad. October of fifty-three it was. I can place it because we bought the house in Daly City that summer, and the wife was frantic because the flat wasn't rented yet and she was counting on the income to put toward our retirement. Our retirement . . . she had such plans." He looked around bleakly, then shrugged. "Ah, well, what's the good of talking about that, either? It's over, God rest her. To answer your question, it was Melissa and her stepbrother who first lived in the flat."

"Do you remember his name?"

The furrows around Fabrizio's eyes deepened as he thought. "Roger . . . something."

"Not Cardinal?"

"No, like I say, he was a stepbrother. A good bit older than her, too—in his thirties. Was only there a month or two. Next thing, Melissa came to me and asked if a couple of girlfriends could move in to help with the rent. What could I say but yes? And next thing after that we had loud parties and a lot of coming and going, and the wife was fit to be tied."

"What happened to the stepbrother? Why did he leave?"

Fabrizio shook his head. "I don't recall that Melissa ever gave any explanation. Somehow I had it in my head that he'd been drafted—Korea, you know. But that couldn't have been right; he was kind of old for the service."

"I don't suppose you have anything with the stepbrother's name on it—the lease, for instance?"

"No, those papers are gone, long gone."

Another dead end. I sighed. "This Roger—what was he like?"

The old man peered at me, eyes keen. "Why are you asking me? Since you've found Melissa, why don't you ask her?"

"Because she won't talk to me. Someone's frightened her, badly. I'm trying to help."

He continued studying me for a moment, then nodded as if what he saw had answered some internal question. "The stepbrother was . . . I don't know how to put this. Disturbed, maybe. Angry, for sure. Made the wife nervous." He paused, watching a pack of children who ran noisily across the grass. "I haven't thought of that Roger in years, but now I remember him clearly. Very thin, dark, intense. Very angry. Unpleasant."

A breeze stirred the branches above our heads; the shadows of the leaves dappled Fabrizio's troubled face. "You know what?" he said. "A goose just walked across my grave."

Nineteen

So where is she?" It was close to seven, and Jack had been pacing around the kitchen at All Souls for at least fifteen minutes. Every now and then he'd step into the hall and stare toward the front door, looking for Rae. I wasn't sure if he was driven by hunger for the pizza she'd promised or by eagerness to get on with preparing the case.

"Maybe there was a long line at Mama Mia's," I said. "Maybe she's following up a lead. What about Judy? I thought you were going to ask her to join us."

His lips tightened. "Couldn't reach her." He might as well have added, "Subject closed."

I got up and poured myself some coffee; it had been standing all afternoon and tasted charred. I made a face but drank it anyway, needing the caffeine boost. On the way back from North Beach, I'd made a few stops relating to other matters in my caseload, then run by my house to reassure myself that everything was all right there. Now the letdown of waiting for Rae made me realize how little sleep I'd gotten since returning to the city, how deep my weariness went.

Jack peered through the door again. "A watched pot," I said. He glared at me but came back and sat down at the table.

172

"How're you coming with the original SFPD files on the case?" I asked.

"I've barely started. Later tonight I'll get into them some more."

The front door opened and footsteps came down the hallway. Rae appeared, pizza box in hand. Jack sprang into action, opening the box and getting out plates. Rae set her briefcase on the table and kicked off her shoes.

I asked, "Where've you been all this time?"

"City Hall—Vital Stats and Voter Registration."

"But they close at five."

"Voter Registration doesn't—if you happen to have entranced a hunk named Tim who works there."

"And you did."

"You bet. I'm a free woman, and on the prowl."

Jack handed us plates. "Okay, tigress," he said, "what'd you find out?"

She pulled a well-filled legal pad from her briefcase and sat down, riffling through its pages while reaching for a slice of pizza. In her absorption she missed her mouth, and a piece of pepperoni slid across her cheek and landed on her white shirt, leaving a tomato-sauce slick.

Jack said, "If only Tim the hunk could see you now."

Nonchalantly Rae plucked the pepperoni from her shirtfront, popped it into her mouth, and continued paging through the yellow sheets. "Okay," she said. "Melissa Ann Cardinal, born January eleven, nineteen twenty-five, to Jane Marie and William Albert Cardinal. Death certificate, William Cardinal, May thirteen, nineteen thirty-two, heart attack. Record of marriage, Jane Cardinal and Lawrence Robert Woods, August eight, nineteen thirty-five. Death certificate on the mother, December eighteen, forty-nine, pneumonia. No death certificate on the stepfather in this county. No further record of marriage for him, or for Melissa."

"So the stepbrother's name was probably Roger Woods," I said.

Rae looked up. "She had a stepbrother? You find that out from the former landlord?"

"Yes. What'd you get from Voter Registration?"

She read the information from the pad. Melissa's mother had described her occupation as housewife, her father as a plumber; over a seven-year period between Melissa's birth and the father's death, they had lived at three different addresses in the Mission district. Melissa's stepfather had called himself a laborer; the Woodses had resided on Shotwell Street, not far away in Bernal Heights.

When Rae finished, I asked, "Anything else?"

"Just their party affiliations. The Cardinals registered Democratic. So did Lawrence Woods. Then in forty-eight both he and Melissa's mother switched to the Progressive party, and that's how Melissa registered, too. After forty-eight, there's no registration for either the stepfather or Melissa."

"Progressive party." I glanced at Jack. "Wasn't that the one that ran Henry Wallace for president?"

He nodded. "Looks as if the Woodses were lefties."

"And they lived here in Bernal Heights." Given what Adah Joslyn had told me about her left-leaning parents, the Woodses would have fit right in—maybe even been a shade conservative.

Rae asked, "Who's Henry Wallace?"

Jack stared at her in astonishment and dismay. "And you call yourself a liberal!"

"Well, how am I supposed to know?" she said defensively. "I wasn't even born until the mid-sixties."

"But you ought to have some sense of history. I presume you've heard of Franklin Delano Roosevelt and the New Deal? Wallace was vice president under him, was dumped in favor of Harry Truman on the forty-four Demo ticket. Wallace went on to oppose what he called Truman's reactionary politics, got branded as a Communist sympathizer, and was roundly defeated as the Progressive candidate in forty-eight."

"So the Progressives were actually Communists?"

"No, they were *not*. The Progressives were victims of a well-orchestrated campaign by the Democratic opposition to identify them with the Communists in the public mind. You might say they were among the earliest casualties of the anti-Communist crusade."

"Huh," Rae said. "That's interesting, but what does it have to do with our case?"

"Probably nothing, but I couldn't resist the opportunity to give you a history lesson." Jack winked at me, then frowned. "Why do you have that weird expression on your face?"

"I do?" I said. "Yes, I guess I do. Something's connecting here, in a vague way."

"What?"

"I can't pin it down yet. I need more information." Quickly I looked around and spotted a long phone cord snaking across the floor, got up and followed it to where the instrument sat behind a stack of dirty dishes on the drainboard of the sink. The kitchen phone was the sole relic of the days when red phones with twenty-five-foot cords had been an All Souls tradition. Eventually they'd been replaced by a more sophisticated system, and I for one didn't miss having to track them down by sorting through a maze of often impossibly snarled cords.

I called SFPD Homicide, but found Adah Joslyn was off duty; there was no answer at her home number. Next I unearthed a local directory from a pile of cookbooks on the floor under the chopping block. A Rupert Joslyn was listed on Powhattan Avenue, only a few blocks away. Briefly I wondered if Adah would resent my contacting her parents without first clearing it with her; then I shrugged and dialed.

Mrs. Joslyn answered. She said she and her husband would be delighted to talk history with a friend of Adah's and suggested I come by in half an hour. I agreed, and went to grab another slice of pizza before Rae and Jack finished it.

·   ·   ·

The Joslyn home was a bungalow faced in the kind of fake sand-colored stone that is guaranteed to make anyone swear off the use of synthetic building materials. As I rang the doorbell, I mentally prepared for an encounter with the sort of people Adah had described as "interesting . . . particularly if you don't have to live with them."

And was pleasantly surprised. Barbara Joslyn, an attractive

woman in a boldly striped caftan, was warm and gracious, eager to put a visitor at ease. Her husband Rupert, tall and muscular with only grizzled hair to betray his age, was quieter but affable. While his wife fetched coffee, he settled me in their plainly furnished parlor, opening windows and commenting on the unseasonable warm spell. When Mrs. Joslyn returned, I apologized for interrupting their evening and got right to my questions.

"Jane and Larry Woods?" Rupert Joslyn said. "Of course I knew them. If you think Bernal Heights is a small community now, you should have seen it right after the war."

"I didn't know them," Barbara Joslyn added, "but I know what happened to all those people. Criminal, just criminal."

"What did happen?" I asked. "The only information I have is that Jane Woods died of pneumonia in December of nineteen forty-nine."

The couple exchanged glances. "Was pneumonia, all right," Rupert said, "but compounded by the situation. Jane just plain gave up on life."

"Had it *taken* from her, no matter how indirectly," Barbara said.

"Now, Barb, don't start."

"Maybe the passage of forty-some years has blunted your anger. Not mine."

"You were only a college girl at the time."

"That doesn't give me the right to be angry?"

I was beginning to understand what Adah had meant when she'd said it was a wonder that her parents had survived, given their differences. I would have hated to get between them during a really heated ideological debate.

A shade plaintively I asked, "What happened to the Woodses?"

Rupert said, "Forgive us. Larry Woods and his wife were good friends of my first wife and me. I feel their story personally while Barb sees it as a political metaphor."

"Metaphor, my ass!"

"Watch your mouth, woman!"

"Then don't go putting me down."

"The way it was, Sharon—"

"When the anti-Communist backlash started—"

"Larry wasn't *ever* a Communist—"

"Didn't matter in those days. All those dangerous labels and catchphrases they had: fellow traveler, dupe, concealed member—"

I held up my hand. "Wait! Please. You've completely lost me."

They both looked startled, as if they'd forgotten they had a listener. "Barb," Rupert said, "one of us is going to have to be designated spokesperson."

"Well, you're personally involved in the story, while I'm taking it to the objective level. Let's ask Sharon which version she'd prefer."

Great, I thought, make me choose sides. "How about if I hear the personal view first, and then you"—I looked at Barbara—"can place it in context."

They both nodded, apparently satisfied. Rupert steepled his fingers and sank deeper in his chair—a storyteller's pose. "My first wife and I came to San Francisco during the war. I worked at the shipyards. That's where I met Larry Woods. He and his wife, Jane, had been married less than ten years—second time for both of them. His boy, Roger, was already grown and out of the house. Jane's girl, Melissa, had finished high school and was working in a plant down in South City. Nice family."

"Rupe, get to the point!"

He winked at me and made a show of ignoring her. "After V-J Day, Larry got on with San Francisco Stevedoring, a big contractor. He joined the International Longshoremen's and Warehousemen's Union. Larry came up fast in the union, got involved with the Progressive Citizens of America, the outfit that the Progressive party spun off of. I suppose he might even have gone to a few American Communist party meetings—more out of curiosity than anything else."

Rupert paused, sighing heavily. As he spoke, the last vestiges of daylight had faded; across the room, Barbara sat in shadow, arms folded across her breasts.

After a moment Rupert went on. "I don't know if you're aware of it, but Communist party members played a big role in organizing the CIO unions—and the ILWU was one of them. A lot of Party members rose pretty high in the union hierarchy. But by forty-eight the tide of opinion had turned against them. CIO leadership condemned them—for the most part, unjustly—as agents of a foreign power. Pretty soon the union leaders got swept up in the hysteria of the times, and even members who had supported Wallace for president were being denounced. Larry Woods in particular was in trouble; he'd been too outspoken for his own good, made too many enemies. Three days before Christmas of that year, he was beaten and left for dead in a South of Market alley by a trio of fanatically anti-Communist ILWU members.

"Of course the beating only made him more vocal, and the harassment escalated. Larry, Jane, and Melissa virtually lived in fear. By the middle of forty-nine, Larry was on a downhill slide: they tossed him out of the union, and he lost his job. Couldn't get another; a blacklist existed in the trades long before it did in Hollywood. Jane had never been strong, and the strain of it all took its toll. When she caught pneumonia, it carried her off. A few weeks after she died, Larry disappeared."

Rupert paused again, pressing his forehead against his steepled fingers. I could feel him fighting for control. "Larry's son, Roger, searched for him for over three years. He finally found him, late in the summer of fifty-three, in an L.A. charity ward—his liver and his mind shot. He died two days later."

Rupert's voice had broken; he cleared his throat. Barbara made a little noise—of understanding as well as of sympathy. She said, "I'm sure you've read about what it was like during the cold war, Sharon. History has, fortunately, been revised so the truth can be told. But to know the horror of it all, you had to live through it. Rupert lived through it as a laborer, I as an intellectual, but believe me, no matter who you were, the horror was the same."

"Not all the anti-Communist union members were thugs like the three who beat Larry," Rupert added. "Most were like me, good union men who knew we had to get the hard-core Party members out in order for the labor movement to survive. Was just the climate of those times. That's not what shames me."

His voice dropped, took on a husky timbre. "What *does* shame me is that I did nothing for Larry. I saw what would happen to my friend. I even warned him. But I never did risk my own hide to help him."

"That was the tactic the government crusaders used on us," his wife said. "They made us afraid of them, and what's worse, they made us afraid of one another. A person who is afraid of his or her fellows is alone, and a lone person is easily controlled."

"Was no excuse for me doing nothing, though."

"Not an excuse—a reason."

For a moment I remained silent, thinking of that dangerous aloneness. Then I asked, "What happened to Roger Woods?"

Rupert raised his head and glanced at Barbara. "No one really knows," he replied. "From what his father told me, I assumed that Roger was very far to the left. After the conspiracy trials in forty-nine, a lot of Party members took their activities underground."

"Are you saying Roger was a Communist?"

"Again, I don't know. I never actually met him. He called me late in fifty-three to tell me his father was dead, and after that I never heard another word."

"That must have been about the time he and Melissa were living together in North Beach. He wasn't there long. Their landlord described him as angry, unpleasant."

"Understandable, given what was done to his father."

Barbara said, "What was done to everyone. Ironic—the 'Red Menace,' Russian communism, is dead today. But because of our government's unreasoning fear of it, so many of our people were destroyed." She went on to talk some more of the cold war and the anti-Communist crusade, and though I had read a good deal about it, I now began to feel what she'd called the horror of those times.

Barbara described a world where the ground beneath the feet of the average citizen was as unstable as quicksand. An atmosphere so oppressive that an individual could be deprived of his or her livelihood for the simple act of writing a check to a charitable organization rumored to have leftist leanings. A time when informing on one's friends, neighbors, and relatives was seen as the only means of survival; when truth was made malleable in the hands of congressional inquisitors; when honest statements of fact were twisted and used as boomerangs against those who had made them. To live in those times, I thought, was not unlike living in a grim fun-house maze, where you would never know if you were making a false move until the chute opened under your feet and you found yourself plunging into oblivion.

By the time I took my leave of the Joslyns, my own world seemed a very precarious place. As I walked to my car, I searched the surrounding darkness—and didn't even mock myself for doing so.

Twenty

■ ■ ■

But what did any of the things I'd just learned have to do with the McKittridge murder?

I sat in my MG in front of the Joslyn house, pondering the question. Had Melissa, like her stepbrother Roger Woods, possessed Communist leanings? Perhaps even been a Party member? And so what if she had? Surely the leftist leanings of a roommate could have had little bearing on the vicious killing of a twenty-one-year-old woman who seemed more inclined toward cocktail parties than political parties.

Or had Cordy been more politically involved than I suspected? I still hadn't found out how she'd met Melissa. What if . . . ?

The lights went off in the Joslyn parlor. I started my car, checked my watch in the light from the dash. Nine-forty. Not too late to run by All Souls and talk the matter over with Jack.

When I arrived, Rae, Ted, and Pam Ogata were gathered in front of the TV set in the front room, watching an old Edward G. Robinson movie on one of the cable channels. I paused in the archway and asked if Jack was around.

Rae said, "Try the Remedy. He went down there to meet Judy." Then she glanced back at the screen, shook her head, and got up. "If you want, I'll wander down there with you. This movie is depressing."

181

As we walked down the hill toward Mission Street, I told her about my visit to the Joslyns.

"Weird coincidence," she commented, "that Adah would tell you about her parents the day before you needed that kind of information."

"As I always tell you, She provides." I pointed to the heavens.

We turned onto Mission and maneuvered our way through the crowd to the Remedy Lounge, a short block away. The locals were out in full force tonight: people congregated in doorways or by parked cars, drinking and talking; music, from heavy metal to salsa, drifted from the bars and clubs; drunks lurched along the sidewalk; junkies lurked in the shadows; old people surveyed passersby with fearful, darting glances; low-riders and patrol cars prowled. San Francisco nights are rarely warm, even when the daytime temperatures soar, and people were taking advantage of the unexpected in their various ways.

In contrast, the Remedy was nearly deserted. Only four customers hunched over the elbow-worn bar. Owner Brian O'Flanagan stood near the front, sipping coffee and staring through the streaky window. He saluted us, eyes lighting up when he saw Rae, his favorite customer.

Jack sat alone in the rear booth, nursing a mug of beer; pleated and shredded cocktail napkins lay in a puddle of moisture. There was no sign of Judy. As we approached, he looked up hopefully; then his face fell into disappointed lines, which quickly degenerated to a scowl.

"Some greeting," Rae said, sliding into the booth next to him.

Jack merely grunted.

I sat down opposite. "Where's Judy?"

"Damned if I know." His mouth twitched as he reached for his beer. "She said she'd meet me here at nine."

"Maybe something came up at the theater."

"I called; she's not there."

Brian came over and set a glass of wine in front of me, a beer in front of Rae. So far as I know, she's the only customer who has ever rated table service from Brian—unless you arrive with her, and then you rate it, too. After enviously observing this phenomenon for over a year, I finally asked him why she commanded preferential treatment. Brian merely shrugged and said, "There's a touch of the old country in her." Since Rae is about as connected to her Irish heritage as I am to my one-eighth Shoshone ancestry, I didn't see much basis to that claim. But I have to admit that it's nice occasionally to be waited on at the Remedy.

When Brian had gone back to the bar, I asked Jack, "Where do you suppose Judy is, then?"

He hesitated a bit before he said, "I have no idea, and at the moment I don't care. Judy's making herself crazy over this mock trial. As soon as she found out her father had involved himself, she started calling me, badgering me to allow her to play herself in court. When I questioned the wisdom of that, she started . . . 'interrogating' is the only way I can put it. Interrogating me about every detail of my defense. Finally I told her we'd talk about it when you, Rae, she, and I got together at dinnertime, and she blew up. That's the real reason she didn't show earlier; I just said I hadn't been able to reach her because I didn't want to go into it at the time."

"But you've spoken with her since."

"Yes. She called around eight, sounding calmer. I suggested we meet here and talk. Then she didn't show up for the second time."

"Why, do you suppose?"

"I don't know, but what I'm seeing is a pattern of periods of rationality followed by periods of irrationality, and I don't like it one bit."

Rae asked, "Has this ever happened before?"

"Well, Judy's an actress and she tends to be melodramatic, but . . . She seemed fine when Lis first got out of prison and moved in with her. Then she started pressuring me about un-covering new evidence and going for a new trial. Lis was totally opposed, as well she should have been; the woman didn't want to spend what was left of her life in court. Judy gave it up for a while, but then she hit on the idea of a mock trial and actually talked with James Wald without warning me she was going to. The pressure started in again. Lis finally bowed to it. I got my back up, started dragging my feet. Finally I caved in." He looked at me. "That's when I sent you to talk with Lis."

"So that's why Lis insisted she wanted the trial for Judy's

sake," I said. "Who besides the three of you and James Wald knew about the possibility of a mock trial?"

"Quite a few. Judy talked it up with any number of people, and I'm sure Wald wasn't shy, either."

"And someone panicked when he heard about it and hired someone else to try to intimidate Lis, Judy, and, later, me. Only it backfired, because you and I realized there had to be something to Lis's claim of innocence and became determined to move ahead with it."

"Right."

Rae had been listening, eyes narrowed. Now she murmured, "Perfect timing there."

"What?" I asked.

"Nothing, just thinking aloud." She turned to Jack. "Maybe you should try the theater again."

"I called just a few minutes before you two came in."

"What about her house?"

"She'd never go there."

"Why not?" I asked. "The police seal's off, and she's free to clean it up. If she's behaving as irrationally as you describe, you don't know what she might do."

Jack toyed with his beer mug, looking indecisive.

"Call her there," I urged.

He glanced toward the hallway to the rest rooms, where the pay phone was, then shook his head. "Shar, I can't deal with her tonight. Things have been deteriorating between us ever since Lis's murder. Before, if you want to know the truth. I'm angry, I've been drinking, and I don't want to chance really blowing it with her."

"Then I'll call." I stood, rummaging in my bag for coins.

"And say what?"

"That I want to come up there and talk."

He looked both relieved and conflicted. "Shar, you shouldn't have to—"

"Jack, she may be your friend, but this is my case." I went back to the hallway.

The phone at the house on Wool Street rang several times; I'd almost given up when Judy's voice spoke a hesitant hello. She didn't seem surprised that I'd known where to find her, but she was adamant against my coming up there. I had to do some persuasive talking before she relented.

As I hurried out of the Remedy, Jack was punching buttons on the ancient jukebox. The strains of his first selection followed me onto the sidewalk: "The Great Pretender."

. . .

The little house on Wool Street was dark and silent when I arrived. As I rang the bell, I realized that the neighboring buildings were dark, too; even though their windows must have been open on this warm evening, I didn't hear radios, music, or TVs. I felt as if I were the only survivor of an atomic cataclysm.

After half a minute footsteps approached the door and Judy opened it. She was again swathed in her mother's black cape and carried a candle in a silver holder. To my questioning look, she said, "We just had a power failure."

Such failures were commonplace in parts of the city where the electrical systems hadn't been upgraded to carry their present-day load; tonight too many fans and cooling units had been pressed into service, and the transformers had blown. "Lucky you could find your candles and matches," I said as I stepped inside. "Mine're always missing when I need them."

Judy didn't reply, merely closed the door and led me down the hall, bypassing the parlor. In her long black cape, taper upraised in front of her, she looked like a creature out of a low-budget horror film. Surprised at where she was taking me, I followed her into the room where Lis had died.

Judy set the candle next to another on the table and sat in the chair I'd occupied the last time I saw her mother. Lis's chair was still overturned on the floor; the chalk marks remained where she'd fallen, scuffed but plainly visible. The shards from the coffee cup and glass door still littered the tiles. Gingerly I picked my way through them and sat on a stool next to the plywood slab covering the opening. Whatever Judy's reason for coming here tonight, I thought, it wasn't to tidy up.

I said, "Jack tells me you're very concerned about the mock trial."

She shrugged, cape ruffling.

"Does that mean yes or no?"

"Does it matter?"

It irritates me when someone answers my question with another, and this was no exception. "It matters—to both Jack and me. We've gone out of our way for you, and you could at least give me a straight answer. Why do you want to play yourself in court?"

She was silent, rubbing a fold of the cape between her fingers. A gust of wind swept through an open window above the sink, made the candle flames shiver. Their light distorted the shadows and glistened off the scattered shards of glass. For a moment the vision I'd had of the interior of the dovecote passed through my mind: shadows moving across rough brick walls, deadly metal flashing. . . .

I shook my head to clear it, concentrated on Judy. Even in the softening half-darkness, her skin looked dry and flaccid; the lines that bracketed her mouth cut deep; her light hair straggled lifeless around her forehead. I might have been looking at her mother.

"Judy," I persisted, "why?"

"Who else could play the role better? Who else knows what I do? I wouldn't have to be coached. It would save Jack a lot of time."

But I suspected saving Jack time was just an afterthought. "There's more to it than that."

Silence.

"Why didn't you meet Jack at the Remedy tonight?"

"There was no reason."

"You're being unfair to him. He cares very deeply for you."

She sighed, as if the thought of him caring was merely a burden. The sigh was overly dramatic and caused me to make a quick connection.

I asked, "Does playing yourself have to do with that one great performance you told me about yesterday? The one performance that might have made a difference?"

". . . Maybe. But there's more. If I could relive the trial, I might be able to remember. And then I could put it all to rest."

"I see. Why'd you come up here tonight?"

"I needed to think."

"Here?"

"It's as good a place as any. Better. I feel close to Lis here."

Close to Lis, in the room where she had died, the death scene virtually unaltered? "What were you thinking about?"

To my surprise, she began to cry—silently, her lips tightly compressed. The tears slid from beneath the round frames of her glasses, made tracks across her cheeks, dripped unchecked from her chin. And then the words began, in stutters and stops, interrupted by shuddering intakes of breath.

"She was there . . . on the floor with the gun. There but . . . not there anymore. And the reasons . . . the reasons why, she left them for me. I looked in and I saw the letter . . . there for me."

She motioned toward me, and I realized she was indicating where she'd been standing. I said, "*You* were the one who broke the door."

"The chain was on in front. She didn't expect me. But I'd been worried. I sold my ticket on the red-eye to an acquaintance in New York, then caught an earlier flight. And when I got here . . ."

"You went down the path to the deck and looked inside and saw Lis's body."

"I smashed the door with a piece of firewood . . . so loud. Too late. She was gone. So still. Maybe at peace. Do you think she was finally at peace?"

"Of course she was. What did you do next?"

"There were sheets of paper on the table. Like the tablets she used to buy for me to take to school. Mama's writing . . . a letter addressed to me."

A suicide note, I thought.

"I couldn't look at it," Judy said. "I picked up the sheets and put them in my purse. And then I . . . I ran away."

"Where did you go?"

"I drove. A long way. Down the Peninsula to the beach where they have the caves . . . San Gregorio. I remembered it from back when I was happy, when Mama and Daddy . . . I sat on the rocks for a long time and then I made myself go back to the car and read the letter. After a while I came home and called Jack."

"Why didn't you tell him about the letter, that Lis was a suicide?"

"I couldn't. Because of what she'd written."

Judy's tears had stopped now; she scrubbed at her damp chin, took off her glasses, and rubbed her eyes. When she removed her hand, I saw they were bleak, unfocused. Quickly she covered them with the glasses.

I said, "Later, when the police came, you let them assume Lis had been murdered."

"Yes."

"Why?"

Silence.

"Judy, what was in Lis's letter?"

More silence.

"Have you shown it to anybody?"

"No."

"Will you let me see it?"

She raised both hands defensively, then dropped them to her lap. For a moment they lay limp; then they convulsed, pulling and tearing at the fabric of the cape. Her mouth twisted in sudden anger.

"I can't show it to anyone! She made a mockery of everything I ever tried to do for her. She lied and lied and lied. . . . She *destroyed my life!*"

I got up, put my hands on hers, trying to calm her. She shoved me away, stood, and wrenched the cape from her shoulders. Then she hurled it on the floor and kicked it.

"I *hate* her! All my life I've hated her and I've felt guilty and she just let me. All my life I tried to make it up to her, and she took whatever I offered. And then she went and made a mockery of everything with her fucking letter!"

"Do you still have it?"

"Of course I still have it! Do you think I'd part with my mother's precious last gift?"

"May I see it?"

She shook her head, face still showing rage and sarcasm. Then abruptly she began to cry again.

"Go ahead," she said after a moment. "It's in my purse. Take it. I never wanted it in the first place."

Twenty-One

My daughter—The time has come to put an end to this. As long as I live, you will continue to resurrect memories that are best left dead. And frankly I am weary of the effort to protect you. Weary of those memories, of the horror that lives within me, and of life itself. For years I've remained silent, and I will continue to do so. I struck a bargain, however poor, and I will honor it for both our sakes. Is it better to think your mother falsely convicted of murder or to know her for the despicable creature she is? Only time and understanding can answer that, and we have neither. How are you to understand that I forged the letter that lured that woman to her death? That I went to the dovecote that night armed with talismans against failure? How are you to understand my rage and frustration, my awful sense of being thwarted at the very last? The knowledge that if I didn't act, she would forever be frozen perfect in your father's emotions? But in some secret place you've always known, although I've never dared ask. And I well know your own rage and frustration. Let it go, Judy. Let it go, as I am. And forgive me. Your loving mother—Lis.

189

I looked up from the flimsy lined sheets. Judy, calm again, watched me, eyes unreadable in the candle glare on her glasses. "See?" she said. "She finally confessed."

"It's a very self-serving letter, but I'm not convinced it's a confession."

"It's all there, written down."

"She admits to writing the letter that sent Cordy to Seacliff. She admits to going to the cote. But she doesn't come out and say, 'I murdered Cordy.' "

"Yes—in typical Lis fashion, she skirts the truth."

"I don't think . . . What's this about a bargain?"

Judy shrugged.

"And 'talismans against failure'?"

"I assume she meant the gardening shears."

"And she says you've always known. Always known what?"

"Always suspected that she did it."

"She says *known*."

"Semantics. Imprecise choice of word."

"I doubt that. This letter was important to her. There're no crossed-out words, no misspellings, no evidence of haste. I wouldn't be surprised if she drafted it more than once."

"What're you trying to say? That you still believe Lis didn't kill Cordy?"

"I don't know what I believe. But we can't base any conclusion on what she says in this letter."

Judy was silent for a moment. Finally she said, "Well, now you see why I need to go ahead with this trial. Need to know more than ever."

"And you don't care what damage that might do your mother's memory?"

"Did she care what damage she did to me? Look at the opening of that letter. She practically came out and said she was killing herself because she was tired of protecting me from the truth!"

"As I said, it's very self-serving."

"That was Lis. She played the martyr. First she was martyred by my father's drinking and womanizing and abuse. Then she was martyred by being falsely accused of murder. That letter makes it sound as if she nearly martyred herself into the gas chamber—and all so she could protect me from God knows what."

I studied the letter some more. "I wonder about this bargain. It supports the cover-up theory. And it fits with something else she said to me one of the first times we talked—that when she was reprieved from the gas chamber she 'knew what was operating there.' "

"You think the bargain was to go to prison but not be executed? In exchange for what?"

I shook my head.

"Who did she make the bargain with? My adoptive father?"

"Not likely. He wasn't all that important then. I think he was acting on orders from someone more powerful."

"The governor?"

"More likely one of those behind-the-scenes people who hold the real money and power."

Judy slumped, a trifle theatrically. "My first parents were an alcoholic and a . . . I don't know what. And then I was adopted by a man who would make a deal with the devil."

"What was your adoptive mother like?"

"Cold. I could sense she didn't really care for me, and she died only a couple of years after I went to live with them."

"He never remarried?"

"He was too busy moving up the political ladder to take the time. I was more or less raised by the housekeeper."

"Okay," I said, "enough rehashing the past. Right now you're going to have to do something that I guarantee won't be easy."

"You mean tell the police about this letter, and the fact that I've let them proceed as if Lis had been murdered." She bit her lip. "Will they arrest me?"

"Maybe, but I think we can persuade them not to, or at least to hold off until after the mock trial."

She nodded resignedly. "Will you call them?"

"Don't you want a lawyer present?"

"The only lawyer I trust is Jack, and I definitely don't want him here. I'll take my chances with just you and the cops."

I nodded and started for the phone. As I reached for the receiver, the overhead lights flashed on. The refrigerator's motor sighed and groaned, then started whirring. In one of the neighboring houses, someone let out a cheer.

I tried to take it as a good omen.

.　　.　　.

"I am so pissed off," Adah Joslyn said. "Does either of you have any idea just how truly pissed I am?"

I said, "To hazard a guess—truly."

"This is no laughing matter, Sharon. I shouldn't even be talking to her"—she jerked her chin at Judy—"without her attorney present. She's admitting to obstruction. That's a heavy—"

"Come on, Adah. You're not going to charge her."

"The hell you say!"

"You are not going to charge her, because if you do there will be no mock trial. And if there is no mock trial, you and Wallace will not accomplish your prime objective."

"Our prime objective was to solve this homicide—which now turns out not to *be* a homicide."

"You have—or at least Wallace has—a more personal agenda."

Her eyes narrowed. I knew what she was thinking: since Lis had committed suicide, they couldn't nail Joseph Stameroff for murder, so what sense was there in pursuing either the old case or the new one?

Speaking slowly, with emphasis, I added, "I know what Benedict said in the letter about being weary of life, but I also know that the woman was literally hounded to death by graffiti and anonymous phone calls. Both Judy and I have lost sleep and suffered property damage. Now, Adah, *someone* is behind all that. *Someone* does not want the facts of that old homicide to be taken out and reexamined. That someone is guilty of illegal acts in the present, and probably in the past as well. I think that you and Wallace could accomplish what you hope to do by attending the mock trial and seeing what's revealed there."

"You sound quite confident that the trial will produce results."

"My investigation points that way."

"Are you sure you aren't promising more than you can deliver?"

I wasn't sure, but I said yes.

Joslyn's gaze flicked to Judy, who was watching us, puzzled and somewhat wary. Then it moved back to me. "Well, it wouldn't be a foolproof way of taking the individual down, but it'd be satisfying nonetheless. I think Bart would agree."

"Does this mean that you'll forget the idea of charging Ms. Benedict?"

"I can see my way to that."

"What about publicity on this new development?" I motioned at Lis's letter, which lay on the table between us. "What's your feeling about that?"

"Keeping it quiet would be difficult. There's a certain amount of media curiosity about the case, as well as a good deal of departmental pressure."

"I'm wondering if publicizing it would be such a bad thing, anyway."

Judy made a noise of protest.

"I know how you feel," I told her, "but if the public assumes that your mother confessed before killing herself, it might put someone off his—or her—guard."

"You're really convinced that Lis didn't kill Cordy," she said.

"As I told you before, we can't base any conclusion on such an ambiguous letter. So why not proceed on our original assumption?"

Judy looked down at where her hands tightly clasped Lis's black cape; she'd rescued it from the floor, folded it lovingly, and now seemed reluctant to let it out of her grasp. "Lis is dead," she said in a small voice, "and very few people believed in her innocence to begin with. You might as well release the contents of her letter to the press."

Joslyn nodded decisively. "We'll just say it's new evidence and skirt the issue of how we discovered it." She looked sternly at Judy. "I don't know why I'm cutting you this much slack, but you've got a powerful ally in McCone here." Then she turned to me. "So where do we stand? What else have you found out since we last talked? As if this wasn't enough."

I related my day's activities. When I got to the part about my visit to her parents, she turned another stern look on me.

"Lot of nerve, bothering them without consulting me first," she commented.

"I tried to consult. You weren't available. You ought to at least get an answering machine."

"I've got one. I just keep forgetting to turn it on. Hate the damn things. What did you think of my folks?"

"I liked them. But I can see why they'd be hard to live with."

" 'Hard' doesn't begin to describe it. Anyway, this Commie connection—you think there's anything to it?"

"It's worth following up." I looked at Judy. "What do you recall about your biological parents' political stance?"

"They toed a strict conservative Republican line, I'm sure. In the fifties, people in the military-industrial-intellectual alliance would have been fools not to; they had little choice in the matter. Security clearances were absolute requirements, both for the Institute staff and for their families."

"Then there's no line of inquiry there." I turned back to Joslyn. "Will you run the name Roger Woods through NCIC and CJIS?"

"Sure. Not much to go on, though, and the feds and state are damned slow. I'll see if I can't get them to expedite this." She stood, picked up Lis's letter. "I'll have to take this," she told Judy, "but eventually you'll get it back."

Judy released her grasp on the cape, moved her hand as if to stay Joslyn. Then she pulled it back, shaking her head. "Take it. Keep it." To me she added, "I meant what I said earlier—I don't want it anymore."

.   .   .

I was home in bed by midnight, exhausted but wakeful. Ralph and Allie sensed my unease and pressed close to me, hemming me in on either side until I felt like a book between furry bookends. The cottage had not been harmed, and there were no messages on my answering machine tape—not even from Hy, which puzzled me. Still, I lay tense, waiting for stealthy noises outside or the ring of the phone or doorbell. And as the hours passed, Adah Joslyn's question kept replaying in my mind: *Are you sure you're not promising more than you can deliver?*

Twenty-Two

■ ■ ▮

Thursday morning there had been a heap of garbage in front of my house; on Friday I found Justice Joseph Stameroff in his gray Towncar. As I went down my front steps, his driver got out and opened the door to the backseat. Stameroff motioned for me to get in. I complied, doubting that a state supreme court justice would harm me in front of the curious neighbors who were eyeing the car while leaving for work.

Like Judy's the night before, Stameroff's face was marked by pronounced strain lines. Arrogance still shone in his eyes, but it was clouded by worry and sorrow. He said, "I've come to ask you one last time to put a halt to this mock trial."

"I can't. By involving yourself, you've ensured that."

"Miss McCone, I'd gladly back off. And I've observed a certain . . . force of character in you. You could stop the trial if you chose."

"Maybe, if only Jack Stuart were involved. But it's Judy who's determined to go forward. Have *you* ever tried to stop her when she's bent on a course of action?"

He sighed. "Tried, yes. Succeeded? No."

"She's given you a lot of trouble over the years, hasn't she? I hope the bargain you struck with Lis Benedict was worth it."

"I struck no bargain with her."

"Come on, Stameroff, we both know there was a cover-up and that you were smack in the middle of it. Why don't you admit it—at least to me?"

"Miss McCone, at the time of the Benedict trial, I was a very small cog in the wheel of justice. If Mrs. Benedict bargained, it was with someone far more important than I."

"Just following orders, were you? Was adopting Judy one of them?"

Wearily he shook his head. "You don't understand at all, do you? I genuinely cared for the little girl. She was alone in the world—or soon to be—and needed me in a way no one had before. It may surprise you, Miss McCone, but even a man of whom you think so little is capable of loving. Judy is going to be badly hurt in the next few days, and I have no choice but to defend myself."

"We all have a choice."

"If I do, then I fail to see it."

We sat silent for a moment, sharing the one thing we had in common—our sense of impending ruin. Finally, surprisingly, Stameroff offered me his hand. "I don't suppose we'll have occasion to speak again."

"No, I don't suppose we will."

I got out of the car and watched it inch away along my narrow, congested street. Then I went about my self-appointed rounds.

.   .   .

The morning had dawned foggy, and like any true San Franciscan, I felt a measure of relief. Long warm stretches are just not natural for our city by the bay; when one continues for more than a few days, memories of the strange mugginess preceding the quake of '89 surface, and we tend to become jumpy and short-tempered. As I waited beneath the closed clamshell dome of the Institute for North American Studies building, I actually enjoyed watching gray salt-laden moisture stipple its curved glass.

Leonard Eyestone was late for our ten o'clock appointment. After twenty minutes I stood and moved restlessly about the lobby. To the far left of the reception desk was a recessed hexagonal area that reminded me of an apse in a church. I went over there and found a small photograph gallery with a cushioned bench in its center.

The photos depicted events in the history of the Institute: furnishings being moved into the Seacliff house; Russell Eyestone accepting a plaque from John F. Kennedy; the groundbreaking here on the Embarcadero; opening ceremonies for the new building. Most of the others showed men at lecterns—delivering speeches, accepting awards, shaking hands with public figures. I recognized one I'd seen on microfilm at the library of the Eyestones with John Foster Dulles. In yet another, of a head table at a banquet, I found an attractive young Lis Benedict. I stepped closer and studied the man to her right. Vincent Benedict had been good-looking in a dark, dissipated way; the camera had caught him in what I assumed was a characteristic pose, cocktail glass halfway to his lips. All the photographs, even the most recent ones, were stamped in their lower left-hand corner with a silver signature: Loomis.

"Ah, there you are." Leonard Eyestone had come up behind me.

I turned. He was impeccably clad in gray pinstripe, but his face looked puffy, his protuberant eyes tired. We shook hands, and he motioned at the bench.

"If you don't mind, we'll talk here," he said. "My office is in chaos. We're getting ready for a press conference, and for some reason my staff are convinced that reporters notice such details as dust."

"Press conference? About what?"

"A major new contract—quite a coup. A five-year, sixty million dollar study of the religious right, with emphasis on their disruptive tactics and potential for undermining established social institutions. If our findings are as we expect, we'll also develop the framework for a teaching apparatus—public seminars, lectures on college campuses—to educate citizens to the inherent dangers."

"This study is funded by the government?"

"Department of Health, Education and Welfare."

"I'm surprised the present administration would take off after the religious right."

"Why? The administration is concerned with stability. The religious right are extremists, have been known to be a source of embarrassment in the past. They're capable of doing incalculable harm to the conservative position."

I could see his point; as a liberal, I too was concerned about the rise of the religious right. But government funding of a study obviously designed to control them smacked of the same sort of intolerance displayed by those who would outlaw abortion, forbid the teaching of evolution in the schools, and ban books that did not agree with their own narrow outlook.

"This study is a far cry from the contract you people announced the night Cordy McKittridge was murdered," I commented. "From taking off after the far left to taking off after the far right is a long way to come in only thirty-six years."

"Ms. McCone, we are not 'taking off after' anyone. Nor have we ever done so. We are merely contracting with the government to determine the facts of the situations we study."

"And after you issue your reports, you don't care how they're interpreted? How they're used—or against whom?"

He sighed, as if weary of trying to explain a simple concept to a slow child. "That's right. We're merely contracting to gather information and apply objective analytical techniques."

"And you have no personal stake in the outcome?"

"Personal stake? No. Now, if you're asking me if I have a personal opinion, that's something else entirely. I believe that all forms of extremism have negative effects on our society. But if we can contain them, channel them, they can be used for the public good. In the case of this study, if we can objectify and quantify the religious right—in layman's terms, find out what makes them tick—we can neutralize their undesirable effects while utilizing those that may bring about greater stability for American society as a whole. It's what we should have done with the Communists and the Vietnam War protesters."

Now I felt distinctly uneasy. "You mean use them without their being aware of it?"

"Essentially."

"To preserve the status quo?"

"To improve it."

"But to preserve the position of those currently in power?"

"Well . . ." He shrugged.

"To discourage change, unless it's government-mandated?"

"For the greater good."

Troubled, I looked around at the photos on the walls surrounding us; they were stark testimony to the Institute's alliance with those in control at any given time. Too much power was contained here in Eyestone's shrine to the intellect. Too damn much power that could be used—abused—to ride roughshod over the rights of the largely powerless individual.

Eyestone said, "You don't like the concept."

"It takes me back to Big Brother."

He made a dismissive sound. "Fictional nonsense—and badly outdated. My point is that extremism has no place in modern society. Terrorists, mass murderers, protesters of every stripe: we can't afford rampant individualism anymore. Nor can we afford unplanned social change."

I'd seldom felt so entrapped by an argument, and I sensed it was structured to accomplish just that. Eyestone had presented me with a thorny dilemma: on the one hand, I abhorred terrorists and murderers as much as I did protesters who resorted to mindless violence or intimidating tactics. On the other hand, when he spoke of curtailing the rights of the individual . . .

"What place would First Amendment freedoms have in this scheme of things?" I asked.

"They're vastly overrated. You're politically naive if you believe they actually exist anymore."

"I'm not as politically naive as you think. What you're talking about here is an oligarchy, where only those approved by the few in power would be granted the right to register an opinion. It hasn't quite come to that yet."

Eyestone's lopsided face skewed in a smile. "Oligarchy! Why, Ms. McCone, I had no idea your vocabulary was so extensive!"

"Why, Dr. Eyestone, one can't help but pick up a few four-syllable words at Berkeley. But to get back to what we were talking about—do your colleagues here at the Institute share your personal opinion?"

"To varying degrees."

"And has that always been the Institute's political stance?"

"You mean, of course, was it the stance at the time of the McKittridge murder? More or less."

"The intellectuals of the cold war era were a fairly conservative breed?"

"Yes, with the exception of a few household names—C. Wright Mills and Erich Fromm, for example. There were a number of reasons for that, from the dramatic—fear of HUAC and blacklists—to the mundane—enjoyment of postwar prosperity. Both were operative here at the Institute. We're a privately held corporation, founded and built by my father. We rely on our contracts for our profit, and the contracts come from the government and big business. Surely you can understand the implications of that."

"Oh, yes."

"You sound disapproving—fitting for one who attended Berkeley and picked up those four-syllable words." He smiled as he spoke, as if trying to take the edge off the conversation. "Now what else can I tell you about my organization?"

"I'd like to talk about Cordy for a minute. How long had you been romantically involved with her before she broke it off?"

He seemed surprised at the change of subject and had to think for a moment before he replied, "About two and a half years."

"She was only a high school girl when it started?"

"Cordy was never *only* a high school girl, and she could be very . . . persuasive when she saw something—or someone— she wanted. In hindsight, I realize I seemed sophisticated to her, and of course the clandestine quality of the affair was titillating. Also, it didn't hurt that I had a good deal of money of my own and stood to inherit more, as well as control of the Institute."

"You say the affair was clandestine. I thought you brought her around to Institute parties."

"As a friend of the family, a surrogate older brother, might."

"So few people knew you were seeing her?"

"Only her younger friends—Louise Wingfield, for example."

"You saw Cordy at the apartment in North Beach, then?"

"Ah, you know about that?"

"Louise Wingfield told me. Did you know Melissa Cardinal, the woman who originally leased the place?"

"Was she the little blond flight attendant? I saw her occasionally."

"What about her stepbrother, Roger Woods?"

Eyestone frowned. "I don't recall any brother."

"Stepbrother. He lived in the flat with Melissa before the others began contributing to the rent."

"Then I couldn't have known him, could I?"

"I guess not. But you may have a chance to meet Melissa if you accept the invitation I'm here to extend."

"And what is that?"

I explained about the Historical Tribunal calendaring the mock trial for the weekend and added, "Since Justice Stameroff is participating, I thought it would be interesting for all of you who testified at the original trial to be there. And Melissa Cardinal, even though she wasn't actually a witness." I doubted Cardinal would accept my invitation, but I'd decided it wouldn't hurt to ask.

Eyestone shot his cuff and fiddled with the cuff link, clearly uneasy. "I wouldn't be required to testify, would I?"

"Merely to observe. As a favor, I'd like you to let me know if anything seems inaccurate or distorted to you. We want the presentation of both sides to be as historically correct as possible."

Eyestone thought for a moment. I waited to see if my blatant appeal to his vanity would work. Finally he smiled. "I'd be pleased to attend, Ms. McCone. I'll see you at City Hall tomorrow morning."

•   •   •

Louise Wingfield said, "I suppose if I don't attend this mock trial, you'll forever suspect me of having murdered Cordy."

"Does it matter?"

"Oddly enough, I like you and care what you think of me." She hesitated, sunk in thought. "Joe and Leonard will be there.

Judy. And you say you're going to try to persuade Melissa to attend. Old home week. God, what a motley group!"

"Will you be there?"

"Yes. I don't like the idea, but I suppose it's all part of the cathartic process. I see from the morning paper that the police found evidence that points to Lis being a suicide." She gestured at a copy of the *Chronicle* that lay on the corner of her desk.

I'd seen the article; it had been written just in time for the city edition. "Lis's death still constitutes a form of murder; she might not have killed herself if she hadn't been harassed." Then I switched subjects. "I need to clarify a point about your testimony at the original Benedict trial, as well as ask you a few more things about Cordy. Do you have the time?"

Wingfield leaned back in her chair and reached for a cigarette. "Go ahead. I don't seem able to accomplish much this morning, anyway."

"First your testimony: when the note to Cordy arrived at the apartment, was anyone else there?"

She thought, eyes narrowed. "Melissa was."

"Did you tell the police that?"

". . . I must have."

"Did the police question Melissa?"

"I don't know."

"Later, did Stameroff ask you if Melissa was present?"

"No. As I mentioned before, the subject of the apartment and the people who shared it was ignored for Cordy's family's sake."

Or someone else's, I thought. "Did anyone ever approach Melissa about testifying?"

"I wouldn't know. The day the note came was the last time I saw Melissa until I went to her apartment last week."

"All right. Now, about Cordy: what were her political opinions? Were they conservative or liberal?"

"What few she had—and that wasn't many—were conservative. All of us who were raised in San Francisco society thought that way. Even on the college campuses we were more concerned with becoming well-rounded individuals—the educational catchphrase of the day—than with exploring new concepts or ideologies." She grimaced ruefully. "That's why they called us the Silent Generation."

"And as far as you know, Cordy never flirted with radicalism? Communism?"

Wingfield raised her eyebrows. "Cordy? God, no! Her flirtations were strictly sexual."

"What about Melissa Cardinal? Did you ever talk politics with her?"

"No. My relations with the other girls in the flat were fairly superficial. And then there was Vincent. When you're closeted in a bedroom with the man you think you love, you're not likely to pay much attention to a roommate's preferences at the polls."

Her frankness about Benedict was an abrupt switch from her previous resentment at my intrusion into her privacy. Acceptance of the truth coming out, I wondered, or more candor calculated to confuse? "Did you ever meet Melissa's stepbrother, Roger Woods?"

"I didn't even know she had a stepbrother."

"And you don't remember anything further about where Cordy and Melissa met?"

She shook her head, exhaling smoke through her nostrils. "I've done some thinking on that, and I have the distinct impression that Cordy didn't really know Melissa well, either. They seemed to have friends in common, though; one time I remember them reminiscing about something ridiculous that had happened at the Unspeakable."

"Where?"

"Coffeehouse on Filbert. It's long gone."

"A Beat place?"

"No, this was a little early for them. More of a Socialist hangout."

"Maybe that's the connection I'm looking for. Do you know who ran it? Or any way I can find out more about it?"

"The only time I was there was one weekend when I came up from Stanford and had a date with a fellow who fancied himself a radical. We didn't stay long; he'd had too much to drink, got loud, and they asked us to leave."

"I don't suppose he was a regular, then."

"He may have been; at least he'd been there before. I can ask him what he remembers about the place."

"You're still in touch?"

"God, yes. His mother was my mother's bridge partner. Once he got over his radical phase, he went into his father's brokerage firm and made millions. I regularly approach him for contributions."

"Would you mind calling him and asking about the Unspeakable?"

"Will do."

An argument had been in progress in the next cubicle for some time now. Suddenly it escalated, Spanish epithets peppering the air. Wingfield glanced that way, said, "I think I'm needed."

"I'll hope to hear from you about the Unspeakable, then. And see you at the mock trial."

Her lips twisted ruefully. "And *I* hope this trial doesn't make a complete mockery of us all."

.   .   .

Back at my office, I checked in with Cathy Potter. She had a few interesting things to tell me about the Seacliff property: the asking price was five-point-five million, prequalifying territory, but the Institute for North American Studies no longer owned it. The new owner was a firm called Keyes Development.

"And have I got the skinny on that!" she added. "Seems the Institute mortgaged it to the max to finance the new facility. During the last year, they got behind on their payments to the lender, plus they owed millions to Keyes, which put together the Embarcadero deal. So Keyes took over the property in lieu of payment, and now they own a piece of primo oceanfront real estate, even if most of it is practically vertical."

"What about getting access?"

"I'm working on that."

"When will you know?"

"Like I said, I'm working."

"Call me back when you know something. If you get me in there, I promise to buy my next house through you."

Cathy, who had been privy to the complicated and peculiar financial finaglings that had gotten me my present house, merely snorted and hung up.

I hung up, too, and contemplated the handful of message slips I'd carried upstairs with me. Two clients, requesting minor things. Another client, thanking me for a job well done. My mother: my answering machine had screeched at her when she'd called my home yesterday, and she feared it was malfunctioning. Would I call when I had the time?

I would, gladly. Since Ma had divorced my father the previous fall and moved in with her new love, a younger man—fifty-seven—named Melvin Hunt, our conversations had become increasingly upbeat and enjoyable. So had my dealings with my father, who every day emerged further from a decades-long shell of depression and isolation. With both of them, I'd been forced to create a new relationship—one where criticizing and guilt-tripping and resentment of parental authority had no place. It was wonderful to have found two new friends in my own parents.

There was one final message: "Linda wants you to call her at Wig Wonderland." Beneath the words, Ted had drawn a big exclamation point and a face that looked remarkably like mine, topped by carrot-colored curls.

Linda? Wig Wonderland? Oh, right—Tony Nueva's woman friend, Linda Bautista. She'd said she'd let me know if she heard from him.

I decided to go over there rather than call.

Twenty-Three

■ ■ ■

Linda Bautista wore an auburn wig today, its glistening tresses woven and piled so high that it looked as if she had a leafless pineapple balanced on her head. She was fitting a mop of platinum curls on a young Asian woman when I entered the store; the effect was ghastly, but the woman turned her head from side to side, smiling. When she saw me, Linda put a finger to her lips and motioned at a curtained archway at the rear of the room. I nodded and went back there; after a few seconds she followed.

The archway opened into a stock room. More disembodied heads sat on the shelves, and wigs lay curled up in their plastic boxes like sleeping animals. Linda leaned against the wall, took off one of her bright red pumps, and wriggled her stockinged toes. "Tony's back," she said. "He wants to see you."

"Where is he—your place?"

She shook her head. "He's hiding at a friend's out by the beach."

"Who's he hiding from? The person who beat him?"

"Yes and no. It's sorta . . . complicated."

"Tell me about it."

"Well . . ." Her gaze slid away from mine, and she leaned down to pick up her shoe. "Tony was in Chula Vista, and him and his cousins, they went over to Tijuana. Coming back, there was some trouble with Customs, so he took off."

"What kind of trouble? Drugs?"

"Um, I'm not sure. But he didn't feel good about staying down south."

For some time now I'd been expecting Nueva to make a serious mistake; he wasn't bright enough to balance indefinitely on the thin edge of legality. "So he came back here, where he knows someone has it in for him."

Linda fiddled with the shoe, pulling out its crumpled, dirty innersole. "Where else was he gonna go? Here at least he's got friends. Will you go see him?"

"What's the address?"

She gave it to me, on Forty-seventh Avenue near Santiago. As she slipped her pump back on, I asked, "Does this mean you and Tony are back together?"

She shrugged, still avoiding my eyes. "What else can I do? He needs me." Unspoken was the corollary: *And I need him.*

I wanted to tell her that she had more options than a semi-slick operator who at nineteen had already begun his downward slide to prison. But I wasn't sure that was true, and she didn't want to hear it anyway, so I said nothing. As I left the shop, the Asian woman was asking to see a wig exactly like Linda's.

.   .   .

The outer reaches of the Sunset district look much like the beach communities of southern California, but everywhere are reminders that the elements impinge more harshly here. Salt-laden moisture and heavy rain corrode the iron railings of the apartment complexes near the Great Highway; wind-driven sand scours the paint and pits the stucco of the small homes sandwiched between them. Even on a sun-drenched day, a vague aura of depression hovers over the area, as the fogbank hovers over the sea; on one like this, when grayness had a grip on the entire city, the shabbiness and outright decay seemed cruelly exposed.

The address Linda had given me was the ground-floor in-law apartment of a pink stucco house. I rang the bell, salt mist dampening my cheeks as I waited. Footsteps crept up to the door; I looked through its peephole and saw a dark eye looking back at me. Then the security chain rattled, and Tony Nueva let me in. Quickly he replaced the chain and turned the dead bolt.

We were in a dark narrow hallway whose floor was covered with a patchwork of different colors and types of carpet. Some overlapped, creating a lumpy surface. All smelled strongly of mildew and more faintly of dog. Tony didn't speak, merely led me to a room furnished with only a mattress and one of those beanbag chairs that were popular in the sixties. There was no kitchen, only a hot plate on top of a small refrigerator; through the bathroom door I could see dishes stacked in the sink. Nueva motioned for me to take the chair and flopped on the mattress.

The draperies on the single window were safety-pinned shut. The light that filtered around them revealed Tony to be uncharacteristically rumpled. His dark hair stood up in ragged points, his eyes were circled and bloodshot, and he reeked of beer. A pyramid of Budweiser cans leaned against one wall.

"So," I said, "you went and did it this time. What happened at the border? Were you smuggling dope?"

He gestured wearily. "No lectures, McCone. I been beating myself up pretty good without your help."

"Who else beat you up?" I could see the marks on his face: cuts that had scabbed over, bruises turning ocher.

"Before I tell you about it, I'm gonna need a stake to get out of town."

"I may be able to help you with that, but first I'll have to hear what you have to say."

"Shit, McCone—"

"Do you want me to help you or not?"

He glared at me, then sighed. "Okay. That Friday two weeks ago when you came around to the arcade about the graffiti? You were right about it being easy to spot the punk on account of his red hands. Name's Enrique Chavez. Big dude, kind of ugly, pretty stupid, too. He'd been bragging to the guys at this bike shop where he hangs out about how he's got this contract from somebody big and is gonna be rolling in it."

Nueva looked around, picked up a beer can, and shook it.

Then he tipped back his head and sucked at the dregs. "So I go see Chavez," he went on. "I figure if whoever's hired him is big, I can make a deal. I talk to him, tell him you're looking into the graffiti. He says to cool it, don't tell you nothin', he'll find out what it's worth. Next day he shows up with five big ones."

"Then what?"

"I keep listening. Chavez's really stupid; he's got a mouth on him. I find out there's been more graffiti. Phone calls. And *then* I hear about the old lady."

"What about her?"

"Just a name. Benedict." Nueva nodded, pointed emphatically at me. "One day I hear Chavez's talking about her. Next day she's dead. Now I know I'm on to something."

Obviously he hadn't seen the piece in the morning paper, had no idea Lis Benedict had killed herself. "So you approached Chavez again," I said.

"Not right off. I think it through for a couple of days. Work it all out in my head. Then I go see Chavez at the bike shop. *Big* mistake. Chavez gives the signal to a couple of his pals, and they all three lay into me. Those guys—killers. No way am I gonna make it in this town anymore, so I take off down south. And if it wasn't for my fuckin' cousin Carlos talking me into helping him move a couple of kilos across the border, I'd still be there."

I was silent, thinking over what he'd told me. As I'd said to Adah Joslyn, even though Lis Benedict had committed suicide, she'd literally been hounded to death. I wanted this Enrique Chavez—and I wanted the person who had hired him. "You know where Chavez lives?" I asked.

Nueva shook his head. "Like I said, he hangs out at Ace Bike Works, on Seventeenth near Folsom. But don't go there, McCone. Those guys'll make dog meat of you."

"Just worry about yourself, Nueva."

"I am. Why d'you think I told you all that? How much're you gonna give me for it?"

"The twenty dollars we originally agreed on for this information."

"McCone!" A wail of pure outrage.

"You went back on the deal, Tony. You wouldn't even have

returned my ten buck advance if I hadn't hunted you down and accused you of selling out."

"McCone, I *gotta* get out of town. Chavez finds out I told you, him and his pals'll kill me for sure."

"I doubt that; Chavez doesn't know where you are. And I'm not going to tell him, because I want you to stay right here."

"Why?"

"Because I may need you, and if I do, I'll pay you well."

Nueva smiled. Even with a drug-smuggling charge hanging over his head, the prospect of dealing could perk him right up.

. . .

Ace Bike Works wasn't much, just a garage beneath one of the dilapidated Victorians on Seventeenth Street in the heart of the Mission. It wasn't doing much business, either. When I pulled up across the driveway at ten to five, I saw only one man inside—a bullet-headed Latino in coveralls, sweeping the floor and allowing the detritus to blow into the street. He glanced uncuriously at me as I got out of the MG, then looked back down at his broom.

As I approached him, I checked out the garage. Definitely no one else there, and only one cycle—an old Harley-Davidson that looked as if it hadn't been streetworthy in years. The man stopped sweeping, leaned on the broom, and regarded me with dull eyes.

"Enrique around?"

No reaction.

"Enrique Chavez?"

It was as if a relay switch had kicked in. The eyes cleared—infinitesimally. "Enrique?" he asked, and I realized he was retarded.

"Enrique Chavez," I said more slowly.

"Not here."

"You know where he lives?"

Again, no reaction.

"His house? The address?"

"Clipper Street?"

"The number?"

Headshake.

"The cross street?"

"Sanchez?"

"Thank you."

The man said nothing more, merely began to sweep again.

. . .

The directory in a phone kiosk near the Sixteenth Street BART station showed only three Chavezes on the blocks of Clipper near Sanchez, and only one named Enrique. I drove, rumbling through potholes, to the listed address.

Clipper is the city's main artery over the hill from the West of Twin Peaks area to the Mission and points east, including the Bay Bridge. I've long suspected that the residents discourage our famed Pothole Patrol from paying too many visits in hope of cutting down on traffic. Chavez's block was one of the worst, and my spine tingled unpleasantly by the time I stopped across from his Victorian cottage. Its paint had peeled away long ago; only splintered wood remained, and if something wasn't done soon, the venerable structure would be good for nothing but kindling.

I went up to the house, rang the bell. No one home. As I turned away, I spotted a neighbor picking up the evening paper from her front steps and called out, "Does Enrique Chavez live here?"

"Father or son?"

"Son."

"Yeah, he's still there. The old man took off with a bimbo six months ago."

"Thanks." I went back to the MG to wait.

An hour passed. The fog spread farther inland, slipping over the hills behind me and riding along their contours. Lights came on in the nearby houses; even though it was daylight saving time, we'd have an early evening. The Chavez house stayed dark.

I stared through the mist dotting my windshield. The house was set in a small hollow, and the fog lay strangely still there, as it had at Seacliff the night Wingfield and I made our pilgrimage. As it might have on the night Cordy McKittridge had died. . . .

I didn't want to think about that night. I pushed the images aside. They came on steadily in spite of my efforts. I said aloud, "God, what's wrong with you?"

I hadn't slept well in days, but by now my weariness felt like an intrinsic part of me, something I thought about no more than the blood coursing through my veins and arteries. Deep down, I was furious with myself for having become so involved—no, face it, obsessed—with long-ago events that I could neither prevent nor change. Furious, too, with present-day events that told me the past was not as dead as I'd like it to be. But my rage was curiously blunted; on the raw-nerve level where I was operating, I felt beyond it all, simply too tired to expend my energies on nonproductive emotion.

Full dark now, and still no one home at the Chavez house. Too much to do this evening to wait it out. I drove over to Bell Market on Twenty-fourth Street and used the pay phone to check in with All Souls.

Ted answered, still on duty at twenty to seven. "Louise Wingfield called," he said. "The former owner of the Unspeakable is Jed Mooney. There's a number where you can reach him." He read it off, then asked, "What is that—one of those rock groups that puke on stage?"

"Just a defunct coffeehouse. Anything else?"

"No. Jack is upstairs, in conference with Judy. He said if you checked in, I should tell you to come by here at eight for a strategy session."

"Tell him I'll try."

I hung up and placed a call to Jed Mooney. He said he'd be happy to talk with me about "the last good decade," and gave me an address on Thirty-first Avenue in the Outer Richmond.

On the way back to my car, I wondered what kind of person would refer to the tacky, conformist fifties in such a manner.

.   .   .

A leftover member of the Beat Generation—that's what kind of person. I knew plenty of die-hard hippies; they were everywhere, living in throwback communes in the hills or going about perfectly ordinary pursuits, like my mailman. But I'd never before met a leftover Beat.

Jed Mooney was in his sixties, tall, very thin, and wearing the uniform of another day: black jeans, black sweater, goatee, and crew cut. From outside, his stucco row house looked the same as the others in its block, but its interior resembled what I imagined his coffeehouse had been like. The living room walls were plastered with blown-up photographs of Ginsberg and Kerouac and Ferlinghetti; a folk singer with an odd nasal voice droned on the stereo. Mooney had lit a candle in a wax-encrusted Chianti bottle against the encroaching dark. He invited me to pull up a cushion to a low table and sat opposite me, hands clasped on its teakwood surface. "You said you want to talk about the Unspeakable."

"Yes. I understand you owned it from—"

"Fifty-two to sixty-six when, regrettably, declining interest forced me to close."

"This was a Beat hangout?"

"In its latter stages. Early on, we catered to a more political clientele—socialists, anarchists, Communists. The repressive climate of the times either sent them underground or forced them to mend their ways, so to speak, and then we attracted a livelier crowd. I preferred them, as you can see." He gestured around at Allen, Jack, and Lawrence.

"A wonderful era," he added. "I suppose you're too young to remember it."

"What I remember of the fifties is more along the lines of Hula Hoops and cars with big tail fins."

Mooney snorted. "Yes, that's what the fifties are usually remembered for. And the sixties—everyone identifies them with the hippie, not his more intelligent predecessor. The brief Beat era"—his eyes glistened in the candlelight—"what a joyous time!"

"I thought Beat meant down-and-out."

Mooney looked sternly down his rather long nose at me. "Young woman, you're sadly misinformed. As Kerouac once said, 'Beat means beatitude, not beat up.' " He moved his gaze reverently to the writer's photograph; if he'd been standing, he would have genuflected. "The Beats felt everything, *dug* everything. They were religious, they looked everywhere for God."

He was right; I had been misinformed about that short but historic movement, and I would have liked to learn more, but my time was limited. "Actually, Mr. Mooney," I said, "it's your earlier clientele I'd like to talk about. Specifically, a woman named Melissa Cardinal and her stepbrother, Roger Woods. They may have frequented your coffeehouse in the early fifties, before fifty-six, anyway."

Mooney pursed his lips; after a moment he nodded. "I remember them. Roger Woods was an interesting man. He had a good deal of training in political science, had worked toward the Ph.D. somewhere. Then he became disillusioned, dropped out. I believe something had happened to his father, and it made him bitter and angry toward society."

"And Melissa?"

"She was less interesting. An airline stewardess. It was said she did a little courier work on the side—documents, that sort of thing. But in hindsight . . . we were all very romantic then. Melissa may have started the rumors herself to avoid being typed as a mere waitress-in-the-sky."

"Are you saying that she and her brother were Communist party members?"

"Roger was, had been for years. I'm not sure about Melissa. And Roger was not a member in good standing. The Party kept a low profile, especially after the conviction of eleven of their leaders in forty-nine on charges of violating the Smith Act. Roger was too angry, too vocal. He openly advocated the violent overthrow of the government. I wouldn't be surprised if it was Party members who killed him."

"*Killed* him?"

"That's what we heard. Summer of fifty-six, I believe. In Seattle. They said he was shot to death on the docks. Some claimed he was attempting to recruit longshoremen for the Party; others claimed he was trying to escape to Russia."

"Did Melissa confirm any of this?"

"She wouldn't discuss Roger. Finally, about a year later, she stopped coming around."

"What about a young woman named Cordy McKittridge? Did she ever come to the Unspeakable with Melissa?"

Mooney's eyes widened. "So that's what this is about—the murdered debutante. Yes, she was a friend of the Cardinal girl, and for a while she came often. But that stopped in the spring of fifty-five, long before she was killed."

"Did she always come with Melissa, or with a man?"

"Wherever those two girls went, there also went a crowd of men."

"But you don't remember anyone in particular?"

"There was a friend of Roger Woods, but he struck me as a dabbler, a hanger-on." He paused. "Sorry, I don't recall his name."

"Can you describe him?"

"No, I can't. When a man stood next to Cordy McKittridge, you scarcely noticed him, except perhaps to envy him. She was beautiful and warm. Fresh as a spring rainstorm, soft as the dawn. . . ." He broke off, smiling ruefully. "As you can see, Ms. McCone, I'm a poet—and an exceedingly bad one."

"You remember Cordy so vividly," I said, ignoring the invitation to comment on his similes.

"Some individuals have that effect. My memories of Cordy are especially strong. For me she'll forever be caught in candlelight—young, beautiful, perfect."

Lis Benedict had said something like that in her suicide note, about Cordy being forever frozen in Vincent's emotions. "You sound as if you cared for her."

He turned the full force of his melancholy smile on me. "Very much, but she never knew. Cordelia McKittridge would never have returned the feeling—not to a man like me. She was special and I, alas, am not."

I sensed he had enough wistful self-knowledge to see through any comforting platitude I might offer, so I asked a question instead. "The coffeehouse—why did you call it the Unspeakable?"

Again the smile came, trembled, and extinguished itself. He said, "I thought it would negate the unspeakable—my loneliness. It didn't. Nothing ever has."

Twenty-Four

■ ■ ■

Jed Mooney insisted on giving me coffee—a bitter Turkish blend that would eat at my stomach lining all evening—and I didn't have the heart to refuse. For twenty minutes he spoke of the days when the Unspeakable was a mecca for the hipster; of poetry readings, improvisational jazz; of drugs, sex, and absurdity. I listened distractedly, my thoughts fixed half a decade earlier than that, toying with the interrelationships among a debutante, an airline hostess, a faceless man, and a Communist who advocated the violent overthrow of the government. By the time I was able to take my leave of Mooney, it was well after eight, and the fog wrapped the city in a smothering embrace.

I was missing Jack's strategy session; by now he'd be furious with me. But I had nothing new to offer—yet. Perhaps tomorrow, after I'd read the original police file on the murder. That would mean another late night, but given the way I felt, I wasn't going to sleep much in any case.

What now? I could call Adah Joslyn, see if she'd heard from either NCIC or CJIS about Roger Woods. But it was much too soon for that, and a call would prompt her to ask about my day's activities—something I didn't care to rehash at the moment. I supposed I could run by Enrique Chavez's house again, stake

217

it out until he returned, but that didn't feel right either. I was restless, primed for action. My earlier exhaustion was now pushed far below my level of awareness.

I stood next to my car, blinded by the mist, feeling the pull. Tried to resist, but couldn't. Gave in to it.

Seacliff was only a dozen or so blocks away. I got into the MG and headed west.

.　　.　　.

The driveway of the Institute's former home curled away from me under its overhanging cypresses. Clotted mist hung heavy and oddly still in their branches. Foghorns groaned and howled up by the Gate, and the cold air smelled of the wild open sea. I stood at the foot of the drive, wondering about the security here.

The property seemed as deserted as it had on the night Wingfield and I came out. If the owners were having it patrolled, the guard's rounds would probably be cursory and very intermittent; police patrols were frequent in Seacliff and besides, the location of the house—on a street with no immediate outlet, dead up against the National Recreation Area—made the prospect of vandalism a slim one.

I started stealthily up the drive, walking to one side of the gravel, my footsteps scarcely audible. The dry leaves of a nearby stand of eucalyptus rattled overhead. As I rounded the curve I saw the house—tall, massive, black as the grave beyond the security lights. Nothing moved here, not even birds in the ivy.

So this was how it had been that June night thirty-six years before. In the dark, through the mist, a killer had walked as I did now.

I skirted the house, glancing briefly at its third-story dormer windows, wondering at which one Judy had stood in fear of the thing that moved in the dark below. I believed her fragmented memories—no exaggeration there. She'd heard someone, seen something. Perhaps witnessed an act so terrible that she'd unconsciously willed herself to forget it.

Beyond the house was a slate-floored terrace, walled at the cliff's edge. I crossed it, leaned over the wall, bracing myself on the palms of my hands. Surf roiled against jagged rocks below; to my right, where the crescent of China Beach and the towers of the Golden Gate were, I saw only mist. I turned away and started walking toward the dovecote.

Didn't matter that it was no longer there. Didn't matter that I wasn't sure of its exact location. I kept going. The ground sloped gradually at first, then leveled off. Some fifty feet beyond that, it dropped steeply—a rocky tumble covered with tenacious Monterey pines—all the way to the sea. Somewhere on this flat expanse had been—

My foot slammed up against stone, pain shooting through the toes in spite of the protection of my athletic shoe. I cursed, hopped a little, then squatted and felt around with my hands. A curving brick foundation. I'd found the place where Cordy had died.

For a moment I stood, my eyes closed. Listened to the crash of waves, sough of branches, lament of foghorns. Images intruded, the nightmare pictures of my dreams. I opened my eyes again, shook my head. What was I *doing* here?

Ignoring my own question, I knelt beside the foundation. Touched it again, gently. Thought of Cordy. Thought of them all: Lis and Vincent Benedict, their young daughter, Judy. Louise Wingfield, Russell and Leonard Eyestone, Melissa Cardinal, Joseph Stameroff. And Roger Woods, even though he had probably never come here. And Roger's father, Larry, who had defied the forces of conservatism and breathed his last in an L.A. charity ward. . . .

And again I thought of Cordy.

So much blood. So much pain. What would drive a person to inflict that much pain? The usual—fear, rage, even hatred—weren't enough to explain it. Insanity? Sheer random acting out of psychosis? That might be so today, but in the fifties? Well, maybe; there have always been monsters. But what kind of monster would inflict such pain, commit such desecration, and then gently lay the victim out, closing either eye with a penny?

I could not reconcile the violent act with the ritualistic one.

And the finger. Good God, the finger . . .

I knelt there on the cold ground for a long time, my hand

resting on the overgrown foundation. Kept thinking of them all, each a victim in his or her own way. Each a predator, too.

Even though I'd found no real answers here, somehow I felt as if I'd gotten what I'd come for. Finally I stood, wiped the dirt of the dovecote's foundation from my hands. Turned and walked away.

Twenty-Five

■ ■ ■

Lights shone in the windows of the Chavez cottage. I parked directly in front, mounted the rickety porch steps, and knocked. A plump woman in jeans and a Hawaiian shirt opened the door. No, she said, Enrique wasn't home.

"When do you expect him?"

She smiled as if I'd made a joke. "Friday night—who knows? My boys, they come and go like they want. Mostly go."

I thanked her and started to turn away. A motorcycle rounded the corner. Mrs. Chavez said, "There he is now."

The motorcycle pulled up to the curb in front of my car. Its rider got off and gave the MG a curious look, as if he'd seen it before and was trying to place it, then glanced up at where I stood on the steps. He was tall and slender, with an acne-scarred face and a thick mane that fell nearly to his shoulders.

It was the young man who had come to the door of Louise Wingfield's cubicle at Project Helping Hands the first time I'd talked with her.

What had she called him? Rick. She'd anglicized his name.

Chavez looked back at the MG, putting it together, too. Then he got back on his bike.

"Rick, stay right where you are!"

221

I raced down the steps. Rick gunned the cycle. I lunged for it, but it moved away from the curb, its exhaust hot through the legs of my jeans. I watched as it careened west up the Clipper Street hill.

Mrs. Chavez stood on the porch, her mouth open. I called to her, "Where would he go?"

She shook her head.

"A friend's? A girlfriend's?"

"You the police or something, lady?"

"I'm not the police."

"Huh." She went into the house and slammed the door.

That was all right, I thought. I didn't need to talk with Rick Chavez now. The person I needed to talk with was Louise Wingfield.

.   .   .

On the night of our pilgrimage to North Beach and Seacliff, Wingfield's car had been in the shop and I'd dropped her off at her condominium on Chestnut Street on Russian Hill. I found the sprawling brown-shingled building easily; it was on the north side of the street, and great expanses of glass and cantilevered decks took advantage of the bay view. No view tonight, however; even here the fog held the city in its grip.

I went to the entrance of the building and checked the mailboxes. Wingfield's condo appeared to take up the entire third floor. I rang the bell. Got no reply. Stepped back onto the sidewalk and looked up. All the windows were dark. No Wingfield. No answers.

Now what?

.   .   .

The mist hung as thick in James Alley as anywhere else in the city tonight. I walked along, sounds from the surrounding congested area oddly muted by the buildings on either side of me. The alley was very dark, and few lights showed in windows; I had difficulty locating Melissa Cardinal's door.

There it was—the one with the iron mesh over its window. I

fumbled with the bells, rang the one I thought was Cardinal's. No answer. I rang the rest, but no one came. The two times I'd come here, I'd seen no evidence of other tenants; possibly the other three apartments were unoccupied.

I started to walk back the way I'd come, then stopped. Melissa had been cautious about answering the door the other day; possibly she was climbing down the stairs. I went back to the door, listened, but heard nothing. Finally I grasped the door-knob and pushed experimentally. The door was open a crack.

I looked down, but couldn't see what had prevented it from latching. I pushed harder, encountered resistance. After locating my small flashlight at the bottom of my bag, I stood on tiptoe and shone it through the window mesh.

What I saw made me put my shoulder to the door and force it. It opened about eighteen inches, enough so I could squeeze partway through. I shone the light downward.

Melissa was the barrier I'd been pushing against. She lay on the floor at the foot of the stairs, head propped against the baseboard, dress hiked up to mid-thigh, veined legs splayed. And the blood . . .

It had spurted, sprayed on the walls. The spatter patterns seemed to jump out at me as I moved the flashlight beam over them. Tacky here, still wet there, and the sickly sweet smell combined with more pungent odors—

My heart did a little skip, then started racing; my stomach revolted. I squeezed back through the door, used a nearby garbage can for the dregs of the Turkish coffee. Then I breathed deeply, leaning against the building's wall. It was several minutes before I could make myself go back inside.

She was still warm, but had no pulse. If it hadn't been for the blood, I would have assumed she'd fallen downstairs and broken her neck. There was no wound that I could see—

Wait, there it was. In the neck. A single puncture to the artery. No wonder the blood had sprayed. The killer—he or she—must have been covered with Melissa's lifeblood.

It was silent in the building—the kind of silence that told me no one else was there. Carefully I edged around Melissa's body and went up to her apartment. Its door stood open; she'd gone down to let someone in, then.

There was a phone on the table next to the recliner. Under the lamp's base my card was still anchored, finger-smudged, as if she'd been toying with the idea of calling me. I picked up the receiver, called Homicide. Wallace was in the squad room; he said he and Joslyn would be right behind the uniforms. I replaced the receiver, turned up the lamp, and looked around.

The first thing I spotted was Melissa's big white cat cowering under the tall cabinet. I hauled the creature out, stroked it. It wriggled from my grasp and ran back under there. I decided to leave it where it felt safe.

As I straightened, the objects on the shelves caught my eye. I looked closer. The animal figurines were not cheap kitsch, as I'd previously assumed, but tasteful and expensive-looking, like the reproductions you see in museum gift shops. And, also contrary to what I'd thought, they had not recently been dusted. A film overlay the carved stone sea lion, Mexican folk-art cat, gold snail with cut-crystal shell, ivory tortoises, fine china dogs, and wood-carved jungle beasts. A large lop-eared jade rabbit, nose pointed into the air, had been moved enough to make miniature footprints.

A costly collection for a woman living on Social Security and disability payments, I thought. Of course, Melissa had probably spent very little on anything else. But even so, she must have had an additional source of income to collect in such a manner. Perhaps her recent extortion attempts were not her only ones. . . .

I heard the first wave of law enforcement personnel in the alley and went down to meet them. Melissa's body seemed strangely diminished now, as if the official presence had caused any lingering vestiges of her persona to flee. I felt a tug of sorrow as I edged around her. Already it was as if she were long dead; soon all traces of her existence would be eradicated. All that would remain was a collection of stillborn animals that would find their way into the city's antique shops, a cat that would end up in the pound.

Outside I identified myself to the patrolmen and filled in the basic details. They asked me to wait in the black-and-white until Wallace and Joslyn arrived; I complied, sitting with the door open, my feet on the pavement. A backup unit pulled in behind it; neighborhood residents began to wander into the alley. When Wallace's unmarked car pulled in from the far end, I got out and waved.

Joslyn hurried toward the building and spoke with one of the men in uniform. Wallace came over to me. "This the angle you were following up?" he asked, motioning the way Adah had gone.

"Yes. Melissa Cardinal, one of the women who shared the North Beach flat with McKittridge."

He glanced around for his partner, who was now entering the building. "You have any ideas about this?"

"One." I explained about Wingfield possibly having hired Enrique Chavez to harass Benedict and me—maybe Melissa, too.

"I'll put out a pickup order on Chavez and Wingfield."

"While you're at it, put one out on Tony Nueva. He's wanted on a drug charge down south, and he may know more about the Chavez situation than he told me."

Bart took down the details about Nueva and went to join Joslyn in the building.

I leaned against the patrol car, watching the all-too-familiar proceedings. Joslyn emerged from the building, conferred with one of the uniforms, disappeared again. The lab van arrived, and then the medical examiner's people. After a while they left with the body bag.

So that's what it comes down to, I thought. A lifetime, and then they zip you into a sack like yesterday's garbage.

Wallace returned. "Adah wants to see you in the apartment."

I pushed away from the patrol car. "You coming?"

"Uh-uh. I want to canvass the neighbors personally."

I went up to Melissa's apartment.

The lab team had already dusted for fingerprints there. Joslyn sat in the recliner, going through an address book. She was dressed in sweats—off duty and at home when I'd called in, unlike her workaholic partner. Holding the address book up, she said, "Mighty slim pickings. She had several doctors, a dentist, and a chiropractor. A vet for the cat"—she motioned at where it still cowered under the cabinet—"and a couple called Mary and Rod in Cedar Rapids, Iowa."

I sat down on the sofa. "They may be family and, if so, the

closest relatives she had. I found out some fairly interesting details about the stepbrother." I related what I'd been told about the life and death of Roger Woods.

Joslyn looked thoughtful. "I'll query Seattle on his murder."

"Did you recover any weapon here?"

"No. From the wound, it looked to be a thin, sharp blade. Now tell me what else you know."

I filled her in on everything. When I finished she said, "You sound like you don't think this Chavez killed Melissa."

"I see the guy as more of a street punk than a contract killer. I think the murderer was someone Melissa expected, possibly someone she hoped to gain from."

"The Wingfield woman? Melissa didn't succeed at blackmailing her before."

"Maybe she tried again. And then there's the man she met at the Haven. What about this: the killer called *her*, gave her the impression of giving in to her demands as an excuse to come over here."

"Could be."

"Let's think about that extortion attempt on Wingfield for a minute," I said. "It didn't work, and one of the reasons is that Melissa had no proof. But with someone else, if she did have proof . . ."

"Wouldn't the killer have searched for it, then? There's no sign of anything like that here."

"Unless the proof was something that wouldn't mean anything if Melissa wasn't alive to explain it." I motioned at the glass-fronted cabinet. "I don't know if you've noticed, but that collection is an expensive one for someone living on a small fixed income. This blackmailing could have been going on for some time."

"So why kill her now?"

"Maybe her earlier demands were modest, but then she saw an opportunity to do large-scale damage to her victim and upped the ante. Lis Benedict's release, the upcoming mock trial—either of those, or something else that we don't know about, could have triggered it."

"But you said Cardinal was afraid. Wouldn't talk about the

McKittridge murder. What was it she told you? That she wasn't suicidal?"

I thought for a moment. "All right—how about this? She attempted to up the ante, and the person—the man at the Haven, Wingfield, whoever—threatened her. So she backed off. But then . . . take a look at that card of mine that's tucked under the lamp. It's well thumbed; maybe she was planning to call me, tell me what she knew about McKittridge in exchange for protection. The person found out and killed her."

Joslyn nodded. "It makes as much sense as anything else does. And if she had some sort of proof, it's probably in this apartment. Let's look for it."

Together we examined the two rooms and their contents, checking the obvious and not-so-obvious places people hide things. The absence of personal items saddened me; there were no photographs, mementos, or letters to suggest that Melissa had had a life beyond these walls. Nothing, in fact, except a small file of paid bills and canceled checks from which to reconstruct the life of the woman who had immured herself here.

Finally the only thing that remained was the glass-fronted cabinet in the living room. I went over, tried its door, found it locked. Joslyn saw what I was doing and produced a key from the drawer of the table next to the recliner. As I fitted it into the lock, the white cat looked up at me, great blue eyes fearful and pleading. *Oh, no, I won't,* I thought, then picked it up and deposited it in Joslyn's arms.

"Hey!"

I opened the cabinet. The dust lay thick enough around an ivory polar bear to resemble a snowfield. The large jade rabbit's footprints were—

The rabbit, I now saw, was actually a vase, its upturned mouth an opening that would accommodate stems. A roll of paper had been pushed into it. I picked the rabbit up, probed with my fingernail, pulled the paper out. A photograph.

It was signed with the same name as those on the wall of the gallery at the Institute—Loomis—and showed the terrace behind the mansion in Seacliff. A cocktail party was in progress: in the foreground Lis and Vincent Benedict were talking with another couple whom I didn't recognize; in the background Russell Eyestone held court, a circle of men surrounding him; at the far right were two young couples. I recognized Cordy from the photos I'd seen on microfilm; she was laughing, head tilted back, the setting sun sheening her blond hair. Leonard Eyestone stood at her elbow, entranced. Louise Wingfield looked plainly bored, and her companion—a tall, thin man with dark hair—smiled politely, but his eyes were intent on some point in the distance.

So what? I thought and showed the photograph to Joslyn.

"Must've meant something to Cardinal," she said, "but what? And when was it taken?"

I shrugged and looked around for a phone book; there was one on the lower shelf of the table next to the recliner. When I turned to the *L*'s, I found a listing for Loomis Photography on Natoma Street in the South of Market district. I called the number, but got no answer.

Joslyn looked questioningly at me. I said, "The photographer's still in business. I'll check with him tomorrow, see if he remembers anything."

She was sitting on the sofa, still holding the cat. Its head was tucked into the crook of her elbow, but it wasn't struggling. "Aren't you going to the mock trial?" she asked.

The trial! I looked at my watch, saw it was after midnight. Jack would really be angry with me by now. "I hope to," I replied. "You mind if I make another call?"

"Be Melissa's guest."

I ignored the graveyard humor, dialed All Souls. When I explained what had happened, Jack's anger evaporated. "I'll be up all night, anyway," he told me. "Come by when you can."

Replacing the receiver, I asked Joslyn, "Can I keep the photo overnight?"

"Go ahead." she held it out to me. "I doubt it has any bearing on my case."

I didn't believe that for an instant. She was trusting me with it because she and her partner had already trusted me too much; all they could hope for now was that I'd deliver something.

"Thanks." I tucked it in my bag, then motioned at the cat. "What're you going to do with it? Take it to the pound?"

Joslyn's hand paused in its petting motion; she looked down. The cat—wily creature—turned adoring eyes on her face. "Oh, hell," she said, "maybe it's time to trade in the tropical fish for something more companionable."

Her words took me back several years, to the apartment of another murdered woman, to a fat black-and-white spotted cat named Watney who had crouched growling under the sofa. I'd taken him home just for the night; last year he'd died of old age and was now resting under my rosebush.

"You won't regret it," I told Adah.

Twenty-Six

Faint music drifted from Jed Mooney's row house. When he opened the door, I recognized the sound of Charlie Parker's alto sax. Mooney looked slightly drunk or stoned; after a moment his expression brightened.

I said, "Sorry to bother you so late, but there's something I'd like to ask you to look at."

"No hour is too late for a woman such as you." The courtliness of his deep bow was spoiled when he lurched into the doorframe. He righted himself, sighed. "You can see why I've never had much success with members of the fair sex."

I smiled and followed in his shambling footsteps to the living room. He turned Parker down and without asking poured me a glass of Chianti from a near-empty bottle that sat next to the wax-encrusted one on the low table. We resumed our earlier seats on the cushions.

"You look pale and wan," Mooney said. "Drink."

I took a small sip of the wine, felt spreading warmth, and mentally cautioned myself against drinking more. Dinner had been a couple of Hershey bars gobbled down in the car, and much too long ago.

"What have you got to show me?" Mooney added.

I took the photograph I'd found in Cardinal's rabbit vase

230

from my bag and passed it to him. "Do you recognize these people?"

He held it close to the candle, studying it intently. After about fifteen seconds he said, "That's Cordy McKittridge, of course. And Roger Woods." He pointed at the dark-haired man next to Wingfield.

I'd hoped he would identify the man as the one he'd seen at the Unspeakable with Cordy; this was even more interesting. So Roger Woods, card-carrying Communist, had visited the right-wing, security-conscious Institute. By whose invitation? Louise Wingfield's? It would appear so, but Wingfield claimed not to have known Melissa had a stepbrother.

"Are you certain it's Woods?" I asked Mooney.

"Oh, yes." He nodded. "He's dressed considerably better than he did around my coffeehouse, but it's definitely Roger."

"What about the other people in the picture? Did you ever see any of them at the Unspeakable?"

"That I couldn't say for sure. A few look familiar because they ran pictures of them in this evening's *Examiner*, along with a story on the Historical Tribunal session this weekend. I wish you'd told me that's what you were working on when you came here earlier. I would have enjoyed knowing I was part of something . . . important."

His tone was so wistful that I said, "I apologize. To make up for that, I'll arrange for you to have a pass to the preferred seating at the trial. We might even need you to testify to Roger Woods's identity when the defense presents on Sunday."

Mooney's face lit up. "Was Woods involved in the murder? No, he'd left town by then. What possible connection could he have with it?"

"That remains to be seen." I truly couldn't hazard a guess, and now I felt my stress level mounting. The mock trial was slated to begin in eight hours; I had yet to meet with Jack and study the original press file, and I also needed to talk with the photographer, Loomis. I would have liked to go up against Louise Wingfield once more, but common sense told me to leave her to the police. God, I hoped Jack had come up with some solid structure for his case rather than waiting for me to make sense of these bits and pieces of evidence!

Jed Mooney was excited now. He wanted to talk about my case and how the mock trial would be conducted. He wanted me to drink my wine, relax a while, and listen to Charlie Parker. I pleaded the need to confer with the defense attorney, and he immediately became apologetic. When I left, he was already fussing about what to wear to tomorrow's proceedings.

.   .   .

"Jesus, I don't like *any* of the ways I can approach this case," Jack said. He sat on a stool in the law library—disheveled, red-eyed, his gray-flecked hair furrowed where he'd clawed at it with his fingers. On the table lay his files on the case, the SFPD files—which he'd barely had time to glance at—and the remains of the sandwich I'd built from somebody's leftovers when I'd arrived. It was now after two-thirty, and my head ached. My skin had that taut, tingling feel it gets when I pass far beyond exhaustion.

"I thought you'd already structured it along the lines of reasonable doubt," I said. "Most of the cases that go before the Tribunal can't be tried on any other basis."

"Doesn't mean I have to like it. I wanted to introduce new evidence."

"We've got plenty of that. Taken together, though, it doesn't add up." I yawned. "Judy's still insisting on participating?"

"Uh-huh. We've cleared it with James Wald and Rudy Valle. Stameroff's waived meeting with her to brief her, which tells me he's planning to proceed much as he did at the original trial."

"Have you seen Rae? Did she find out anything further from TWA in Kansas City?"

Jack shook his head. "They refused to give out any more information on Cardinal."

"And now she's dead."

The phone buzzed, and I reached for it; as I'd expected, it was Adah Joslyn, whom I'd called when I arrived over an hour ago. "Sorry it took me so long to get back to you." She sounded as ragged as Jack. "Bad news. Nueva and his girl are gone. He sold his car, TV, and stereo to a neighbor of theirs around seven; by now they could be anywhere. And we haven't located Chavez."

"What about Louise Wingfield?"

"She has an alibi for this evening, and we've already verified it. Admits to knowing Chavez, but only as a former client of Project Helping Hands. Says she doesn't know why he showed up there that day you were in her office; by the time you left, he'd vanished and never came back."

"You believe her?"

"She was convincing, but who knows?"

"Adah, that photograph from Cardinal's apartment?"

"Yes?" She spoke in a lower tone now.

"I have an I.D. on the man with Wingfield, Eyestone, and McKittridge. He's Roger Woods."

"The Commie. Huh. Funny thing about him, Sharon: I queried Seattle, and they've got no record of him being killed in fifty-five, or for a three-year period either side."

"So he might still be alive. And that might make the picture very important. Is it still okay if I keep it overnight?"

There was a silence. Then Joslyn said, "As far as I'm concerned, there *is* no picture."

"But if it's evidence—"

"We'll rediscover it at Cardinal's apartment."

"Aren't you going out on a limb—"

"Sorry, Sharon. Got to go."

Annoyed, I hung up the receiver. "Where were we?" I asked Jack.

"Reasonable doubt."

"Right. About that new evidence you want—how likely is it that Judy'll remember anything else that might help us?"

"I can't tell what's going on in her mind." The words sounded bitter.

"I take it the two of you still aren't getting on."

He hesitated. "As a matter of fact, I feel damned angry at her. Right now I could give a fuck about going through with this trial, but I'm into it up to my nuts, and my reputation is on the line. Those assholes at the Tribunal have been grabbing all the press they can; the whole legal community will be sitting back and watching me duke it out with Stameroff. I feel manipulated—by the Tribunal and by Judy. She's been playing with my emotions the way you play with a rubber band—stretch them out, let them snap back. I'm just glad it'll be over on Sunday, whatever the outcome." He paused, then grinned ruefully. "Listen to me. Good old Smilin' Jack, whining like you were Dear Abby."

"If I were Dear Abby, I'd just tell you to get counseling. As it is, I have a more concrete suggestion—about the trial, not your love life. Judy will be called as a witness for both the prosecution and the defense, right?"

"Yes."

"And you'll be putting her on first?"

"Right again."

"Okay, as I recall, during the Patty Hearst bank robbery trial, they all left the courtroom and went over to the apartment where the SLA held her to look at the closet where she was confined. Can you do something like that at this trial? Move it to the Seacliff estate for Judy's testimony?"

"I can make a motion to move the trial for viewing the crime scene. It's done in cases where a point can't be proven by photographs, diagrams, or direct descriptive testimony."

"I'd say this is such a case, wouldn't you?"

"Well, there are subjective factors that would come across more clearly if we went to the scene. That's generally why it's done. But I'd have to back that up in giving the reasons for my motion, and then it'd be at the judge's discretion."

"Do you think he'd go for it?"

Jack rubbed his stubbled chin, thought for a moment. "Normally judges resist. They're big on control, and they know that if they leave the courtroom they'll lose a measure of it. On the other hand, this is only a mock trial; the proceedings are more relaxed. Rudy Valle's a good jurist and inclined to bend the rules in the interest of getting at the truth. I'd say there's a good chance. But are you sure we can get access to the property?"

"My real-estate broker's still working on it. I'll know early tomorrow."

Jack sat up straighter, looking more animated than I'd seen him in days. "Then I should approach Valle and Wald at the morning recess, alert them to the possibility. When should we plan on going out there?"

"That's something else that's a little irregular. I'd like to go tomorrow night, after dark. Given today's fog, the weather should perfectly re-create the conditions on the night of the murder."

He frowned. "That makes the timing awfully tight. I'll have to open the defense in late afternoon rather than on Sunday morning, but I think I can manage it. If necessary, I'll waive my opening statement—it's a bunch of bullshit, anyway."

"In the meantime," I said, "I'll be in and out of the courtroom, following up on a couple of other things. I'll keep you posted on what develops. Tomorrow night, if everything works out, we'll go to Seacliff and you can have Judy walk through what she did and saw on the night of the murder. That should convince the jury that there're big holes in the prosecution's case. And Judy may remember something significant that will strengthen the rest of your presentation on Sunday."

"You really believe all this about repressed memory?"

"Don't you?"

He looked away from me. "I don't know what I believe anymore."

"Well, I talked with a therapist about it; it's a more common occurrence than you'd imagine. The Susan Nason case—"

"I know about that." He shook his head. "I guess it's hard to believe something that bizarre is happening to a person you're close to."

"Well, don't brood on it tonight; you need your rest." I stood and picked up the thick file from the SFPD.

"You going home?"

"Yes, but not to sleep. I have some reading to catch up on."

JUDY BENEDICT: Mama's dress was red in front. It was a white dress, but there was red all the way down to the hem. She said it was ink. . . . The ring was in the delphinium dress she wore last Christmas. . . .

RUSSELL EYESTONE: The child came downstairs with the ring. She said she'd found it in the delphinium—

that was the color of the dress. She said she should have thrown it away, too. . . . I guess she meant that Mrs. Benedict should have thrown that dress away with others she gave to Goodwill. . . .

DR. ROBERT MCDONALD (Lis Benedict's personal physician): No, Mrs. Benedict didn't consult me about her case of food poisoning. Frankly, that surprises me. She's always struck me as a bit of a hypochrondiac. . . .

LEONARD EYESTONE: All of us, with the exception of Mrs. Benedict, were present at the Blue Fox and later at the St. Francis. The only time the party was separated was in transit, and as you know, that's only a short distance. . . .

RUSSELL EYESTONE: Interrogate the secretary of state? Are you insane?

AARON OVERTON (deputy coroner of San Francisco County): Whoever killed her would have been covered in blood, literally soaked. Unless they dressed in protective garments and even then . . . Dismembering a body after death, when it doesn't actually bleed, is a messy proposition. Hacking a person to death . . . well, you saw the inside of that cote. Which wound was inflicted first? How do you expect us to be able to tell?

TOM DECK (head groundskeeper at the Institute): Those shears, they was always in the garden shed when I locked it up at five. But now that I think on it, I might've left them in the cote, near it, anyway. I was working there that afternoon trimming back those larkspurs that grow around it, and I could've stuck them inside or leaned them against the wall. I was in a hurry, see, 'cause it was my kid's Peewee baseball night. . . .

LEWIS WELLMAN (rare coin dealer): In late fifty-four—I think it was November—I sold a mint pair of nineteen forty-three war-issue pennies to Vincent Benedict. I remember it well, because Mr. Benedict knew the pennies were made of zinc-covered steel, wanted them because of that. He was a chemist, you understand. He said he was buying them as a gift. I assumed it must have been a joke gift, because he seemed highly amused at his selection.

I pushed away from the kitchen table and stretched. Shaded evidence, vague evidence, suppressed evidence—it was all there in the SFPD file. Glancing at the clock, I saw it was almost five in the morning. I felt curiously alert in spite of a slight headache.

My purse sat within reach on the counter. I fumbled in its zipper compartment for some aspirin, and my fingers encountered the piece of coral Hank had brought me from Hawaii. For a moment I rubbed its rough surface; then I smiled. Everything was coming together now. I had only two pieces of information to look up.

Forgetting about the aspirin, I went to the closet off my home office and located the old Funk & Wagnalls encyclopedia that my mother had gotten for us with Blue Chip stamps many years before. I dragged out Volume 15, *Lace to Maots,* and Volume 25, *Watfo to Zymol,* and perused a couple of entries while sitting cross-legged on the floor. Then I left the books there and went back to the kitchen, where I poured myself a small snifter of brandy.

The couch in the sitting room looked inviting. I curled up there, thinking how I should have tried to get hold of the police file long before, read through it immediately. The typed reports, transcripts of interviews, autopsy reports, and scribbled notes of long-retired or dead detectives had begun to take on a certain shape and definition. What wasn't contained there was significant, too. Now the facts enmired in my subconscious had begun to filter loose and merge with what I'd discovered; soon they would flow freely toward a solution.

But at the moment I needed to sleep, if only briefly. I'd sleep more soundly, I was sure, than at any time since Hy and I had flown back from the Great Whites on Wednesday.

Hy, I thought suddenly, what's happened to you? Where are you now, and why haven't you called? My body missed him, but more than that, I needed him intellectually. If I could talk this through with him, utilize his objectivity and keen perceptions . . .

But that wasn't possible, and I'd have to accept the fact that I would never be able to rely on him, any more than he'd be able to rely on me. A poor relationship? Maybe, to most people's way of thinking. But deep down it satisfied a restlessness in me— a need to be free that had caused me to chafe at other, more settled unions.

I sipped brandy, stared at windows that grew light with the dawn. All was quiet, and I had no further fears of vandalism. Enrique Chavez, if he hadn't already been apprehended, was on the run.

On a cushion by the fireplace, Allie snored. Ralph, a true couch potato, lay beside me. I stroked him and, as I had in the early hours of the morning after Lis Benedict's death, thought about the victims and the predators. About how I now knew most of the reasons why. . . .

Part Three

All the Reasons Why

Twenty-Seven

■ ■ ■

At eight-thirty that Saturday morning the rotunda of City Hall was jammed. Security measures—always heavy since the 1979 slayings of Mayor George Moscone and Supervisor Harvey Milk—were in full force. As I pushed through the crowd beneath the dome, voices babbled around me and rose to echo off the archways framing the three tiers of galleries. I glanced upward but saw no familiar faces peering over the rails.

Before my gaze returned to those around me, it rested briefly on one of the building's many sculptural details: the city's initials, entwined so that the S resembled a dollar sign—a wholly unintentional effect, I was sure, but apt for a city that hustled so energetically for the buck. I smiled, then looked at the broad marble staircase that swept from the rotunda floor to the chamber of the Board of Supervisors and spotted Justice Joseph Stameroff.

He stood in its center, a few steps above everyone else, pontificating to a knot of admirers. A woman elbowed through them, followed by a man with a Minicam, and I recognized Jess Goodhue, co-anchor of the KSTS-TV evening news. She went right up to Stameroff and thrust a microphone in his face; he moved up a step before beginning to speak. Goodhue kept clos-

241

ing in, intruding farther and farther into his space, and Stameroff was forced to retreat even higher in order to maintain the superior position. Finally he was rescued by James Wald, a balding man verging seriously on obesity, who planted himself between Stameroff and Goodhue's microphone. As I weaved and dodged over there, Jess seemed to lose interest in what Wald was saying—probably the Tribunal's standard press spiel. By the time I reached them, she and her cameraman were turning away.

"How come you're out on this story?" I asked Jess. As an anchor, she rarely worked in the field.

She grinned when she recognized me. "Hey, Sharon. I'm thinking I might put together one of my special reports on the mock trial." The greeting, while hearty, contained an element of reserve. A while back I'd saved Jess from a potentially disastrous situation, and like most people who felt they owed a debt they could never repay, she was vaguely uncomfortable in my presence.

She added, "You care to tell me about your investigation or the co-op's courtroom strategy?"

I shook my head.

"What about this murder in Chinatown last night—the Cardinal woman? What's the connection?"

"No comment."

Jess didn't press me, merely asked, "You seen the judge yet?"

I opened my mouth to say no, but just then Rudy Valle appeared at the top of the staircase and beckoned to Wald. The Tribunal's organizer tapped Stameroff on the arm and ushered him up toward the second-floor elevators.

"Too bad. I wanted to talk with him," Jess murmured, turning practiced eyes on the surrounding crowd, her gaze skipping from person to person in search of fresh quarry. I followed its direction and spotted Jack and Judy waiting at the bank of elevators in the lobby on the Civic Center Plaza side of the building.

Judy was plainly in the pull stage of their push-pull relationship. She clung to Jack's arm, plucking at his sleeve like a hungry street waif. Jack was ignoring her; from the set of his mouth and the impatient way he stared at the elevators, I sensed he would have liked to shake her off. Goodhue started over there without saying good-bye, leaving me alone on the bottom step of the staircase.

Now Rae and Hank entered from one of the side archways, which were still shored up by plywood against structural damage done by the Loma Prieta earthquake. I waved; he noticed me and waved back, pointing me out to her. They separated, Hank heading behind the stairs where the concession stand was and Rae coming toward me. As I waited for her, I glanced up at the galleries again; Leonard Eyestone was leaning against a pillar on the second floor, staring over the ornate gilt railing.

Even from below I could tell that the Institute director's eyes were preoccupied and unseeing. I wondered if they were focused at another point in time, some three and a half decades before. Certainly the weary set of his mouth indicated that he was thinking of the dead. I would have given a great deal to be privy to those thoughts.

Rae joined me. "Hank's grabbing a cup of coffee and going upstairs. You'd better hurry, before somebody steals your seat." I'd been assigned one in the row directly behind the defense table.

I nodded and followed her toward the elevators.

"Judy's in top form this morning," Rae added as we waited for a car to arrive.

"How do you mean?"

"Hank and I ran into her and Jack on the street. 'Oh, I don't know what I'd do without Jack's support. Oh, Jack, you've *got* to help me get through this.'" Her voice parodied Judy's breathy tones. She broke off and made a gagging sound. "God, what a manipulator!"

I frowned at her, surprised that such an expert manipulator as she would dare to criticize.

"Yeah, I know," she added cheerfully. "Takes one to know one. Well, how else could I catch on to what nobody else apparently sees?"

As a vacant elevator arrived and we stepped on, I said, "Doesn't it bother you to admit that you're—"

"Sure, sometimes. It's certainly not my most desirable character trait. But at least I know what I am and admit to it. Judy's either incredibly deluded about herself or thinks she can fool everybody—and I'm banking on the latter."

I thought about that while the last few people squeezed onto the elevator, preventing its doors from closing. As two of them stepped back off, I said, "Do you think Jack has caught on to her?"

"Smart men can be total idiots when they're in love, but I'm pretty sure he's starting to. And when he does, it's going to be painful."

I remembered Jack's verbal explosion the week before about Rae's own manipulative behavior in the matter of the skylights. Even then it had seemed too strong a reaction. Now I wondered if his anger with her wasn't actually displaced anger with Judy's similar behavior. If Rae was right about all this, hard times were once again ahead for Jack.

The elevator doors finally slid shut, and the car rose to the fourth floor. The people in front of me seemed to spew forth into the area by the pay phones and concession machines. I lost Rae in the crush and hurried toward the north corridor, fishing my pass from my bag. The mock trial was to be held in one of the larger superior courtrooms; I'd testified there myself a time or two, had spent many hours in these hallways, sitting alone on the oak benches or chatting with other witnesses and attorneys. Today I was struck by the absence of staid business suits, high heels, and briefcases. The people who gathered here were casually dressed, and their talk was of dinner reservations and theater tickets rather than countersuits and out-of-court settlements. As I attached myself to the tail end of the line entering the courtroom, I spied Jed Mooney, dressed in full Beat regalia. He waved and smiled as the guard studied the pass I'd had messengered to his home early this morning. I'd now seen all the principals in the case except Louise Wingfield.

Inside the courtroom, the golden oak paneling, institutional green walls, and high judge's bench had a subduing effect on those who entered. They filed in sedately and took their seats with a minimum of conversation. I hurried up the aisle, the soles of my athletic shoes squeaking on the worn brown linoleum, and folded down the wooden seat of the chair directly behind Jack. As I slipped into it, he glanced back and nodded.

I'd seldom seen him so tense at a real trial. His shoulders were stiff, and his hands moved aimlessly among the piles of documents on the table before him, as if he were trying to keep afloat in the mire of facts and theories that so far constituted our case. I smiled reassuringly, but too late; Judy, who was sitting a few seats down from me, leaned forward and tugged at his sleeve, and he turned to her.

From the judge's chambers, Stameroff and James Wald entered. Wald sat at the end of the jury box, while Stameroff took his place at the prosecution's table. He twisted around and smiled at his daughter; Judy avoided his eyes. Stameroff frowned, then nodded cordially to Jack. Jack's return greeting seemed nervous, shifty. So far, All Souls was looking none too good.

The jury filed in next. I checked the handout given me at the door. Today's panel was indeed impressive, included professors from several U.C. campuses, Stanford, and San Francisco State as well as a Los Angeles *Times* journalist who had won a Pulitzer for court reportage and a well-known author of true-crime accounts.

The jurors settled into place, and the courtroom grew still. I glanced around, noting the row of reporters behind the prosecutor's table. Behind them sat Bart Wallace, arms folded across his chest, face stern and unreadable. His topcoat lay on the seat next to him, probably reserving it for Joslyn. There was still no sign of Louise Wingfield.

I turned toward the front, about to give my full attention to the proceedings, but a thought popped into my mind: *How ludicrous!*

Quickly it was followed by another, equally heretical: *And offensive.*

Solemn as this assemblage might be, what we were actually doing here was *playing*. As I'd said to Jack before, the Historical Tribunal was nothing more than an intellectual game for adults, a brief weekend's amusement. Today we would toy with and possibly damage the memories of the dead—Cordy McKittridge, Lis Benedict, and Melissa Cardinal. And we could also tarnish the reputations of the other, still living victims.

As James Wald faced the court and began a self-serving

speech about his role in establishing the Historical Tribunal, I thought, *Don't dignify this game.* Don't brag about how we're helping to set history straight. What we're actually doing is providing entertainment for people before they use their dinner reservations and theater tickets.

I wondered what the reaction would be if I stood up and voiced my thoughts, told them to end this travesty.

Fortunately Wald's speech was a short one. Judge Valle entered. We stood, were told to be seated.

Valle wore full judicial robes. He mounted the bench, sat, adjusted his microphone. Then he stared sternly down his Roman nose at the courtroom, dark eyes searching.

In his gravelly voice, the judge began, "As Mr. Wald has said, we are here this weekend to decide a point of history. And while this tribunal is an avocation for me, I do not take my responsibility lightly. Nor do our jurors, our prosecutor, or our attorney for the defense. We hope our audience will conduct themselves with equal seriousness. While ex officio, we are nonetheless a court of law, and the law is not to be toyed with."

I relaxed somewhat, letting go of my reservations.

Valle's eyes once again searched the courtroom. "In the retrial of the *State of California versus Lisbeth Ingrid Benedict,*" he went on, "we encounter unusual circumstances. Until ten days ago, the defendant was still living. Her daughter and others who were involved in the original trial are presently in this courtroom. A woman who, the defense tells me, was closely connected with the case was brutally murdered just last night. These circumstances lend the matter before us both an immediacy and a potential impact that we seldom see at this tribunal."

He paused to let the words sink in, then continued, "In light of these circumstances, I am going to take an unusual action. At this point we will take a five-minute recess during which the prosecution and the defense may reconsider their willingness to proceed. When I return, I will call for their decisions, and those will be final and binding."

Valle rose, surveyed the court once more, then stepped down and went to his chambers.

For a moment the crowd remained silent. Then a buzzing began—primarily in the area where the press was seated. I watched Jack and Judy. He turned toward her, spoke in low tones. She listened, then shook her head vehemently.

I glanced at the prosecution's table. Stameroff gazed at the empty bench, hands laced in front of him. His eyes were narrowed, as if he was weighing the consequences of withdrawing against those of proceeding. After a bit, he turned his head and looked seekingly at Judy.

She was clutching Jack's arm, speaking swiftly, her face grim and determined. Jack whispered something, and she looked over at her adoptive father. I couldn't see her expression, but it made Stameroff turn away. Judy spoke some more to Jack, and finally he nodded in resignation.

The buzz of voices escalated throughout the courtroom. Ebbed, then escalated again. Stameroff, Jack, and Judy all stared at the bench now. When Judge Valle returned, the voices cut off and we rose. After we were seated, the judge's eyes swept the crowd; then he directed his attention to the defense table. "Mr. Stuart, what is your decision?"

"The defense is ready to proceed, Your Honor."

"Justice Stameroff?"

"Ready for the prosecution, Your Honor."

"Then the court will hear your opening statement."

Joseph Stameroff rose, approached the jury box, and began to speak. I listened in amazement as—without the aid of notes—he began reciting words I'd reread only two nights before in the Benedict trial transcript.

Apparently he was so confident of his original case that he planned to reprise it verbatim.

Twenty-Eight

■ ■ ■

I watched Stameroff, listened carefully. The words certainly sounded the same as those in the transcript; even his gestures had a studied quality, as if he remembered exactly how he'd moved his hands and body thirty-six long years before. It was like watching the enactment of a play that I'd only recently read.

To my right, Judy sat white-knuckled, staring at the man who had raised her. Her face seemed varnished, lines of strain cutting deep. Did Stameroff realize what he was doing to the daughter he'd adopted out of the ashes of this old tragedy? Did he *realize*?

Did he care?

I couldn't take this any longer. I scribbled a brief note, passed it to Jack, and got out of there.

In Civic Center Plaza a chill wind blew. It had swept away the last tendrils of fog, leaving a glary white overcast. A few ragged souls huddled under the gnarled plane trees and on benches by the reflecting pool, but otherwise the area had that deserted Saturday-morning look. I turned toward Market, deciding to walk the few blocks to Natoma Street, where the Loomis photographic studio was located.

I'd called first thing this morning and spoken with Nell

248

Loomis, daughter of the Institute's original photographer, who had inherited the business upon the death of her father. She'd be there all day working on a rush job, she told me, so I could stop by at my convenience—preferably after ten. She sounded grumpy and unfriendly, but I was hoping that was just an early morning mood.

Natoma is one of the many alleys that crisscross SoMa—as the South of Market district has been dubbed. Most are lined with warehouses, automotive shops, and small business concerns, interspersed with the occasional surviving Victorian residence. The block of Natoma between Tenth and Eleventh streets was entirely commercial; I found the blue door Nell Loomis had described halfway down, next to a TV repair shop.

The woman who answered the buzzer was about my age; her carroty hair was cropped close to her head, she wore no makeup except for dark green eye shadow, and a rubber apron protected her jeans and T-shirt. She barely glanced at me, merely motioned me into the gloom behind her. Then she slammed the door and secured it with a pair of dead bolts.

"Damn precautions," she said, stepping around me. "You can't even leave the door open while you go out to get something from your car two feet away. City won't do anything about the crime problem, so who pays? People like me who are struggling to get by. Watch that step there."

The dark hallway led into the studio: a large room of whitewashed brick, with a sofa, desk, and chairs in one corner and the rest of it an open space cluttered with lights and tripods and rolled backdrops and a variety of props. In the middle sat a display of canned artichoke hearts such as you'd find in a supermarket.

Loomis saw me looking at it and said, "The rush job I mentioned. National ad campaign, and it's got to be off by FedEx tonight."

"You mainly do advertising work?"

She perched on the edge of the desk and waved me toward the sofa. "I mainly do anything that'll bring in the rent money. Don't get as much ad work as I'd like. Pretty much I'm stuck with the kind of crap my dad did—weddings, parties, special events."

"The Institute for North American Studies is one of your steady clients?"

Her mouth twisted disagreeably. "Not anymore. I did my last job for them when they dedicated that building on the Embarcadero. Bastards can overextend themselves by moving into a place worth millions, but they can't be bothered to pay my piddly little invoices. If I don't get the money soon, I'm turning it over to a collection agency."

"How much do they owe you?"

"Thousands. They claimed they were waiting for a big contract and would pay up soon, but I didn't get a dime. Look, what is it you want? I need to get back to the darkroom."

"How far back do your business and negative files on the Institute go?"

"All the way to when my dad opened the studio in fifty-one. Why?"

"Would it be possible to look up some work he did for them?" I showed her the photo I'd found in Melissa Cardinal's rabbit vase and also explained about the banquet and reception for Dulles.

Loomis frowned. "It's possible to look that stuff up, yes, but not today. The files're all boxed." She motioned toward the high ceiling, and for the first time I noticed a railed loft at the far end of the space. "My old studio on Minna Street was hit hard during the big quake. Took me six months to find this place. Since then I've been busting my butt just to make ends meet, and I've never gotten around to setting up the files again."

"How much would you charge to locate the files and negatives that I need?"

Loomis thought, running her thumb over her lower lip. "My hourly rate, anyway. But this rush job—"

"I understand that, but couldn't you take some time—say, while your prints are drying?"

She considered.

"I'll double your hourly rate."

"In that case, okay." She stood up. "Let me do a couple of things in the darkroom, and then I'll climb up there and give it a try."

"Thanks, I appreciate it. Do you mind if I use your phone while I'm waiting?"

"If it's a local call."

As Nell Loomis disappeared into her darkroom, I sat down at the desk and called Cathy Potter. When I identified myself, she said, "Sharon, where've you *been*? Keyes Development has agreed to let you tour the Seacliff property, but they want to know when."

"I'd like to see it tonight, but here's the catch: I want to bring a number of other people along." I explained about my idea of moving the trial to the estate.

"I don't know if they'll go for that. There's sure to be publicity, and reminding people that a murder happened on a property isn't such a great way to sell it."

"There'll be publicity anyway. If they cooperate, it might actually help to interest a buyer who isn't squeamish."

"Maybe," she said skeptically. "Call me back within the hour, okay?"

In five minutes Nell Loomis emerged from her darkroom and climbed up into the loft. I called after her, offering to help, but she said her insurance wouldn't cover it if something happened to me. So I remained on the sofa, watching her silhouette move among the stacked cartons, backlit by a single bare bulb. It took her about half an hour, but finally she climbed back down, clutching a thick file folder.

"I can't find the order on the print you have, and there's something odd about the order for that banquet and reception," she told me.

"What?"

"The order sheet shows that the prints and negatives were to be destroyed."

"Why?"

"Doesn't say."

"Who made the request?"

"Doesn't say that, either." She showed me the order sheet. It was a simple form with blanks to be filled in for the number of prints and their sizes. Across it someone had written: "Destroy prints and negs" and the date—June 25, 1956, three days after Cordy McKittridge's murder.

I asked, "Is that your father's writing?"

"My mother's. She helped out in the studio but she died in seventy-one."

"Do you know who they usually dealt with at the Institute?"

"No. I dealt with Leonard Eyestone's secretary, so I guess Dad would have gotten his instructions from one of the support staff, too."

"Would there be anything in any of your father's other files that would tell us who that was?"

"Maybe." Loomis glanced at her watch. "I can't look now, though. I've got to get back to the darkroom."

"Well, if you'd check later, I'd appreciate it." I stood, picking up my bag.

"Wait," she said, "don't you want to look at the negatives?"

"I thought they were destroyed."

"Dad would *never* have destroyed negatives of his work. I have them here." She held up a sheaf of glassine envelopes. "I'll turn on the light table, and you can have a look while I tend to my printing."

I took the envelopes from her, removed a strip of film from one, and laid it on the illuminated opaque plastic. These appeared to be of the head table at the banquet; the speaker was recognizable as Dulles. Quickly I laid out the other negatives: more head table; people shaking hands and posing; a reception line; more posed group shots, including the ones of both Eyestones with Dulles. In reversed black and white, details were difficult to discern, but none appeared particularly incriminating or even unusual. I went through all the negatives carefully, then turned the light out, straightening and sighing. I would need prints in order to figure out what had prompted the request that these be destroyed.

Nearly an hour had gone by since I called Cathy Potter. I dialed her office, got her voice mail, and left a message that I'd call back after lunch. As I hung up, Nell Loomis came out of the darkroom, scowling fiercely. "How the hell do they expect me to get this done in time?" she muttered. "Took them all week to deliver their damned artichokes, and now they want—" She broke off, looking embarrassed, as if she'd forgotten I was there. "You find what you're looking for?"

I shook my head. "I need prints of these. Today."

"Can't do."

"I'll triple your hourly rate." I took a couple of twenties from my bag and offered them as a deposit.

"Well . . ."

"I'll also triple it for the time you spend finding out which person at the Institute usually gave your father instructions about the photographs."

Loomis bit her lip and worried at it for a moment, then nodded. "I'll do it. How soon do you need the prints?"

"Right away, but I'll settle for a couple of hours from now."

"I can't guarantee how good they'll be, but I'll get onto it as soon as I can."

On my return walk to City Hall, I tried to convince myself that I now had the lead that would salvage Jack's case. I tried to reassure myself that Keyes Development would allow us to move the trial to the Seacliff estate. I told myself that by the time I entered the courtroom Jack would have regained his customary confidence and be building a solid foundation for the new evidence I planned to produce.

All I accomplished was to give rise to a whole new crop of doubts and insecurities.

Twenty-Nine

∎ ∎ ∎

The witness was being badgered by the man who had raised her. Stameroff loomed aggressively over Judy, jabbing his index finger at her while he posed his question. As I came down the aisle, Jack said, "Objection. Counsel is arguing with his own witness."

"Sustained."

I slipped into the seat reserved for me. Stameroff stepped back from the witness box, executed a half turn, and looked ruefully at the jury. I knew that trick: a glance that said, "What *am* I to do?" It elicited little sympathy, however; this panel was far too experienced to fall for prosecutorial theatrics.

Stameroff realized his error and quickly returned his attention to his daughter. "Let us try," he said, "to confine this testimony to what you actually saw on the night of the murder. As you were saying, your mother had blood on the front of her dress—"

The old man had forgotten none of the sneaky ploys of his trade. Jack said, "Objection. Witness made no such statement."

"Sustained."

"Allow me to rephrase. What was your mother's appearance when she returned to the house?"

Judy's expression became confused.

254

"Miss Benedict?"

She didn't reply. I leaned forward, watching her intently. There had been something about the question. . . .

After a moment she said, "She had stains on her dress. They were ink, red ink."

"How do you know they were red ink?"

"She told the police—"

"Miss Benedict, confine yourself to what you saw."

"I'm sorry." Still confused, she looked to Jack for help. He was studying a document on the table in front of him.

"Now," Stameroff went on, "you and your mother were the only people present on the estate that night—is that correct?"

"I . . . don't know."

The justice frowned. "You don't know?"

"I've remembered standing at the window of my room, and something being below in the darkness—"

"Some*thing* or some*one*?"

"I don't know!"

"Could this . . . thing merely be the product of an overactive imagination?"

"Objection!"

"I'll allow the question."

"No, it was real. I remember—"

"Yes?"

Judy was silent.

Stameroff leaned toward her, placing his hand on the edge of the witness box. "Isn't it a fact," he said, "that you remember very little of what happened that night?"

"I . . ."

"Isn't it a fact that aside from the bloodstains on—"

"Objection!"

"I'll rephrase. Isn't it a fact that aside from the *red stains* on your mother's dress, you remember very little indeed?"

"I remember . . ."

"*What* do you remember, Miss Benedict? *What?*"

Judy hung her head. She was shaking—from rage, I thought.

Stameroff said, "I'll withdraw the question. Now I would like to move forward to the night of July seventh—"

Judge Valle interrupted. "Since this portion of the testimony will undoubtedly be lengthy and it is now nearly noon, a lunch break is in order. Court will recess until one-thirty."

After Valle had left the courtroom, I slipped around the rail to speak with Jack. Judy stood in the witness box, her angry gaze riveted on Stameroff, who was gathering papers at his table. He straightened and started for the aisle, and I came face-to-face with him. His expression showed no satisfaction, only a sadness and something else that hinted of desperation. His eyes met mine, a long measured look; then he nodded and stepped aside. I joined Jack at the defense table.

"It's going quickly," I said.

"Yes, he whipped right through the first few witnesses, and he's playing it pretty much by the transcript."

"Did you speak with Wald and Valle about moving the trial to the crime scene?"

"At the recess. Looks as if it's a go. You hear about getting access yet?"

"The broker's still working on it." I took a sheaf of notes that I'd made while reading through the police files in the early hours of the morning. "You may want to look at these in preparation for tomorrow."

He nodded and stuffed them into his inside pocket.

Judy came up to the table, her lips still taut with anger. I said quickly, "I've got to talk with Hank."

My boss was sitting in the last row of the courtroom. When I sat down next to him, he commented, "Stameroff's giving Judy the hostile-witness treatment."

"In case you haven't noticed, she *is* hostile. Unlike when she was a child and easily lead, she now has a mind of her own. I'm convinced he controlled her original testimony, maybe even fed her some of it."

"Wouldn't surprise me." Hank watched the remaining spectators leave the courtroom, then stood and went to look out the window. "I made those inquiries that I promised you."

"And?"

"Stameroff's been bought, several times."

"Who told you that?"

He shook his head, picked up one of the poles used to open

and close the old-fashioned windows, and hefted it experimentally. "All I can say is that they're good sources, ones I trust."

"Who was he bought by?"

"No one whose name you'd recognize." Hank sighted along the pole, made motions as if he were a javelin thrower. "The real powers-that-be keep a low profile. Often our elected officials aren't sure who they are. And they're almost never held accountable. Makes them damned hard to fight."

"I used to think theories like that were just paranoia. Not anymore."

"Yeah." Hank jabbed angrily at the air with his pretend spear. "Anyway, Stameroff was promised the district attorney's job for a victory in the Benedict case, and that gave him a taste for trading favors. He bartered his way right on up to the state supreme court."

"So why did he involve himself in this mock trial? Common sense should have told him it would only draw attention to what he did. The Tribunal may be publicity-hungry, but it doesn't really get that much press; if Stameroff weren't part of this, it would only rate a column in Monday's paper."

Hank propped the pole up next to the window, looking thoughtful. "There's got to be something very damaging that he's trying to keep under wraps, but I haven't the foggiest."

"Me, either." I stood, and Hank followed me out of the empty courtroom. "Did you see Bart Wallace leave?" I asked.

"The homicide inspector? As a matter of fact, he and his partner asked me to tell you they'd be at Tommy's Joynt. If you don't mind, I'll go over there with you. It's been years since I had some of their buffalo stew."

■   ■   ■

Tommy's Joynt on Van Ness Avenue has long been a San Francisco institution. Garishly painted with slogans and ads on the outside, noisy and comfortable on the inside, it's been serving some of the best food and drink around to both locals and tourists for decades. Hank and I had to fight our way through a crowd before we found the inspectors at a table near the back. Joslyn was wading into a thick pastrami sandwich, but from the appearance of the glass of dark liquid in front of him, Wallace was drinking his lunch.

Hank went to place our orders, and I sat down next to Adah. "So what do you think so far?" I asked.

"I think Stameroff is a grade-A shit," Bart said. "If the son of a bitch ever had any humanity, he lost it long ago."

"Other than that," Adah added, "Bart thinks Stameroff's a hell of a nice guy."

"Any progress in the Cardinal investigation?" I asked her.

"Zilch. Nobody in the neighborhood saw nothin', nobody heard nothin'. They—surprise!—just don't want to get involved."

I glanced at Wallace. He wasn't paying any attention; his eyes searched the depths of his drink as if it contained the answers to the world's problems. I supposed that was as good a place as any to look for them.

Adah said, "I do have one piece of news for you. NCIC actually came through on my inquiry on Roger Woods."

"My God." The FBI crime information network was notoriously slow. "What did they say?"

"Woods's file is classified."

It was the last thing I'd expected to hear. "What do you suppose that means?"

"Could be any number of things. He might have been involved in some sort of covert work, or been placed in a protected witness program."

"You mean he might have been FBI or an informant?"

"Or had something to do with any one of a number of other agencies or operations."

Hank returned with coffee and bowls of buffalo stew. I stared at mine, realizing I'd lost my appetite. "You know," I said to Joslyn, "I have an idea about Roger Woods. That Cedar Rapids couple in Cardinal's address book—Mary and Rod. Could you have misread the name? Maybe it's actually Mary and *Rog*."

"It's possible."

"Have you called them?"

"Tried to. There wasn't any answer."

"Why don't you try again?"

She frowned. "You think Roger Woods has been hiding out in *Cedar Rapids* for thirty-some years?"

"It's as good a place as any. Besides, maybe he's not hiding."

Joslyn nodded and tossed her napkin on the table. I stood so she could squeeze past me. As I sat down, Wallace muttered something, still staring into his drink.

"What did you say?" Hank asked him.

"I said, the bastard's going to go on and on untouched, no matter what anyone does."

I realized he hadn't heard a word of Adah's and my conversation. "Stameroff, you mean?"

He nodded.

I glanced at Hank, who was wolfing down the last of his stew and greedily eyeing my untouched portion. "Bart, isn't it time you explained the history between Stameroff and you?"

He was silent, hands cupped around his glass.

Hank now wore an expression worthy of a Famine Relief Fund poster boy. I sighed and traded my full bowl for his empty one.

Wallace echoed my sigh. "Story time, huh?" he said. "Do you want I should start it with 'once upon a time'? Once upon a time I had an older brother—Burton. Burt and Bart. Cute." His tone was laced with bitterness.

I waited.

"Burt was in private security. He and another guy had their own firm. In sixty-seven they got a contract to provide the security for a rock festival at a big arena. Riot broke out, Burt was killed. Plenty of witnesses saw the kids who were responsible. I was only a rookie at the time, but Homicide let me review the file; plenty of evidence. But when the file went over to the D.A.'s office, they declined to prosecute."

Wallace raised his glass, took a sip. "Lack of evidence, they said. Bullshit. What it was was our D.A. making a deal. One of the kids' fathers was a big honcho in the aerospace industry down the Peninsula. Few months after that, Stameroff bought his house in Presidio Heights."

He was silent for a moment, then added, "One thing it did, it made me the cop I am today. Before Burt died, I was thinking of leaving the department, joining his firm. Afterward I decided to be the best damn cop I could, build cases that couldn't be dismissed for lack of evidence. And I swore that one day I'd bring Stameroff down. Watching him in that courtroom this morning, though, I realized it'll never happen."

"You don't know that," I said. "Stameroff looks good only because the defense hasn't presented its case."

Wallace shrugged, drank some more. I knew he didn't believe me. I wasn't sure I believed me, either.

"Sharon?" Joslyn stood by the table.

I moved my chair to let her by. "Did you reach anybody?"

She nodded. "You were right—the geezer in Cedar Rapids is Roger Woods. He's been in a nursing home for a couple of years now, but I spoke with his wife. She didn't sound too upset about Melissa, and she wouldn't say much about Roger."

"Did you ask her why his FBI file is classified?"

"She claims she didn't know he had one."

"What about the rumor he died on the Seattle docks in the fifties?"

"That surprised her. And when I mentioned the possibility of a connection with the American Communist party, she damn near threw a fit. Said they've always been 'decent Republicans' like everybody else around there."

"Interesting." All sorts of odd twists there, and none that I could reconcile with what people had told me about the man.

I glanced at my watch: approaching one-thirty, no time to think this through. "Thanks for checking, Adah," I said. "I'll keep you posted." Then I hurried back to City Hall, sticking Hank with the tab for the buffalo stew he'd so cleverly made off with.

Thirty

■ ■ ■

Nell Loomis sounded harried when I called her from one of the fourth-floor phone booths at City Hall. The artichoke-heart shots, she said, were all screwed up, and she hadn't gotten to my prints yet, much less searched the files in the loft. When I pressed her, she promised to start on it within the hour. After all, she really needed the money. I said I'd call back at three.

The news from Cathy Potter was better. Keyes Development had gone for my proposal. "You were right about them thinking the publicity might attract a buyer," Cathy added. "And I just hope I'm the one who brings him through."

I told her I'd get back to her later to finalize the details, and left her to dreams of an enormous commission. Then I hurried to the court room.

Judy was on the stand again, and Jack was beginning his cross-examination. It went well. During the lunch recess both had recovered their customary poise, and from the smoothness of their performances, I assumed they'd rehearsed. In spite of frequent objections from Stameroff, Jack managed to establish reasonable doubt on several points of her direct testimony—points that the justice wasn't able to undermine in redirect.

Stameroff approached the actress playing Louise Wingfield,

routinely leading her through testimony that was almost identical to that in the trial transcript. Jack's questions on cross deviated markedly from those of Lis Benedict's inept public defender.

"The note summoning Cordelia McKittridge to the Institute's Seacliff estate arrived when, Ms. Wingfield?"

"June twenty-first, the day before the murder."

"And *where* did it arrive?"

"At an apartment in North Beach that Cordy and I shared with several other women." The actress gave the address.

Stameroff looked up, his mouth tightening; it was obvious he knew about the apartment and didn't like this line of questioning one bit.

"Was this apartment a full-time residence of Ms. McKittridge?" Jack asked.

"Objection. The question pertains to matters not covered—"

"Your Honor, the door to this line of inquiry has been opened by the prosecution. We will demonstrate relevancy."

"Overruled."

"Ms. Wingfield?"

The actress explained about the apartment and described the kind of activities that went on there. Voices murmured, and Judge Valle called for order.

"So various men were frequent visitors at the apartment?" Jack asked.

"Yes."

"Vincent Benedict?"

"Yes."

"Leonard Eyestone, son of the Institute's director?"

"Yes."

I glanced at Eyestone, who sat in the fifth row. His face was unperturbed.

"Did anyone else connected with the Institute for North American Studies visit there frequently?"

"Not that I recall."

"Let's get back to the day the note arrived, Ms. Wingfield. Was anyone there at the apartment besides you and Ms. McKittridge?"

"Melissa Cardinal was there. She saw the note."

"Was it your impression that she knew it was from Vincent Benedict?"

"Objection. Calls for a conclusion from the witness."

"Sustained."

"Let me put it this way, Ms. Wingfield. Had Melissa Cardinal ever mentioned Vincent Benedict's notes to you?"

"Yes. She said—"

"Objection. Hearsay."

"Sustained."

Smoothly Jack switched to another tack. "Now, Ms. Wingfield, you stated on direct examination that you knew the note was from Vincent Benedict because you recognized his handwriting?"

"Yes."

"Are you a friend of Mr. Benedict? Have you had occasion to receive notes from him?"

"Objection!"

"I'll allow it. Witness is directed to answer."

"I was a friend of Mr. Benedict."

"And you have received notes from him?"

"Occasionally."

"For what reason?"

The actress, one of several who frequently appeared before the Tribunal, did a stagy impression of a witness in distress. She wrung her hands, wet her lips, looked for a way out. Too many reruns of "Perry Mason," I thought.

"For what reason, Ms. Wingfield?"

"To set up . . . assignations."

Jack drew back, feigning shock. We'd have to curtail his late-night TV viewing, too. "Ms. Wingfield," he said, "are you admitting to having had an affair with Vincent Benedict?"

The little ham hung her head, then told her—Louise's—sorry tale. It made me glad that Wingfield wasn't there to see her reputation soiled in such a careless way, no matter how little she claimed reputations mattered. But by the time the witness was dismissed, Jack had instilled more doubt in the minds of the jurors.

Stameroff had sunk into a moody silence during the latter part of the testimony, scarcely objecting at all, and then only in a routine fashion. When he called the man acting the part of Leonard Eyestone, however, he became more alert. I glanced back at the real Eyestone, saw he was leaning forward in his seat, interested and vaguely amused.

During the direct examination, Stameroff tried to skirt any opening that would allow Jack to ask about Eyestone's personal relationship with the murdered woman. Nonetheless, Jack found a small one, and by the time he was through cross-examining, Eyestone looked as bad as Wingfield. In addition to bringing out the director's affair with Cordy and the fact that he'd paid for her to abort their child, Jack also planted in the jurors' minds the idea that it would have been impossible to account for the presence of every person attending the Dulles banquet and reception at all times during the evening. Stameroff, I thought, must be growing tired to have allowed that.

When Jack returned to the defense table, I leaned over the rail and said, "It's all set for tonight. We just need to give Keyes Development's security people a time."

"Good. Stameroff's going to rest his case after testimony from the gardener—which I'm going to demolish with what you culled from the police report. I'll have time to make my opening statement and my motion to view the crime scene."

"I'm sorry I'll have to miss that, but I've got to leave now." I handed him Cathy Potter's business card. "Have Wald firm up the arrangements with her, will you? I'll check in later."

As I hurried up the aisle, my gaze rested on Leonard Eyestone. He was staring at me, his eyes cold and analytical. I nodded, but he turned to the front of the courtroom. Finally, I thought, the mock trial had ceased to amuse him.

From one of the pay phones by the elevators, I called Nell Loomis. It took her a long time to answer. Things, she said, were "coming along," but maybe I'd better not stop by until six, after her FedEx went off.

"Did you check the files yet?"

"That much I managed. There's nothing, just order sheets with the number and size blanks filled in."

"What about my prints?"

"Come by after six, okay?"

I said I would, trying to keep annoyance out of my voice.

Next I tried to reach Louise Wingfield at the various numbers for her foundation that were listed on her business card, but got only machines. Her home number turned out to be unlisted, so I left City Hall and headed for Russian Hill.

.　　.　　.

Wingfield came to the door of her condominium looking haggard and smelling of gin. She admitted me sullenly, saying, "Thanks for setting the police after me last night."

"I had no choice. Can we talk?"

She shrugged and led me to a living room full of good but well-used furniture that no decorator's hand had touched. Without asking my preference, she set a martini in front of me, lit a cigarette and propped her Reebok-shod feet on the coffee table, took a deep drink from her own cocktail glass.

"I don't usually drink this heavily or this early," she said defensively, "but after last night everything came crashing down on me, and I'm badly in need."

"Everything?"

"My whole rotten miserable past. I hadn't realized what a hypocrite I am."

"In what ways?"

She shrugged again, moodily sipped her drink.

I took the photograph of her and Roger Woods from my bag and pushed it across the coffee table. "Do you remember when this was taken?"

She picked it up and studied it intently. "This must have been at one of the Institute's cocktail parties. Cordy was still with Leonard, I see, so it would have been when I was with—"

I waited. When she didn't go on, I said, "When you were with Vincent Benedict."

Her chin dipped in confirmation. She placed the picture on the table. "God, I hate to remember how foolish I was."

"Where does the man in this photo fit into things?"

"He was just someone Cordy fixed me up with. A friend of Leonard. I don't recall his name."

"Did Cordy do that often—fix you up?"

"Now and then. I'm beginning to remember that evening."

She gestured at the photo. "Leonard had asked Cordy to get the fellow a date so he could attend the party without seeming like a third wheel. I had the impression he was looking to make contacts there, perhaps get on staff. He must have been, because he spent the entire evening wandering around meeting people and dropping in on their conversations. That picture was snapped at one of the few times we were actually together. I didn't care; I'd only gone to be perverse."

"Why?"

"Vincent and I had quarreled that afternoon. I wanted to go to the party and dangle myself in front of him, make him sorry he had to be with his wife instead of me. Or so I thought." Her mouth twisted bitterly and she lit a second cigarette off the butt of the first.

"*Was* he sorry?"

"No. He was polite and distant. They both were, he and Lis. It was that night that I realized things weren't . . . that he would never leave Lis for me."

"Are you sure you don't remember your date's name?"

She picked up the photograph again and scrutinized the man's face. "Sorry, no."

"Could it have been Roger Woods?"

"Didn't you ask me about that name before? Well, maybe it was Roger Woods. That was so very long ago."

"But he was Leonard's friend?"

"That's what Cordy said when she fixed us up. But I don't know—they didn't act all that friendly."

"Was he a friend of Melissa, by any chance?"

"Well, when he came by the flat he seemed to know her. By the way, have they found out who killed her?"

"Not yet. I think this picture may have something to do with her murder; it was hidden in her apartment. Can you think of any reason she'd have had it?"

"No, I can't. To my knowledge, Melissa never went to the Institute. I can't imagine where she would have gotten this, unless she took it from the things Cordy kept at the apartment. Cordy was fond of keeping pictures as souvenirs." Again Wingfield studied the photo, as if its time-frozen figures could give her an answer.

"Can you pinpoint exactly when this was taken?" I asked.

"Well, in the spring of fifty-five, before Cordy took . . . before it ended with Vincent and me."

"Did you see the man again?"

"Never." She drained her glass and went to a bar cart for the martini pitcher. After she poured for herself, she glanced at my glass, saw it was still full, and set the pitcher down.

I said, "Let's talk about Rick Chavez now."

"I already told the police—"

"I know what you told them, but there may be something they didn't think to ask. Chavez was one of your clients?"

"Yes, and not a particularly promising one. I liked him, though; he'd had a rough time—family problems and a girlfriend who died of an overdose—and would often come to me just to talk."

"Did you place him in a job?"

"I sent him through our general maintenance—janitorial—training program; it's run out of our Potrero Hill center. He was placed in a couple of positions; the first didn't work out."

"But the second did?"

"I don't know. Maybe not. That might have been why he came by the day you were there. I hadn't seen him in quite a while."

Or he might have come by, I thought, because he had a bigger problem than losing a job. He might have been worried about how much trouble he'd gotten into by taking money to harass an old woman. "Is there some way you can find out today if he was working, and for whom?"

"I could go to the Potrero Hill center and check the files, I suppose."

"Would you? It's important."

"Then I will. I can have the information for you by this evening."

I watched her as she lit yet another cigarette and waved the match out, then asked, "How come you didn't attend the mock trial?"

"This morning I was angry with you because you told the police about my connection with Rick Chavez. Then I got depressed." She motioned at her cocktail glass. "I know, it's a poor solution to one's problems. I always caution my clients against it. But like most people, I seldom take my own advice."

"You might want to consider coming to Seacliff tonight." I explained about the trial being moved to the crime scene.

To my surprise, the news badly unnerved her: her mouth twitched and she leaned forward, elbows on knees, forehead pressed against the heels of her hands.

"I can't go," she said.

"Why not?"

"I can't face the horror of it again."

"Louise, decades have passed. The house is empty, the dovecote's gone—"

"And the feelings are still there. You know it. You connected with them that night two weeks ago. I could tell; you were shaken. And I . . . connected, too."

"What specifically did you connect with?"

"Hatred. Rage. Pain. Terror. The sick pleasure that you feel at the death of a person whom you detest."

I bit my underlip. Took a small sip of the martini. It tasted as bitter as the residue of a thirty-six-year-old hatred, as sharp as the bite of an old, well-nurtured rage. I set the glass down and waited.

Wingfield sighed deeply. Raised her head and straightened. "All right," she said. "Truth time."

I continued to wait.

"Melissa was right about me," she said. "I hated Cordy. When she died, I was *glad*. And the pleasure I took in her death never went away." She paused, sipped her drink, contemplated.

"Over the years," she went on, "I would take an emotional inventory whenever something particularly good happened. When my son was born, for instance, I told myself, 'You now have someone whom you love totally, who will return that love. Isn't it time you let go of this baggage?' The answer was always no. Every few years I'd take that inventory, but the hatred and sick pleasure were still in stock."

"And are they now?"

"Yes." She set down her glass, faced me unflinchingly. "I hate Cordy as much at this very minute as I ever did. She took away everything I ever cared about and turned my life to dust."

Wingfield rose, went to the window wall behind her, and stood silhouetted against the early-evening light. Finally she said, "All right. I'll go to Seacliff tonight. I'll face it one last time. Either tonight will set me free or I'll be caged with my hatred for the rest of my life."

Thirty-One

■ ■ ■

It was well after six when I reached Nell Loomis's studio. Shadow and silence had claimed Natoma Street. A sheet of paper fluttered from where it had been tacked to Nell's blue door.

"Took package to South SF drop-off for FedEx," it said. "Back soon. Don't try door—dog is loose inside." I hadn't seen any dog earlier, so I assumed this was Loomis's idea of how to ward off would-be burglars—providing they could read well enough to decipher the note.

For the next half hour I sat in my car, fretting. I needed to talk with Jack about tonight, but I didn't want to leave. If Loomis returned and didn't find me there, she would go home, and I'd never get hold of those prints. And the prints had assumed greater and greater importance in my mind as the hours passed.

This, I thought, presented the best argument I'd come up with so far for having a car phone. On Monday I would buy one and request reimbursement from All Souls. If they balked at paying for it—as they so far had—I'd foot the bill myself. And make sure to inform them that as far as I was concerned, all their talk about moving forward into the twenty-first century was just so much overblown rhetoric.

At ten to seven, a car entered the alley and pulled up behind me. Nell Loomis and I got out of our vehicles simultaneously. She gave me a stingy smile and thanked me for waiting. Inside the studio she excused herself and went into the rest room; I used her phone to call Jack.

"Are the arrangements all set?" I asked.

"Yes—for nine o'clock. Wald's having a fit because Keyes Development wants the number of people admitted to the property kept to a minimum. That means only participants and those with preferred passes. No press. Have you come up with anything that I should know about?"

"Nothing conclusive yet. How're you going to handle it out there?"

"Have Judy walk through it from the beginning, starting at the window of her old room. And hope we score points with the jury."

"How is she?"

"Cool and confident."

"How are you?"

"A wreck. I think she's feeding on me."

"Well, hang in there. Judy's our only living witness. Let's let her memories speak for themselves." Loomis emerged from the rest room and went into the darkroom. I told Jack I had to go, then followed her.

Nell was slipping a strip of negatives into the enlarger's holder and blowing off surface dust with canned air. She glanced at me and frowned.

"Can I watch?"

"I guess. Just don't get in my way." She inserted the holder in the enlarger and switched from fluorescents to an orange safelight. The timer whirred, light flashed and disappeared, and the timer clicked off. Loomis moved the sheet of photographic paper from the enlarger to the tray of developing liquid.

"I want to check the exposure," she said.

I moved closer, watching over her shoulder as images appeared and sharpened on the submerged sheet. The banquet table at the Blue Fox, Dulles speaking at the lectern. To his right, Russell Eyestone. To Russell's right, his wife and then Leonard. And to Leonard's right, Vincent Benedict—bleary-

eyed, probably drunk. The men were formally attired in dark
jackets, white shirtfronts, and bow ties. Dulles's shirt, as be-
fitted a conservative, had small, austere pleats and plain studs,
as did Russell Eyestone's; Benedict and Leonard—wild and
crazy young guys that they'd been—had opted for something a
bit more froufrou.

Loomis said, "Exposure's good," and moved the paper to the
stop bath. "You sure you want regular prints and not just contacts?"

"Contacts won't give me the detail I need."

She shrugged. "It's your money." Then she returned to the
enlarger and began printing in earnest.

Enlarger to developer, developer to stop bath, stop bath to
fixer: Eyestone Senior shaking hands with Dulles at the banquet table; Dulles with Benedict, with Leonard, with people I
didn't recognize; couples chatting in the restaurant lobby; Dulles leaving amid a phalanx of Secret Service men.

I said to Loomis, "Cut to the shots of the reception, would
you?"

More couples chatting in what looked like the ballroom of the
St. Francis. I recognized a younger Joseph Stameroff, the then-
mayor of the city, and other public officials, including a man
who would later be a two-term governor. A receiving line: Dulles,
Russell Eyestone and spouse, other Institute staff members and
their wives, whose faces were now becoming familiar. One of
the arrivals passing along the receiving line was familiar, too:
Roger Woods, lean and somewhat sinister-looking in his black
formal attire. And there was the photo the newspaper had
picked up of the Eyestones with Dulles: impeccably clad, smiles
correct, but Leonard looking diminished. . . .

I stared at the last two prints until Loomis grasped them with
her tongs and fished them out of the developer. Stared some
more as they sank into the stop bath. Went to the prints floating
in the fixer and fished around until I found one of both Eyestones and Vincent Benedict in the Blue Fox lobby.

And saw what had made these photographs incriminating to
someone on the Institute staff.

Loomis jostled me. "Told you not to get in my way," she muttered irritably.

I moved aside. "How long will it take to run these through the dryer?"

"All of them?"

"No, just this and this, these two also."

"I can do them pretty quick, if that's all you want."

"Thanks." I went out into the studio. Sank onto the sofa, but immediately sprang to my feet. Wandered aimlessly among the light stands and tripods and around the mountain of canned artichoke hearts. All the while thinking of how to play it at Seacliff.

After a few minutes I called Adah Joslyn at home. Laid out for her what I knew but couldn't prove. Asked that she and Wallace meet me at the estate.

I now knew who.

I thought I knew why.

But many things were still inexplicable. Might remain that way forever.

Thirty-Two

■ ■ ■

Joslyn, Wallace, and I leaned against the unmarked car. The street in front of the Seacliff property was clogged with vehicles; neighbors stood at the windows of the nearby buildings; the area was nearly as bright as day, and at the foot of the driveway a reporter from KPIX-TV spoke into the microphone. The mood among the press was ugly.

A few minutes before, Judge Valle had addressed the crowd, warning them that only those who held preferred passes to the trial would be allowed onto the grounds. "This is an ex officio court of law," he said, "and a court of law must not be turned into a media circus." Beside him, James Wald nodded agreement but drew his lips down discontentedly.

Joslyn said, "Big night for the Tribunal, and then the judge and the development company go and spoil it."

Wallace grinned and slapped Joslyn's shoulder. "Big night for you, too, partner. You get to make the collar, and no judge or development company is going to go and spoil *that*."

The comment answered my question about what concession Bart had given Adah in return for taking all of the risk on the case: she'd also take all of the credit for the collar. I'd get little

274

thanks, if any, but that was all right with me. My visibility in the community was already uncomfortably high.

Joslyn said, "Don't get ahead of yourself, Bart. We've got nothing to bring charges on, much less take to court."

"Like Sharon said, something'll go down in there tonight"— he motioned at the estate—"that'll blow it wide open."

I felt nervous, irritable, tired of talking about it. "Let's go," I said.

We pushed through the crowd of glowering reporters and started up the drive, showing our passes to one of the security guards provided by Keyes Development. The fog was in again; it hung thick in the trees, blurring outlines and shadows. I lagged behind the homicide inspectors, fighting off images.

The house loomed ahead, a halo of light spreading through the mist from its front door. Indistinct figures milled about before it. I stopped, glanced into the blackness where the dovecote had stood. Foghorns groaned up by the Gate—two long, dolorous notes, underscored by the boom and hiss of the sea.

If I'd ordered the weather, it couldn't more perfectly have replicated that of the fatal night thirty-six years before.

Ahead of me I saw Joslyn and Wallace split up, going to find the persons they were to keep under surveillance. I moved toward the group by the door, where Judy and Jack stood with Judge Valle. The judge was speaking, but a chill wind scattered the sound of his voice; he motioned for people to gather closer and began again.

"Tonight," he said, "we are re-creating a crime scene. And while this is a somewhat melodramatic demonstration, we do so with utmost seriousness. I remind you that court is still in session and no disturbances will be tolerated. Are you ready, Mr. Stuart?"

Jack stepped forward and explained that we would enter the house and proceed to the third-story room once occupied by ten-year-old Judy Benedict. Ms. Benedict would serve as our guide to the crime scene and tell us what she witnessed on the night of June 22, 1956.

As Jack spoke, I looked around at the others. The jurors were clumped together, bundled in heavy coats; some of their expressions plainly said that this cold Saturday night outing was more than they had bargained for. Jed Mooney stood on the fringes, his black neo-Beat attire merging with the shadows. Louise Wingfield and Leonard Eyestone watched from the far left, their faces pale and apprehensive. Behind them was Adah Joslyn. On the other side of the judge, Bart Wallace surveyed Joseph Stameroff with narrowed eyes. Rae and Hank stood a yard or so beyond them.

Suddenly I recalled a dream I'd had in the early hours of the morning as I dozed on my couch. In it, Judy had been kneeling near the foundation of the cote as Jack and I watched her. She told us she was afraid, and Jack said, "Just because it happened that way before doesn't mean it'll be the same this time." I said, "The truth can't be changed." Judy said, "I'm afraid," and the conversation repeated itself in one continuous loop.

Wrapped in her dead mother's black cape, blond head held high, Judy didn't look afraid now. When Jack finished speaking and nodded to her, she turned and led us into the house.

It was colder in there than outside—that dead, down-to-the-joists chill that you feel in long-vacant houses. Lamps in wall sconces showed scuffed hardwood floors and high ceilings with bas-relief coving. An unlit wrought-iron chandelier hung on a long chain in the bow of the curved staircase.

Judy paused, looking around. Seemed to hug herself under her cape—more, I thought, against memory than against the cold. She said something in a low voice, and Judge Valle asked her to speak up.

"I said, the lighting is right. These sconces were always left on all night." She moved toward the stairway, touched the newel post lightly, then began climbing.

The second-story hallway was wide, railed on the side overlooking the staircase. Judy hesitated again, staring down its length, where dark doorways interrupted the light-colored walls at regular intervals. At the end was a double door that probably led to a master suite. Judy's eyes rested on it for a moment; then she touched her fingers to her brow and shook her head as if to clear it. Quickly she faced the other way, toward a second staircase.

Now what was that? I wondered. Some half-realized memory?

We all followed Judy upstairs. The third-story hallway was narrower, with doors opening on either side. The room Judy led us into was small—probably intended for a servant—and had a sloping ceiling. The dormer window showed the mist-draped tops of pine trees. Judy crossed to it and looked out.

Jack joined her. He said, "It's June twenty-second, nineteen fifty-six. You're ten years old and you can't sleep, so you're looking out your bedroom window. What do you see?"

"It's foggy. I can barely see the lights of the bridge. There's something outside. Moving under those pines. I'm afraid of it."

"Why?"

"The way it moves. It creeps, as if it doesn't want anybody to see it."

"Is it an animal? A person?"

"A person."

This sounded too slickly rehearsed to me. I glanced at the members of the jury. Several of them looked skeptical, as if they were entertaining the same thought. As if they were remembering that Judy had been an actress.

Jack asked, "What do you do now?"

"I go back to bed. But I still can't sleep. Mama tucked me in hours ago. She was sick. Said she was going to bed, too. But now I can hear somebody at the front door. Going out? Maybe coming in. That can't be—Mama's the only one home besides me."

Judy's voice had begun to change, its pitch climbing until it was the childish singsong I remembered from my dinner party, when she'd told about finding Cordy's ring. I watched her carefully, trying to gauge if this was also rehearsed or if she might actually be retreating into memory.

"What do you do now?" Jack asked again. I couldn't tell from the way he spoke whether the change in her had surprised him.

"Pull the covers over my head. I'm scared to be up here all alone, because of the man out there."

"The *man?*" Jack's tone told me that the response had genuinely caught him off guard. A couple of the jurors noticed it, too, glanced significantly at each other.

"The man under the pine trees," Judy said impatiently.

"It was a *man?* You're sure?"

She looked at him, eyes flashing with irritation. "It was a man! It moved like a man."

"Okay," he said quickly, "you're scared and you have the covers over your head. Now what do you do?"

Judy was silent. The only sound in the small room was the whisper of our collective breath. From outside came the lament of foghorns.

She said, "I'm going to find Mama." As she moved toward the door she seemed as focused as a sleepwalker.

I caught Jack's eye. He shook his head. If she was acting, she hadn't told him her intention.

We all followed her at a short distance, down the stairs and along the second-floor hallway to one of the open doors. Judy pantomimed opening it and looking inside. "She's not there," she said. "I'm going down to the library. Sometimes she reads there at night."

Again we followed her, but at more of a distance now. Even Jack hung back, as if afraid of breaking her concentration. She stopped a few steps from the bottom of the stairs. I glanced at Stameroff and Eyestone, who now stood together. Eyestone's expression was unreadable, but Stameroff frowned.

Judy said, "The front door's open. Mama must have gone . . . Oh, no, she wouldn't go there."

"Where, Judy?" Jack asked.

"I was going to say to the dovecote, but she'd never go there."

"Why not?"

"Because that's where Daddy goes to meet Cordy."

A couple of the jurors grunted. Judge Valle coughed. Stameroff's hands tensed into fists. Judy noticed none of the reaction. She crossed the foyer to the front door and stepped out into the strange, still mist. Began walking toward the vacant lot on the bluff above the sea.

As the group followed, Louise Wingfield fell in beside me. "I never expected such a performance tonight," she commented. "She has to be acting."

"When they started, she was. Now I don't know. Did you get that information on Chavez for me?"

"Yes—it's a funny coincidence. You remember I told you that I rely heavily on my old social contacts to provide positions for our clients? Well, the place where Chavez got hired—and worked up until he failed to show this morning—was Judy's theater, the Artists' Showcase."

I stopped, staring at her. Her words tumbled in my mind. Tumbled together with other words I'd heard over this two-week period. And fell into a perfect, chilling pattern.

Up until now I'd known who. I'd thought I knew why. But I'd feared that other factors might remain unexplained forever.

Now I almost wished they could.

Thirty-Three

■ ■ ■

I left Wingfield behind and moved swiftly over the uneven ground. Toward the foundation of the dovecote, where the group now huddled against the cold sea wind. Moved to stop this before it went too far. . . .

Judy was kneeling, as she had in my dream. Touching the circle of bricks, as I had the night before. I began edging through the people around her. Jack saw me, shook his head, motioned me back.

"I came out here looking for Mama," Judy said in her little-girl's voice. "The light was on inside the cote. The door was open."

I kept moving. Jack grasped my arm, stayed me.

"Mama came out of the cote. Her dress was all red in front. I hid in the trees." She crawled backwards, ducked under the branches.

I tried to pull away from Jack. He held firm. "No, let her."

"You don't understand—"

"I understand more than you think."

"She'd left the light on," Judy said. "The door was open." She came out from under the branches, stood, moved forward. "I went over and looked inside." She leaned across the foundation. Recoiled.

The group was caught up in the drama now. No one moved or even whispered. I felt a chill on my shoulder blades, tried once again to shake free of Jack's grip. He tightened his fingers, hurting me. His eyes were on Judy, full of something implacable, cruel.

"It's Cordy!" Hushed voice now. "She's lying there like she's asleep, but there's all this blood. . . ."

I looked around for Wallace and Joslyn. Tried to signal them, but neither saw me. Eyestone's expression was wary now, gaze skipping from Judy to Stameroff. The justice stood with his head bowed, as if awaiting a fatal blow.

"Cordy's dead," Judy said in a stage whisper. "She's got Mama's good-luck anniversary pennies on her eyes." She stepped back, looked down at her feet.

Silence. Judy kept looking down. Finally she added, "And there's Cordy's finger with the amethyst ring Daddy gave her."

A current of unease rippled through the spectators. My own foreboding heightened. Judy continued looking downward, at the ground where larkspur had once grown. Larkspur, which are also called delphiniums. . . .

Stameroff raised his head, made a sudden lurching motion toward her. "Judy, don't—"

She looked up at him. "Why not? You know what I did."

"Judy—"

"I picked up Cordy's finger, and I took the ring off of it. Then I threw the finger off the cliff. And then I went back to the house and hid the ring where nobody but me could ever find it."

The ensuing silence made it feel as if we'd all fallen into a void. At the bottom of the cliff, a high wave boomed.

Judy faced her adoptive father squarely, lips twisted in contempt. "I lied," she said. "I lied for years and years. And *you made me do it.*"

Jack's fingers loosened; I wrenched my arm away. Stameroff moved toward Judy at the same time I did. And stopped as her right arm shot out from under the cape and pointed a long-barreled pistol at him.

"You made me lie," she said. "For all those years, every time I tried to get at the truth, you stopped me."

The crowd gave a collective gasp, pulled back as one—shocked, suddenly confused. Even Wallace and Joslyn froze.

My first thought was that Judy's gun, the one Lis had shot herself with, was in the hands of the police. That this gun was a stage prop, more calculated melodrama. Loaded with blanks, if it was loaded at all. But what if it was real, loaded with real bullets? What if she meant to kill him?

Wallace recovered from his shock, shouted, "Nobody panic! It'll be all right. Just don't move!"

Stameroff ignored him, starting toward Judy, his eyes flicking wildly around. "I did it to protect you! Your mother made me promise—"

"You both did it to protect yourselves." She grasped the gun with both hands. Stameroff froze.

Everyone except Jack and me was within her line of sight and fire. Jack seemed incapable of speech or motion.

Should I go for the gun? Risk its being a deadly weapon? Risk her firing at Stameroff or into the crowd?

I took a slow step toward her. She caught the motion in the periphery of her vision. "Don't come any closer, Sharon."

I stopped, watching the gun. No way to tell if it was real or not at this distance—stage props were that good. *Should* I chance it?

If I were the only one involved, perhaps. But I couldn't risk the others' safety.

Reason with her, then? Feed into the heavy drama she'd constructed?

Try a little of both. Maybe she'd give me an opening.

"Judy," I called, "I know he's a bastard and deserves to be punished, but not that way. And not in front of all these witnesses."

"Why should I care about witnesses?"

"Because your life is valuable. You don't want to throw it away."

"My mother threw it away when she murdered that woman."

She didn't know. The memory gap had not fully closed.

And that gave me my opening.

"Judy, your mother didn't kill Cordy McKittridge. Are you going to let the person who did get away with it?"

The words seemed to confuse her. Still, she kept the gun aimed at Stameroff.

Quickly I asked, "After you disposed of the finger, you went back to the house, right?"

". . . Yes."

"Who did you see?"

Silence.

"Who, Judy?"

"Not Mama. Her door was locked."

"But there was someone else, wasn't there?"

She hesitated, then shook her head, taking her left hand off the gun and touching it to her brow as she had earlier in the second-floor hallway.

"Was someone *upstairs?*"

A gust of wind whipped the black cape around Judy's slender body. The gun wavered. She frowned, steadying it.

"Think, Judy," I said. "The second-floor hallway. You're standing there with Cordy's ring in your hand. Your mother's door is locked. How do you feel?"

She kept her eyes on Stameroff, but after a moment she said, "Cold. I'm barefoot in my pajamas. And I'm scared. Mama and I have done this terrible thing." Again she spoke in her little-girl's voice, but it now held genuine helplessness and fear.

"What do you hear?"

". . . Water running, I think in Mama's bathroom."

"Anything else?"

"Footsteps. Up here, at the end of the hall. In Dr. Eyestone's suite."

"And?"

". . . I move back. To the stairs to where my room is. It's dark there. I get down behind the newel post."

"What happens then?"

"The door opens."

"Who comes out?"

She looked at me, shock and comprehension flooding her face. In her adult voice she said, "Leonard."

More gasps and murmurs ran through the crowd. Eyestone took a step backward, shaking his head.

Judy swept the gun from Stameroff to Eyestone. "Leonard

was wearing a tuxedo, and his hair was wet. I was afraid he would see me. I thought if he saw the ring, he'd realize what my mother had done. Only she hadn't—had she, Leonard?"

Eyestone spread his arms in a wide gesture of bewilderment and innocence.

Judy put both hands on the gun again, readying to fire. The crowd suddenly broke apart and began to scatter away from her.

I ran toward her.

She turned my way, but too late. I slammed into her shoulder. Grabbed her arm, smashed the gun from her grip. She cried out and then wrenched away from me, scrambling after it.

I hurled myself at her again, knocked her sideways. Kicked out at the gun and sent it skittering toward the foundation. Judy tried to fight her way around me, but Joslyn ran up, grabbed her arms and pinned them behind her, then forced her to the ground with a knee in her back. Judy lay sobbing, her face pressed into the dirt.

Another commotion broke out behind me. I twisted in time to see Stameroff rush at Eyestone.

The justice grabbed Eyestone by the shoulder, raised his fist, and slammed it into his face. Eyestone staggered. Stameroff hit him again with every bit of his old-man's strength. Eyestone went down on one knee, then toppled over.

I felt the full force of thirty-six years of anger, shame, and self-loathing behind Stameroff's blows. He wasn't a man who could turn his rage upon himself where it belonged, so he swung out at his corrupter.

Before Wallace could subdue him, Stameroff had kicked Eyestone in the head.

I got to my feet and went over to the foundation. Picked up the gun. Not a stage prop—a .22 Colt Woodsman. I broke it open, checked its load.

Not blanks—real bullets.

More melodrama or a genuine attempted murder? I didn't suppose I'd ever know for sure.

But of one thing I was certain: Judy had finally delivered her one great performance.

Thirty-Four

■ ■ ■

On Sunday afternoon, in the police ward where he was recovering from the injuries Stameroff had inflicted on him, Leonard Eyestone confessed to killing Cordy McKittridge but firmly maintained his innocence of the Cardinal murder.

"And he'll never admit to it," Adah Joslyn said when she stopped by my house to tell me about the confession.

The weather had again turned unseasonably warm. Joslyn and I sat on my deck, Ralph lying companionably at our feet while Allie stalked an imaginary bird in the gnarled apple tree.

"The scenario of the night of the murder was pretty much as you figured it," Adah added. "Like you said, it's all there in Benedict's suicide note, once you know what to look for."

"In the suicide note and the photographs Eyestone suppressed."

In my mind's eye, I pictured the scene in the upstairs hallway of the Seacliff house: ten-year-old Judy watching Eyestone come out of his father's suite, fresh from his blood-cleansing shower. Judy, much too afraid he would realize what she and her mother had done to wonder why he was there. And Leonard, newly clad in formal wear borrowed from his father, his fresh shirtfront austere with tiny pleats rather than the ruffles that were soaked with Cordy's blood.

Eyestone had returned to the St. Francis too late to join the reception line, but in time to pose for a picture with his father and John Foster Dulles. A potentially incriminating picture, he'd realized when he saw it in the paper the next day, because someone might notice the change of clothing. So he'd called the photographer and requested that all negatives of the evening's photos be destroyed. I'd always wonder what excuse he'd given.

But something must have puzzled Eyestone in the days that followed, intrigued him in spite of his fear of discovery and arrest. He'd stabbed Cordy, yes, but he had not hacked her to death. Someone else had mutilated and then laid out her corpse—and Eyestone had a good suspicion of who that person was.

Is it better to think your mother falsely accused of murder or to know her for the despicable creature she is? How are you to understand my rage and frustration, my awful sense of being thwarted at the very last? The knowledge that if I didn't act, she would forever be frozen perfect in your father's emotions?

A despicable creature, Lis Benedict had written, because she had mutilated a lovely young woman's corpse.

Rage and frustration . . . thwarted, because she'd been denied her confrontation with Cordy. Perhaps been denied the opportunity to do to her what had already been done by some unknown person.

Forever be frozen perfect, because even in death Cordy was beautiful, and such perfection had to be destroyed.

But then at the last she hadn't been able to leave what she had desecrated—because, to the thinking of a superstitious woman like Lis Benedict, the dead staring eyes were looking for the next to die, looking at her. So she placed her talismans over them.

Armed with talismans against failure, the 1943 good-luck pennies of zinc-coated steel that Vincent Benedict had purchased as an anniversary gift to her in 1954. Pennies minted in the year they were married. Pennies for the eleventh anniversary because it called for gifts made of steel. An unusual gift, but Vincent Benedict and his wife were unusual people. And as the coin dealer had told the police, Benedict seemed to take ironic pleasure in the gift—coins that many collectors considered false, to commemorate a marriage that contained its own degree of falsity.

"You were right about Eyestone's motives, too," Joslyn added. "Bastard made one mistake early in life, and it just kept compounding."

Leonard's mistake was a youthful flirtation with Communism. In 1953 he began dabbling in radical politics, and by the time he met Roger Woods at a Party meeting in 1955, he was in love with the idealism and intrigue. He even tried to enlist Cordy in the cause, but she dismissed it as merely one more of Leonard's strange enthusiasms. Soon Woods asked Eyestone to take him to the Institute and introduce him to his father and the other staff; this bastion of bourgeois pseudo-intellectualism, Roger claimed, must be infiltrated. Leonard, who had kept his two worlds strictly segregated, balked—until Woods reminded him how much harm it would do him and the organization if his radical connections were made public.

The point was further driven home when the Institute began negotiating for the contract on the domestic security threat and background checks were run on staff members to be assigned to the project. While Leonard wasn't one of them, he now fully realized the danger he'd placed himself in and tried to break with Woods and his other radical associates. But Woods had an irritating habit of popping up unannounced at Seacliff and insinuating himself into any gathering. Leonard was particularly horrified to learn that his former comrade had wangled an invitation to the Dulles reception.

Joslyn said, "When you think of it, Leonard's involvement with the Commies was pretty innocent. He said he never even joined up."

"Didn't matter back then," I told her. "McCarthy and his followers destroyed people for far less than what Leonard did."

"True." She stretched out her long legs and propped her feet on the deck railing, squinting up at the sun. "But I still think Leonard would have been all right if McKittridge hadn't known about it."

But Cordy had known, and in time she began to perceive Leonard's radical fling and Roger Woods's continuing presence at Institute affairs as a personal danger. Vincent Benedict had decided to leave his wife and marry her; the divorce would be costly, and Cordy knew that her conservative, publicity-shy parents would cut her off once Lis named her as corespondent. Vincent would need his job; therefore the Institute must be protected. In June of 1956 Cordy put her former lover on notice: get rid of Woods and resign from the staff or she would tell his father everything.

"Cordy was rough on Leonard," I said, "and there was more than a little self-interest operating there, but I think in a way she thought she was—excuse me for using an overworked catchphrase—doing the right thing. She's always struck me as a woman whose moral sense was black-and-white."

Joslyn snorted derisively.

"No—think about her background. Conservative old money. Proper upbringing. All those rules. Early influences like that can't help but have had a strong effect. What happens with kids who are raised that way? They rebel and sow their wild oats, but eventually they find they can't escape who they are. Look at Leonard."

"Maybe."

"Louise Wingfield said something telling to me: that Cordy didn't love anyone, least of all herself. A lot of that self-hatred could have been because she was going against everything that, down deep, she believed in."

"You're quite a psychologist, McCone."

I ignored the dig. "Did Eyestone admit to premeditation?"

"No. He claims Melissa told him that Cordy had an appointment with Vincent that night—Melissa didn't know that Lis actually wrote the note. Eyestone found it odd, considering they were holding the banquet, so he asked Vincent about it, and Benedict said Cordy must be confused. Eyestone took advantage of the opportunity to leave the banquet early and go over there. Just to talk, he says. But sneaking out of the Blue Fox was tricky, and he'd have had to think it out well in advance. Why the secrecy if he didn't plan to off her?"

"Of course he did, but he'll never admit it. That way his

attorney can build a heat-of-the-moment defense. Given how long ago the crime took place, he's likely to get off with a reasonably light sentence. As for Cardinal, there's no proof he killed her."

"Oh, don't you worry. We'll get it." Joslyn nodded sagely. "You and I know Cardinal'd been hitting him up for years, and somewhere in his bank records there has to be proof of that. My partner's a great one for building meticulous circumstantial cases. As to why he killed Melissa—as you suggested the other night, he probably found out she was planning to talk to you."

I felt a stirring of guilt. "Indirectly, it's my fault one way or the other. I told Eyestone that I was going to try to persuade Melissa to attend the mock trial."

Joslyn grunted. After a moment she said, "Well, you couldn't have known."

"No." But the guilt remained—always would.

We both fell silent, watching Allie, who was practically hanging upside down in the tree. After a moment I asked, "Did Eyestone say who put the fix in with the D.A.'s office?"

"Old man Eyestone's political buddies. Leonard kept quiet until Benedict was charged with the murder. Then he went to his father and confessed; he said he couldn't allow an innocent woman to go to the gas chamber."

"So Russell Eyestone went to his political friends and arranged a deal. A prosecutor who could be bought would be assigned to the case—probably a public defender who could be bought, too. Lis would be convicted, and the question of who killed Cordy would be settled. But Lis would not go to the gas chamber."

Joslyn nodded. "Lis knew that; it was part of the deal they cut with her."

"But why would she accept what she knew had to be a life sentence? That's bothered me from the first."

"Felt as guilty as if she had done it, I suppose. Probably thought she *deserved* life in prison." Joslyn gave me a bright, mocking smile. "See? I'm a psychologist, too."

I smiled back at her. "There's another reason: Lis had her daughter to think of. You can't tell me she didn't know how that ring came to be in her attic. In her suicide note she said, 'you've always known, although I've never dared ask.' That implies she knew Judy was on the scene. And Stameroff did say that he'd promised Lis to protect Judy against her memories of that night."

Adah shuddered. "What kind of a kid would pick up a severed finger and . . . plus frame her own mother?"

I'd given that a good deal of thought, and there were quite a few things about Judy that I didn't intend to reveal to Joslyn. She'd find them out soon enough. "Well," I said, "she really believed Lis had killed Cordy. As far as Judy was concerned, her mother wrecked her life."

"It was going to be wrecked anyway, when her parents divorced."

"Kids don't think that way; they focus on one thing at a time. I'll bet it never occurred to her that Eyestone murdered Cordy. When she saw him in the hall, she focused on him telling on her mother and her."

"I'm glad I don't intend to have kids," Adah said.

"Melissa's cat is enough for you, huh?"

Damned if she didn't smile like a fond mother.

I turned my thoughts to the past again, to Judy's recollection of a night in late July of 1956, one day after the collision of the *Andrea Doria* and the *Stockholm*. Vincent Benedict came home drunk that night after a period of relative sobriety, and he continued to drink at the kitchen table until he passed out. Then he gave Judy over to the care of the Eyestones, who placed her in a foster home where the prosecuting attorney could have easy access to her. I asked, "Did Eyestone say whether Vincent Benedict knew what Lis had done?"

"He suspected, because of the coins, but at first he wanted to fight the charges anyway. Then Russell Eyestone laid it all out for him, presented a done deal."

"And that was the end of Vincent Benedict."

"You know, Sharon, the whole thing disgusts me. Depresses me, too. What's the point of little people like me fighting for justice when the biggies like Russell Eyestone and his buddies can put the fix in and not be held accountable?"

I shrugged. "I don't know, but what're you going to do—give up?"

"Sometimes I want to."

"Well, you can't; you don't have it in you. Me either." I paused, remembering. "You know what Stameroff calls those biggies? 'The people who count.' Implying, of course, that the rest of us don't count. But you know what else? He's wrong. He just doesn't get it."

"What do you mean?"

"I think that we allow ourselves not to count—by letting it get us down, by giving up. And I think we *can* count—if we get angry enough, brave enough, or maybe are just stupid enough to believe we can make a difference."

Joslyn looked curiously at me. "You really believe that stuff?"

I shrugged again. "Like they say, everybody got to believe in something."

Thirty-Five

■ ■ ■

On Monday morning before I left for the office, I did some persuasive phone work and finally spoke with Roger Woods at the nursing home in Cedar Rapids where he was a patient. Woods confirmed he'd become an FBI informant infiltrating Communist circles in San Francisco after the death of his father from what he referred to as "Dad's addiction to radical causes." Melissa had never suspected; to the last she'd thought her stepbrother true to the cause.

Woods had infiltrated the Institute for North American Studies after he'd met Leonard at an American Communist party meeting, in order to investigate unconfirmed reports that others on the staff shared Leonard's political leanings. "The irony," he told me, "is that I was about to give the Institute a clean bill of health and let Leonard off with a lecture when the McKittridge girl was murdered."

After the murder, Woods's FBI contact asked him to relocate to the East Coast; the Bureau arranged for rumors of his death to be circulated among his former associates in San Francisco. For several years he worked as an informant in New Jersey; then he married and moved with his new wife to her home state of Iowa and raised wheat on a farm near Cedar Rapids until arthritis crippled him in the late eighties. Out of sentimentality he reestablished contact with his stepsister when he retired, but, as he put it, "she wasn't one of our kind; she'd stayed a Commie sympathizer. And I didn't really like her."

Woods was talking to me, he said, only out of patriotism. He wanted it known just how much harm the Commies did back then. As far as he was concerned, they were still up to plenty. This democratization in Russia was just a smoke screen.

I didn't bother to tell him that in my opinion, his kind had been the ones to wreak havoc in the fifties. Woods wouldn't have cared.

.   .   .

When I arrived at All Souls, I went directly to Jack's office. He knelt on the floor, rolling clothing up and stuffing it into his backpack. His rock-climbing gear lay nearby.

This was bad news. With Jack, rock climbing was as much of a danger signal as heavy drinking was for some people. "Going on vacation?" I asked.

He glanced up, went on packing. "Yes."

"You want to talk about it?"

"What's to talk about?"

"Judy paid Chavez to harass Lis and me, didn't she?"

"Yes."

"Why?"

"Because she's fuckin' crazy, that's why."

But she wasn't crazy, and he knew it. Manipulative, yes. Jack had been dragging his feet on the case when the harassment began; it had made him angry and spurred him to action. With me, I suspected Judy's motivation had been slightly different: she wanted me to believe in a present-day danger so I'd press harder with my investigation.

"She was obsessed," Jack added bitterly. "Totally obsessed with getting back at Stameroff for what he did to her and Lis. Just as she was obsessed with getting back at Lis for what she imagined Lis had done to her when she was a child."

I had a certain feel for the motives behind Judy's actions,

having become well acquainted with obsession during the past two weeks. The thought of living in a prolonged state of it was horrifying: being pulled toward something, driven relentlessly by forces you couldn't begin to comprehend. . . .

But still it didn't justify what she'd done.

"Jack," I said, "what about her performance out there the other night? When did it stop being a performance?"

"When you asked her if there had been anyone else at the house. Before that she was acting—damned well, too. She certainly had me fooled." He rocked back on his heels, naked pain on his face. "Afterward she admitted everything to me. She's been seeing a shrink for years. The memories came back with the aid of hypnosis even before Lis got out of prison. All except that last. Up until then she had believed Lis murdered Cordy."

"Do you think Judy would have shot Stameroff?"

"Now that she's in custody, she claims she only wanted to scare him. But, Jesus, Shar—you saw her, you heard her." His eyes clouded; on some level he'd always be haunted by the memory. "I *know* she would have blown Eyestone away," he added. "She's . . . so full of hate."

Hate. Wasn't that really what this case boiled down to? Intolerance and hate, breeding fear and violence. In the fifties we hated the Commies; in the sixties it was the hippie–drug fiend–protesters; in the seventies, fledgling feminists were vilified; the eighties saw backlash against liberals; and now in the nineties, our government was commissioning studies on how to control and use the religious right. Left, right, or smack in the middle—as a nation we don't discriminate in our hatreds. . . .

Jack stood, hefted his packpack.

"How long will you be gone?"

"Till I feel sane again. Maybe sanity's all I can reasonably hope for in life."

"Maybe it's all any of us can reasonably hope for."

After he left, I sat on his sofa thinking for a while. Then I went back to my office.

Rae was waiting for me, lying on my chaise longue looking more than a little blue. "You see Jack?" she asked.

I nodded. "You suspected about Judy being behind the harassment, didn't you?"

"Yeah. How'd you know?"

"Something you said that night we were at the Remedy, about the timing of the harassment being perfect."

"Oh, right. Will Jack be okay, do you think?"

That was what I'd been pondering as I'd sat on his sofa. "Maybe," I said, "if he doesn't try to climb Half Dome."

Rae wasn't in the mood for light comments, though. She merely stared moodily at the ceiling.

I sat down at my desk. "So how's by you today?"

"Oh . . . okay."

"Do you want to tell me what happened between you and Willie? I heard a rumor that a diamond ring was in the offing."

She sat up suddenly, eyes flashing. "Oh, you did? Well, you know what, Shar? Willie's about as romantic as a . . . toaster!"

"No ring?"

"Oh, yeah, there was a ring. And flowers. Champagne, too. But you know what the asshole wanted before we could get married?"

Dumbfounded, I shook my head.

"A prenup, that's what!"

"A prenuptial agreement?"

"Yep. He claims that he created a monster in me when he taught me about credit, and if the marriage doesn't work out, he doesn't want me getting my hands on all his money!"

I told myself that if I laughed now I'd blow our friendship for life. With an effort I said seriously, "Hank tells me prenups are a fad since Donald and Ivana. Maybe Willie'll come to his senses."

"Tough if he does. He knows what he can do with his prenup!" She got up and strode to the door, then turned. "Oh, that Adah Joslyn called while I was waiting for you. She wanted to let you know that Chavez is in custody and Tony Nueva was picked up on the drug charge at a wedding chapel in Reno."

"Before or after the ceremony?"

"How the hell should I know? I hope it was before. Or, if not, that he didn't have time to get the woman to sign a prenup!"

After she'd left, I allowed myself to laugh. Rae's life often resembled the plot of a soap opera, but compared to Jack's, her worst day was a bed of roses. . . .

Roses. I stared at the wilted tangerine-colored blossom in the bud vase. Hy's latest tribute, delivered last Tuesday by long-standing arrangement with a nearby florist, while we were still high in the Great Whites. Tomorrow there would be another. On impulse I picked up the phone receiver and dialed the office of the Spaulding Foundation in the town of Vernon, near Tufa Lake.

When I asked for Hy, Kate Malloy, his executive assistant, sounded strained. "He's not here, Sharon," she said. "In fact, I was about to call you."

Foreboding made my skin prickle. I thought of a small high-winged plane falling from the sky, of twisted and burning wreckage. . . . "What's wrong?"

"Hy's disappeared."

"What?"

"It looks deliberate. His house is closed up, and he paid his ranch hands two months in advance. Left instructions with his accountant to take care of bills as they come in. And his plane's been tied down at Oakland Airport since last Wednesday."

Oakland? He'd told me he was going to refuel and fly directly on to San Diego. "You called General Aviation at Oakland?"

"Yes. I knew he was dropping you off on Wednesday, and I thought he might have filed a flight plan."

I clutched the receiver, shaking my head. Hy Ripinsky was fooling me again, just when I thought I had him figured out as much as was necessary.

"Look, Kate," I said, "is there some reason you need to get hold of Hy right away?"

". . . No. I'm just worried."

"Well, don't be. We both know Hy can take care of himself. I'll let you know if I hear from him."

I hung up. Leaned back in my chair. Contemplated the wilted rose.

In a way Hy's disappearance didn't surprise me. Maybe I was getting to the point where nothing Hy did would ever surprise me.

But how could I resist such a challenge?

"Hy, you rascal," I said, "you're not going to get away with this."

I took a fresh folder and a strip of labels from my stack tray. Swiveled over to my old typewriter and rolled the strip into it. Typed.

Then I swiveled back to the desk and opened a new case file labeled "Ripinsky, Heino."